Praise for *Mary*

In *Mary*, author Shannon McNear contin[...]ry colony of Roanoke begun in Elinor, wea[...]or-ough research with insightful and suspense[...]ity of early European settlers might have be[...]nd mindsets of two strikingly different people g[...], [...]ng Native woman, Mushaniq, and a young English man, Georgie, as they navigate the complicated middle ground between their peoples—as shifting as the sands that form the barrier islands of their coastal home—seeking a path firm enough to carry them forward into a shared future. The resulting story is as pleasing as a skillfully woven sweetgrass basket, and hints of more to come. I cannot fail to mention how vividly this setting is brought to life; I can still smell the salt-sea air and hear the gulls and feel the warmth of tide-washed sand.

–Lori Benton, Christy Award-winning author of *Burning Sky*,
Mountain Laurel, and other historical novels

Heartwarming and heartbreaking at the same time, *Mary* is the next satisfying tale in the Daughters of the Lost Colony series. The wild lands of the New World are a dangerous place to be, for body, heart, and soul. New relationships are forged between the natives and the colonists as they struggle to figure out life together—all while dodging the ever-present threat of attack. A story that you won't soon forget.

–Michelle Griep, Christy Award-winning author

In *Mary*, the second book of the Lost Colony Series, Shannon McNear focuses on a native maiden and the English youth with whom she falls in love. Again, the reader is quickly immersed in the mysterious, haunting primeval coastlands of North Carolina through evocative descriptions and realistic, relatable characters. The depth of McNear's research is impressive. But what affected me most was her depiction of what might have been if later European colonists had chosen to work with the indigenous peoples to build communities based on mutual respect and cooperation instead of, as happened in too many cases, taking the land by force, with the consequent stain on American history. McNear doesn't offer a utopian interpretation of the possible fate of the lost colonists, but portrays honestly common human virtues and flaws, failures and successes in both native and English characters. In *Mary* we are given a bright vision of what can happen when we see those of other races and cultures as image-bearers of the Creator equally precious in our Savior's sight, and neither bludgeon them with our faith nor neglect to preach the gospel through word and action so that some may come to a saving knowledge of Christ.

—J. M. Hochstetler, author of The American Patriot Series and coauthor
with Bob Hostetler of the Northkill Amish Series

With *Mary: Daughters of the Lost Colony*, author Shannon McNear blurs the demarcation between history and fiction in such a way that the saga is both fully believable and beautifully written. I loved how the story questions deepen as McNear picks up where her novel *Elinor* ends, twining the fates of two women from different cultures and beliefs who hold the same needs and yearnings. *Mary* pulses with drama, romance, and spiritual insight. I highly recommend it to any lover of historical fiction who has ever pondered the mysteries surrounding the Lost Colony of Roanoke.

–Naomi Musch, author of *Season of My Enemy (Heroines of WWII)*,
Song for the Hunter (sequel to *Mist O'er the Voyageur*),
and *Lumberjacks and Ladies (Not for Love)*

Explore the history and lore of Roanoke in Shannon McNear's *Mary: Daughters of the Lost Colony Book 2*. Young orphan Georgie Howe and Mushaniq, the precocious daughter of Native leader Manteo, force the Indian and English peoples to explore how to mesh two different cultures into one cohesive unit. That joining doesn't come easily. McNear deftly weaves history with fiction to create a compelling tale of times gone by. Don't miss this one!

–Jennifer Uhlarik, award-winning author of
Love's Fortress and *Sand Creek Serenade*

This honest and thought-provoking exploration of a long-standing mystery of early American colonization serves up not only a rich coming-of-age yarn but also not one but two romances, including the resolution of Elinor's rescue in Book One. The union of two cultures, while fraught with challenges, births many a beautiful moment. Mary immerses readers in a perspective on the Lost Colony as colorful as the North Carolina wilderness and as fresh as the baptism of the native new believers.

–Denise Weimer, author of *The Witness Tree* and *Bent Tree Bride*

Shannon McNear once again transports readers to the 1590s in the wilds of a yet unexplored continent. Her new book, *Mary*, returns to the lost people of Roanoke and explores what might have happened using their known history and expanding into the possibilities. Readers reengage with the characters they grew to love in *Elinor* and follow their lives as they adapt to the strange and wonderful place they learn to call home. Experience their struggles to survive in both body and spirit alongside these brave men and women of two very different cultures. A captivating read for anyone with a love of history, mystery, and imagination.

–Pegg Thomas, award-winning author of *Abigail's Peace*

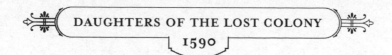

DAUGHTERS OF THE LOST COLONY
1590

Mary

*A Riveting Story Based on the
Lost Colony of Roanoke*

SHANNON MCNEAR

BARBOUR
PUBLISHING

Cover Design: Kirk DouPonce, DogEared Design

Published by Barbour Publishing, Inc., 1810 Barbour Drive, Uhrichsville, Ohio 44683, www.barbourbooks.com

Our mission is to inspire the world with the life-changing message of the Bible.

Member of the
Evangelical Christian
Publishers Association

Printed in the United States of America.

Dedication

To a vanished people whose story begs to be told

*"Thus sayeth the Lord (even he that maketh a way
in the sea, and a footpath in the mighty waters):
Remember not the things of old, and regard nothing
that is past. Behold I shall make a new thing, and
shortly shall it appear, and shall you not know it?
This people have I made for my self, and
they shall show forth my praise."*
ISAIAH 43:16, 18–19, 21

and

To all my sons and daughters: the ones I birthed, the ones
adopted in by friendship or marriage, and those in youth
group who I've loved and prayed over and preached at.
May you follow the leading of the Spirit always.

*"Those who are well have no need of a physi-
cian, but those who are sick. I have not come to
call the righteous but sinners to repentance."*
LUKE 5:31–32 ESV

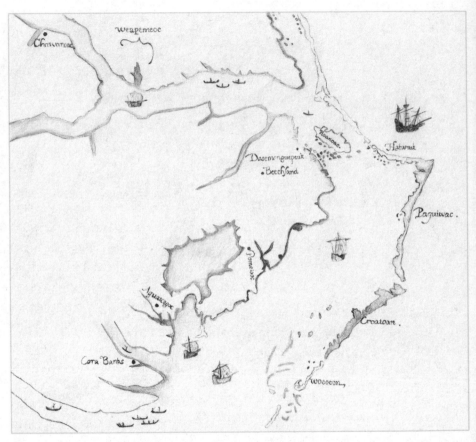

OSSOMOCOMUCK by Corrie McNear, after John White, La Virginea Pars, used by permission of the British Museum.

Dear Reader,

In 1587, twenty years before the landing at Jamestown, 117 English colonists were dumped unceremoniously on Roanoke Island, a part of what is now the Outer Banks of North Carolina. To understand why they did or did not want to settle there and why the colony was being established at all, one must recognize that England and Spain were bitter enemies. Spain held most of South America and ruthlessly exploited its land and people, using forced native labor to mine for gold and other resources. Spain made her riches from the New World, and England increased her vast wealth by taking prizes of Spanish ships returning through the West Indies.

The animosity between the two nations was not only political but religious as well. Queen Elizabeth, a Protestant like her father King Henry VIII before her, refused to submit to the Catholic Church. Mary Stuart, Elizabeth's own cousin, subscribed to Catholicism and used religious differences to foment rebellion against Elizabeth, for which she was executed earlier in 1587 (a fact I somehow neglect to mention in *Elinor*).

The question of religion wasn't just a struggle across the water. It was manifested in the very soil of England. The Catholic Church by definition ("catholic" meaning "universal") believed itself to be the only valid expression of God's people, while Protestants viewed the Pope as "the Spanish Antichrist." Other permutations of Christianity were also viewed with disdain if not outright hostility. One Spanish account refers to Simon Fernandes (at least we think it's him) as "the Lutheran Portuguese," but then the Englishman John White viewed him as vulgar, vile, and heathen.

Modern believers in Christ can be just as harsh toward those who walk their interpretation of His teachings in ways they disagree with. This can extend even to fictional portrayals of history. It has long been my conviction, however, that in order to be true to history, it's necessary to show people as they would have been—products of their own culture and society—and not impose modern ideals and sensibilities on them. Sometimes this also means not imposing even Christian ideals and sensibilities.

Scripture is full of examples of how God chooses and uses flawed and sinful people in all their frailty and does not whitewash the struggle or even the ugliness of their actions. If it bothers you to read stories where such things are portrayed with honesty, this may not be the story for you.

But I would appeal to you to read it anyway, to remember what it felt like to be young, with all the passion and struggle, and to have compassion for their journey, just as others had compassion on us (or should have) in that same season.

One writer whose Lost Colony work I have closely followed has said he would love to see a "tremendous love story" told in fiction between the two peoples—how the Natives welcomed the beleaguered English and how they all sought to live together, as John White envisioned, as one community, of one heart, one mind. And so I offer you *Mary*, which serves both as a parallel story to *Elinor* and a sequel. I recommend you read that one first, but even if you haven't, mayhap you will be curious enough afterward to read Elinor's own story, with that of her father, John White, and the Secotan warrior Sees Far.

Thank you, as always, for taking this journey with me!

My most earnest regards,
Shannon

* For author notes and glossary of characters, people groups, and terms, see end of book.

Chapter One

G *o! Protect her!"* she'd said.

Protect her, he would.

Two-year-old Virginia Dare was no burden at all in Georgie's arms, even as he dived through thick underbrush in the wake of the Croatoan women and children fleeing toward the river.

Near the edge, he hesitated for but a breath. *"Pyas!"* came an urgent whisper, and the pert, round face of Mushaniq peered from the reeds. He waded in, heedless of the *sluck* of his feet in the mud.

'Twas better to be muddy than dead or taken.

Just short of the water's edge, they hunkered down, Mushaniq at his elbow. Ginny Dare whimpered, and the native girl breathed a word— *ehqutonahas*—their equivalent of *shush!* Wide-eyed, Ginny reached both arms toward her, leaning so abruptly that Georgie nearly pitched over, but Mushaniq took her without hesitation, flashing a look of apology at Georgie.

It mattered not. If the girls huddled together, then that freed his hands to fight. If it came to that.

Da's life had ended in a marsh. Would his as well?

9

Quiet settled. Still, they waited. At last, they heard others creeping back to dry ground. A man's voice called out from nearby, "It is safe now! They have gone."

He exchanged a glance with Mushaniq. She rose, still holding Ginny, but Georgie found his own limbs strangely uncooperative. What if the call was but a ruse, and they'd emerge from the reeds to find themselves ambushed once again?

But he must be brave. Since God saw fit to put them here—

He unfolded his body and peered over the top of the reeds. Behind and beside him, the Croatoan women and children were slowly making their way back to shore, where several men stood, both English and Croatoan, as far as he could tell. At the least, none wore paint to indicate their intentions of making war.

He trailed Mushaniq and Ginny through the reeds. Families met and embraced. Georgie swallowed back an ache.

"Here is little Virginia, but where is Elinor?" The question came from William Berde, who gripped a pike, its trembling tip betraying the man's lingering distress.

Georgie hauled his feet through the mud and stepped onto firmer ground. "She was—taken. I saw it and snatched up Ginny to carry her away."

Would they reproach him for not fighting? But nay, the intake of breath all around bore sorrow, giving way to cries of dismay. None offered rebuke. Were they busy enough with their own shock they did not think of it, or did they remember how he himself had suffered the first of the colony's losses at similar hands?

Come to think, might all their losses be at the same hands?

Well, that could not be, given the loss of Thomas Archard.

The old hurt bloomed once more in his chest, but he resisted attempting to rub it away. 'Twould do no good anyway.

"What terrible hap! How did it occur? Did Elinor say anything?"

Georgie gulped a breath. "We were clearing the field for planting, she and the other women on that side, the little children on this." He glanced over to see Margery Harvie clutching little Henry to her chest, despite his wriggling and begging to get down. "The savage seemed to appear from nowhere, out of the forest, and while many of the women ran for the river, she hesitated—or did not see him in time. The savage seized her arm and began dragging her away, but she looked back—" He swallowed. "She looked back and shouted to me to protect Ginny. I—I already had the child in my arms but also hesitated."

The eyes gazing back at him were grave, pitying. "There was naught else you could have done," Master Bailie said, as if he'd heard the doubts in Georgie's own mind.

Georgie tucked his head for a long moment. Elinor—Mistress Dare, rather—was nigh well a mother to him as well.

"We shall pray for the soon return of Manteo and the other men before deciding how best to respond to this outrage."

"How many others are taken? How many killed?"

"None killed—that we know—although Griffen Jones has a nasty wound to the head. Roger Prat and at least two other men taken. Two of the boys, I think. And Emme Merrimoth and Elizabeth Glane both gone." Frustration shone in Master Bailie's eyes for the girls, about Georgie's own age.

"Any Croatoan?"

Timqua and Wesnah conferred quietly in their own tongue, and word was passed amongst their sister natives. At last, shaking heads gave the answer—it appeared the only targets were the English.

At least for now.

In Mushaniq's arms, Ginny began to whimper. "Mama?"

Mushaniq's eyes met Georgie's over the child's head as she sought to comfort the tiny girl, but Ginny broke into full cry, scanning the faces around her. Without thought, Georgie reached out, and Ginny came into his embrace. "Mama!" she wailed, and he snuggled her closer.

"I know, little one. I know."

There was nothing like the feeling of being completely alone in this world.

He closed his eyes to the pity in Mushaniq's face—and everyone else's.

Mushaniq could hardly believe it had all truly happened. In one instant, they were running about, minding the little ones and pretending to help with clearing what would be the field for *pegatawah* and other crops—in the next, peril and fear and running to hide.

And well was she practiced in hiding. Years of running the island and either squatting in brush or stands of reeds and grass or climbing trees—although the latter were by no means thickly leaved enough to provide the best cover—and being utterly still had sharpened her ability to not be found. She was the best at all those games.

But this was no game. Even now, shock and sorrow rimmed the faces of the women, both Aunties Timqua and Wesnah, and *Nunohum*—her *weroansqua* grandmama—although she hadn't been near the field when the attack happened. Mushaniq's own belly felt so sour she nearly wanted to return to the reeds and empty it, though morning meal had been hours ago.

Instead she stood, watching the *Inqutish* boy, who—finally—was taller than she and who also stood cuddling a crying Ginny to himself as if her tears were for both of them, his long-lashed eyes tightly shut, his bright head bent over hers. Timqua also watched and at last edged forward, easing the tiny girl from his arms. "Pyas. We will go find food."

He trailed along, head still down, not looking at Mushaniq. She had never seen him so subdued. So dejected. Even after the great storm two summers ago when his friend was lost.

At the *yehakan*, Timqua tried to set down the still-sniffling Ginny, but the child went to wailing again. Before Mushaniq could offer, Georgie swooped her up, dancing in circles and bouncing. A hesitant grin parted the tiny lips despite her still-wet eyes. With a nod, Timqua gathered foodstuffs and an earthenware pot for cooking. "Kindling, Mushaniq. But do not go far."

She lingered for a moment—that should be a boy's task, and she was nearly a woman—then darted off to fetch what Auntie needed.

Never mind that Georgie was nearly to manhood himself—or would be if his people would let him go on *huskanaw*. Many of them, however, decried it as being contrary to their religion. Mushaniq sniffed as she gathered small branches. How could venturing out with the most sober of preparations to seek one's God and an individual's own place in the spirit realm be disapproved of?

Of course, with their town so freshly under attack and half the men gone to the aid of others, this was no time for anyone to be venturing out, no matter what the reason.

At the edge of the town, she stared into the forest. All seemed calm and peaceful now, but a shiver coursed over her skin. How could it be that here she felt so confined, where the land lay vast beyond her imaginings, while on their small island out at the edge of *yapám* she felt safe and free?

She mouthed the syllables. *Kurawoten. Kuh-rah woh-tuin.* Oh, how she missed her old home.

Chapter Two

THE PAST:
Kurawoten Island, August 1587

S he ran, hopping over fallen branches and ducking beneath gnarled limbs of the island oaks. The sun was warm upon her skin, the wind cooling. Ahead of her, a small herd of *wutapantam* lifted their heads, then startled away into the underbrush. A laugh bubbled from deep in her chest.

How good was life, and how beautiful their home, surrounded by both sea and sound. She topped a hill and stopped, soaking in the shush of waves and miles of blue stretching beyond the pale sand edging the forest where she stood.

Nunohum and the aunties would be wanting her back very soon, but none begrudged her this daily run up the hills and back again. In fact, it was customary for all of them to roam, sometimes on a mere whim, but more often for the sheer joy of simply rambling about. Being yet a child meant she could do so with more speed and freedom.

With a sigh, she turned back and made her way down the slope. A white heron took flight from a nearby pond, gliding across the water.

As she neared the town, shouts and cries came to her ears. She hesitated. An alarm, or—no, they carried the distinct ring of happiness and not warning. Running then, she burst from the trees into the town, where several people gathered.

Timqua—*Numiditáq*—turned from where she stood at the edge of the gathering. "Mushaniq! There you are. Come quickly—your father has returned!"

Her heart leaped into her throat. *Nohsh*, here? The great Manteo, who had been snatched away by destiny when she was nearly too young to comprehend what was taking place or who the strangely garbed men were on their giant *kanoe*?

Suddenly her feet would not move, and she stood, rooted, until the crowd parted and she saw him.

He turned, dressed just as the Inqutish around him, a tall, wide-brimmed hat on his head and a fire stick in his hand. Foreign, yet. . .his smile the same. His eyes sparkled as he crossed the ground between them with long strides. It truly was Nohsh—so tall, so handsome!

And *here*!

He caught her up in his arms, murmuring in her ear. "Mushaniq—*Nunutánuhs*, my little daughter!"

Inexplicable tears sprouted, and she clung to him in return.

Through the rest of the day, she could not bring herself to stray far from his side, his being surrounded by the Inqutish, whose eyes devoured them as if they were the ones dressed strangely. So long it was since he left, she'd not even been sure she remembered what he looked and sounded like. In odd moments as he spoke in both the People's tongue and that of the Inqutish, she had to peer closely to know it was him.

At the same time, bursts of pride flared within her chest. This was her father. The one chosen for a very great journey and purpose—the hope of bringing two peoples together, of learning more about the world across Mother Ocean and carrying that knowledge back in order to make their own People stronger and wiser.

But what was this they discussed? One of the Inqutish men had been slain and most cruelly. She remembered talk of the coming of the

Inqutish from boys and men who wandered and fished the sound, and how they'd seen a war party cross from Dasemonguepeuk on a day not long ago. Someone had been close enough to be certain that one of that party was Wanchese of the *Roanoac*, with his *Sukwoten* brother warriors.

Mushaniq watched the Inqutish faces as they heard the news. Shock, anger, disbelief. A tendril of fear went through her. Would these people bring war with them?

But they all went away the next day, taking Nohsh with them, and life settled back into its previous rhythm.

Except that now she knew he dwelt on another island to the north of them. And she missed him.

THE PAST:
Roanoac Island, August 1587

How good it was to be out on the water again in a kanoe, watching the fish swirl lazily in the pale green shallows of the sound, both big and small, sometimes in schools and sometimes intermingling. Manteo lifted his spear, narrowing his eyes against the glare of the sun.

Would his arm remember its craft?

In an instant, he was transported back to that moment when the first great winged kanoes appeared near Chacandepeco, off of Kurawoten. The strange, glistening armor worn by the bearded strangers. The inner nudging—and years of watching his elders dispense hospitality to any and all visitors—that led him to spear and gather two heaps of fish, one for each of the ships.

Who could have guessed he'd be carried over the sea on such a ship not only once but four times?

He drew a deep breath, let it out slowly, then threw the spear. A large *chingwusso* wriggled against the floor of the sound, pinned there by the hazel shaft. Well, that was fortuitous! These were of a kind not usually in season for another moon or two yet.

He kept fishing, next taking a *manchauemec,* and another chingwusso after, his body falling into the easy rhythm of spear following where eye and arm sent it.

Did the waters of his homeland welcome him back? How very odd that water should be a symbol of passage from one identity to another— and yet, not odd at all. When he considered the change in himself, from the very moment he accepted the task of journeying across the sea with the Inqutish, indeed, from the moment he accepted it was even possible, it seemed fitting. Did his own name, *Snatched,* not reflect that—how he felt snatched from his old life into this new one. Accepting the rite of what they called *baptism* was but one step of many on this journey. And yet, as explained to him by Thomas Harriot and others, it was as weighty and needful as huskanaw had been in his youth.

Harriot, however, had emphasized that it was to be a choice. One came to faith and knowledge of the Great Creator and God above all by being drawn by His—how had Harriot put it? By His Sacred Breath. The idea intrigued Manteo—Wanchese too, he believed, though the two of them debated it often enough. And yet, Sir Walter Ralegh had commanded that Manteo be baptized if not while they were still in England then once they landed back on Ossomocomuck and established the town named after him.

Commanded. As if a man's heart and soul could be dictated to so. To perform obeisance and ritual, perhaps. But if that were all faith in the True God was, where would be the difference between Him and the various *Montóac* and *Kewás?* Harriot said that men were told to love with all their heart, soul, and strength. A command, true, but one inspired not only, the Englishman had said, by God's greatness but also His goodness—and the sacrifice of His own Son for the sins of mankind.

Manteo could not conceive of giving his own child for the wrongs of another, but Harriot and others assured him that this was so with God.

He thought of Mushaniq, with her bright and lively manner. Well was she called *Squirrel.* Would she choose to change that once she came of age?

How tall she was already. Would she remind him even more of her mother as she grew? The longing stirred within him to see her, though it had been but days this time, but as always, he pushed it away. So close he was and yet bound to obligations that would not release him. *Snatched*, indeed.

He had sailed across the seas in their great winged kanoes. Felt the chill of winds more northerly than those that reached Ossomocomuck, and marveled at dwelling places so piled in upon one another he could hardly walk between without feeling short of breath. Seen hordes of their people—bearded men decked out in glittering splendor, and women so trussed in their clothing he could not be sure whether they truly were *crenepo*.

He had been presented to their weroansqua, the *queen* Elizabeth, herself seeming a fantastical construct with only hands and face showing. Her hair was a flame red and her eyes the color of the sky—or what passed as the sky in that drab land—but her smile drew him in and reminded him of his own mother.

And now he was home—or near enough—and had gotten barely a night and a day visiting with his own daughter.

This was where he had been placed, however, by fates or Montóac or *Ahoné* or the God of the English. *Yehovah*, Harriot had said His name was. *I am that I am.*

A God who merely—*was*. Spanning time and eternity. But vitally interested in the affairs of men, he was told.

He nearly could not comprehend such a thing.

Like one's father, Harriot had insisted. Or mother, Manteo had added. Harriot owned that could be so, since their God was referred to in at least one instance as a mother bird, spreading her wings over her offspring.

God in heaven, Creator of all—I believe You are. I have always believed. I am told I need no other sacrifice but Kryst—*yet I pray You, accept mine.*

He speared fish until the bottom of his kanoe was covered, then returned to shore.

For better or worse, today was the day. They'd told him not to try providing single-handedly for dinner to celebrate his own baptism, but it was something to keep his hands busy while his mind yet sorted it all out.

At last, he stood before the others, waiting. Why did his innards tie themselves in knots? He had done far more daring things than get up before a gathering and allow water to be poured over his head while ceremonial words were spoken.

And yet, this felt like more. So much more.

He spoke as he was prompted and listened to the congregation's responses to the call and answer, and then he bowed his head over the bowl. Water—such a simple thing. It shimmered, reflecting the sky, before Nicholas Johnson's hand disturbed the surface and dipped. Once, twice, thrice. It trickled over his head, down his neck, and across his face, sending an unbidden shiver across his body.

And something else, which he could not name. A stirring—nay, a burning—in the middle of his chest and spreading outward.

He straightened, his gaze skimming everyone's faces as wonder overtook him. Nicholas Johnson lifted a bottle of oil and traced a cross upon Manteo's forehead.

Wonder and joy filled him until he could scarce stand still. What was this?

With this sort of strength, he could run from one end of the island to the other. Swim across the sound to Dasemonguepeuk and then run some more. Would the God of the Inqutish—any god, for that matter—show His presence so? Such open favor?

His throat thickened. Whatever men said, whatever they did—and he had seen many who used the name of this God and of His Christ as a weapon—

You truly are God alone. And I will indeed follow You all the days of my life.

Chapter Three

THE PAST:
Kurawoten Island, Winter 1587–88

I t was complicated with Nohsh. Now that she was a little older, she hardly recalled his leaving, except that it was cause for one of many great celebrations the People threw at the slightest notice.

Aunties Timqua and Wesnah and the other women, as well as Nunohum, filled in the gap. The men were gone so often anyway, hunting and visiting and all, that she did not mind. The women and other children were always busy enough with or without the men there.

Unlike the other men, though, he went—and came—in the summer, always in the summer, until this year, when they were told women and children came along. But though Nohsh and the others made several trips back and forth from Roanoac, rarely did they stay more than a night, and never long enough for her to spend much time with him.

He returned again as the wind coming from the west began to have an edge, with the same Inqutish men in tow. There had been attacks from Dasemonguepeuk, and the Inqutish were in trouble, he said, as they sat long into the night, smoking the *uppowoc*.

Nunohum, who was weroansqua, and the others made the surprising suggestion that the Inqutish move to Kurawoten—men, women, and children alike. Mushaniq listened as excitement grew, and they talked of bringing even their strange houses to make their own town, overlooking the sound as others did. Some of the men would also rebuild the fort on the ocean side to keep watch for more of their kanoes.

Mushaniq did not know what to think about that. With more people on the island, there could be more friends to run and play games with. But the Inqutish men—were they good men or evil? She'd heard stories of awful things done by the *Span-ish.*

And she did love her freedom to run about the island.

But if the Inqutish came to live nearby, then she could at last satisfy her curiosity about them. Who were these strangers, and why was their skin so pale? Why did the men let their face hair grow instead of plucking it as the People did, and for what purpose did they all wear so much clothing? Were they cold even in summer? Wesnah and others who had seen their women reported that they covered even more of their bodies than the men. How did the mothers feed their babies if their breasts were wrapped up so tightly all the time—or did they even have breasts like normal women?

Her questions were endless. She'd heard whispers—that they wore all manner of clothing even while sleeping and did not wash every day as people should, while their kanoes and weapons were wonderful beyond description.

How could a people be such a contradiction? But she wanted to see them for herself.

Roanoac Island, Winter 1587–88

It began as an adventure. Then—in one day—it became a nightmare.

Georgie kept expecting to wake up and find it had all been a bad dream, but that never happened.

Though everyone was so kind, he hated the pity in their eyes. Especially the women. It was easier after a while to stay with the men and boys who hadn't come with wives or mothers, to work alongside and stay busy, or to simply disappear into the woods when he found himself idle. Most of the boys wandered and explored whenever they could. They were oft scolded for it—as if Georgie needed the reminder of how his father was slain—yet many a time it was one of them who saw the savages slipping through the trees, bristling with weapons and war paint, before ever the guards knew an attack was coming.

Now they were leaving Roanoac, which everyone said could not support their people for very long anyway, and removing to another island, fifty miles to the south. An island already inhabited. With savages. Taking refuge, the Assistants and other men called it.

Georgie was not so sure. The Croatoan seemed friendly enough, but what if they turned upon the English and slaughtered them all?

None seemed concerned about that, however. Or if they were, no one said anything about it.

On the other hand, Georgie wasn't sorry to be leaving this particular island, where there was nothing but nightmares.

They made him board the pinnace with the women and girls. He remembered when they first landed at Roanoac—how Governor White tasked him with looking after his daughter, Elinor Dare, very round at the time with child. She'd been there that day they'd carried his father's battered body back to the town. Though he wound up biding awhile with the Archards, whose son Thomas was nearest Georgie's age, it was the pretty Mistress Dare he felt the most drawn to and protective toward—her and the sweet, golden-haired Virginia, the first English babe born in the New World.

Baby Ginny, as they called her, charmed everyone. Georgie, however, hadn't expected to find himself so taken with her, but 'twas no hardship to watch over her and Mistress Dare, whether tagging along on foraging expeditions or just to hold the babe upon occasion.

At the moment, she lay safely tucked inside her mother's cloak, and Mistress Dare herself perched where she could watch the waves and shore, so nothing remained to hinder Georgie from climbing into the rigging of the pinnace.

The sea voyage here had been long and rough, but he missed the open water and having the wind in his hair. The endless rise and fall of the waves, the green of the deep—lighter here where the shoals lay—and the cry of seabirds who glided the wind above the pinnace. It soothed in ways he could not put words to and at least for a little while made him forget the knot in his gut over what had been and what was yet to come.

This was the day. Mushaniq could hardly contain her excitement. Despite Timqua telling her repeatedly that most of the day would pass before they could expect the kanoe to come, she spent a good part of it running the beach from ocean side to sound side, accompanied by her cousin Kokon, then up the hill to try to catch a glimpse of the great white wings.

The sun hung very low in the sky indeed by the time she saw them. A cry burst from her throat, and her entire body quivered. They were here at last! Kokon on her heels, she ran down the beach, past the swirling inlet where the ever-churning waves of the great ocean met the ripples of the sound.

With the larger, winged kanoe remaining out in the sound where it was a little deeper, a smaller craft brought several people to the shore. Mushaniq crept closer, Kokon matching her step for step, then sank down to peer through the sea grasses. Her heart pounded so, it felt as if it would leap from her chest, and she found herself clinging to Kokon's hand.

These people would change everything. She felt it to her very bones.

The women climbed out of the kanoe, one by one, helped by the men. She knew they must be women because of the way their clothing wrapped about their legs, all the way to their feet, while the men dressed alike in coverings that allowed their legs to be free. How odd! And how inconvenient for the women, who had to pull up the strange, long kilts in order to even step across the sand.

Timqua, Wesnah, and the others welcomed them and led them along to the town. Mushaniq and Kokon crept along behind.

As they walked and finally as they were brought into the women's yehakan and served cups of spiced, sweetened drink, the women stared at them—and everything else—as intently as the girls watched them. There

23

was a small child, boy or girl Mushaniq could not tell, as it was covered neck to toe in clothing, and a babe in arms.

Her fingers itched to touch the strangers' clothing and hair, but Timqua had warned her severely to stay back and give the newcomers room and time. She did not understand that. She was only curious! But even she could see by the widened eyes, the furtive glances, that these women were more than a little frightened and wary.

The strangers had just begun to settle in when a second group of women arrived. There was another baby, a wee thing with the palest skin and hair and eyes the color of the sky. Mushaniq crept closer and crouched where she could better watch. After suckling—so these strange women did indeed have breasts under all that clothing—the little one pushed up to look around and caught Mushaniq's eye from across a short space. They exchanged a mutual grin, and the baby's arms flapped in delight.

Georgie sailed with the pinnace farther down Croatoan Island, past the first of the savages' towns, where just opposite a broad, shallow cove, they dropped anchor. There they took the longboat ashore, laden with various supplies and baggage—or such as they'd been able to carry along with the women, who would stay the night at the Croatoan town while the men finished unloading and diverse other preparations. Thus the women and little children would be cared for and then have a full day's light to move to their own dwellings and sort through baggage.

He lifted a chest from the bottom of the longboat, hefted it, and trudged in the wake of Ananias Dare, up a sandy path through the reeds and into a scrubby forest.

This island was different from Roanoac in small ways. For one, no large land could be seen across the sound, which lay calm as glass this evening, so calm that they'd needed to break out the oars. And then the trees—

"The trees are shorter here," he said, between huffing breaths.

Ananias glanced back with a wry smile. "It is because of the sea winds. Roanoac is more protected."

"And closer to the mainland."

"Aye, very much closer. But here we are more protected from other perils." Something shone in his blue gaze that might have been either pity or speculation. "I do not believe the people here are to be feared, if that is your thought."

He would not admit he had entertained that very thought, and more than once. But Ananias only nodded and led on to the town site.

Several of the houses were already up or mostly so. After setting down the chest where Ananias indicated, at the base of a sprawling oak, Georgie wandered about to view the progress made. Plats lay already measured and marked out, with holes being dug for posts.

Beyond the immediate town site, pens edged in rails kept the pigs confined, while chickens scratched and pecked here and there, roaming about even as the shadows grew long. One of Georgie's tasks on Roanoac had been to make sure they were herded into their coop for the night and to look about for eggs laid elsewhere than the boxes provided for them inside the coop.

William Wythers, one of the older boys, came trotting around the corner. "Georgie! I think we're all here now, are we not? Come to the fire—we've fish a-broiling."

In the deepening twilight, the flickers from the bonfire illuminated not only properly clad English bodies but Croatoan men as well, their bare skin gleaming. Georgie's feet dragged nearly to a stop.

"Come," Willie said, beckoning, before Georgie thought he'd even noticed the hesitation.

The fish—and some accompanying bread of the grain they called pegatawah—did smell beguilingly good. If the savages thought to win their trust for ill purposes by feeding them, it was sound strategy. Georgie could not bring himself to refuse.

A round, yellowish cake was offered him by a savage whose entire face creased with a grin. "*Apon!*" he said.

Georgie repeated the word, lightly tossing the thing between his fingers, still hot and steaming it was. He took a bite, and the sweet-salty flavor of the coarsely grained cake burst inside his mouth.

He'd had these before, after the attack on Dasemonguepeuk that had gone so badly, but for some reason these tasted better. Far better. He wolfed it down, caring not that his tongue was a little burnt.

After sating himself with more apon and some broiled fish, he slept that night in the upper floor of one of the houses, swathed in a cloak that had been his father's. 'Twas still odd to him that all those belongings were now his, but his father was not here. On this night, however, he thankfully had but a moment to dwell on that before weariness claimed him, and when he next opened his eyes, it was to a pearly dawn.

"We are to fetch the women from the Croatoan town," Arnold Archard said. "You lads may come along and explore a bit, but don't run too far. We'll be a-needing you before long."

Georgie fell in with young Johnnie Sampson and Thomas Humfrey. 'Twas but a short stroll to the Croatoan town, and the aroma of cooking food drifted to them on the morning breeze.

As the various houses came into view, rounded roofs and sides all covered over with woven reed mats, a feeling of strangeness overcame Georgie. Here they were at last, among the people who, if they were not the ones to have slain Da, were nearer in relation to them than the English.

His feet dragged to a halt. Could he truly do this? Live with a people who were a daily reminder of Da's brutal death? Although nothing at this point was not a reminder of that.

John and Thomas stopped and looked back. "C'mon, Georgie, what are you waiting for?"

The treble of women's voices floated from somewhere ahead of them. Georgie swallowed and forced his feet to move. He must do this. He *would* do this, even if he too were killed. He would be brave and leave no room for any to say he was chickenhearted or that he had not done Da proud.

The other boys jostled him as he caught up with them, but before either could rib him about his slowness, a pair of young girls came darting from behind a house. The taller, leading, skidded to a stop so that the other collided with her. Two pairs of glittering dark eyes took them in, mouths hanging half open, but he was trying desperately not to notice.

"Gor!" John said. "They both be nekkid!"

Well, they each wore strings of beads, both copper and shells, and a bit of moss tied up between their legs, but that hardly counted.

While both John and Thomas sniggered, the shorter of the girls nudged the other, and she drew herself up a little straighter and crowed, "*Wingapo!*"

It was their greeting, he knew. With the barest nod, he replied, "Wingapo," but John and Thomas only went off into another round of laughter. Georgie shot them a dark look. "Don't mind them—they be but swine."

Not that the girls would comprehend, but the other boys would.

He set off walking again, John and Thomas trailing behind this time. The girls accompanied them, skipping and gamboling and resembling nothing so much as newborn lambs. Or magpies, because they chattered aplenty as well. And the sleek black of their hair reminded him of birds' wings.

Around the next corner, the women all came into view, with familiar English forms and faces mingled with savage. A tightness around Georgie's chest eased—and there was Mistress Dare, with little Ginny in her arms.

She looked up nearly at the same moment, and a smile lit her round, pretty face. "Georgie!"

A grin tugged at his mouth—he could not help it. Mistress Dare was always so kind and her baby so sweet.

The native woman beside her pointed at one of the girls and said something. While Mistress Dare was distracted in the exchange of conversation, Mistress Archard caught sight of them and brought a stack of apon, giving one to each of them, girls included.

Even under their strange clothing, very much like that worn by the grown men only without the shining armor, Mushaniq could see the boys were lean and wiry. How many years had each of them? They did not appear to be very close to adulthood.

Under their caps, two of them had darker hair, and one of those had dark eyes, while the other's eyes were light. But the third boy—the one who had tried to talk to her and Kokon but then refused to look at them as they'd skipped along beside—had hair the color of the sand along the ocean and eyes the color of a clear summer sky. It was a fascinating combination.

The light-haired woman with the baby came forward as if to speak with the boys, then looked aside at one of the Inqutish men approaching—also with sandy hair and blue eyes. Were they this boy's parents? But the boy stood back and did not greet either of them as the woman ran to the man's embrace. Then—as if the night and morning had not already held enough strangeness—the man and woman kissed. Why would they do that? Only a mother or father would give such a token of affection. And right on the mouth as well! For a moment, the sweet and savory apon tasted as ashes on Mushaniq's tongue.

She shot a glance at Kokon. Her cousin's face reflected her own disgust.

This, in addition to the strangers' reluctance to bathe properly, did not recommend them in the least. But Auntie Timqua and Grandmama said they must be kind, that perhaps they didn't know any better.

Perhaps it would do these *wutahshuntas* good to be with *Tunapewak* and learn better ways.

Chapter Four

Kurawoten Island, Spring 1588

As the strangers built their town between Mushaniq's and the next Croatoan village down the water's edge, life settled back into something of a predictable rhythm. Mushaniq found much opportunity to observe them, either from Timqua sending her over on some errands, accompanying Timqua or Nunohum, or sneaking over alone to watch through the bushes.

She wanted to talk to Nohsh. He was so busy though, always deep in conversation with either the men of the Inqutish or the adults of their own people, and something made her oddly reluctant to interrupt. He was so changed from his time away, and his continuing to dress as the Inqutish was off-putting. What was wrong with their people's way of adorning themselves? Was it that after so much time away, he, like the Inqutish, was too cold to go back to freer clothing?

She felt sorry for him if so.

Another that she felt sorry for was the boy with the sand-colored hair, whose name she learned was *Chor-chee*. Timqua told her it was his father who had been so brutally slain by Wanchese and the Sukwoten shortly after the Inqutish landed on Roanoac Island.

That was partly why his people had sought refuge on Kroatoan. While Roanoac was closer to the mainland, here they were farther away, and it had been a long time since war had come to this island.

She hoped Chorchee felt safe here and came to love it as much as she did.

"What does it mean, then, that you are *weroance* of Dasemonguepeuk and Roanoac?"

What indeed? Manteo walked the shore with Towaye, whose return to the ways of their people was so complete he nearly did not recognize his cousin.

A moon had passed and then some since the Inqutish moved to join the Kurawoten. The weather, always fickle during this season, warmed enough that the men fishing out on the sound in their kanoe had bared their upper bodies. Would that he could be among them, soaking in the sun and the joy of providing for his family and the town.

"It is a fair question," he said slowly. "With the recent attacks coming from Dasemonguepeuk, my thought is that the English are, how should I say it, hopeful?"

Towaye gave a laugh. "Have you told them this?"

Manteo blew out a long breath. "No—*mahta.*"

"Well. Perhaps it is not such an unlikely thing, that we should make war on the Sukwoten and others and push them from Dasemonguepeuk."

"In time. I am in no hurry to go to war again."

Towaye eyed him.

"Perhaps," he went on, "once our Inqutish have settled in and grown stronger. But there is a certain pleasure in just being here and enjoying our lives again that I am reluctant to give up."

Still Towaye said nothing, and Manteo studied him.

"What is it?" he said finally.

His cousin rubbed the back of his neck and turned away, shaking his head.

"Speak, already."

Towaye gave another little laugh before shifting toward him again. "Timqua. And the other women. Well—we all wonder, really."

Manteo folded his arms. Obviously, this might take awhile.

"She told me to ask, and if I do not, she will."

"Such weighty matters we have already discussed this morning without benefit of uppowoc," Manteo said, letting a bit of a growl edge his voice. "What difference one more?"

"Well. We want to know—she wants—which of the women you have been seeking out for comfort?"

Was that all? A smile tugged at his mouth. "None," he answered after a moment.

Towaye's mouth dropped open, then, "Do not say it! Surely you are jesting."

"I do not jest." Oh, he would hear about this later from his sister. "But there is a being set apart that God desires of His followers, and I wish to be obedient to that."

"God. You mean, the Inqutish god. He is opposed to a man having a woman?"

"No, but He wishes men and women to be married and to be faithful to each other."

Or so Nicholas Johnson— and Harriot before him—had said.

Towaye gripped the back of his neck and squinted at Manteo. "The Inqutish do not so with each other. Surely you remember, especially on their cold island and crowded towns."

"Mahta, and I own that full well. I simply wish to do better. It is not their actions I answer for, but my own."

Towaye nodded slowly.

And hear about it he did. They'd barely returned to the town, with preparations for evening meal nearly complete, before Timqua cornered him. "What is this about the Inqutish God disapproving of a man having a woman? How then are we to get children?"

When Manteo could stop laughing long enough, he drew a breath and answered, "It is not that He disapproves. He wishes men and women to marry and be faithful to each other."

His sister's expression remained severe. "So do you have plans to marry again?"

"Not yet."

Her eyes softened a little. "How is a man—or a woman either—supposed to go without comfort?"

He had to think about his answer. "So far, I have felt no need. Or," he amended, to her upraised eyebrow, "very little."

Her chin tucked as she continued to gaze at him.

"Truly. It is a wondrous thing, that we can know the Maker of all. But I trust that when the time is right, there will be a woman to be my wife."

She did look away at that.

"You do not believe me?"

Her eyes cut back to him. "I have never known a man who did not—need. You are my brother, and I have high regard for you, but this?" A smile quirked her mouth.

His thoughts flashed back to his time in England—both times. He would not tell her how frequently he and Wanchese—and later Towaye as well—were approached by the women there, as often by what Harriot referred to as "high born" as those who were little more than slaves. The attention was flattering, and while Wanchese thought it amusing, Manteo felt only hesitation and at times outright disgust. These females who wore so many layers and yet so rarely washed. Not that he and Wanchese were able to wash as often as they liked either.

And none were the sweet, winsome girl who had been mother to Mushaniq.

"Do you still mourn Shines Like Sunset, or is there another who catches your eye?"

Timqua, as always, saw more than he guessed. He shrugged and gestured to his raiment, which even now felt strange but he was reluctant to give up. "Who would wish to be my wife, after everything?"

Pity colored her gaze again. "Do I have your permission to inquire?"

He huffed but then said softly, "I suppose you might as well."

She smiled again, only a little, a shadow of her customary openness. "Do you ever regret going with the Inqutish that first time?"

"Mahta," he said, without doubt or hesitation.

And it was true. Though none of them knew how this venture would go, the meeting and building of a community of strangers and family, he was glad of his part in it.

He would not be like Wanchese, who determined the threat these strangers would be and set his face to be their enemy. And he would go to whatever lengths necessary to protect them—and his own people.

It was Nohsh who sought her out first, after all.

"Come, let us walk," he said, beckoning, and set off for the ocean-side beach.

Was this not what she'd been longing for? And yet now that the moment was here, nervousness shivered through her.

Where had all her questions gone?

Before they crossed the dunes, he bent and removed his *mahkusun*, and she did the same. The morning had started cool enough for footwear but warmed, and it was easier to navigate loose sand with bare feet.

The sea grasses rippled with the wind coming off the sea, and as they made their way to within sight of the waves, her hair swept straight back. How good it was, though, that she'd thought to bring a mantle, the warmth of the rabbit fur on the inside soft against her skin. At the top of the dune, she paused, tipping her face to the sun, gaze tracing the wisps of white clouds floating against the winter-blue sky.

Nohsh ambled past her, sinking a little and sliding as his feet hit the band of loose sand above the tide mark. Mushaniq followed, scanning both near and far, as was her habit, for anything interesting. Scattered small shells and clumps of dried vegetation were all that immediately met her eye.

On any other day, wading through loose sand would have been fun, but she wanted to keep pace with Nohsh, and so she crossed as quickly as possible to the strand edging the waves, where the sand lay smooth and packed from the tides. They both trod so close to the water that the sea-foam swirled over their feet as they walked. Mushaniq yelped at the first cold rush of it, but then the second wave was not so bad.

Nohsh looked back and smiled. The tracings across his cheeks stood out in the sunlight, familiar and comforting.

"Are things well with you?" he asked as she neared, raising his voice over the wind and waves. "I have been so occupied, I neglected to ask after your well-being, but Timqua assures me you grow and thrive."

Those were strange words for him to use—but she supposed it was true. Life was happy enough, and they all had plenty to eat and wear, despite last year's lack of rain, and so she nodded.

He set off walking again, mahkusun dangling from his fingertips as he clasped his hands behind his back. "And how are you getting on with the other youths of the Inqutish?"

Her thoughts skipped back over the past moon and more. There were girls, only a bit older than Mushaniq, that she had not realized that first day were not already grown because they dressed so much like the older women. It surprised her that even a few of the older ones came unattached from any of the men. But Nohsh was waiting on a reply.

"We get on fine. It will be easier once we can speak each other's tongue. Some of the boys are curious, of course." She wrinkled her nose at the thought of allowing liberties with any of *them*—even if she were of age already. "But there have been no real difficulties so far."

Nohsh nodded, but distractedly.

"I know you want us all to be—*nitáp*, friends."

"*Kupi.*" Even that was spoken absently. At last, he stopped and turned toward her. "More than friends, I wish us to be as one people. One heart and mind. One purpose."

Mushaniq rubbed her nose. What exactly did that mean?

He chuckled. "We do not have to clothe ourselves like the Inqutish or they like us. We do not have to look like each other. But to—help each other. Work together. Fight together."

"Play together?"

"Kupi. That. All of that."

She nodded hesitantly. "But how can that happen when we cannot yet speak the same tongue? You cannot be everywhere to translate."

"Mahta, but people are learning. You—you will learn more quickly than those of us who are grown." He smiled, and it was full of fondness, his dark eyes sparkling. "Go to the Inqutish women, offer to hold their babies or carry their baskets. Ask what things are called."

Mushaniq frowned. She knew to do all those things. At least, she knew with Timqua and the other aunties and women of the town. "So I should consider the Inqutish women as our own people?"

He nodded vigorously, smiling broadly. "Kupi, exactly!"

She turned her face to the wind, for a moment only letting herself savor the tug on her hair and clothing, then folded her cape more snugly about herself and took off down the beach. Nohsh fell into step beside her.

"So," she said, "I have wished to ask you."

He leaned closer. "Ask, then."

"This new religion —" She'd longed to voice these questions and now, how did she say it? "Do you truly believe it, or have you taken it just to please the Inqutish?"

"Hmmm." His expression, when she peeked at him, was grave. "There was something of pleasing the Inqutish, I suppose, at least in the beginning. But it has become more." He fixed her with a look. "Much more."

Something in his face dragged her feet to a halt. "Tell me."

He brushed aside strands of hair blown across his face and smiled, but wistfully this time. "This is not just religion, little one. This God is real and true."

"But—" She stared at him, the sparkle of his dark eyes. "Of course God is real and true."

He laughed. "Kupi, but He is different from what we have always been taught. He is not far away and uninterested in what we do with our lives. He is very much near to us and very much interested. So much, in fact, that He came to this world as a baby and grew to be a man who would defeat death for us. He died but then was raised again to life, nevermore to die."

Mushaniq took a step back. She had never heard such a thing! How could that be?

"But. . .the dead do not come back." A shiver took her at the thought of their *machicomuck* and the dead lying there until flesh and sinew could be flayed from the bones and all bound up in mats, ready to be buried at the proper time.

An image flashed through her mind of a desiccated corpse, rising up and walking. She shuddered again.

But Nohsh's smile was patient and steady. "It is not how you are thinking. He truly was living and breathing—even eating food to prove to His followers that He was still a man such as they, only undying ever after."

She found herself shaking her head. "I will think on it" were the only words she could find to say.

"I would not expect anything different." Nohsh's smile remained undimmed.

Had he taken leave of his senses?

She'd ask Auntie Timqua about it later. For now, she mimicked Nohsh's stance, hands clasped behind her back, and kept walking down the beach.

Why was it so difficult to talk with her? Simply to explain what he had experienced? She was his daughter, after all. Should there not be some sort of understanding between them?

God of heaven and earth, why can I not tell her properly of You? I thought this would be easy. Or at least not quite so difficult.

Truthfully, though, he was torn between dismay and yet laughter at how she struck such an adult pose and strutted down the beach. So proud, so—queenly. She minded him of a very young—and Kurawoten—version of the Inqutish queen, Elizabeth.

And of Shines Like Sunset as well, of course.

How lovely she would be when grown. Or even in a few years.

A few long strides, and he caught up to her.

"Nohsh, tell me about the great Inqutish weroansqua."

Manteo laughed softly. "I was just thinking about her."

Mushaniq glanced up, waiting. He blew out a long breath. A tiny woman in a great dress. But how to translate that into his own tongue?

"Does she look like the crenepo of the Inqutish here?"

"No. She is smaller and older. She dresses in the finest of their clothing, so much that she is nearly lost beneath the weight of her wealth."

Mushaniq looked thoughtful. "Well, that is nothing new. Grandmama likes to dress up as well."

"The Inqutish also do not prick their skin to mark it, but do often paint their faces. Especially the women or those who put on plays of great deeds."

Of course, their people did similar things, and Mushaniq nodded as if she already knew this.

"Is she a good weroansqua?"

Well, there was a question.

"I think she tries to be, Nunutánuhs. She is much loved by some, hated by others because they think she should not be weroansqua. In that land, women do not often lead."

Disapproval flashed across her face. "That is stupid."

He chuckled. "It may be, but it is their land and not ours."

Her expression did not change. "That makes it no less stupid."

This time his laughter completely overcame any reply he might have offered.

Chapter Five

Nohsh's suggestion on approaching the Inqutish women lingered with her. The very next day, as soon as morning oblations and the meal were finished, she made an excuse and trotted down the path along the sound toward the strangers' town until the approaching clomp of their curious footgear sent her scurrying into the underbrush.

She was not quite ready to face one of them on her own just yet.

Huddling behind brush grown sparse with winter's leaf fall, she kept still and watched the oddly clad men stomping loud and clumsy down the path where she had just been. Once they'd passed, she hurried on, this time under cover and not on the path proper, until voices and the noise of work came to her ears. She slowed to a creep and made her way stealthily until she could peer between the branches and observe the activity of the town.

Men moved about carrying tools and building materials—at least she thought they were—and even now a house was being built nearby. How fascinating its shape, all hard angles and not the rounded warmth of their own longhouses. A few fowl wandered about then scattered, chased by a dog that someone scolded. A pair of women took a basket of—was that their clothing?—to a central fire where a large pot hung, made of what looked like *wassador*.

Mushaniq fingered the loops of beads adorning her neck, made also of wassador but a different color. How wealthy they must be, to use the rare substance for something as common as cooking!

A repeated ringing sound, as of something being struck over and over, echoed from the other side of the town. She hesitated then flexed her body to crawl backward out of the thicket—

"Hai."

A boy's voice, behind her, spoke the single word. Mushaniq startled with a flurry, twitching around and biting back a squeak. It was the one she'd seen before, in her own town, with the sand-colored hair and sky-colored eyes. *Chorchee.*

He squinted at her, bending to peer at her beneath the bush. A string of words came from his mouth, not a single one of which she understood. With a huff, he stepped back and motioned her out.

Did she trust him? But perhaps what Nohsh had said began here. . .now.

She studied him, even as he studied her, then tapped her chest. "*Nutuduwins* Mushaniq." She said it again, drawing the syllables out. "*Mush-ah-neek.*"

He repeated it clearly enough. She pointed at him. "Chorchee?"

He laughed shortly, a reddish flush sweeping up his cheeks. "*Georgie.*"

She too laughed. "Chorchee." It was close enough, was it not?

He made a flip-flopping motion with his hand and shook his head, rattling off something else. Then he beckoned, and taking a few steps away, pointed to a tree with stiff, glossy leaves. "K-ka. . ." He cleared his throat and tried again. "*Ka ka torwawirocs yowo?*"

The words were halting and garbled, almost as if he were chewing instead of speaking, but his intent seemed clear enough: *What is this called?*

"*Ascopo,*" she said. *Sweet bay.*

"Ascopo," he repeated, haltingly, then walked a little farther and pointed to another tree, gnarled and bent with prickly, fragrant greenery that did not fall during winter.

"*Andacon.*"

"Andacon." He pointed back at the sweet bay. "Ascopo."

Much better now. She smiled and, taking a few steps away, beckoned. "Pyas. I will tell you more."

When he hesitated, she repeated the command to come, but he did not move. With a little huff, she returned. This time she offered words for *hand, foot, hair, leg,* and other bodily features and articles of clothing and adornment. Georgie grew bolder, offering in turn words such as *shirt, dub-let,* and *hose.*

He was not, by any inducement, going to follow an unknown savage, be she ever so young or friendly, into the woods alone. But her efforts surprised him, both to speak and make herself understood, and the trading of words was a pleasant enough diversion.

What burned most in his thoughts, though, was the question—why was she hiding in the bushes, spying on the town? Was it childish curiosity or something more?

There was a way to find out.

After they'd traded words for clothing and parts of the body, he cocked his head toward the town. "Will you come?" he asked.

Dark, glittering eyes were watchful, alert, but she did not move.

Ah. She'd not yet comprehended that. But what was it she'd said when beckoning him? He'd heard others use it. "Pee-ahs." He motioned to her and took a step toward the houses.

Her lips quirked. "Pyas?"

He nodded and took another step. "Pyas. Come."

Her gaze swung toward the town, then back to him, the conflict playing openly across her round face. She shifted to peer through the bushes and trees again, then gathered her cape about her and gave an answering nod. "Kupi."

He felt vaguely foolish leading her into the village but held his shoulders square and kept his steps purposeful as he made his way between the houses. Mistress Jones and Mistress Dare smiled and waved, and after the briefest hesitation, he angled toward them. After a properly polite greeting, he asked, "Where might I find Manteo and the Assistants?"

Mistress Dare bounced little Virginia, who favored both him and the native girl with a grin. "Last I looked they were gathered at the forge, discussing something or other, but—"

Even as she spoke, a group of the men were walking through the town toward them, Manteo in their midst. And to his surprise, the savage-turned-English—or so he was considered by most of the older men, to Georgie's eye—smiled at the girl and greeted her in their own tongue.

Well, of course they would know each other.

Georgie marched up to Manteo and pointed at the girl. "I found her watching the town through the bushes. I wished to make sure she wasn't spying on us."

His surprise doubled when Manteo laughed softly. He addressed the girl in their tongue again, and she chattered back, then, smiling, both turned toward Georgie. "This is Mushaniq, my daughter, and she has come to begin getting to know you and the other Inqutish."

Georgie felt his mouth fall open and stared at first one then the other. "Your daughter."

Manteo laughed again then spoke to Mushaniq in a tone that was so obviously chiding—albeit with a smile and much obvious affection—it brought an ache to his chest.

Da. Rough he might have been at times, but fatherly affection had been there as well.

"I have asked her whether she was watching your people, and she told me she wants to learn of your ways. To learn your tongue and be able to speak with you."

Georgie shifted from one foot to another and considered the two pairs of sparkling dark eyes looking back at him.

He was at least a fast learner. It was not many days later before he and the other boys, and occasionally the girls too, as they could escape their usual work, joined Mushaniq and Kokon and their companions on their daily run across the island. When they all went from making signs to each other and naming various things to something like actual talk, she could not say. But Nohsh had been right—it happened far more quickly than she would have thought possible.

She learned the names of the others, although some were harder to say. The Inqutish had a strange sound in their tongue that her own did not, and it made many of their names and words especially difficult. They spent much time practicing, and Mushaniq would murmur the names to herself while busy with her tasks. *Wityam*. . .or was it *Wiryam*? She tried to flatten her tongue across the roof of her mouth as the others instructed for that particular sound, but it didn't work for that name. On the other hand, she could almost say *Elinor* instead of *Errinor*.

And *Georgie*. It was *dgee* not *chee*.

She chuckled to herself.

He was still her favorite. The other boys—they were annoying and infuriating by turns. Most of them preferred the company of the older boys and girls of her people. But she didn't care about that. How the older ones, the boys and girls of age or nearly so, chose to spend their time was no concern of hers.

And so day flowed into day, with tides coming and going and moons waxing and waning. The first spring came, and then summer, and all were busy preparing fields and planting crops in addition to the never-ending tasks of gathering wood for fires and spearing fish in the weirs. Gathering oysters through winter and spring gave way to hunting for crabs in summer.

Squabbles arose over this point or that between her people and the Inqutish. She heard whispers that the men of both were worried over how the Inqutish comported themselves toward the women of the People, but again, that was not within her interest. She cared only for the predawn run through the forest and over the dunes then back again to wash herself in the sound before helping Timqua with the day's tasks.

Nohsh visited often, sometimes alone and sometimes accompanied by the Inqutish, and the Kurawoten often visited the Inqutish town—both from her own town and the others across the island. Nohsh told many stories about what they had seen in *En-ga-land* and elsewhere. Though they tried and tried to say the name, it would still only come out for some of them as *Inkurut*, which led to much laughter between their people and the Inqutish, who could not quite say Kurawoten properly either.

Nohsh told not only of the cold islands of the north but of those to the south, which were warm all year long. Of seas so blue it made his eyes ache to look at them. When she later asked Georgie whether that was so, he smiled and nodded. "'Twas beautiful," he said, a wistfulness in his voice.

Nohsh tried to describe the people of these lands—the Inqutish and others all covered in clothing and armor, and peoples to the south who wore nothing at all. That made all of them laugh. Now that she was old enough to wear a doeskin kilt, she could no longer imagine running about all bare as she had when she was a child.

Then, at the height of summer, came the awful storm which threatened to wash all their towns, Kurawoten and Inqutish alike, into the sea.

Chapter Six

Summer 1588

'T is been a year," Roger Prat said. "We've kept watchmen at the fort over the hill yet have caught sight of nothing but a lone Spanish vessel."

Manteo took a thoughtful pull of his pipe. The other men seated and lounging about the wind-tugged fire did the same. Nearly all had adopted the custom of taking uppowoc during these long talks, and to his mind, conversations were calmer and more reasoned when they did.

"It has been a good year," Chris Cooper said, "even if the governor has not yet returned to us."

Manteo nodded, still turning the thoughts over in his mind. Of all the talks he'd had with the other weroances—his mother and those who led both her town and the others along the island—it was a different thing altogether to serve as "Lord of Roanoac and Dasemonguepeuk," or so they had titled him a year past. To be weroance to this people. When he was not overseeing the work of building and planting and tentative explorations to seek resources over on the mainland, he sat with Nicholas Johnson and sought to learn to read and to learn more of the book they called *Holy Scriptures*.

Several of his people were discussing the possibility of being baptized. Timqua and the girls often attended Sunday meetings and others with her. It always required a good part of the remainder of the day to explain more fully what had been said and talk through what they thought of it.

Timqua was open and curious about this God he insisted could be known and felt. His mother and other sisters as well. Only Mushaniq remained closed, although the girl voiced her curiosity about nearly everything else. What was she afraid of? Or was it even fear?

In the meantime, Timqua had, unsurprisingly, failed to present even a single possible woman to be his wife, while several of the Inqutish men had approached him to inquire after his people's marriage customs.

It was a fair enough question. After about the third or fourth one and a spate of grumbling from the other townspeople about men looking at and behaving improperly toward the women of his own people, he gathered all the Inqutish adults—the women needed to hear it as well—and gave as complete an explanation as he could.

"If a man wishes a woman to be his wife, he will go to her and tell her all the ways he admires her. And then he brings presents to her and to her family. If she agrees to be his wife, he will move into her house. It is always her house. If she decides she does not wish to be his wife any longer, she will put his things outside the door. Also they have three days of sleeping together to decide if they really want to be married."

The Inqutish people all murmured one to another.

"So," Chris Cooper said, "a pair could be married for, oh, two or three days and then just be done?"

Manteo blinked. "Aye."

"What about 'till death do us part'? And what if one commits adultery?"

He thought about how to answer. He knew the Holy Scriptures taught that a man should contain himself if he had no wife, or if he did, he should keep himself to his wife only. But that was not what Manteo had observed among the Inqutish.

"And what about the next man? Does he not care that his wife is no longer a virgin?"

"What do you mean? I do not understand."

"I mean that. . ." Cooper stammered and spluttered, apparently trying

45

to find the words. "Will he not care that there were men before him?"

Manteo gave a short laugh. "That is of no account. All young people have play with each other until such a time as the boys have gone on huskanaw and are allowed to choose a wife." He looked from one face to another. "Your people make free with one another as well. I have seen this."

And witnessed it for himself in England. It still astonished him, how many women offered themselves, from those considered "ladies" down to housemaids, some bold and some shy.

"But that is licentiousness and ought not to be so."

Manteo lifted a hand, palm up. "Yet it is, and you know this full well."

Their expressions ranged from shock, likely that he would dare say so, to indignation, to agreement, and several nodded.

"What is the answer, then?" Roger Prat asked. "We do not want our boys thinking it is an accepted thing to sport with the girls."

While the others exchanged looks, Manteo spread his hands. "I will leave that for you to decide. Rafe Lane made it punishable by death for a man to take any woman by force, and rightfully so. My people have similar laws against such things. But play that is agreed to by both?" He shrugged. "Both Harriot and Johnson have read to me where the Scriptures say a man should keep himself to his wife only, however. If this is what the Great God asks, I say for myself that I will certainly keep to my own wife, whoever that will be."

He would not add how it was at times customary for men to borrow other men's wives if their own was in a season of carrying a child or nursing one. They did not need to know everything, not all at once.

Summer 1588

The mildest winter Georgie could ever recall flowed into spring and spring into summer. The uneasy truce he had forged with Mushaniq and the others became an easy camaraderie, where they chased and hid and sometimes simply raced, where they hunted and talked and sometimes sat nestled in the dunes without speaking, watching the endless surge and ebb of the ocean waves.

Those waves, which had brought them here and had taken so many lives.

Those waves, which lay between him and all the family he had left in the world.

The thunder of the surf, like his mother's half-remembered lullaby, bathed him in solace yet stirred the ache of longing, while the changing colors of the water, grey to blue to green and back again beneath wind-driven clouds, offered endless fascination.

Sometimes he sat alone. Other times the too-pert Croatoan girl would find him—and how did she always know where to find him?—and settle herself at his side. Not touching but still *with* him.

Today, the breeze was light and the waves almost lethargic.

"Yapám, she is playful but sleepy," Mushaniq murmured, nearly at his elbow.

He was not entirely sure of all the words, but he nodded anyway.

Soothed by the waves and the shush of the wind in the grasses, they sat in companionable silence until a growl behind them caused them both to startle. Georgie whipped around, on his feet in a moment, and Mushaniq scampered away with a shriek, but it was only Willie Wythers, Thomas Archard, and Tom Humfrey. Having accomplished their aim of scaring the daylights out of Georgie and the girl, the three boys climbed to the top of the dune, cackling.

Willie grinned. "What do you out here alone?"

"Watching the waves." Georgie lifted one shoulder. "And you?"

"We came to find—" Willie's gaze slid toward the girl. "You."

He addressed Georgie, of course, but the meaning of his glance was clear. Georgie felt the heat rising in his face. "Well then? You've found me. What of it?"

The three of them sniggered. Willie's chin lifted, and he called out to Mushaniq, "Hie, maid! Come and share some of wha' ye were offering Georgie-boy here."

With a quick sliding-step forward, Georgie shoved Willie's shoulder. "Leave her alone. Weren't nothing happening like that."

They all sniggered again. "Could be. Did you know some of the older girls are puttin' out? They seem to not mind at all—all of them do it."

Georgie felt his jaw fall open. "Nah," he said, challenging.

Willie's eyes narrowed. "Aye. 'Tis so."

He glanced again at Mushaniq. How much did she understand? But her expression did not change.

A sudden, fierce need to protect her surged inside him. "Go back to your town," he told her, and when she hesitated, he made shooing motions. "Go, now—go away! Leave!"

She looked at all of them in turn, sadness stealing over her face. Georgie scowled and made the motions again, more urgently. "Get thee gone!" He pointed at her and then in the direction of her town. "You—go away—there!"

Looking back over her shoulder, she set off down the beach. Willie made a move as if to go after her, but Georgie blocked his way. "Leave her be. She's nothing but a babe yet."

His eyes still glinted. "She waren't be for long."

Georgie shoved his shoulder again. "Stay away from her."

Willie's grin widened. "I won't need to. She'll give it up on her own. Just wait and see."

He moved off, back into the forest, the other two following, but in the opposite direction from Mushaniq. Georgie remained where he was, a heavy, sick weight in his belly. When the other boys were out of sight, he turned and stared back out across the sea.

This time the rolling surf and tugging wind did nothing to give him ease.

She did not understand what was said, but Georgie's shift from calm to caution to anger was clear enough. And his frantic motions urging her to leave? She did not like the feeling the other boys had given her the moment they showed up on the beach. She only hesitated to leave Georgie alone with them.

Making her way back toward the town slowly, she thought through the exchange. The way the older boy looked at her and spoke in what was unmistakably an invitation—or an insult.

Probably both.

It made her shiver just remembering the glint in his eyes and the tilt of his head.

"Manteo! *Sá keyd winkan?*"

He looked up from sharpening a knife to Towaye's called greeting and, after excusing himself, walked out to meet his friend and kinsman, who was accompanied this time by Swims Deep Water, one of the older weroances. "I am well. How do you also fare?"

They both nodded and bowed. "We have come on a matter of importance," the older weroance said.

Manteo inclined his head. "We will sit, then, and hear you out."

Accompanied by Cooper, Prat, and a handful of the other men, he led them to the house that many of the unmarried men shared. Once they had settled together, pipes packed with uppowoc and lit, he waited for them to speak.

Eventually, they did. Swims Deep Water released a long breath and lowered his pipe. "We wish to ask—is there provision being made for your men and boys who may wish to marry our women?"

He stilled. More lay behind that question than was being said, he was sure.

"What provision would you wish made?" he asked after a moment, then translated both the question and his answer for the other men.

Their mouths fell open and air rushed out of them in either surprise or shock. Manteo met their gazes directly. "Is this not what we have been talking of for some time now?" He turned to Towaye and Swims Deep Water. "Have any inquired of such?"

Towaye rubbed the back of his neck, and a rueful smile curved his mouth. "It did not take long for the older boys to be at play with the girls. Most of them do not see it as serious, but one or two of the girls have expressed their willingness to talk of more."

Swims Deep Water blew out a puff of smoke. "We wish to speak of what marriage might mean to the Inqutish. And when do they consider the boys to be men? When do they go on huskanaw?"

Well, this would be interesting. Manteo turned to the other men and translated.

A breath of silence, then—

"*What?* The boys—are *what?* When did this happen?"

"The better question is, what is to be done?"

"We must speak to them immediately! This is not to be borne!"

Towaye and Swims Deep Water peered with concern at the Inqutish men, quarreling among themselves. Towaye, of course, could comprehend much of what they said, but lack of knowledge of their tongue did not keep Swims Deep Water from catching the gist of their talk. "Do you not wish your people to marry with ours? It was our understanding that would follow naturally with our communities living so closely."

Manteo translated, and one by one, beginning with Prat, the men stopped speaking and their mouths closed, and they collected themselves once more.

He looked from one to another. He had some idea of what the answer would be on either side, but still the question begged to be asked. "What do you consider the greatest hindrance to one of our peoples taking one of the other in marriage?"

After he had addressed the Inqutish, he turned to Swims Deep Water. "What do our people see as the most needful condition to be met for our women to accept an Inqutish man as husband?"

The older man puffed soberly at his pipe. "It is said your boys do not go on huskanaw. How then can they be proved as men?"

Manteo turned to Prat and Cooper and related what had been said, then waited for their reply. All the men looked indignant to varying degrees. "'Twould be heathen," Cooper muttered.

Prat shifted. "We would of course require only what you yourself have done, inasmuch as you have submitted yourself to the holy ordinance of baptism."

"Aye, faith in Christ is the paramount thing," Cooper said.

"At what point would you deem a boy ready to take a wife?" Manteo said. It was too important a point to lay by.

"Well. Perhaps when we know he can hunt and fish and has learned a trade in order to keep a family."

"But what measure do you propose to ensure he has learned enough?" Swims Deep Water countered when Manteo translated the reply.

Prat was flustered at that. "When the elders of the town have deemed it so."

Swims Deep Water nodded sagely. "So it is with us. But we send the boys on huskanaw as the final test."

Prat looked hard at the man. "Are there particular boys in question here?"

A long, slow nod. "Perhaps. We have yet to see."

"And what of the girls or women in question? Many of your people have attended meeting with ours. Do they wish to be instructed further in the faith of our Lord Christ?" Prat leaned forward. "Do you, perchance?"

Swims Deep Water sucked the stem of his pipe. "The old ways have served well enough. But perhaps the Great God has sent your people to show His way more perfectly. We are still talking upon it."

"Well then," Prat said slowly, "we will be talking upon the question of huskanaw."

Towaye and Swims Deep Water took their leave shortly after, and after walking them to the edge of the town, the Inqutish men turned to each other. "We must speak with the boys and other men and soon," Prat said.

Chapter Seven

Georgie had spent the morning gathering wood for the blacksmith, Tom Ellis, to make charcoal. He wished he were still doing so, or out on the water mending weirs, or even pulling weeds from the fields or gardens. Anywhere but here.

Nicholas Johnson, who served as the town's minister, had preached many a sermon about the temptations of the flesh—lust of the eyes and the pride of life, and suchlike—but at the behest of Master Prat, Georgie and the other boys had been gathered up and plunked down beneath a spreading oak. Master Prat and Master Johnson speared each of them in turn with their steely gazes.

Master Johnson spoke first, hands set upon his hips. "It has come to our attention that some of you—or mayhap all—have made free with the girls of the Croatan. This ought not be so. Would you behave thus toward a proper English girl? Know and understand that if you are caught taking liberties with a girl—any girl, whether English or Croatan—you will wed her.

"In the meantime, we will be assigning additional labor, since it is clear you have not been kept busy enough, and such idleness has led only to licentious behavior."

Again with the hard gaze, meeting Georgie's for a moment before moving to John Prat beside him. Did Master Prat think him guilty of such? His innards wrenched at the thought.

He had seen plenty of "taking liberties" between men and women on the streets of London. But the very idea of doing so for himself? Nay. A thousand times nay.

At last the men let them go. Georgie caught a look of thunder from Willie and slipped away. Best to remain in the town today, under the watchful eye of the grown-ups—but he would not be able to avoid the older boy forever.

As it turned out, avoidance lasted not even the rest of that day. Come nightfall, as Georgie walked from the central fire, a pair of hands reached out from behind the smithy and yanked him into the shadows.

Willie Wythers thrust his face into Georgie's, with Thomas Archard and John Sampson flanking him. "Was it you who snitched?"

"I did not," Georgie hissed. "I know not who did, but 'twas not me!"

"Liar!" Willie shook him. "Own up to it already!"

"'Twas not me!"

A fist landed in his middle. Georgie bent, gasping and retching. "I—didn't—"

A flurry of blows this time, and he curled in on himself. This was it—he'd die here, not at the hands of any peoples native to this land but his own cronies who had themselves turned savage.

"Hie there! What goes on?"

Space cleared suddenly around Georgie. He fell to his knees, but hands grasped him, lifting him. Despite his best effort, he cried out. "There now," a man's voice, soothing, then calling, "Bring a light!"

Other voices, farther away. Georgie could only shiver.

"Gor, what 'ave they done?" Arms scooped him up, though he was no longer a small child, and carried him to one of the houses where the men stayed.

In the flickering lamplight, Master Prat bent over him, examining his face, then arms and chest. Saltwater was brought to bathe his bruises and scrapes. "Whatever did you do to arouse the ire of the other lads, Georgie?"

He glanced about to see if any of said lads were in the room, but only the older men were there, peering at him from round about.

53

"'Tis safe, lad. Chris Cooper and Ananias Dare went after them and are giving them what for."

Georgie's teeth chattered, but he clenched his jaw with the effort to be still and speak. "They—think I snitched," he whispered. "About the Croatoan girls."

Understanding smoothed Master Prat's features. "Ahh. Well, that shall be made clear. 'Twas the Croatoan elders who sought us out, inquiring after possible marriage alliances between our peoples." His mouth twisted. "Might I gather that you are not one of those responsible for this being an issue?"

"N-nay, sir." He flexed his jaw and pushed up. "They made rude comments about Mushaniq. I made her go away. She's still but a little girl, and I did not know what they might intend."

Master Prat's head came up, and muttering rippled through the men around them. "You did the right thing, lad." He huffed and dabbed a wet cloth to Georgie's cheekbone again. "So who did this to you?"

He dropped his voice to a whisper again. "Willie, sir. A pair of the others were with him."

He'd not mention Thomas Archard. Thomas had been his friend. Why he ran after Willie, whom nobody liked, was a mystery.

Master Prat grunted. More mutterings went around the room. "...knew he was getting too high and mighty of late," one said.

After they'd looked him over, Georgie put his shirt back on and sat up. "Go sleep in the loft," Master Prat told him, not unkindly, then he rose and beckoned to Master Cooper, who had just come into the house.

Manteo stood back, watching. There had been minor disagreements before now, scuffles over belongings and suchlike as the planters settled in both on Roanoac and here on Kurawoten, but this was the first outbreak of actual violence among the Inqutish themselves.

Notwithstanding it was merely the youths, of course. Manteo suspected this ran deeper and would affect the Kurawoten as well.

Listening to the defensive snarl of the tall oldest boy, Manteo had his suspicions confirmed.

"'Twas no different in England. Women offer and men take, and it makes no matter whether they be lawfully wed or no," argued the one called Willie.

"We are not in England any longer," Cooper said, his words slow and deliberate. "We are here to follow more fully the laws of God and to live peacefully with the peoples who dwell here before us."

The youth's eyes flashed to him, insolent, then his gaze fell and he made no reply.

Cooper's voice fell. "Recall, if you will, that I left behind a wife. I know full well the burden of a man's need for a woman's softness, and having none, yet being constrained to self-control. These girls and women are not ours to use as we will. And whatever their people's customs in the matter, Christian temperance must hold the final rule."

While Cooper spoke, Prat walked up and stood at Manteo's side, also listening.

Cooper turned from addressing the youth. "Master Prat, have you anything to add?"

"Not at the moment." He straightened. "William, get thee to the house and to bed. Downstairs, if you please. We will speak of this more fully later."

The youth murmured something—presumably his assent—and vanished into the darkness.

"Georgie seems to have sustained no lasting hurt, thanks be to God," Prat said, more quietly, as Cooper joined him and Manteo. "I admit, though I know too well how boys will scuffle, this has me shaken." The older man scrubbed a hand across his face. "It is more than the lads sporting with the girls. Georgie tells me that William cast an eye toward one of the younger girls, not even yet of age." He peered at Manteo. "It is Mushaniq. Your own daughter, I believe?"

An unpleasant jolt went through Manteo. "Aye. Nunutánuhs, my daughter."

Prat nodded. "Georgie says he defended her, sent her away. Although it was Towaye and Swims Deep Water who came and told us what was taking place, William and the other boys think Georgie was the one who spoke."

This would require delicacy indeed. "I know that your laws do not approve of a woman being forced."

"No, nor of a girl being—being used—when she is not even of age." Prat looked uncomfortable.

"It is the same here, with the People. This is considered a very great wrong."

"How do you suggest we deal with it?"

"I must think on it. Talk with the weroances of the other towns again as well."

There was another assembly, the next day. Georgie sat in the back—though he could hardly sit, could hardly focus on the words. But try he did. Manteo was the one speaking this time in his slow, measured way, the words accented but clear enough.

"It has been told me that there is a lack of respect from you, the young men, toward the young women both of your people and mine. Let me tell you what our people teach about women. They are not weak. They are strong. They carry new life, and bear it and nourish it from their own bodies. They are the ones to bring life from the earth in the form of food and to prepare it for us to eat and enjoy. Their bodies are to be respected.

"One way of showing respect is that just as we cannot eat the pegatawah before it is ripe, so a woman is not to be approached before her season of readiness. This would include before her monthly courses have come, or for our people, while she is growing a child or nursing a child. It is up to us the men to possess ourselves in patience during those times." He was quiet a moment, his gaze sweeping their faces. "Even your Scriptures speak of this, 'that every one of you should know how to keep his vessel in holiness and honor.'"

Some of the boys in the front bent their heads, although Willie sat as he had from the beginning—perfectly straight, posture stiff.

"Some of you wonder why this is being talked of now. It is because the elders of the Kurawoten, the weroances, have heard that some of you go out and speak with some of the Kurawoten girls. There is talk of marrying between you. This does not displease them, but they wish to know how the Inqutish judge readiness for marrying." Manteo smiled. "If any of you feel ready to marry and wish a certain girl to be your wife, you should come to us, the elders of this town, or to your fathers. It is not a thing to feel shame over. Wishing to marry is a natural part of becoming a man."

"No, it is like this. Make your weave a little tighter." Mushaniq held her basket so the younger girl could see, slowing her fingers to make their motion more easily followed.

Timqua strolled past with an indulgent smile. "She is doing very well, Mushaniq. Do not be too hard on her."

"Yes." Mushaniq sat back and huffed a little. "But she does need to weave more tightly."

"She will learn." Timqua went on her way, chuckling. "She will yet learn."

"I try again," Little Shell piped.

They bent over their respective baskets, and another set of footsteps approached and stopped. The feet were bare, and skin markings across the lower legs peeked from beneath Inqutish-style hose.

It was Nohsh. He crouched, smiling, and nodded at her handiwork. "Do not let me keep you from your task."

She looked at Little Shell and then at her own work in progress. "I think it would not suffer if we rested from it for a little while."

The younger girl gave a squeal and leaped up and scurried away so quickly her poor basket was sent tumbling across the ground. Nohsh caught it as it rolled past and, laughing, handed it to Mushaniq. "A walk would be welcome, if you are sure."

She flashed him a smile in return, and nesting one basket inside the other, she set both aside and hopped to her feet.

"Ocean or sound side?"

"Ocean," she said, and led off.

She loved watching the waves, but on some days, she only felt safe with Nohsh there.

Or Georgie, but she wouldn't think about that. She'd not so much as seen him since the afternoon he'd sent her away. And she wasn't sure she wanted to.

Up through the forest and its underbrush, thick in places, and then to the edge of the dunes and over. The wind blew warm but strong, and the waves crashed hard with an undertone of grey and green. In the distance, clouds piled tall.

"Feels like a storm brewing," she said, tipping her face to the wind.

"It does." He stepped up beside her. "How do you fare these days, Little Squirrel, Nunutánuhs?"

"I am well," she answered without thought.

"It is good to hear this."

She peered up into his face. He was not smiling now.

"We have a trouble with the Inqutish," he said after a few moments. "I would like your thoughts about it." His gaze was warm upon her, yet searching. "You have gotten acquainted with the one named Georgie, yes?"

And here was Nohsh mentioning him. Was the trouble with Georgie? She nodded a little uncertainly. "He is often sad. I feel sorry for him because of his—his father. I remember that he is the one slain by the Sukwoten when they first came to our country."

Nohsh's gaze remained steady. "It is often hard for him. Some of the other boys are here without much family as well." He hesitated. "Has there been trouble with any of them? Or with Georgie?"

A chill swept her, and she turned to look out to sea. "There was a day, not long ago," she began at last. "Georgie and I were watching the ocean. Three other boys came upon us—the tallest, older one they call *Wirr-am*—" She shook her head, tried again. "I know that isn't quite right. He spoke to me in words I did not understand but in a way that made me uncomfortable. Georgie quarreled with him, then shouted at me to go away." She chewed her lip. "At least, that is what I thought he was saying. I am still learning the words. But he pointed and seemed angry and stood in the other boy's way when he seemed to make a motion to follow me."

Nohsh nodded, slowly at first, then with more firmness. "That is the story he told us." He took a few steps and bent to free a broken whelk shell from the water-packed sand, then shot another glance at Mushaniq, squinting against the sun. "It would seem the older Inqutish boys have been going out to talk with some of the Kurawoten girls. Have you heard anything of this?"

Mushaniq felt her lip curling. "That is the older girls. I think what they do is—" She made a gagging sound.

Nohsh burst out laughing.

She huffed and stomped a foot. "Auntie Timqua does the same when I tell her that."

Nohsh swiped the back of his forearm across his face, but a grin remained. "You will feel differently when you are older."

"I do not wish to be older," she said stiffly.

"Perhaps, but it happens to all of us. Except," and he sobered, "to those who remain children in mind or body, and you would not wish that."

She scuffed a toe in the sand. "Perhaps not." His laughter still burned under her skin.

"Georgie said that the other boys hinted that you and he were similarly sporting."

That brought her head up with a sharp snap. The burn intensified. "What? No! I would not!" She made another sound of disgust.

He laughed again but softly, and then the humor vanished from his face. "He said they intended to make you do so for them. So I must know, Nunutánuhs, have they approached you thus?"

She stared at him, her mouth falling open. "That is—a very great wrong!"

"It is. And it must be known if they are indeed doing so with you or any other girls who are not of age."

A slow nod overtook her. It would explain much about that day with Georgie. "They have not with me. As for the other girls, I cannot say. But I promise to come tell if they do or if I learn of anything."

A slight smile came and went. "It is good." He brushed a hand across her hair. "You are a good girl, Little Squirrel. Do not give of yourself too easily when the time comes."

"Ugh! No, I shall not give of myself at all."

Again the laugh, but this time it did not sting so much.

She looked up. "You are a good father. Thank you for coming to talk with me about this."

He drew her in for a quick embrace, and she leaned into it.

Chapter Eight

I ron-grey clouds stacked higher, now blocking the sun, with nearer, lower bands scudding fast over the water and across the island. The wind, always tugging at them without end, blew with more intent than an hour ago, and spitting rain had already driven the men who kept watch at the easternmost fort back to the town. But Georgie and Thomas held fast their perch. "It is like the tempests at sea before we came to Roanoac," Thomas said.

Georgie shifted, arms clasped about his knees. A thread of excitement danced with that of fear through his middle. What would such a storm look like on this island? It had not been so terrible on Roanoac the summer previous, but here, on what amounted to a sandbar jutting out into the ocean?

The waves gathered and rolled, gathered and rolled, breaking and washing high up on the beach. Much like Georgie's own thoughts.

'Twas a year, or nearly so, since Da's terrible death. And though the planters had left clear token on Roanoac of where they had moved to, there had been no sign of Governor White's return. Things were still uneasy between the English and the Croatoan, though they visited often between towns.

For that matter, things were uneasy between some of the English, himself and the other boys, included.

"So why are you not running about with Willie?" He blurted the question before he could lose his nerve.

Thomas shrugged.

"Is he still chasing after the girls?"

"Aye." Thomas shifted forward.

"What, he isn't afraid of getting caught and having to marry one?" Georgie could not keep the scorn from his voice.

Thomas made a rude noise in his throat. "He thinks he can sneak about well enough."

"And what of you?"

Another shrug. "I've decided 'tis best to wait until Emme and Libby grow a bit."

Georgie snorted. "As if either would look twice at the likes of us. Girls grow up faster'n boys anyway, you know this."

Thomas gave Georgie a long look. "Seems t'me you weren't lacking none for a girl's attention, at least awhile back."

"Mushaniq is nothing but an infant yet."

Thomas's mouth curled in a smirk, and Georgie punched to his feet.

"Hey, hey—don't be angry with me. There are more girls yet to come from England—"

Thomas glanced over Georgie's shoulder and fell silent. Georgie turned and found Willie himself approaching.

"Speaking of the girls," Willie said, his smile slow and wide.

Georgie turned, backing up so he could keep both Willie and Thomas in sight. It was instinct—he couldn't help it.

"Master Prat wishes us back before the rain starts in earnest," Willie said as if he'd not just a moment before spoken of something else entirely.

"Fine," Georgie snapped but did not move.

Neither did Willie.

"What do you want? Truly? You aren't here simply to deliver a message from Master Prat."

"I suppose not." The smirk did not alter. "I heard what you said. And no, I do not plan to marry a savage."

Georgie held himself still. "The elders have said, as long as they are baptized into our faith—"

"They're still savages. I'm with Thomas—I'll wait for Emme or Libby, or for more girls to come from England."

He didn't necessarily disagree with Willie about the preference of waiting. But the way he thought it acceptable to—to *use* the Croatoan girls while deeming them unfit for marriage—well, it rankled. "Then leave off. They are still women, worthy of your deference and respect."

Willie laughed outright. An ugly sound.

"Would you do thus to Emme or Libby? Were either not your wife or intended to be?" He wasn't sure where the question had come from, but the words simply burst from him.

Willie took a step forward. "So were you one who snitched, after all? Even Manteo came to your rescue and said you didn't, but I don't know whether to believe a savage."

Fury wormed its way under Georgie's skin. "You call them so and yet continue sniffing around their girls."

"Ha! They are willing. Are you only an infant to not understand that? Run back to Mother Archard, then, or Mistress Dare, and cry to them!"

Willie was taller and heavier. Georgie couldn't hope to take him. But he could bear it no longer and threw himself at the older boy. They went rolling, across the packed sand and into the fort wall.

In the scuffling, Georgie found himself straddling Willie. "I am no lover of savages," he hissed into Willie's face, "but neither am I a user of them. And you are worse than Rafe Lane and his ilk if you do not cease."

Willie growled and shoved upward. "You know *nothing!*" He landed a blow, but Georgie pressed in. Willie wrenched free and rolled to his feet, then backed up, chest heaving. "Is it not enough that Manteo defended you?"

"You are the one who would not leave off," Georgie shouted over the wind.

Willie spat to the side—downwind, fortunately for him. "You are not even a man."

"If being a man requires preying upon others—"

It was Willie who came at him this time, knocking Georgie off his feet. The world went black and the sound of the wind faded. . .

And then Willie was hauled off him, and Thomas stood there, shouting at the older boy. Georgie fought for breath, chest and throat burning, and tried to sit up, but the pounding of his head sent him back to the ground. He curled on his side, retching.

Willie broke away from Thomas and landed a kick to Georgie's side before Thomas tackled him again. "Get up, Georgie!" Thomas said. "Run!"

Crawling was all he could manage, out through the opening of the fort and around the corner, where he collapsed against the outside of the wall, breathing hard.

Willie emerged first, looming over him. "Tell you what. You two stay with me out in the woods tonight, through the storm, and I'll leave off."

At the moment, all Georgie wanted was to curl up and sleep. Willie did not wait for a reply but set off up the hill into the trees.

With a little moan, Georgie slumped over and let the wind howl about him.

He awakened with a start, clothing soaked through by sheets of rain. Peering into the near-darkness, he sat up, the wind now a scream.

Where had Thomas gone? And Willie, for that matter? He rose, swaying, and stumbled toward the opening of the fort, one hand on the wall for support. He shouted Thomas's name, but the sound was lost in the howling gale. At the gate, he could discern nothing of the interior of the fort in the gloom, only that waves were breaking over the far wall, the floor of the fort awash with seawater.

Oh God, what is happening? And where is Thomas?

His continued shouts were lost to the buffeting wind. A sob tore his already-aching throat, but there was naught he could do here.

"Gracious God, preserve us!"

Fixing his gaze on the smudgy shadows of the forest, he half crawled up the slope, whimpering with every step.

At last he gained the shelter of the forest, its branches clacking and creaking about him.

Dawn found him dozing in the lower branches of a gnarled oak. The wind had died to a mere zephyr and the rain to a drizzle.

He looked around before climbing down, every muscle aching. He'd think it a simple summer shower were it not for all about him being completely drenched and the drifts of fallen branches and other vegetation heaped about.

Thomas. He would stroll about and first seek his friend.

The aches in his body eased as he walked, retracing his path back to the fort. A few birds and squirrels twittered and chittered here and there, but for the most part, the forest was oddly quiet. Or was it the dripping wetness masking the usual array of sounds?

He reached the edge of the forest and stopped. The entire oceanside of the island, as far as he could see, looked wet and rumpled, with even sea grasses bent over.

There was no sign of Thomas—or anybody else.

The waves still foamed and roared up to the dunes and sprayed over, the sea beyond, a dark green. Tall, puffy clouds still sailed overhead in shades of iron grey, but the sun was just peeping over the horizon and washing that half of the sky in brilliant color.

He went on more slowly. The walls of the fort looked worse for wear, worn through in at least two places, although the palisade near the opening still stood. Georgie tiptoed in. Completely deserted—but he walked about the inside perimeter and peered into dark corners, calling Thomas's name, just to be sure.

There was nothing. Back outside, he called louder and set off down the strand, weaving between the dunes and the forest edge.

A half mile down, he stopped, the sun a little above the horizon now. He should return to the town, seek help in looking for Thomas.

Would the town still be there? And what of the people?

Not waiting to catch his breath, though the suddenness of the thought left him aching anew as if bowled over again by Willie, he set off at a run and dived back into the forest.

Just over the ridge, he struck a familiar trail, washed clean and made soggy by the storm, and followed it down.

The town was still there, and yet—

Emerging from the forest, he blew out a breath and surveyed the wreckage. Water lapped at the opposite edge of the field where he stood, and the entire crop was flattened. Beyond, the town stood in disrepair, and people moved here and there, wading through the tide still swirling among the houses.

No crops, and days and days of work to rebuild the houses.

But where was Thomas? Had he returned on his own?

As he picked his way around the field, another figure slipped out from under the trees, following the path or what remained of it, on the other side of the ruined crop. Willie—and was it Georgie's imagination, or did the long look the older boy gave him bespeak humility and regret?

Something in his face smote Georgie to the heart.

Please, gracious God, let Thomas be here after all!

They went on down to the edge of the water and waded in, toward the houses. With each step, his blood pounded more painfully.

Please, God. . .please, God. . . .

He did not want to face Mistress Archard.

"Have the sea storms always been this bad?" Mushaniq asked, as she and Kokon helped Timqua carry the reed mats they'd retrieved from around the town.

The weather remained fair and warm enough that, for the Kurawoten, sleeping a few nights without a roof was no hardship. Of greater concern was the damage done to the machicomuck and the dancing circle.

She set down an armload of rolled mats on the pile of pieces they'd already found and watched as two of the men carefully measured distances and dug holes for the sagging posts marking the edges of the sacred circle. Only four had remained, with two found washed up at the edge of the forest, and yet another still missing.

"What will they do about the last post?" she asked.

Timqua gave the working men barely a glance before she turned back to considering the empty longhouse frame before her. "The priest will make a new one."

"Why do they carve the faces at the top, with the funny shrouding around the head?"

"I do not know, Little Squirrel. Some say they are the spirits of our ancestors."

"Or representation of Montóac?"

"Kupi, or that."

Mushaniq went back to unrolling mats and laying them out so Timqua could see the ones still closest to whole. "I think we can still use most of these for now and then repair as we can before winter."

Timqua looked over and gave her a smile. "You are right."

She riffled through the remaining stack of mats. "I wonder how the Inqutish fared in the storm."

"Towaye and a couple of others went over to see. We will hear soon."

When they did hear, it was with somber faces and the news that one of the boys, Thomas Archard, had disappeared during the night. Searchers were setting out to look, although many were still needed at the town to begin repair of what wind and waters had torn down. Towaye gathered a few more men and left again.

Mushaniq's heart thudded uneasily. Thomas was one of the more winsome boys. Or had been, until he began running with the older Willie. Of course, Kurawoten boys were pushy and obnoxious at that age as well.

But she could not help a moment of relief that it was not Georgie gone missing.

Thomas was not found, and after three days of searching, the Inqutish held what they called *church* to pray in case he was still out there alive and for the continued safety and guidance for their own community. Timqua, Wesnah, Grandmama, and several of the other elders wanted to attend, and so Mushaniq went as well.

She enjoyed their singing and often sang along, wordlessly. This time, however, a sorrow so overlaid their music that all she could find expression for were tears. Georgie stood off to the side, looking desolate. Willie too. What had happened between them? Word was that the three boys had stayed out, sheltering who knew where during the storm. Mushaniq shivered. She'd not want to endure a night alone out in the woods with the thunder, pouring rain, and howling winds. She'd think it some form of huskanaw, if she did not already know his people did no such thing.

She could ask Georgie—but a strange reluctance gripped her. Perhaps she did not want to know.

Chapter Nine

T he days flowed on, and as the houses were repaired, talk came from the Inqutish about dividing their group and some settling elsewhere. Nohsh made plans for an expedition to explore Dasemonguepeuk to see if the Sukwoten had withdrawn, as some said they had, and whether there was situation likely enough for a town over on the mainland.

In the meantime, the Inqutish determined to stay on Kurawoten had decided, with Grandmama and the other weroances, to rebuild their houses closer to Mushaniq's town. It was odd to live and work alongside the Inqutish on a day-to-day basis now. Georgie still did not speak to her. Often his glance would meet hers but then slide away. Willie ignored her around others as well, but at odd moments she would find him staring at her.

But then, he stared at the other girls as well.

"Why do the Inqutish boys stare so rudely?" she finally asked Timqua one day.

Auntie did not answer at first, and Mushaniq was about to ask again when she straightened and began to speak. "They believe we should wear clothing that covers more of our bodies."

A scoffing sound escaped Mushaniq's throat. "But it is summer! And the weather is hot."

A little smile curled Auntie's mouth. "Yes, and they are miserable enough in all their layers. But they think men and women's bosoms alike should be covered. That it is. . .improper to go about uncovered."

69

"Improper?" Mushaniq gaped. "I mean, I have heard you and the older women murmuring about this before but. . .a breast is for feeding a baby! What is so improper about that?"

Auntie smirked more fully now. "You have yet to learn, then, that men find them very attractive. And thus distracting."

She could not think at all for a moment, and then—

"That is ridiculous. Wutapantam feed their young from their bodies, as do all furry creatures. How would such a thing be distracting? It's just stupid."

Auntie Timqua went off into a peal of laughter, but Mushaniq huffed.

"Well? And what is to be done about it?"

Auntie's expression went thoughtful. "You will be of age in another year or two. It certainly bears considering what might be done."

Of age? Mushaniq's stomach knotted, and she wrinkled her nose. Auntie saw it and laughed again.

"Do you not want babies of your own?"

"Well, of course, who does not? It's the getting them that's stupid."

Auntie laughed so hard, Mushaniq thought she would fall down.

"You will see, Little Squirrel," Auntie said at last. "You will see."

Good Creator, give me strength. Give me wisdom. You tell us to ask, and I am in need of both.

Manteo found it increasingly harder to slip away for solitude and reflection, much less prayer and meditation on the bits of the holy book Nicholas Johnson was helping him read and understand.

Sometimes Johnson felt too vague or too set on a certain way of interpreting a passage for Manteo to grasp its meaning or application. This afternoon had been particularly trying with what Johnson called *doctrine of sanctification*. Granted, they were all weary, with patience stretched by rebuilding and cleanup after the tempest.

And then with new questions arising—those who wished to press into the mainland, as John White had originally planned for the colony, to locate a place where they might build a town and clear fields and finally live as a truly English, God-fearing community. But where they had cast their eye put them in the heart of what had once been the purview of the Sukwoten.

If the planters removed to where greater opportunity lay, then greater danger followed.

Some days he wished heartily that the English had never come to Ossomocomuck.

But then there were nights like this, where after a long hour and more at the community fire with the people of his birth, sharing stories and hearing their own heart for fostering love and friendship between them and the Inqutish—they could no longer be called strangers after months of dwelling together on the same shore—his own heart and spirit were full and content. As the conversation wore down, many wandering away to sleep, Manteo took his leave. He too would sleep, eventually, but for now he wanted to walk along the ocean, watch the rising full moon, and hear whatever the Great Lord of creation might murmur to him.

He was not the only one out for a night walk, but he smiled to himself and tried to avoid the others. How long ago it seemed when Mushaniq's mother agreed to accompany him on such a walk, when blood ran hot and before long, soft words led to touch, and the next he knew, he was laboring to gather up what he thought might please her and her family as a bride gift.

Mushaniq herself reminded him more and more of her mother. How long until her sweet face drew the attention of some youth who would overcome shyness to win her?

And how would he feel if it were an Inqutish youth who caught her eye? There were only six of them now, with the Archard boy gone missing.

Six, who would in time need wives if more ships from England did not come.

Manteo ducked beneath the gnarled boughs of the oaks and pushed aside the yaupon edging the forest above the beach, emerging slowly enough to scan this way and that before exposing himself in the moonlight. The island held no predators large enough to endanger him, but there was always the chance of a stray boat with men of unknown origin—and he was yet a warrior, first and foremost.

The strand was clear as far as he could see, with the waves rolling in, glittering under the moon. He stepped out, tipping his face to the wind and sky, letting himself be dazzled by the array of stars, like a celestial sea above the moon swam in reflection of yapám beneath.

Creator of all that I see and more. . .help me to lead with courage and wisdom. Preserve us from our enemies. Give us victory in war, if it comes to that. . .but for now, help us to find a place for these people to live. Help my daughter to find her way in life. And if it please You, give me a wife as well.

For a moment, the loneliness that lurked ever beneath the surface, like water beneath the sand if one dug too deeply, welled up and swamped him.

It was odd, how even months later, the Kurawoten women remained shy of him, despite the handful warming to the attentions of Inqutish men.

When it is time, he had said before. He would abide by that. And until then, he would trust the Good God to sustain and nourish him.

There were prayers and music to send them off—their first serious voyage since the storm and nearly the whole summer long. Shortly after dawn, they launched out on the pinnace, following the wind and tide. Towaye and three other Kurawoten men accompanied the dozen Inqutish comprising the expedition to Dasemonguepeuk.

Despite the prayers—his own and those of others—the fear gusted its cold breath across him at odd moments, though there was nothing but joy to be found in the morning light playing across the rippling waters as they wended their way between the shoals. After a time, the western shore became visible, and ahead they could see the first of the tiny islets strewn across the space between Roanoac and Dasemonguepeuk.

Most of them weren't sure they trusted their memory of the channels and shoals enough to make a sure passage around the west side of Roanoac, but one of the Kurawoten warriors insisted he and the others had paddled it recently. Manteo shook his head and ordered them to use the eastern passage. Both would have changed greatly after the storm, and to the east would be deepest and safest.

They made a brief stop on Roanoac proper, just to confirm that the artillery and iron and lead still remained inside the old town walls, but no one else inhabited the island.

Shortly moving on, they went west and a little north, sailing round the point of Dasemonguepeuk, closely watching the shore. The land did indeed seem deserted, but Manteo knew too well how deceptive appearances could be. At the least, nothing seemed amiss with the call of birds and other creatures.

At the mouth of the first river leading inland, to the south, they anchored and let down a ship's boat. Half stayed with the pinnace and half climbed down into the boat, Manteo with them, keeping his arquebus to hand and motioning for continued silence as they set off upriver.

The old familiar alertness took him again, eagerness mingled with a swirl of dread. His gaze swept the shoreline, where yaupon and laurel grew beneath tupelo, pine, and cypress and could easily hide the presence of anyone who crept down to the water's edge to mark their passing. Only the sounds of nature came to their ears between the muted dipping of paddles, but Manteo remained watchful.

The river narrowed, and at last he directed them toward the mouth of a creek, where they tied off the boat and climbed out. Manteo took a deep breath. Oh, how he had missed these woods! The marshy areas with the cypresses and their pointed knees, the pines, the way butterflies and dragonflies flitted about while the air rang with birdsong.

He met Towaye's gaze and that of the other Kurawoten who had not stayed with the pinnace. They all knew the way from here, from their youthful years of rambling the coast. How long ago that seemed. Before the English, almost before the threat of the Spanish, when the worst that could come upon them, beyond the havoc wreaked by the Pomeiooc upon their brother warriors of the Sukwoten and others, were the dreaded Powhatan to the north.

He thought he heard something, and stopped, motioning for the others to do the same. One long, slow breath in, hold it, then an equally long and soundless release. Somewhere on this side of the water was Wanchese and his band. Menatonon and Okisco, both wronged by Rafe Lane in matters small and great. It still brought the bile to Manteo's throat to think of the killing of Wyngyno, and even before that the burning of a village and its fields over a missing silver cup.

He knew well, however, that Wyngyno, who had taken the name Pemisapan, Wolf-Who-Watches, to indicate his change of heart about trusting the English, would have exerted—and did—any measure of subterfuge to preserve his own people and had been in the midst of planning to slaughter the English unawares. Manteo had been given permission for no such thing from the weroances of the Kurawoten, and the English were still valuable—despite Rafe Lane's almost sure lunacy and despite his own opinion that a more useless band of men he had never met when it came to providing for themselves in the richness of Ossomocomuck.

Harriot and his men had proved the exceptions. Willing to listen to the People and learn of their ways even as he averred the One True God, Harriot alone seemed to view people of a simpler lifestyle with value equal to that of his own.

Manteo missed him, missed the conversations where they would wrangle over the meaning of some word or another, or where Harriot would endeavor to explain the intricacies of faith in his beloved Christ.

Harriot had dared walk the solemn depths of the forest here, seemingly unmoved by the dread that pressed itself even now upon Manteo's heart and soul. *Beware*, it murmured. *You might have been born and raised upon these shores, but you have given up what it requires to belong.*

The fear deepened, soaking the corners of his being. He turned a slow circle, searching the forest, but there were none but the Inqutish and Kurawoten with him.

Was the voice that of a seen enemy lurking in the shadows or of one wholly unseen?

"'Greater is He who is in me,'" he whispered back, barely above a breath, "'than he who is in the world.'"

"You know not whereof you meddle here, little one."

But he did know. He recalled the long preparations, the sacrifices, the desperate need to satisfy the spirits of the forest before venturing out for a hunt or war. The terror of huskanaw. The awe of merely walking through the woods, as they did now, or paddling the streams.

Holding up a hand for the staying of the others, he turned another slow circle. "Gracious, all-mighty God, Maker of the heavens and earth and all that we see, we claim the ground that we walk for You. We beg the covering power of the blood of Your Christ and the overshadowing of the Holy Ghost. We trust that we are here by Your will, Your behest, and submit ourselves to You and Your protection. Help us to walk worthy of that as we seek a place for some of our people to dwell here and be Your ambassadors among those who may not yet know You as they ought."

The uneven echo of "amen" rippled about him in varying tones of surprise and agreement. Peace and courage settled as a garment around Manteo once more, and he continued on.

It was a hard thing to contemplate later. Did he indeed no longer belong to this land? And, given how thoroughly the reality of this God had taken him by surprise upon the moment of baptism and confessing his faith before others, did he even truly mind?

That night, as most of the men settled in to sleep but Manteo and a pair of others took a turn at watching, Towaye edged up beside him. "What did you hear, that moment in the forest? Why did you stand so long, and then what stirred you to speak those words?"

He sighed. "There are moments," he said at last, "that I am sure more is at stake here than simply one people seeking to make a home among strangers. I feel a presence or a gathering of presences who resist change. Certainly, they resist any whisper that they are not the final word on how our people should live. And so they set themselves against any who represent contradiction to their authority."

Towaye stared at him, the flare of eyes and nostrils all that betrayed his inner response, then he nodded slowly. "It would follow. We are told by the priests that the spirits of this land—and the ocean—will be favorable to us if we continue to acknowledge them. But these people who speak of another God altogether?"

"Or that this God rules all, including them, and it is they who must bow the knee to Him, not us to them."

Silence fell, with insects churring and an owl hooting not too distantly.

"What a thought," Towaye said at last. "That alone makes me wish to look more deeply into this belief in the Christ."

Manteo smiled at the irony of it. "Truly? This?"

"Well, think on it. Does it not make sense that if what they say of God and this Jesus is true, it would stir up the ancient spirits?"

"It does, indeed. Although I would not have thought of it that way before."

They both then just sat together, letting the sounds of night wrap them about.

Chapter Ten

There were houses being built at the edge of Mushaniq's town. Houses made of brick, and lath and plaster. Ugly, blocky things that lacked the grace and simplicity of the rounded Kurawoten dwellings. But since the storm, her people and the Inqutish had agreed with one heart and mind to combine their living spaces.

She watched, half in fascination, half in dismay at their progress. It was odd to be so close to them on a day-to-day basis—the men and their faces covered with hair, the women and their—well, their everything covered with clothing and whatnot.

Worst, however, was having to bump into Georgie so often, at odd moments, only to have him meet her gaze and then look away, while Willie and the other boys not only continued to look but did so far more openly and intently than was proper.

At least they had been scolded about watching the women during their early-morning bathing in the sound, although Mushaniq was sure they managed to creep close enough at times anyway. It was the Inqutish women who scolded the loudest over it, surprisingly enough—especially when they took to joining Mushaniq and the other women in their washings. They often still wore the thin, pale garment that served as the innermost layer of their garb, but at least they kept themselves cleaner than they had before.

And then, on a day when Nohsh had been gone for several days, scouting for a new Inqutish settlement in Dasemonguepeuk, she realized she'd grown more accustomed to their ways, and they no longer appeared as strangers. The cadence of their speech still took effort to catch, but she was recognizing more and more of the words.

It was also still hard to say some of their words and names. Like the tiny girl-child with hair of sun and eyes of sky—the long form of her name was something like *Vur-cheen-ya* but everyone called her *Cheeny*. Only it wasn't quite a *ch* sound but more like the beginning of Georgie's name. Speaking the sound felt like crunching sand between her teeth.

The girl herself was the most darling thing, with a smile for everyone as she took her first steps. The other Inqutish baby, a boy, seemed content to crawl or be carried, but it would not be long before he too was toddling about.

Nohsh and the other men returned safely, and then the town was full of talk about which of the Inqutish would make the move and how soon. Mushaniq was used to evening gatherings being lively, but this brought a new level of commotion.

The strangest turn, however, was Towaye suddenly asking questions about the God of the Inqutish, when he previously had listened with polite interest at best. The customary singing and dancing gave way sooner rather than later to a spirited discussion, Nohsh sitting at its center with the Inqutish's holy man on one side and Towaye on the other.

More than half the town, lingered to listen, Kurawoten and Inqutish combined, with Timqua and Nunohum and others occasionally asking questions. Kokon leaned into Mushaniq's side, and she allowed it, savoring the warmth and comfort and community despite her disquiet at the intensity of conversation.

The grown-ups talked until far past sunset. A few wandered away to sleep, but most stayed. Even Mushaniq found herself leaning in as Nohsh related, in both Inqutish and the tongue of the People, how while traversing the swampy woods of Dasemonguepeuk, he felt a presence so strong he thought it must be enemy warriors ready to attack them. And when he stopped and saw that truly no one was there, he still heard a voice, menacing.

At that point, he told them, he began to pray.

Chills swept Mushaniq's skin, and snugged up against her, Kokon shivered.

Not only did the fear and dread leave, Nohsh said, but the rest of the expedition went so smoothly they thought it nigh a dream.

A moment of silence fell, with only the wind and the crackling of the fire, then a flurry of questions came. "But how could that be? Why would the spirits of the land set themselves against the Creator?"

Nohsh spread his hands. "For the Maker of land and sea to come down and become a man, then shed His blood for the final sacrifice of our wrongdoings—that is powerful magic. Thomas Harriot and Nicholas Johnson both have shared from the holy book that in Christ, we are free of our sin and guilt. We no longer have to strive to please Montóac or *Okeus*, or whatever name the gods may go by among the Tunapewak. Perhaps it is the fact that we look to our true Master and not to them that displeases them." He smiled. "I only know, as I have said before, from the moment I accepted baptism, I felt free as I had never before in my life."

Towaye scooted forward. "So it is the baptism that determines this change?"

Nohsh looked at Master Johnson and exchanged a few words with him. "In truth, we do not know for sure. It is—how do they say it? A mystery."

Master Johnson said something else, and Nohsh went on. "He says the holy book says simply, if you acknowledge with your mouth that Jesus is Lord and believe with your heart that God has raised Him from the dead, that is enough to begin."

"Then. . ." Towaye swallowed hard. "I too felt the difference out there in the forest. Have seen the calm you have carried since we returned from England and you took the baptism. So—I believe."

More silence, and then inexplicably, Towaye's head went down, and his shoulders shook with weeping that soon became audible.

"I also believe," rose another voice above the crowd, and others joined in agreement.

Against Mushaniq's side, Kokon began to tremble, but a terrible coldness swept through her own belly. What was this madness?

Could it be that what Nohsh had been saying was indeed the truth? Or was this something even darker and more treacherous than what they had been taught of Montóac?

"I wish to be baptized," Towaye cried.

Nohsh turned to convey his words to Master Johnson, whose mouth fell open and worked before he finally replied. Nohsh argued with him, and at last he spread his hands. Nohsh turned back to the others.

"A formal service may be held later, but for now, nothing hinders you from going down to the sound and putting yourself under the waters there."

In the ensuing commotion, Kokon leaped up and bolted forward, but Mushaniq crept backward, away from the incomprehensible rush of her people toward the shore.

Across the fire, Georgie glimpsed Mushaniq's wide, panicked gaze just before she fled off into the dark. He was torn—this was too great a curiosity to miss, with most of the older folk suddenly collapsing into tears and begging to be baptized—and good Master Johnson and the other elders so obviously flummoxed at it all. And it wasn't as if she'd likely be in any danger. But with unease stirring in his gut, he edged his way out of the crush and trailed her into the forest.

It felt a bit like the days after they'd first come to Croatoan, with both of them seeking each other out after his discovery of her watching the town from the bushes—but with the pace she was keeping, it was very like a game of tag or hide-and-seek as well.

At what point should he warn her he was here? She was old enough to carry a wooden knife or shell fragment, both capable of damage with enough force.

She scurried along under the low-hanging branches of the gnarled oaks like the creature she was named after, only stopping at the top of the ridge, where he knew a break in the trees afforded a view of the ocean beyond. It was now or never, if he wanted to not startle her beyond repair—

"Mushaniq!"

She twitched toward him, hand to the waistband of her fringed deerskin skirt, as he'd anticipated.

"It is I, Georgie."

She relaxed only a measure, keeping her hand at her side. A stream of words rattled from her mouth. He shook his head and lifted a hand to express his lack of comprehension.

She tried again. "Why—you follow?"

He was trying, but she was certainly better at English than he was at Croatoan, yet. "I—saw you run away." He gestured behind them.

Her chin came up, but she did not move otherwise.

"Do you wish to walk down to the ocean?" He pointed this time past her.

She tipped her head oh so slightly, as if considering his words, then gave a single nod.

"Pyas," he said, and closing the distance between them, moved past.

She followed without a word.

He avoided the path to the fort. It was too unsettling since the tempest and Thomas's disappearance. Instead, he angled toward the northernmost shore, and once past the wood's edge, he tucked in at the edge of a dune as was their previous habit.

She dropped to the sand, hugging her knees to her chest and shivering. He hesitated but a moment before tugging off his shirt and draping it about her shoulders. She angled him a look somewhere between confusion and annoyance, then laid her cheek against her knees, face turned away from him.

For a while he simply watched the stars and listened to the wind and waves. At last he ventured, "What ails you, then?"

She peeked at him but did not reply.

"Were you angry? Afraid?" He attempted the Croatoan words for those two terms, since past lessons in their mutual tongues had included emotions. Recalling the contortions of facial expressions they had exchanged to accomplish this nearly brought a chuckle to his throat, but he suppressed it. This was not the time.

She was quiet so long he was unsure whether she had even heard him or merely chose to ignore him. But at last, "Kupi. Angry and afraid." She turned her face toward him. "What—" She shook her head, said something entirely in Croatoan that he could not follow, then propped her chin on her knees.

After a few moments, she tried again. "Do you have—mother?"

His gut churned. "In England. She died."

Her eyes came back to him. "What was her name?"

He felt a curious reluctance, as if answering made it more real. "Mary," he said at last.

"Mah-ree." She made a sound, then nodded and smiled. "Is a good name."

When had she gotten so skilled at speaking English?

"Do you miss her?"

He snorted. "Of course."

"How old were you when she die?"

Another hesitation. "I was but ten."

She sighed. "I miss my mother sometimes, even though I too young to remember when she die."

For some reason, that made his eyes and throat burn. "I am sorry."

She merely looked at him at that.

It was passing strange to be speaking with her yet unsure how much she understood. But he would sit here with her all night if needed.

Mushaniq woke with the dawn, the wind tugging hard at her and the sun not yet over the horizon. She uncurled from her nest in the sand, still wrapped in the shirt Georgie had put around her and—

Her head had been pillowed against Georgie's shoulder.

He stirred at the same time she did, sitting up to gaze around them, then eyes widening. He moaned. "I will be in dreadful trouble over this. You need to return to the town without me."

She rose, then shook out the shirt and handed it to him. He took it without looking up. Had he given it to her to begin with because he could tell she had a sudden chill or—because he was too ashamed to look at her?

Failing words this early in the morning, she pointed as he clutched the garment to his chest. "Why—give?"

His eyes flashed surprise. "You shivered."

She did not know that word, but then his quick shake, mimicking, made it clear. With warmth suffusing her for the unexpected kindness, she dipped her head. "Thank you."

He smiled, the tiniest bit, before making shooing motions. With an answering grin, she sped away. She too would be scolded by Auntie Timqua if she did not return quickly.

Strangely enough, Auntie barely seemed to notice. She and the other women were already down at the water, splashing and chattering and in general raising a commotion. Mushaniq shed her skirt and slipped in among them.

They were all full of jubilation about what had taken place the night before. Laughing, singing, calling back and forth. Mushaniq waded in as far as her waist before sinking beneath the warm water. A breath, then she went completely under.

The water filled her ears, its hum and roar of distant waves soothing and comforting. But after several heartbeats, she had to come up again.

Behind her, one of the women had begun a song about the rising sun. Suddenly the words were no longer about the breaking dawn but about the Creator God and how great and wonderful He must be to provide all that they had.

Mushaniq stayed submerged to her chin as the song began again and became a call-and-answer with the other women echoing each line. A heaviness settled in her gut.

She loved singing and the evening dancing, especially. But all this enthusiasm was overwhelming, and she could not say why.

Perhaps in time it would all die down, and life would return to normal.

If anything could ever be normal again, with the Inqutish living right there in the same town.

Chapter Eleven

T his is," Roger Prat pronounced, "a most unexpected hap."
Manteo sat with the Inqutish men out under a spreading oak.
Across the circle, Georgie and another boy edged in, plopping down to
watch and listen. He must needs speak to that one later. In the midst
of all else the night before, he'd noted Mushaniq's flight and Georgie's
departure after.

As if he knew the bend of Manteo's thoughts, Georgie met his gaze
and held it for a heartbeat or two, then glanced away.

Now he truly was curious what had passed between the boy and his
daughter.

"'Tis unfitting, is what it is." Edward Powell swiped his forehead
with the back of his hand and replaced the tall hat upon his head. "Such
overflow of feeling. One's faith should be sober and steady. How can we
be sure that this is a true change of heart on any of their parts?"

"If this is how we plan to conduct the savages' conversions," Ambrose
Viccars said, "perhaps we should simply throw out all the rest of our prin-
ciples as well."

Several of the men, Manteo included, fastened stern gazes upon Viccars and Powell, but it was Ananias who growled, "Mayhap if that is your
feeling, it truly is best for you to remove across to the mainland and soon."

Predictably, Powell bristled at that. "Are you forcing us to leave?"

Ananias did not budge. "No one is forcing anything. You are the ones unhappy that somehow, in our wish to live at peace with these people and bring them gently along the path to true faith, we are not English enough. Or—righteous enough."

Powell's eyes glittered. "The Holy Scriptures tell us to hate the filthy vesture of the flesh. And to be holy as He is holy."

"The apostle Paul also spoke about fashioning himself to all men, to save at the least way some."

The man drew in a long breath, squaring his shoulders. "Some things are simply not meet, even so."

"Well then," Prat said, "I suppose we shall know them by their fruits, eh?" He gave Powell and Viccars a smile that set them sputtering with indignation.

Manteo understood their reticence, their scramble to comprehend what had taken place. He had his own questions and reservations. He had seen initial exuberance before, from others of the People. When first presented with the concept of the One True God, they had thought it merely another form of ritual and not only joined the Inqutish in kneeling for prayer but also took the holy book to rub against their skin, as if its virtue could be transferred by mere contact, like a talisman or personal totem.

Such things were useless, Manteo knew by now, although simple kneeling was proper enough. But this was different—and the Kurawoten had taken at least half a year to hear and consider before coming to such a decision. Certainly, that had to count for something.

The calm, steady dark gaze of Manteo struck a not-unexpected terror into Georgie's middle. He knew he'd done nothing amiss. If anything, his concern had been wholly for Mushaniq's well-being. But would the tall native see it thus?

After the men's meeting had broken up—interrupted, really, by a group of Croatoan come clamoring for Master Johnson to speak to them from the Scriptures—and it was decided that Towaye understood enough English to help with translation for the time being, Georgie tried to slip away unnoticed. Manteo made a beeline for him, however.

Georgie stopped near another oak, resisting the urge to hide behind it and instead leaning back against its trunk, feigning nonchalance. But Manteo tucked his chin, his gaze intent, pinning Georgie in place as surely as if he'd used spears or arrows.

"Was all well with Mushaniq last eve?" Manteo asked finally, deep voice rising and falling in that musical way his people had.

But Georgie would not let his guard down. Manteo might yet be wroth with him. "She was confused—and afraid—by what was happening with your people."

Manteo nodded slowly. "It is to be expected. There is much to understand in all this."

"I wished to make sure she was not alone. That—she came to no harm out there."

Another slow nod. "I thank you."

Something in his eyes told Georgie that speculation still brewed in his thoughts, however. And Georgie couldn't blame him, not after the issues with the other boys. "I—I hold her in very high regard. I would not see her used ill."

At that, Manteo's stance and gaze shifted. "For that as well, I thank you," he said at last. "See that your care continues."

The older man walked away, and Georgie's breath left him in a rush.

The boy came about to his chin now, Manteo noted. A full hand taller than when they'd arrived at Roanoac.

His willingness to face Manteo, despite his obvious nervousness, was heartening. Now to see what Mushaniq had to say.

He found his daughter studiously boring holes in pieces of shell, as if the task were all she should give attention to this fine day. She did not look up until he stopped beside her, then her gaze fell again.

Not his usual Little Squirrel.

"Come for a walk?" he asked.

She hesitated, then bobbed her head and set the bowl of shells aside.

He did not even need to ask. "Everyone has lost their minds!" she burst out as soon as they were set off down the path. "You—you told us stories, but it seems this is all anyone can think about—this *Kryst*—this God whose love and peace they say they can now feel." She flapped her arms. "Is it terrible that I do not want to follow just yet? That I do not want it to be just a matter of I must because everyone else believes?"

"No," he said carefully. "Although it began somewhat so for me, and then was more."

She stared at him. "Is it terrible that I think half of those who followed last night did it only because others went?"

"Also no. But only time will prove whether their trust in God is a genuine thing or whether it might grow into such."

Mushaniq sighed loudly, half a groan. "I will not pretend." She shot him a frown. "Not even for you, though I love you."

He laughed but quietly. "I would have it no other way, Little Squirrel."

Her expression became thoughtful. "Some are even changing their names. But you did not. Why?"

"Because—" Again, he needed to choose his words. "You were almost too young to know, but when I was first chosen to go with the Inqutish, I chose to keep the name that came to me during huskanaw because it was appropriate. I think the weroances chose me as much for that name as for my heart and spirit. And when I chose to follow God in this way, again, *Snatched* was the best description of what I felt my life had become. I did not choose so much as I felt chosen. Does that make sense to you?"

She nodded after a bit of thought. "It does." Another sigh but less noisy. "I just do not want life to change. It was happy before; why does everything need to be different?"

He tried not to smile. "That is a good question, and one I should think upon before trying to answer."

That seemed to soothe her.

"But why do you think this means less happiness?"

She drew herself up. "The Inqutish, they are so worried about silly things. Whether or not a woman is covered. And—the boys." Her eyes fairly flashed. "They do not understand the honor of the women. We are the ones who work, who take care of the babies—and them!"

Manteo did laugh at that, at least a little. "No, and you are right. They have much to learn about what even their own God says about such things."

"So why should we listen to them about God Himself?"

He sobered. "Because. The idea that God is closer than we know, that He truly cares about us. . . Why would the spirits of the forest feel so threatened were there not something to this?"

"Well, they can take it and go back to their land, then."

He snorted softly. "They might be tempted to. Except that there have been no ships this summer, and the season grows late for one. So we must continue extending kindness at least for one more year."

She huffed but did not comment this time.

"Speaking of extending kindness, it is my understanding that young Georgie accompanied you last night merely to watch over you?"

Her shoulders both sagged and hunched at the same time. "Kupi. He said he did not want me to be lonely. We talked and watched the waves. I was cold, and he gave me his shirt."

"You would tell me if he spoke or acted amiss?"

She peered at him, then gave a quick nod. "Kupi. He has been good if not a little shy."

"I am glad to hear it."

It gave him much to think about in the coming days.

Even Auntie Timqua was not unaffected by what had taken place that one night, but despite her fears to the contrary, life did settle much as before, except for the added joy and exuberance of Auntie and many other elders. Evening dancing and prayers still took place, with most of it aimed more directly at God and not all the attendant spirits, and much discussion between the people and the priests over what was now fitting in their various customs. Mushaniq did her best to ignore it all—and for the most part, even Auntie let her be.

Little Ginny toddled everywhere, babbling happily even as her mama cast longing looks to the ocean. But Elinor was so sweet and kind

Mushaniq found herself lingering in the woman's house when she'd nothing else pressing, marveling over the various devices the Inqutish woman used or playing with the bright-eyed child.

And so the summer faded to autumn, and autumn into winter, which did seem merrier for the company of the Inqutish, and then suddenly it was spring again and summer. Mushaniq and Kokon and the others fell back into an easy rhythm of work and play and running about the island with the Inqutish boys and girls, hunting and gathering and soaking in the wind and waves.

The adults, especially the Inqutish, watched the sea with even more vigilance. Two years, they all said to each other. For several days in late summer, Georgie looked more somber than usual, but Mushaniq did not press him about the cause.

Then came the sea storm, worse than the year before, with the water sweeping in from the sound so quickly they all barely escaped. The breakers already rolled high on the ocean side as they went inland, seeking shelter under the tangled oaks along the island's highest ridge, and there they huddled all the night through as the wind howled, lightning crackled above them, and the thunder shook the entire forest.

When it was over, the town lay in great ruin, but all lives were accounted for. Curious though was the way the machicomuck had been half swept away, and while most of the human remains were still there, the Kewás figure was gone.

Much consternation and squabbling ensued between the weroances and the priests, especially between those who had taken the name of Christ and the handful who had not.

The most pressing argument, though, was over whether to stay on the island. With all their stores ruined, they'd little enough to sustain themselves through the coming winter, and the saltwater washing over most of the island meant that crops likely would not grow the next year and possibly the year after that.

After much talk, with heavy hearts, Mushaniq and her people said goodbye for the present to their beloved island and made their way west.

They settled not too far from where one of the Inqutish expeditions in previous years had found several Sukwoten towns, or so it was said on a map that Elinor's father had helped draw from those journeys. They named it not after the Sukwoten, however, but *Cora Banks*, partly for the people whose towns lay not far through the swampy mainland forest—the Cwareuuoc, *Kwah-ray-yuh-wock*, or Corée. They had taken the boats straight across the sound as the sun set. Mushaniq was not afraid, but there were perils to be found on the mainland that they'd never known out on their beautiful, sandy islands.

The Cwareuuoc met them on the shore, where both Kurawoten and Inqutish had agreed to build a new town, with gifts of food and fire already kindled. At first, as evening came, it was a little like old times, but then off in a crowd, she noticed Georgie glancing away into the forest, then around at all those who were strangers to both of them, and she was reminded.

This was meant to be home, at least for a little while—but it was not home yet.

She missed the island already.

Chapter Twelve

THE PRESENT:
Cora Banks, Spring 1590

The trouble with removing to the mainland, Manteo knew, was not so much whether they would find enough food to support themselves through autumn, winter, and the following spring until they could plant crops. It was how exposed they suddenly were to the forces that had driven them from Roanoac to begin with.

And it was not that they had forgotten. The Inqutish men, to their credit, remained ever mindful. But then the tranquility of that first season at Cora Banks dulled everyone's sense of alarm just enough that when the first breath of threat arrived, it caught them off guard.

While they were drawn away by the claim of an attack on Beechland, where their Inqutish brothers had made a town deep in the woods of Dasemonguepeuk, Cora Banks itself was struck. In a moment, an unknown enemy had swooped in and taken nearly a dozen townspeople. All Inqutish, curiously enough.

Almost as if there had been planning and those taken chosen aforehand.

For a while now, thoughts of Wanchese had lurked in the back of his mind. Manteo knew deep in his heart that his old companion must certainly have some part in this. How many others had allied themselves with him yet remained to be seen.

Also hard upon his thoughts—and heels—was Ananias Dare, keeping pace by sheer will alone, he was sure. The grim desperation in the man's blue eyes chilled Manteo. Ananias was not the only one to suffer fresh loss, but he certainly seemed to bear it as more of a personal affront than the others.

"We all go together or not at all," Manteo had warned him. *"You will die otherwise."*

But the man's face had merely hardened. Only the great God knew what foolishness he would commit.

Lastly was the weight of the chase itself, the peril to which even now they were running. All the way back to Cora Banks from Beechland, it had pressed upon him—the silence of the forest, the knowledge that in truth a threat lurked there, but where? And what form would it take? Did the spirits of the forest take on the very form of Wanchese and others in order to exact their vengeance at last?

Manteo would not shrink from the war, but the dread of it settled heavy in his gut.

Three days later, after speaking with hunting parties and other travelers, Manteo led the others away from the old path he remembered and tracked the party they sought through almost trackless wilderness.

And then, as night fell, Manteo judged his own men close enough that they might cross paths with the captors. Unwilling to risk one of them stumbling across the enemy camp, Manteo positioned them a distance away from the path tracing the river. Henry Berrye and Anthony Cage both drew first watch, and without a word, Ananias joined them. Manteo suppressed a sigh. The man likely would not be able to immediately sleep anyway.

Still, the unease niggled at him as he stretched out on the ground with the others. Most of the men, Kurawoten warriors included, settled and fell almost instantly into slumber.

His own eyes fluttered closed. *Good God. . .most gracious One. . .*

He'd nearly drifted off when a crashing in the woods drew him up. It was Berrye, eyes and mouth wide. "We've found them—just a short distance away! Cage and Dare sent me to get you."

Half a dozen other men were awakened as well, and Manteo beckoned to them as he rose to his feet and seized his gun, heart pounding.

They ran forward to the sounds of sharp voices and then a bellow that Manteo wished he did not recognize—

Oh God, no! Please, no. . .

Drawn by firelight through the trees, they scrambled over a low ridge to a scene below, where bound Inqutish captives sat huddled beyond a cluster of warriors—Sukwoten or otherwise? In the midst of them knelt Elinor, facing a similarly restrained Ananias across the fire.

For a moment, it seemed the whole world held its breath.

Then a knife flashed in the hand of a warrior—one of steel, both blade and warrior's face familiar to Manteo's eye. Blood flowed dark, and Ananias fell heavily.

A cry ripped from Manteo's own throat. Lifting his gun, he leveled it at those below. But the warriors were already in motion, one snatching Elinor from the ground and the others dragging the rest of the captives into the dark. Manteo could not shoot and be sure of his target.

Oh holy and good God—

He tore down the slope and past the fire, heedless at first of the heap that was Ananias's body. Into the darkness, following the warriors slowed by their burdens to the river's edge, where he could see them piling into their kanoes. One stopped. Straightened. Looked back.

Wanchese!

Manteo swore he heard a laugh as his former companion leaped into the kanoe and pushed off. And then they were lost to the night.

Chest heaving for breath, he retraced his steps to the fire. Weeping shook him as he dropped to his knees beside Ananias's body, turned the form over, and registered the look of mingled disbelief and determination on the now-lifeless face. His blue eyes now glassy and staring. What began as a growl deep in Manteo's chest rose to a howl as he threw back his head and gave himself to the grief.

Around him, the other men likewise found their own expression of such in tears or curses.

"So close," Henry Berrye muttered later, sitting before the fire with legs loosely crossed. "So blasted close."

Anthony Cage swiped a hand over his face, bloodstained and begrimed from the task of wrapping Ananias's body for burial. "I tried to tell him to wait. Tried to hold him back—" His words ended with a strangled sob.

Tears still sheeted down Manteo's own cheeks at regular intervals. "There was no holding him back. He was set on vengeance."

"The warrior who seemed to be leading them was using Elinor rather harshly, shouting right in her face. Ananias could no longer bear watching. And so he thought to intervene."

More weeping, quietly, all around them. Manteo could scarcely take it all in, much less accept it. This man, often stubborn but always faithful—slain in but a moment.

"What now?" one of the other men asked.

He shook his head, slowly at first, then more firmly. He could find no words.

"We must bury Ananias first," Berrye said. "It would never do to try to carry his body back to the town."

"We shall, indeed." Manteo drew a long breath. "And then we will give further chase to the others to see what might be done."

Night fell with uneasy grace outside the longhouse as Mushaniq disentangled herself from the sleeping little girl. Ginny gave a last shuddering sigh and stirred but did not otherwise move as Mushaniq eased away and stood watching for a few moments.

Outside, the community fire burned, the smoke helping keep the mosquitoes and gnats away, but talk was muted, as it had been every night since the attack. A bit of song came to her ears, and Mushaniq knew there would be prayers lifted as well, but nothing as boisterous as often took place.

She tiptoed out of the longhouse and almost ran into Georgie standing near the entrance. "How fares Ginny?" he asked while she was still recovering her balance.

"She misses her mama and papa. But she sleeps now."

He nodded and looked away. "Thank you for tending her."

"Why would I not? She is much beloved to me. Elinor as well."

Georgie's gaze came back to hers, held for a moment, then he turned to walk away. He stopped when she called after him.

"How fares John Prat?"

He tucked his head. "Missing his papa too, of course, though he is much older."

"As it should be."

He peeked back at her. "And yourself?"

How to answer? For so many years, she did not miss Nohsh because he was off doing important things—but more recently? Despite her frustration with his continued attempts at persuading her to accept his view of God, she had more than grown accustomed to his everyday presence.

She did miss him. And fiercely.

Her eyes burned. Tears trickled down her cheeks before she could stop them.

Georgie stepped closer. His arms came up as if to embrace her, then dropped. "'Tis no shame to miss your da."

"I—" She gulped. "What if he does not come back? What if he too is taken or—killed?"

His hands were suddenly on her shoulders, his face bent near hers. "If he does not, then you will survive. And live on. He would wish it."

It was truth he spoke, but oh—

She sagged against him, cheek to his shoulder, the texture of his shirt soft and oddly comforting. As she gave herself to the weeping, one of his hands shifted to the back of her neck while his other arm loosely encircled her.

"I cannot even think on it," she said.

"I know," he murmured. "How well I know."

She drew away, feeling suddenly shy. When had he gotten so tall? And what a long time since they'd even spent more than a few moments alone together, much less talked with such openness.

He likewise seemed to sense the awkwardness, straightening and yet not quite withdrawing completely. "I can sit with Ginny if you want to go back to the fire."

A giggle escaped her throat. "No, you cannot. It is the women's longhouse."

His chin came up. "I can sit outside."

"Well, then." She felt a curious reluctance to leave, but with a nod, she trotted off toward the gathering.

She had been right—they were praying and singing softly. Tucking into a corner against the wall of one of the houses, she folded her arms around her legs and settled to watch. Nearby, a man who was formerly one of the priests murmured and swayed. Having long since been infected by the beliefs of the Inqutish, he no longer wore the blackbird on his head to denote his status and had gone so far as to grow out his hair.

A year and more ago, she'd sought his insight on the dilemma of Auntie Timqua and others suddenly following this new belief, but he had only looked at her before commenting on the power of the Inqutish God and His Son. "What? Even you are moved by this?" she had demanded. And he only smiled, to which she had stomped off in disgust.

If those who taught the old ways could not hold faithful, where was she to go?

She sighed and let the sound of their devotion wash over her. The customary internal kick against all of it was less strong than usual. . .or was she just weary from the shock of the attack days ago and having care over Ginny?

And she was very weary. Almost enough to wish she could accept God being loving and attentive, like Nohsh and Auntie Timqua, rather than great and lofty and distant like the moon and stars. Because how could a Creator who set those lights in the heavens and spun the world into motion truly have any interest in the lives of people here?

Her eyes burned again. She missed Elinor. She missed Libby and Emme, both about her own age now when they'd first arrived not quite three years ago. She missed the kindly face of Roger Prat, John's father. She even—well, while she could not say she missed the troublesome Willie Wythers, or Tom Humfrey and Robbie Ellis—neither did she wish them ill, under the circumstances.

Was there any sort of prayer or oblation she could make that might persuade Montóac to ease their plight, since the vast majority of the Kurawoten seemed to be neglecting that side of things? It seemed to her the strong spirits of the land and air would have more influence on their captors than the great and high Ahoné.

"And why should the Great God who made it all not have the strength to do the same and more?"

Mushaniq lifted her head and looked around, but everyone remained absorbed in their own songs or prayers or meditations. There was no one nearby to have spoken those words, and yet they were as clear as if someone had.

She shook her head and rose, brushing off the back of her skirt. She should be slumbering already, alongside Ginny.

Georgie sat leaning against the outside wall of the women's longhouse, still awake, listening to the sounds of the town, when Mushaniq returned. Her gaze trailed across him, but she kept walking and did not speak as she passed.

That was noteworthy. The "Squirrel" with nothing to say. But she had labored as much as he these last few days, perhaps more.

He let out a long breath and tipped his head back against the wall. Just a moment longer, and he'd go walk the perimeter of the town.

"Hie! Why you here? Get up! Go! You no sleep here."

Georgie startled awake to find one of the Croatan grandmothers—not Mushaniq's own, since she wore far more ornamentation than this woman—standing over him, one hand on her skirted hip and the other waving in an energetic shooing motion.

"Yehakan for crenepo only. You go!"

He scrambled up, dipping his head in deference, and strode away.

At the edge of the dark, he stopped, scrubbed both hands over his face, and swiped his hair back, retying it. Then he stilled and simply listened.

The town, behind him. Ahead, an owl, hooting at uneven intervals. Somewhere between, the rustle of some small creature in the leaves.

No threat there. He set out walking, stepping slowly and deliberately as he'd watched the Croatoan do, keeping ears and eyes open all the while.

Squirrel she might be called, and too exuberant and talkative by half, but oh, did she get under one's skin.

Well, his in particular. And why he felt such a need to help look after her was anybody's guess. To his relief, Willie and the other boys had given her a wide berth, especially after the town's removal to the mainland. Mayhap it was the terror of her being Manteo's own daughter, although that made no difference before, and mayhap it was the loss of the extravagant freedom they'd enjoyed on the island, but whatever, they did seem marginally more respectful in all ways.

It could be too that Georgie simply felt more responsibility as he'd grown older. Certainly, he'd applied himself more thoroughly to learning as much of the men's trades as he could—blacksmithing, carpentry, tile and brickwork, weaving and tanning. So far he could not name a favorite. Even tanning he did not hate, despite the stench, because it was so useful a skill. Yet no matter how absorbed he became in the men's company, in gaining knowledge and craft, that one girl was always at the edge of his thoughts and, it seemed, of his sight. No matter where he happened to be.

To make matters worse, he had noticed—and he could not help it— how the Croatoan women persisted in clothing themselves. Or not clothing themselves, more to the point. But Mushaniq was no longer the little girl she'd been when they first came to the island. She'd grown taller—the top of her head came just about to his mouth—and the outline of her body had begun shifting to something that could only be described as womanly.

And yet she was still completely without any sort of shame or even consciousness of her state. Of course, neither did she flaunt it, as some did, however subtly.

While he had hesitated earlier to comfort her in her distress, neither did it feel unseemly in the moment. And there was something strangely endearing in the way she'd laid her head upon her shoulder.

And Mushaniq gladly helped care for Ginny, whom Georgie had been tasked with watching over. Whether Elinor had intended her cry to apply only in the moment or not, he would not hold that responsibility lightly. They were all still shaken over the suddenness of the attack. He could hardly believe Willie and Tom and Robbie were all taken, as well as Libby and Emme. It could have as easily been himself or Mushaniq. And still could be.

Thus his present task.

He walked on through the forest, circling the town as silently as he could. Movement ahead froze him, but it was only the passing of another owl, silent. Then, a whisper of sound, and he dropped into a crouch.

A figure glided through the trees, stealthy but sure, the silhouette lean but unmistakably native and male. An enemy warrior? Georgie thought not but would not give himself away regardless.

He sank lower, hand drifting to the dagger at his side, then held his breath as the figure came closer. His fingers curled around the hilt—

"Two Feathers!"

The other youth went into a similarly defensive stance as Georgie rose from his hiding place, then relaxed. "You! I smelled your Inqutish stench from away over there."

"You lie." Georgie gave a low laugh, though the insult was not entirely in jest and they both knew it. "I wash as well as you."

The Croatoan stripling made a scoffing sound. "That I doubt heartily."

The two of them stood looking at each other, assessing, measuring. Georgie refused to be the one to speak next.

"What do you out here?" Two Feathers asked at last.

"Keeping watch."

The other boy gave a quick nod, grudgingly, Georgie thought. "Did you see anything? Or did your bumbling about warn all our enemies and even now they might fall upon us?"

Georgie snorted softly. Their whole conversation was barely above a breath, and Two Feathers was no quieter than Georgie himself. "What of you? I heard you coming half a mile away."

Two Feathers's head came up. "You did not."

"I did hear you."

The other boy stared at him, dark eyes almost menacing in the gloom. "It does not matter. I will learn all the ways of manhood soon while you—your people may have all sorts of devices beyond belief, but they do not even believe in huskanaw."

Georgie forced himself to shrug and move as if to walk past Two Feathers, but the boy's hand snaked out and seized his shoulder.

"And you shall not have Mushaniq. I will win her—you will see."

He couldn't help it—his jaw dropped right open. "What?" was all he could manage after a moment.

The grip on his shoulder tightened. "You are not stupid. You comprehend what I mean. And I mean for Mushaniq to be mine." He released Georgie with a little shove. "Even if you persuade her to play with you."

With that, Two Feathers stalked away into the forest.

Georgie stood for a very long time, tumbling all those words about in his head whilst his gut burned.

Chapter Thirteen

M ushaniq discovered the next morning that she would not be leaving the women's yehakans but would be spending a few days in the smaller of the houses set aside for their various needs.

She took her shell blade, made from the half of a whelk she'd found on the beach so long ago she could hardly recall, and scraped a shallow hole in the sandy earth to sit over. Though tiresome to face being still for days on end, this was the most efficient way they had found to deal with a woman's regular flow—and it was their people's way.

Timqua took charge of Ginny as soon as Mushaniq's situation became apparent, but she returned with food for their morning meal, sitting across from Mushaniq with a hungry Ginny next to her. As she helped the tiny girl scoop a portion of the *apohominas* and fish, she favored Mushaniq with a thoughtful look. "How many stays have you had here in the women's house?" Timqua asked.

"This is my fourth," Mushaniq said, feeling almost as petulant about it as Ginny might be over having to wait to eat.

Timqua chewed, nodding. "It is time for your *huskanasqua*, but I am reluctant to carry it out with Manteo and the others gone."

Something in Mushaniq's gut seemed to turn over. "Or with Elinor and the other girls taken."

Timqua's gaze turned sad. "I miss my friend. And I know she was as another mother to you as well."

They both bent their heads for a moment before continuing to eat.

"Can Nohsh find them and bring them home, do you think?"

The older woman sighed. "I do not know." She hesitated, fingers going still in the common dish for a moment. "God is with Manteo. Of course, God is with us all. It does not seem so when we are all suffering such sorrow, but I heard that the holy book says all things work for the best to those who love Him."

Coldness edged around Mushaniq's heart, as it always did whenever they spoke of their God. "If He is so good and strong, why did He not stop them from being taken?"

"Oh, sweet girl." Timqua sighed. "There is nothing so terrible that it can separate us from His love."

Mushaniq just looked at her. How could she believe this? How could she even say it? Elinor had been torn from her family—the other Inqutish as well. She just could not imagine a caring God allowing such a thing.

No, it was more likely that the world was a playing ground, and they were merely the balls being tossed back and forth between the various gods and spirits.

She hated the sitting still. No matter how much weaving or stitching Timqua brought her, they never kept her hands busy enough for her thoughts to stay occupied as well. And she found herself thinking about things that would never otherwise occur to her.

"Do we finish planting the fields while the men are gone? Are we to go hunting in their stead? Fishing? Are we allowed to go foraging in the woods? Do we try to carry on with life as usual until they return?"

The two older women who shared the space during her time merely laughed and shook their heads.

"What?" she asked.

"Little Squirrel, all these questions have already been asked and talked about many times. But it is good, and a sign you are truly becoming a woman, that you think about them now, for yourself."

She huffed and sat back. That answer was not satisfying at all.

"Since you are now become a woman," the other said, "are there any of the young men who catch your interest?"

She grimaced, but in truth, the thought did not disgust her as it once did. "Perhaps."

Both women chortled. "Well," said the older, "when you are ready for your first, do not give over easily. Make him court you."

Mushaniq blinked. She knew, despite much talk over what was good and proper, with many now saying it was not right for couples to sneak out together, that many still did. But she still wasn't sure how adventurous she wished to be just yet.

"Those are wise words, and I thank you," she said.

The women just looked at each other and chuckled again.

A few more days, and Mushaniq could leave. She made straight for the river to their usual bathing place.

She could not get clean quickly enough. Skirt discarded on the bank, she waded in and sank down with a sigh. The loops of her beads, heavier and more numerous now than even a few months past, swished and clacked gently around her.

A splash came from behind, and she turned to see Timqua joining her. "What? It is the middle of the day!"

"It is not, Little Squirrel." Timqua laughed but then grew quickly serious. "I wished to speak with you alone. We will wait until your father and the other men return, and then we will plan your huskanasqua. You have had four stays in the women's house, and it is time."

Her heart leaped. She would soon be considered a woman! Which meant—

"You already help with all the work. You are already as capable as any of the other girls your age."

Work was an everyday thing and not to be shirked. That would not change.

"And—perhaps—there is a young man who has caught your interest?"

Mushaniq turned away, swishing the water with her hands. "Perhaps."

Why were her cheeks turning warm? She ducked deeper into the water, up to her eyes, to cool them.

Auntie laughed, a soft, gentle sound and not like the knowing chuckles of the women in the lodge. "It is very different now, is it not?"

Mushaniq blew water noisily like a dog. "I still do not wish to think overmuch about—that."

Her laughter pealed this time. "It is not so bad. Or at least. . .it does not have to be. And with the right man—" She sighed, a dreamy sound that Mushaniq had never heard before.

"Why have you no husband?"

"What makes you think I have none?" When Mushaniq stared, Timqua snorted and shook her head. "That is a talk for another time. It is enough to say, it is better to have no husband than a bad one."

More wisdom, of a certainty.

Pursuing Wanchese and his company through the tangled, swampy woods was akin to seeking phantoms on a foggy night. Even the fact of them dragging along several Inqutish did not help overmuch, for Wanchese and the others knew where best to travel so their path was not marked so clearly. Sometimes they went through waterways and wetlands where no trace at all of their passing remained after just a few hours, and sometimes they boldly took the main pathways.

Three more days they pursued after burying Ananias, stopping only when it was too dark to track. On the third night, they made camp. Manteo felt they must be close, and yet they could not continue without clear direction.

While others circled outside the camp, keeping watch, Manteo huddled over a small fire with Chris Cooper, John Sampson, Henry Berrye, and Anthony Cage representing the Inqutish, and Towaye and Menatoan speaking for the Kurawoten. "We have advantage with our weapons," Cage said, "and we have advantage with Manteo and the Croatoan warriors leading us who know this land. Those alone would grant us much success. But the difficulty is that we are running short of powder and shot for our guns. There is a certain amount of time needed to make both—if we can find what we need to do so and avoid attack in the meantime."

Cooper looked around the circle and turned at last to Manteo. "My most fervent wish is to not back away from pursuing these miscreants. We have swords yet, and bows and arrows." He sniffed. "Arrows too require time to make, although less so than powder and shot, to be sure."

Manteo examined the array of possibilities. "To make shot requires lead, which we have yet at Roanoac. And powder?"

He knew already, but it gave him time to think.

Sampson answered this one. "We aren't badly lacking in powder, since we recently found resources for such through the Cwareuuoc—gypsum and coal, and saltpetre. If we need more, it simply requires getting to them and carrying them home."

How he longed in this moment for a pipe in hand and some good uppowoc. The councils of the Inqutish were so hasty and filled with more distress than they ought to be.

He drew a long breath. It could not be helped. "We will continue to one of the trading towns I know. I will send Towaye and the others for word while the rest of us remain back."

That foray proved less than fruitful—Towaye had gained word of the captives, but they'd been taken deep inland, up toward the mountains from where Manteo knew copper was dug from the earth and beaten out.

Ananias would have been profoundly unhappy. For that matter, Manteo was unhappy. But they were not prepared to bring war so deep into the home territory of strong adversaries such as the Mangoac.

"We should go back to Cora Banks and look in on the welfare of the rest of the town," he said firmly. "And then we may know best what to do next."

Chapter Fourteen

S pring was always a wondrous time, with the earth reawakening. Even Mushaniq's ever-present longing for the ocean eased a bit with a newfound fascination for the unfolding of tree leaves, the springing of various flowers from the forest floor and riverbank, and the migration of the geese and ducks. Of these she had seen plenty out on the island, but so many wintered here the sky was dark from their wings and full of clamoring as they prepared to fly north.

Even before the attack, the elders warned the younger ones not to stray far from the town and, when they did venture out, to be as silent and watchful as possible. Now, though the elders wished to forbid it altogether, they did not, only warned more strongly. For Mushanig, the days were full enough of work—fetching of wood and cooking and the mending and making of baskets, all with Ginny in tow. She was also learning how to shape earthenware vessels but often felt the tug to slip away alone, wrapped in her mantle if the air held a chill, and watch the slow changes the season wrought upon forest and waterway.

She made sure to work hard enough for the aunties to be tolerant of her wandering or to go only when Ginny napped. And unlike many other girls, who took advantage of the opportunity to go walking with the boys—both Kurawoten and Inqutish, despite the elders' warnings— Mushaniq had too much to think about. When she sneaked out, she made sure to be alone.

On one such day, warmer than many before, she tossed her mantle over one shoulder and walked with deliberate slow quietness, as she had been taught. Such tall trees here, compared to the island! Small birds filled the branches above her, with squirrels chasing here and there. She smiled. She was once as cheerful as they, before the burden of worry over Elinor and Nohsh and the others.

Oh, how she missed the days of running free on the island. But while not quite the same, wandering about did soothe some part of her spirit.

A scuff somewhere behind her brought her feet to a halt. Scanning the forest, she turned, forcing herself to calm despite her suddenly racing heart. One hand curved around the handle of her shell knife. "I know you are there, so you should come out."

A lean, masculine figure stepped from behind a tree.

Oh. Two Feathers. Not who she expected—or wanted.

He held a bow but lifted it to the side, both arms outspread. A crooked smile lifted his mouth. "I only wished to walk with you, Little Squirrel."

She let her lips compress with annoyance. "I wish to be alone for now."

He drifted closer. "It is too dangerous for that."

A dozen sharp retorts came to her tongue, but rather than choose one, she turned and began walking again.

She had no patience for boys today.

He ran past and shifted to face her, walking backward, offering what she was sure he thought was his best charming smile.

"Go away," she said.

The smile didn't waver. He did, however, stop in her path. She angled around him, yet he caught her arm and swung her back.

She struck his hand away. He only edged in closer. "You will be doing huskanasqua soon."

"So?"

He fairly loomed over her now, so near that the edges of the markings across his cheeks and forehead were crisp and clear. The darkness of his eyes glimmered like deep water. A shiver went through her—dread, or a tendril of excitement at his nearness?

Whichever, she was not having it. She thumped both palms into his chest and kept walking.

Of course he was undeterred and caught up to her again. "You are the bravest and cleverest girl in the town. And beautiful."

"Do not waste your words. I have not gone huskanasqua yet."

Again somehow he blocked her way, dancing to keep in front of her as she attempted to sidestep. "Anyone can see you are already a woman. Have you chosen someone for your first play? Let it be me."

Again she shoved him, then broke into a run.

"It should be me, Mushaniq! I am strongest. I am bravest!"

A third time he cut her off, catching her with both hands to keep her from knocking him aside. And just as one hand reached toward her chest, she slapped him, hard, across the face.

That did give him pause. He stared at her, a breathless moment with open-mouthed shock, then a slow grin took over his idiot face again. "You will warm to me. It needs only time."

She stomped. "Do not touch me again. Do not approach me unless I give you leave, or I will tell the elders you seek to force me, and they will cast you out."

His jaw dropped, and while he was still looking for more words, she fled.

Later she saw him, swaggering about the town, exchanging a few words with Georgie, who glared at him, then gazed across the open space at her.

Lackwit and braggart! What could he be saying? An ache lodged beneath her ribs. Somehow Georgie was the one Inqutish boy whose ill opinion she could not bear.

But she would not go to him and ask. She had quite her fill of boys for the day.

Mushaniq had walked alone in the forest with him, Two Feathers had said. In his preening way, he'd given Georgie those words and no more, but the implication was there.

And it burned more than Georgie thought possible.

He was nothing to her, he knew. Although something in the way the other boy made sure he was assured of his inferiority to him or any other Croatoan niggled at him. Like there was some aspect of it he should be aware of but was not.

'Twas not his business whom she walked with. But somehow the memory of Willie's ugly leer and uglier comments haunted still. Was he obligated, then, to try to save her from any of the other boys' attentions?

And what if she had sought the company of Two Feathers? She wasn't an infant any longer. It was, he knew too well according to her people's ways, within her rights to choose.

That didn't mean he had to like it.

The gathering at the fire that night seemed particularly happy—or maybe it was that they were all recovering from their initial shock after the attack. Prayers were made for the men still out and searching and for the safety of the ones captured. One brave soul raised a prayer for the repentance and salvation of those who had done the capturing, and although a bit of grumbling followed, it was pointed out that such was no less than their proper Christian response.

Across the fire, Mushaniq put her arms on her upraised knees and laid her head on them. It reminded him so sharply of that one night, out on the windswept dunes—

He missed the island. There was something comforting about being here, anchored on land, but the town was too crowded, too restrictive, and his nightly walks outside the palisade walls barely eased the craving for freedom.

The Croatoan weroansqua stood up, raising her hands for attention. She spoke in her own tongue, then waved for one of the younger chiefs—actually the chief's wife, the one called Wesnah—to say it again in English.

"We are preparing this summer for huskanasqua, for those girls who have come into their womanhood in the past turning of the sun. We have not done so since our two peoples have begun dwelling together as one town, and it is past time."

"Will we wait until the men return?"

"We will try, but several of us are feeling we should go ahead with it." She looked around at the group. "It is the men's business to see to huskanaw for the boys, but it is my thought we should look to preparing for that as well, before the year is out."

Georgie glanced around. Two Feathers sat very straight, his expression stern and proud. No doubt he was thinking of the advantage that was sure to give him with Mushaniq.

'Twas no business of his whom she chose.

Before he'd given it thought, he pushed to his feet and walked away from the fire.

Senseless it was to let it trouble him. None of them could remain children forever, free of care and encumbrances—not that Georgie himself had known any ease of heart since the day his father was so cruelly slain. But Mushaniq—she would be a woman and conduct her life as such, including choosing a husband and bearing him children. It was necessary for life to continue.

His feet took him of their own accord through the town, finding the shadows and avoiding the light. People's talk and laughter floated to him and washed over him.

What did he have, truly? No mother or father now, no family. It was approaching their third summer and still no ships had come from England with girls he might consider choosing a wife from. He shared the anxiety of the older folk over that point.

He came to the outside of the smithy and sank down against the back wall, well in shadows.

Was he simply destined to be alone?

They came out of nowhere, the deep shadows of the forest exploding with shrieks and howls.

Recognizing all too well the attack patterns of Tunapewak, Manteo ordered the men around him to drop, to huddle back-to-back, and shoot at will. The pop and flare of gunfire filled the night, with clouds of smoke rising about them. The cry of their attackers changed in pitch as lead shot found its mark.

Out of the gloom one figure emerged, the flash of an unmistakably Inqutish blade in his hand. Gritting his teeth, Manteo rose to meet him, blocking the arm holding the knife.

There they grappled, nearly nose to nose, the dark eyes of Wanchese—for truly it was he—glittering into Manteo's own. "Betrayer of our people," Wanchese hissed against the lull of arms being reloaded.

"Slayer of the innocent," Manteo whipped back. "The earth will offer no peace to you for what you have done."

"You think not? The earth will thank me! These people are a plague and a scourge upon it, and we will flourish only if we make an utter end of them."

"I will fight with them to that end, and our fate will rest in the hands of God Himself."

Wanchese laughed, an ugly sound. "Prepare yourself to meet Him now!"

He threw his weight against Manteo, driving him back a step before Manteo recovered, blocking yet another blow that would have landed in his side. He countered with a matching thrust to Wanchese's side, his own Spanish-made blade sliding between sections of woven reed to flesh beneath, then yanking the dagger free, he used his arquebus as a club to Wanchese's head.

The Sukwoten buckled and did not move. The rest of their attackers were taking flight. "Pyas!" he shouted to his own company and took off down the path.

He would not think about the tall warrior, once his companion and now bitter enemy, who lay bleeding on the forest floor behind them.

Chapter Fifteen

A new doeskin dress must be made, and apparently Auntie had prepared for just this thing. Out of the rafters she drew two hides, both tanned to rich softness, and began instructing Mushaniq in the fashioning of them into a garment.

She would also be responsible for the baking of apon and overseeing the broiling of fish. Each of the girls had a food or two to prepare for the feast held in their honor.

There would be footraces and tests of skill and ingenuity. Prayers would be offered, although there was much discussion over which ones and whether the customary oblations were to be made as well. The Inqutish women listened with much interest and gave their own opinions.

"Something else of great import," Grandmother said as she had the group of them gathered about her one rainy afternoon, "is the new name you will choose to define your life as an elder. Pray and meditate on it— and then choose wisely."

Misses the Ocean. That was what Mushaniq would like to be called. Or *Craves Freedom.*

Both were unwieldy and likely unworthy of her. None of the other women complained about being land-bound with only marshes and rivers—or if they did, she never heard them. And so she held her tongue and kept her own counsel while the other girls chattered among themselves about names.

Auntie noticed and asked her about it.

"I miss Nohsh. It is nearly full summer, and he has not returned."

Timqua looked grave and did not try to brush aside Mushaniq's worry.

"When we rise each morning," she said at last, "do we know what that day will hold, whether good or ill?"

"Mahta," Mushaniq whispered.

"This is why it is better to trust our days to the Good God who sent His Son to die for us. Because He walked the earth as a man, He knows what we feel. Our fears, our doubts, our uncertainties. He is worthy of your trust, sweet Squirrel." She drew a long breath and sat back. "I pray every day for my brother and for his safe return and that of the other men. But in the meantime—we *live*. And whatever you think of this God and our belief in Him, your papa would want that. You know this to be true."

Mushaniq tucked her head and nodded.

"I do not understand," Timqua went on softly, "how you can be so tender to your own father's love and yet resist that of the Great God. That is something I encourage you to meditate on as you prepare for huskanasqua. Let this be more than a passage into a new portion of your life. Let it be a passage into Life itself."

"I will think upon it," she murmured.

With so many of the men gone and the others employed in guarding the town, it fell to the older Croatoan men and boys to venture out fishing. On one such day, Georgie was enlisted by one of the Croatoan elders to accompany him and none other than Two Feathers.

Georgie sat in the front as Two Feathers and the older man paddled the narrow, heavy *kah-noe-ay* carved from a massive cedar downriver and out toward the sound, where they still built weirs to ensnare the fish.

It was a calm day and bright, with the breeze stirring the barest ripples across the water. Georgie's spirits lifted with the dancing waves despite the glares he could feel aimed at him from behind.

The elder Croatoan began to sing, a chanting ditty about the water and the fish and aiming well his spear. Two Feathers joined in, although perhaps with not as much strength as he might have if Georgie were not there.

Georgie was fairly sure that Two Feathers would sooner pitch him into the sound as look at him. He glanced back and was surprised to see an expression of open longing on the Croatoan youth's face.

They all missed the island and the ocean.

Of course, that didn't mean Two Feathers wouldn't toss him in the water, anyway. Georgie had long since ceased to fear the natives that had become more like brothers—at least, that they would do to him what had befallen Da.

The old ache stirred, more feebly than before. How Da would have loved this land. Mama too.

As they passed where the river widened into the sound, a large black eagle with a white head took off from a branch and dived for a fish. "Ka ka torwawirocs yowo?" the Croatoan elder asked Georgie, pointing.

"*Nahyápuw*," he answered.

The older man grinned. As they went, he drilled Georgie in the names of other birds and the fish they caught and what various trees were called. As his approval became more evident, Two Feathers glared all the more.

Georgie did his best not to gloat, but the elder's favor was strangely satisfying.

Huskanasqua was but a day away. Mushaniq had fully despaired of Nohsh returning in time, when a stir at the edge of the town with shouts and cries drew them from the task of shaping earthenware. And again she was a small child, running to his arms once she espied him striding along between the houses.

But even as he embraced her, she felt the tremor in his strength and heard his great sigh at the crying of little Ginny behind her. "Papa! Papa!"

A chill touched her. She drew back, hands still on his shoulders, and examined the furrows carved in his face. "What is it?"

"We have not regained the captives, and we lost Ananias as well."

She shrank completely at that, fingers covering her mouth. Her gaze strayed to the small girl with hair of sunlight dancing about and peering into the men's faces.

Manteo scooped her up and held her close. Strangely, Ginny did not protest.

"Lost?" Mushaniq repeated.

Perhaps he only meant taken captive. . .

"He was slain." Her father's voice was husky but gentle. "He would not listen to my admonitions to remain patient, and he threw himself in the way of harm for Elinor's sake. It did not save her."

Mushaniq's heart dropped completely. "Is she. . .?"

"Still captive. They were being taken to Ritanoe."

"Where there is life, there is yet hope." She had heard that so often over the years. *"If you are ever taken, do not fight. Submit! Stay alive."*

It was something all women of the People were told by their elders, and frequently.

"Is there any hope of getting them back?"

One hand stroking Ginny's pale hair, her father looked older than she had ever seen, and the slow shake of his head told all. "I do not know, my daughter. I do not know."

With heavy hearts, they finished preparations for huskanasqua. All agreed they should go ahead, although any joy Mushaniq might have felt for it had fled.

On the day of, she and the other girls rose before dawn and made their way down to their bathing spot at the river, accompanied by the other women, singing and praying. In the water, they scrubbed down, head to toe, loosening their hair. Every ornament had been laid aside for the time being, and when they came up out of the water, they squeezed out their hair and were helped into the doeskin dresses they had made.

Then they returned, single file and in silence, to the town, where each of them was attended by at least three other women who made them kneel and sip cups of strongly brewed yaupon, while they combed out their hair, made sure the fringes about their faces were just so, then bound up the length in back, tying it into a knot at the nape of their necks.

Then, still bare of ornaments, they set to the task of grinding pega-tawah for the making of apon as the men stirred and set out fishing and hunting.

When the sun was up, the girls were led outside the town and made to run four times around its perimeter. Then it was down to the river for a quick dip, back to the houses for paint—even for Mushaniq, who because of her status had no permanent markings on her skin—and orna-ments. Timqua hung long, dangling clusters of copper beads and pearls in Mushaniq's ears, while Grandmother draped strands of the same around her neck and tied bracelets on both arms.

Then it was time to make the dough for apon and see to the fish. This would be the first course, and all the town gathered to eat while the girls stood and watched.

After were the races and games of skill. Mushaniq proved herself with a bow, did not do badly with throwing, and was still as fleet of foot as any of the other girls, although she could have done better were they still on the island with the freedom to run about.

Then came the final preparations—more food, this time deer along with fish—and as the sun met the horizon, the girls were finally seated around the fire.

Before they were allowed to eat, however, each must get up and announce her new name and why she had chosen it.

Mushaniq sat, outwardly poised, but her insides churning. As the daughter and granddaughter of weroances, she would be last. Kokon was the next to last, rising gracefully beside her and proudly announcing she had chosen "Bright Star" for her love of the night skies. Heads nodded and approving murmurs rose about them.

Then it was her turn. She rose, gazing about. The entire town was present, including the Inqutish. Eyes shone in the light of the fire.

She squared her shoulders and faced Grandmother and Nohsh. "I choose—not to choose at this time."

Little gasps greeted her pronouncement. "What? Little Squirrel! Why would you wish to keep that?"

There were whispers and even some laughter. Grandmama's eyebrows had disappeared up under the fringe of her hair, and Nohsh merely gazed hard at her from across the fire.

"A squirrel," she said, "is quick and cunning and wise in the ways of caring for its young. Is that not honorable enough?"

Grandmother's brows came down to something like normal. "We will talk of this later. But for now—Mushaniq it is."

She understood. She was now Stubbornly Refuses to Change.

And talk later they did. Grandmother stood over her, hands on hips, radiating displeasure with all of her being. "If you refuse to take another name," she said, "you put yourself above the ways of the People. You are denying all the symbols of what huskanasqua is meant to be—the passage from child to woman, dying to all that was and embracing what is to be."

"Surely I can do that without taking a new name."

Grandmother flapped a hand. "Your milk name was never meant to be permanent. It is childish."

The more she pushed, the more Mushaniq wished to dig in. That too was childish, but she could not seem to help it. "So? You have already declared us women before the town and our People."

"That is disrespect," came Nohsh's low voice from the doorway.

She let her shoulders sag. "You are right. Please accept my apology, Nunohum." Her gaze flicked toward Nohsh. "And Nohsh."

His mouth remained a firm line.

Grandmother turned to Nohsh. "She is too much like you. Flouting tradition with the skin markings you decided you could not live without."

Mushaniq's ears perked. This was a story she had not heard. Nohsh only shook his head, and Grandmother turned back to Mushaniq.

When they said nothing more about the matter of Nohsh's skin markings—he would never tell her why he bore them, though she had often asked—she took a different angle. "If we are to be one people with the Inqutish, who do not change their names, then what does it matter?"

Both of them only continued looking at her.

Why had she never noticed how much Nohsh resembled Nunohum when he was being stern?

She lifted a hand as well. "What if the name I wish to choose is—Inqutish?"

Their gazes sharpened. "And what name is that?" Nohsh asked.

She hesitated only a moment. "Mah-ree."

Grandmother did not react, but Nohsh's head came up a little. "Mary?"

"Kupi."

"Why?"

"It is—is it not the name of one of your sacred crenepos?"

"Kupi, it is the name of the woman who bore Jesus the Christ." He hesitated. "It is also the name of the sister of the great weroansqua of *Inkurut*—England—and of the cousin who was slain for her betrayal and treachery." A muscle in his cheek twitched. "Do you believe yet in Jesus the Christ? If not, why do you want this name?"

She struggled not to fidget. "It—it was the name of Georgie's mother."

Nohsh straightened slowly, breathing in a long breath, folding his arms over his chest, looking every inch the weroance despite his Inqutish clothing. "And why is that of interest to you?" he said at last.

She lifted one shoulder in a shrug. "It is a pretty name."

"Do you know what it means?"

"Mahta."

"I am told it means *bitter*. Is that how you wish to be marked?"

Bitter. It summed exactly how she felt about leaving their beautiful island. About the loss of Elinor and Ananias.

"Not all tastes are sweet," she said.

His eyes glittered, and a corner of his mouth lifted slightly.

"I will think on it," he said. He turned to Nunohum. "*Nek*, are you in agreement that we consider and wait—and pray?"

She nodded but stiffly. "I do not like it."

"The Inqutish do not change their names," Mushaniq reminded them.

"Crenepo take the family names of their husbands," Nohsh said, just as stiffly as Grandmother.

"Well, I am not yet taking a husband."

He sniffed and turned away. "Perhaps it would be for the best if you did."

"But I am not ready!"

Nohsh swung back toward her, his face as thunderous as she'd ever seen. "You just completed the sacred rite of huskanasqua. Why did you agree to do so if you were not ready?"

There was no good reply to that.

"Does Georgie know you wish to take the name of his mother?"

"Mahta."

"Then you best go ask his thoughts on the matter first."

Chapter Sixteen

T he very last thing he wished to contend with at this moment was a willful, contrary girl-turned-woman who thought she understood the ways of their people. How had they failed in this one thing? What had been taking place in her over the past moons—or years—that she would refuse so simple a thing?

Although she was right on one thing—*Squirrel* did continue to be fitting.

But there was too much to be done. Since their return, he sat down with the men to review first how those left behind had scrambled to assess which tasks were most crucial and allocate those. With Manteo and the others back from the chase, they did so again, mourning the loss of Ananias.

Ananias was not the only man experienced in the making of brick and tile, but he was arguably the most skilled—and much loved for many other reasons. The town as a whole seemed to nearly lose heart altogether at the news of his death. Of the original Assistants, only four now remained, with Thomas Stevens having accompanied those gone to Beechland. Chris Cooper and Roger Bailie seemed the most likely to take the lead among them, although Dyonis Harvie and John Sampson both appeared more resolute than they once had.

"Think you that your uncle will return this summer?" someone asked Cooper.

Hands on his knees, he lifted his head. "We all most heartily hope it will be so. But if not, we are not yet beaten." He glanced across at Manteo. "It is the thought of Manteo and Towaye and others that we consider taking the war to Wanchese, not to wait for them to strike here again. We have some powder and the means to make more but should return to Roanoac for more lead for shot."

They all looked around at each other. "Not a single man among us," John Sampson said, "was under any illusion that we would have no struggle to plant the City of Ralegh. We did in fact choose many of our number for their skill in defense. Let us not shrink from putting it to the test."

Manteo knew they had borrowed that phrase, *take the war to Wanchese,* from him. The Kurawoten had been so long a peaceable people. But now...

He had used that same argument when speaking alone to the elders last night, his mother and her fellow weroances. *"Let us not shrink from defending what is ours."* He had even added, *"Let us not fail to trust the God we have sworn to serve—whether we live or die in the doing of it."*

And die they might. The nations to the west and north of them were mighty and fierce. But Manteo would make it clear they had allied themselves with the Inqutish in good faith and would not abandon their friends in hardship.

In the middle of that, he truly did not have the wherewithal to quarrel with Mushaniq. Not that their women weren't known already for their willfulness and wisdom in their own right, but where did she get such strange ideas?

And was she truly so averse to taking a husband? Or was that also a moment of being contrary simply because she could?

Georgie could hardly believe Ananias was well and truly gone. It was like the early days after the attack all over again, after watching Elinor being taken and feeling the loss like fresh wounds in his own belly and side.

Worse, he hardly knew how to occupy himself each day. Early on, with the other men gone, it was easy. He had pitched in with the immediate efforts to complete the palisade around the town as speedily as they could. Now there were other projects to accomplish, including the making of more brick for houses, which had been left at a standstill with Ananias's departure.

Georgie had learned a little of the trade from Ananias, along with many other things. But not enough to carry it on single-handedly.

After a meeting where the possibilities of war were gravely considered, Manteo walked around the town with Cooper, Sampson, and Bailie. Georgie and Johnnie Sampson trailed behind, listening. Georgie knew that Johnnie longed as much as himself to be useful.

They stopped outside the little house that had been the Dares'. It stood unkept since Elinor's capture, except for the occasional visit inside to fetch Ginny's things. The men stood near the front and stared at it as if fearful of what they might find there.

"I suppose we ought to give the house to another," Cooper said, "but I can hardly bear the thought."

Manteo shook his head. "She was your nearest of kin. If you wish it kept a little longer, I will not say you nay. Besides, we know not how the matter might turn out."

The other men peered at him, waiting for him to elaborate, but he turned and walked on, leaving the dwelling.

Georgie lifted the latch and peered inside. Nothing appeared amiss other than dust, but he felt an intruder and quickly shut and secured the door before hurrying after the men.

He'd nearly caught up with them when a slim figure stepped out from behind one of the houses and almost into his path.

He slid to a halt. 'Twas Mushaniq, wearing the one-shoulder dress of deerskin from the other day but slightly less bedecked with ornaments. "Georgie," she said, before he could think to speak, "would you come and walk? I would speak with you."

Her English was clear enough, but her request—for what purpose? Heat swept his skin at the half a dozen different notions that came to his mind. He glanced after the men, doubly dismayed to see Manteo looking after them, but the Croatan merely waved him away and continued on with the other men.

"I suppose," he said, and without another word, she turned the opposite direction and led on.

How curious. She had never before been so formal with him.

His gaze traced the lines of her dress, the fringed edges with bits of shell, and the way her hair was caught at the back of her head—the very picture of a perfect Croatoan female.

She turned her head and met his eye—demure, yet something so unyielding in her face it made him drop back a step. Not a word did she speak until they had passed out through the palisade opening and over toward the river's edge.

Even there she looked this way and that before being apparently satisfied they were alone and facing him. "During huskanasqua, we girls are told to choose new names. It is the way of our People. But I did not want to change my name."

He watched her face, the arch of delicate brows over the shimmer of dark eyes, the pink fullness of her small mouth, the high, rounded cheekbones and determined chin.

"Nohsh and Nunohum were not happy. I told them finally there was a name I might want to take, but they said I must ask you." She huffed, glancing away and then back. "What would your mind be if I took the name *Mah-ree*. Your mother."

His mouth fell open. She wanted to take his mother's name?

"But—why?"

Her face hardened. "It is a good name. And. . ." Her gaze skittered away again. "It is a name that is precious to you."

Something thudded in the center of his chest like the report of a ship's gun.

"Nobody uses the name Mary anymore." He found himself babbling. "It is—papist. It's meant to honor the mother of Jesus, but in the Romish church, they see her as—I don't know, some kind of goddess, when she was just a woman. A good woman, true—a great woman—but—"

She frowned, eyes intent. "What are you saying? You do not wish this?"

He stopped, jaw still slack.

"Do *you* wish it?" he asked at last.

A quick nod. "Did I not say so?"

He forced the question out. "Why. . .does it matter that the name is precious to me?"

She leaned closer as if studying him, putting one hand up to his face, fingertips tracing the edge of his jaw, his cheekbone and temple, his brow.

He could not breathe.

She brought her other hand up, riffling his hair. Her gaze fair burned him in its intensity, dark as obsidian, long lashes falling then rising as she seemed to examine every inch of his features.

And yet she did not reply.

Her fingers came back to his cheek and chin, and he realized she must be exploring the beginnings of a beard he'd recently noticed springing there. Then she touched his mouth and stilled, eyes coming fully to his again.

He felt the shock all the way to his toes.

Before he could think, he cupped the back of her head and neck, her hair softly tickling his own fingers, and bent to press his lips to hers.

A heartbeat, two, three. . .

She sprang back, eyes and mouth wide, her hand flying to touch her bottom lip. "What—is—that?"

For a half dozen more beats, he could only gape at her as well. Then he realized—did her people even understand a kiss?

"It is—how my people show affection." He swallowed. "Love."

Slowly, understanding replaced the shock in her expression. "I have seen this. But I did not realize—"

Quiet hung between them for barely a breath, and then with a gleam of fresh intent, she again stepped close and this time pulled his head down to hers.

It was nothing more than simple pressure at first, one chaste kiss after another, but then a subtle change took place, a shift here, an angle there. . .

With a gasp, Mushaniq stepped away, several paces this time, one hand pressed to her chest and another to her middle. "I—feel strange."

Georgie was panting as if he'd run the length of Croatoan Island and back. He could only nod.

Grasping at the fragile threads of his sanity, he cast about for something to distract himself. "Who has care of Ginny?"

"Timqua. She—she knew I needed to speak with you."

He swiped a hand across his face and smoothed back his hair. "Did you truly only wish to ask me about my mother's name?"

She nodded, but with a hint of hesitation that he could not read. "I did not intend"—she gestured between them—"this."

His throat burned. Did she not?

It was fascinating to watch how the black center of his eyes widened and narrowed, with the blue becoming almost smoky. And she could still hardly breathe.

At her last words, though, a pinched expression came across his face, and something about it made her ache deep inside.

"What is it you call"—she tapped her mouth—"this?"

His eyes flared again, just for a moment. "A kiss."

"It is very pleasant."

What was he thinking, to appear in such pain? And if a mere embrace with him caused such a tempest inside her, was it safe for her to move closer, to try to soothe that pain away?

She thought of that night she had been so distraught over Nohsh leaving. Georgie's arms around her then were comforting, brotherly—nothing like what had just passed between them.

Did she cause him pain? And if so, for what reason?

Hesitantly, she reached out her hand and placed it this time against his shirt, over his chest, where she could feel the thudding of his heart beneath her palm. He winced.

"Did you truly go walking with Two Feathers?" His voice sounded half-strangled.

Was that it? Could he be—jealous?

A gladness stirred inside her, leaping wildly, but she held herself still, hand on his chest. "He followed me. He wanted to be—my first. I told him to go away."

Georgie's breath went out of him in a rush, and his eyes snapped shut for a few moments. When he opened them again, his eyes were bright and glossy. "So you have not yet—given yourself to anyone?"

She shook her head slowly. "The other girls laugh at me. The elders tell me to guard myself."

He gave a short laugh and scrubbed at his face. "The elders speak wisdom."

Watching his expressions, listening to his voice, the tempest was building inside her again. He was at once strange and exotic and yet so familiar and dear to her, with his hair that was almost yellow and eyes the color of the sky. And yet, his arms made her feel safe, and his—his *kiss*—she had never known it could feel like that.

A new determination rose within her. She eased close to him once more, and his eyes widened.

"Will you be my first?"

His mouth parted, and that agony crossed his face again. "Mushaniq. . .Mushaniq, I can't. If—if I did this—I would have to marry you."

She started to draw back, stung, then realized he was not understanding her thoughts. "What if I wished that?"

His eyes burned into hers, hot like the summer sky. "I could not bear if you took any others. I would—I would want to be your only. And—I would promise to be your own." His throat worked, and his tongue came out to wet his lips. "I know it is not always this way with your people. But I would want that, with you."

"I want that as well," she whispered. She took his hand in hers, glancing around. This place—it was not nearly secluded enough, but she knew of somewhere that was. "Come with me."

Chapter Seventeen

What sweet alchemy was a girl's touch—or was it just the particular magic of Mushaniq herself? Whichever, from almost the first moment that she kissed him back, he was lost.

Later—much later, after they had returned to the town and he went back to seeking an occupation for the afternoon like nothing had happened—he sat at the edge of the light cast from the community fire and gazed across to where Mushaniq gathered with a pair of her young cousins and little Ginny. She looked up, met his eyes across the space between them, and smiled softly.

He smiled in return, holding the look as long as she did, then with arms braced behind him, he leaned his head back with a sigh. They had exchanged promises, true, but was he any better than Willie? Yet, he had not sought her out. He had not sought out any of the girls and had indeed resisted her—at least, he had tried, until he could be sure that this was not a light thing on her part as well.

She had gone so far as to say she wished to be his wife. Did she know what that meant?

Did she mean it, in true?

How daring she had been and yet at once shy. How sleek and lovely her form. And how would he bear being apart from her, now that they'd tasted the sweetest each had to offer?

Because there was no entertaining the thought that they'd be able to be together anytime soon. Or that they could continue slipping away alone. His eyes popped open, and he sat up. What if the adults found out? Particularly Manteo? A heaviness swirled in his gut. And yet he couldn't imagine just carrying on as if nothing had happened between him and Mushaniq...

And would she truly take his mother's name?

She'd chosen it because it meant something to him. He could still hardly take it in.

Over across the fire, she got up, laughing, and hoisted Ginny to her hip, then weaved her way through the crowd as the little girl rubbed her eyes. Georgie got to his feet as she approached. Her half smile was partly shy, partly secretive. "Ginny is sleepy, so I am taking her to bed."

Every night they did this since Elinor had been taken. Georgie ran his hand over Ginny's downy head. "Good night. *Winkan nupes.*"

"Winkan nupes," Ginny answered, and Mushaniq's smile tweaked wider.

Georgie wanted to repeat the gesture for her, but he dared not reach out. "Winkan nupes," he said.

She tilted her head. "Pyas. Walk to the house with us at least."

He fell into step beside her. At the edge of the gathering, Manteo seemed to come out of nowhere.

Georgie's heart hammered, but after but a glance at him, Manteo turned to Mushaniq. "Has he agreed to the name, Nunutánuhs?"

She adjusted Ginny on her hip. "He has, Nohsh." Very demure, but Georgie could see the glitter beneath her lashes.

Manteo smoothed Ginny's hair much as Georgie had done. "It is well. We will speak later. Winkan nupes, little one."

His eyes went to Georgie again and back to Mushaniq, then he walked away.

They both released a breath, exchanging a glance, then she led on to the longhouse and into the shadows beyond.

Only there did he feel safe enough to face her and venture a touch to her hair. To his shock, she responded by sinking against him.

He put his arms around both her and Ginny, who, also to his shock, did not resist.

"When will you tell him we wish to marry?"

He drew back a little. "Is that how it is done?"

Her head bobbed. "There are many ways. But in our case. . ." She snuggled in again. "What is the Inqutish way?"

"I should go tell him. Or rather, ask."

At last, Ginny did grow restless, and after a not-so-quick kiss, Mushaniq took her inside.

Would he even be allowed to have this beautiful creature as his wife?

Mushaniq lay staring into the dark long after everyone else had settled in.

The other girls talked so easily of their play with all the boys. After what had happened that afternoon, however, she could not imagine giving herself to any other.

Is that what it meant to love? Georgie had said the word when trying to explain the kiss. And Mushaniq had longed to say it afterward, when they lay relaxed in each other's arms, almost unable to move. *Kuwumádas.* I love you.

"*I will marry you,*" he had said. "*Are you sure this is what you want?*"

And she had murmured back, "*Kupi.*" Yes.

Strange how their word for becoming husband and wife sounded like the name of his mother—the name she was even more determined to take as her own.

She thought of Nohsh stopping them as they left the community fire. Did he suspect there was more between her and Georgie than they had yet spoken to anyone but each other? And what would he think once he knew?

The next days dragged out, however, without Nohsh or Grandmama or anyone else bringing up the issue of her choosing a name. In the meantime, Bright Star was being courted by an older brother of Two Feathers, a young man who had completed huskanaw just as the Inqutish were coming to Roanoac. He had been through two trial marriages already, but Bright Star was dazzled by the attention and the gifts he brought her.

In the meantime, Two Feathers paraded and preened before Mushaniq, though she made a point of not noticing.

She was not sorry they hadn't pressed her about the change of name, which would not be a set thing until the community recognized it, but why was Georgie being so slow about speaking to Nohsh? Of course, they'd hardly done more than catch each other's eye across the community fire for the past several days. The other men kept him busy as if—almost as if they knew.

But they could not know. Could they?

And would his people really be as upset as all that over the fact that she'd taken him? It was the nature of life, strange though it was, and now that all was said and done between them, she felt a curious impatience to be able to call him her own openly.

Auntie Timqua had been right. It was very different now.

The men worked feverishly over the next few days to make shot and powder with all available supplies as well as catch up on necessary maintenance around the town. The weather grew hot, and as the women worked the fields around the town, with extra guards accompanying them, Captain Stafford and the other men skilled with the pinnace helped Manteo plan a foray to Roanoac to fetch extra lead.

They'd no sooner set out, however, than the wind changed, and clouds piled up in the southeast. Manteo shook his head—he would not risk being out during a sea tempest. And so they went back and battened down at Cora Banks just in time for a downpour that lasted a full day and a night.

He then directed the men to give themselves to making more arrows. Most of the Inqutish were skilled enough with a bow, at least. Some had swords as well. He did not want to depend wholly upon their firearms, especially when so much of the powder had already been spoiled or lost during the sea tempest the year before and supply was yet uncertain.

When the Cwareuuoc visited, as they often did, he made his request to them for warriors to accompany the Inqutish and Kurawoten. They would not give an immediate answer, as he knew they would not, but at least they had not immediately refused.

He did not know what would happen if they refused. But at this point, after holding council with both the Inqutish and his own people and giving the matter to continual prayer, he could do no more.

Chapter Eighteen

G eorgie kept thinking an opportunity would present itself, but nearly
a week went by, and it did not.

He could delay it no longer. And there was no way to know how to
even begin the process of preparing if he did not ask.

The morning after the long rainstorm, he gathered all his courage
and approached Manteo while he was finishing a talk with the Assistants.
When the older men all looked at him, he turned to Manteo and asked as
respectfully as he could, "May I speak with you, sir?"

Mild curiosity shone in the man's eyes but nothing more. He nodded and waved to the others before walking away from the group with
Georgie.

There was no other way to approach it besides to simply jump in. "Sir.
I wish to marry Mushaniq."

Manteo straightened, folding his arms across his chest as a slow smile
overtook his face. "I wondered whether there was more between you than
either knew or was willing to admit."

He felt his cheeks burn. "In truth, it took us both by surprise, I think."

The Croatoan's expression remained mild. "It is good for our peoples
to become as one, to make marriages between us. I have seen your care for
her, and it pleases me. Yet this is not my decision alone. Because you and
Mushaniq are so young, the community will have a say as well."

His gut soured at the prospect.

Manteo patted his shoulder. "You have her favor and mine. I cannot imagine the community would oppose it, at least for long."

Mushaniq had expected questions. She had not counted for all the women of the town to fall upon her at once.

"You only just passed through the rite of huskanasqua. He is but a boy! Their people do not allow huskanaw—how will you know he can hunt for you? Why will you not consider a young man of the People?"

And then there were others. "Have you yet been baptized? You were resistant to this before, but it is important to his people. Will you then be Inqutish? How will you live?"

Why must they make it so complicated?

The other girls crowded about her, nudging. "You and Georgie, eh? And how was it? Do you think him handsome? Do you truly wish to marry him? He is so pale!" And they laughed.

That only kindled her anger. "I know how many of you went walking with other Inqutish boys."

More laughter, at least from some. "That was only play. It was amusing for a time."

Nohsh, however, just gazed at her in that way of his. "I thought you were not ready to take a husband."

She flopped a hand. "That was before I knew Georgie's mind on it."

His quiet laugh brought the heat to her cheeks.

Everyone had an opinion. The English men's responses ranged from sniggers that he'd want the newly of-age Mushaniq as a wife to insistence that Georgie was too young, to objections that she'd not yet been baptized—and oh, the outcry once it became known that despite more than half the Croatoan population gladly accepting Christ in one night, she'd quietly *not*. "So why does she want to take an English name? It doesn't make her any more or less Christian."

And then there was much debate over that.

The response from the Croatoan was equally vocal and full of feeling. "He must go huskanaw. No man of our People would even consider himself worthy had he not accomplished that!"

Two Feathers was the one who got right in Georgie's face. "You are worse than a child and a simpleton. You know nothing! You cannot just ask. You must bring gifts, sing the songs and dance the dances, and you know none of these things." He thumped his chest. "I will still win her."

Something hardened within Georgie under the sting of those words, so closely an echo of Willie's. Mushaniq had sought *him* out, asked him to be her first. It was he whom she favored. "We will see. It is her choice."

Even Nicholas Johnson cornered him. "Have you behaved yourself improperly with her? Did you learn nothing from our lecture back on the island?"

Georgie kept his shoulders square. "I am asking to marry her. Not sneaking about while avoiding any sort of responsibility in the matter."

Master Johnson shook his head slowly. "Your father was an Assistant. It is past time for you to be more than a wild boy at the beck of others. I will take your education in hand right away."

"And marrying the daughter of a chief isn't honor enough?"

The older man's gaze was sharp upon him. "It is precisely because of such honor that you should make of yourself more."

Oh.

The English, then, as well as the Croatoan, had their ideas of his making himself worthy of Mushaniq. And he could not argue with that.

Amazingly, it was Manteo who provided calmness in the midst of it all. "While I might be inclined to merely let you two marry, both our peoples have concerns I cannot ignore. I made a promise to my daughter to not force her to take faith in Christ and be baptized, and likewise I cannot force the Inqutish to accept the requirement of huskanaw as necessary." His gaze was steady and kind. "It would be another matter were you older."

Georgie swallowed back the burn in his throat. "I understand."

"And in this moment"—Manteo spread his hands wide—"we have no time to address those concerns."

The Cwareuuoc and some of the men from Beechland had shortly gathered at Cora Banks, ready to join the effort to seek Wanchese and his men. Georgie realized they might already have gone were it not for the fuss over him and Mushaniq.

But Manteo only looked again at Georgie and said, "Watch over her while we are away. As I know you always have."

Of course he would. How could he not?

Watch he did, every day, whenever Master Johnson would let him go from the unbearable task of reading and working sums. While the women went out to work the fields—which they continued to do in defiance of danger, because the town needed to eat, after all—when they went to the river, when they made their meal preparations in the afternoon and evening. Mushaniq was so busy with Ginny and other womanly tasks, he hardly had time to exchange a word with her.

They stole moments, such as when she asked him to accompany her to the Dares' house so she might find some item for Ginny's care. The child ran to the door and inside, calling, "Mama! Papa!"

Mushaniq and Georgie followed behind more slowly and stepped in after Ginny, watching her run to and fro, looking.

"I miss her," Mushaniq murmured. "She would have been for us in all this, I think."

"I think so too."

"Margery, she says my wanting your mother's name is not 'meet.' I do not understand. How does it dishonor her?"

Georgie shrugged. He could explain it no better than anyone else.

"It has to do with how differently they believe in Jesus" was all he could say.

She faced him, her gaze uncharacteristically sober. "Why does it matter?"

If he gave her the wrong answer, would she turn from him and ultimately choose Two Feathers after all?

But she only heaved a sigh and went on. "Grandmama and others say you must go huskanaw as well. And nothing can be done as long as the men are off to war."

Ginny came running back. "Mama?"

Tears in her eyes, Mushaniq picked her up. Georgie gathered them both into his arms.

"Kuwumádas," she murmured into his shoulder.

The sweetness of it settled around his heart, warm and strong. "And I love you," he murmured back.

"I will wait as long as necessary," she whispered fiercely.

He embraced her more tightly. "Me too."

She lifted her head, pressed a kiss to his lips. "Meet me here tonight, after Ginny has gone to sleep."

"Mushaniq. . ."

"Please." Her eyes glimmered with both longing and sorrow.

How could he refuse her?

The summer had begun to wane into the earliest sense of autumn before Manteo and the other men returned. That night, after they had well feasted, everyone settled about the community fire to hear what had transpired. Georgie and Mushaniq found places next to each other and near her father.

"When we left from here," Manteo began, "we went a little east across the Pumtico, then north through Aquascogoc."

"Was the old town ever rebuilt after the Inqutish burned it?" his mother asked.

Georgie exchanged a glance with Mushaniq. They had talked of that incident, how, two years before the colony led by Governor White, Sir Richard Greenville had ordered a whole town burned over a silver cup gone missing.

Manteo shook his head. "Mahta. Very few live there now. We then went around the western edge of the great lake of Paquippe and went north and back east from there, around Beechland and Dasemonguepeuk. What towns remain of the Tunapewak were sparse, but their weroances seemed willing to talk. At least, they did so at first.

"Then we went down into Pomeiooc. There they told me that I was not a warrior as any of the mainland Tunapewak count being one—not them nor the Sukwoten and Weopomeioc. With our own Kurawoten and Inqutish, however, accompanied by the Cwareuuoc, we were no small force, and they could not rise up against us. Yet—they tried, and we pushed them back."

He gave a sigh as he gazed around the fire at them all. "I am ashamed. I have used the tricks of Greenville and Lane and set fire to the towns of the Sukwoten and others. I was not willing to take lives or captives, and so we did neither, but we did burn the towns remaining on Dasemonguepeuk."

He scrubbed a hand across his face.

His mother spoke again into the quiet. "Did you meet with Wanchese?"

"Mahta. But I heard word that he was yet being sheltered by Okisco."

"Well." She sat back. "It is enough for now. The autumn is coming, and we have need to finish harvesting and hunting for winter."

Manteo nodded, looking weary beyond his years.

The next morning, they started into the work of tending the field—the same one where terror had broken out so many months before. But it was nearing time for harvest, and the entire town would help with that.

Mindful of that day—as they'd been every time they'd accompanied the women in their work—Georgie stood watch at one corner and Two Feathers at the other. The Croatoan youth still glared daggers at him, but they guarded with unspoken agreement—and shared vigilance.

Manteo had said nothing regarding Georgie and Mushaniq, but it was early yet. And the harvest must be attended to.

About midmorning, Mushaniq came round with large gourds full of drinking water. She did not linger with Two Feathers, though Georgie could see him trying to engage her in conversation, but came straight to Georgie with a smile. He scooped his fill and thanked her, and she returned to the field, sun gleaming on her bare shoulders.

A rustling from the brush drew his attention and had him reaching for bow and arrow. In a moment he had the arrow nocked and was about to bring the bow up when—

The ragged figure of a woman—an English woman, thin but with rounded belly—stumbled out into the open. A tangled braid of fair hair fell down her back. "I am back! I am come home!"

For a moment, they all froze, and she hesitated. Her breast rose and fell as she gasped for breath.

"It is I—Elinor," she panted.

With a cry, they all dropped what they were doing and ran to her.

Chapter Nineteen

THE RETURN:
Autumn 1590

On her knees in the middle of the field where Sees Far had first taken her, Elinor could do nothing but hold Ginny and weep.

Sweet Ginny—alive and well, clinging to her in return.

Manteo and her cousin Chris were there. "How can this be?" Chris asked. "What of the others?"

Swiping away tears—oh, she must look a mess—she climbed to her feet, lifting Ginny to her hip. "'Tis just myself. I—we—there is one who risked much to redeem me from my captivity and bring me home. He is Secotan, but he has had a change of heart. Will you receive him and hear his story?"

While the others murmured and exclaimed, Manteo rubbed his chin, scanning the forest, looking thoughtful. "We will hear him, for your sake."

She called out to him. Would he come?

Incredibly, he did. The tall Secotan warrior emerged from the cover of the forest, looking both proud and as vulnerable as she had ever seen him.

Unable to douse her smile, she held out her hand, and he came forward to take it.

This was the moment when her present met her past.

She led him toward the others, already murmuring to each other.

Manteo and her cousin Chris stood as if ready to defend, but Manteo stepped forward, gaze fastened upon Sees Far. "I know you," he said in Croatoan. *"Uunamun.* He who sees."

"Sees Far, kupi."

"There is much to talk of."

Sees Far inclined his head. "Kupi. But I would see her tended, first."

Elinor's eyes burned. She could scarce take it all in. She looked about at the crowd—familiar faces, yet her mind refused to produce names for all.

Was that Georgie—and Mushaniq? Gracious, but he had the beginnings of a beard—and she with her hair tied back so properly—so grown, both of them!

But everyone stared at her as if waiting. She could not think. Her feet turned a slow circle.

"Is my house. . .?" She could not finish the question.

Chris's blue eyes were grave. "'Tis still there. We left everything. . . hoping. . ."

He led the way toward the palisade that she could see now they'd finished. She followed, reluctant to release Ginny, great big girl that she was, but they'd gone no more than a dozen steps before she wiggled to get down. Elinor set her on her feet and took her hand.

The flowers and foliage at the doorstep bore the expected degree of autumn wither, the marigolds still in full bloom while the irises had long faded.

Ginny tugged at her grip. "Mama, want go."

When Elinor hesitated, Mushaniq swooped in. "Go on. I take her."

With a huff, she relinquished her hold. 'Twould accomplish no good for her to wrestle with her daughter already. Mushaniq lifted Ginny to her hip and nodded, eyeing her. A few paces behind, Georgie and Sees Far also watched, with Chris and Manteo behind them.

She blew out a breath and unlatched the door, then pushed it wide and stepped across the threshold. The smell of dust and damp assailed her nostrils. All sat as it was—or mostly, tidy anyway, as if she'd gone outside but a moment before. Closing her eyes, she could almost believe that was so.

That fateful day, six months before, after seeing Ananias and the others off, she'd set the household to rights, then gone with the others to the field to help clear and prepare for planting, never knowing she would not soon return. That she would never again share this space with the man whose strong hands set the posts and assembled the panels—

Nay. She could not allow herself to think such thoughts. But the grief washed over her like a wave, had already pushed its way in like the surge from a tempest. She would be no more able to deny the sorrow than they could turn away the clouds and wind.

Drawing a ragged breath, she swiped at the tears and looked again around the room, now appearing dim and shabby with neglect. Near the small table and chairs, Mushaniq and Georgie hovered, Ginny's head tipped to Mushaniq's shoulder. Sees Far lingered in the doorway, his gaze intent.

It was he who had stolen her away. But it was also he who had brought her back—and she herself who had invited him to stay. She must remember that.

Oh merciful Father in heaven. Let me not rue this path.

Gathering her ragged skirts, she climbed the narrow stairs to the upper rooms of the house. Her heart beat painfully with every step. She had not realized until she stood inside the house how much she'd expected Ananias to be there to greet her or to come in behind from outside, but never again on this earth would she look upon his face, hear his voice, or feel his strong arms about her.

The upper room was even more dusty than below. A few clothing items lay scattered across the bed—Ginny's, where someone had come and doubtless sifted through her things in due course of caring for her. Were Elinor's own belongings still here?

She approached the bed, eyes burning, throat tight. Never again to be Ananias's wife. At this moment, neither could she bear the thought of sharing this bed with anyone else.

Crawling across both clothing and coverlet, which come to think was less dusty than expected, she reached for the stuffed bolster that had been her husband's pillow, curled on her side, and pressed the cushion against her face. Did his scent linger here even now? She thought she could still discern it, that unique blend of earth and smoke and musky sweat.

And then the tears would not be denied.

How strange it was, after so many months, to lie upon a bed of English make.

A scrambling up the stairs preceded Ginny's blond head popping through the doorway. The child trotted over and climbed onto the bed as well. "Mama," she said, snuggling in.

Everyone else followed, but while the rest lingered in the doorway, Sees Far walked brazenly across the floor and lay down next to the bed. "Nupes," he said, then pointedly closed his eyes and folded his hands across his chest.

To Elinor's amazement, she did sleep.

She woke sometime later to the murmur of voices below, English as well as Croatoan, and the smells of food. Untangling herself from Ginny, she rose, carefully stepped across Sees Far, and tiptoed to her chest.

Clean clothing she would need. A bath would be the first order of business.

She lifted the lid, and the scent wafted upward of the herbs she'd placed there, both for freshness and to keep out pestilence. In the top tray lay a linen coif—the one she'd laid aside for Sunday meetings and suchlike, as her everyday had been lost long ago and she'd never gotten around to sewing a new one—a ruff, once crisp and now wilted into sad folds, and a headdress, edged in red velvet and gold ribbon. Fripperies from what seemed another age altogether, of colors and textiles allowed her under the laws of Queen Elizabeth because of Papa's position as governor. She lifted the headpiece, gingerly, and setting it atop her hair, she peered into the small silvered glass hanging on the wall.

How strange she appeared to her own eyes! How gaunt her cheeks and deep the shadows around her eyes.

The image of Sees Far loomed in the glass just behind hers. With a broken laugh, she stepped aside to let him goggle at himself while she tucked the headdress back into the chest and watched him from the corner of her eye.

He leaned close, turning his head this way and that, fingering the once-shorn stubble along the sides of his head and the raven-black locks curling over his shoulders from the longer portion in the back, and then the stray whiskers around his mouth and chin. Muttering something in a tone of dismay, he gathered the length of his hair and tied it up at his nape with a thong he unwrapped from his arm.

Elinor smiled a little. Native men were not without their vanity. She lifted the tray out of the chest and set it aside, then riffled through the layers beneath. At least one shift remained, and her favorite red wool kirtle, another thing she had saved for meeting and other important occasions.

Did she still hold status enough to wear such a color? Was it even of consequence here? With a sniff, she set aside the red kirtle in favor of a more practical green one, lying beneath, and gathered both kirtle and shift into her arms.

Meanwhile, Sees Far had lost interest in his reflection and poked about the room, peering into her chest and examining various other things lying about. He turned and tipped his chin toward the half-open door, where quiet conversation was yet taking place down below. "I am very out of place here."

"Give them time."

He sniffed and gave attention to a row of hooks, where an embroidered doublet and shirt still hung, from Ananias. With slight but obvious hesitation, he reached out to finger the fabric.

Her heart contracted, but she did not stay him. There was no sense in another not getting some use from Ananias's things—although she had not properly considered the ache stirred by the simple sight of someone else touching garments she'd last seen on her husband.

He lifted the doublet and turned it this way and that, then looked over as if to inquire of her. She could not speak, could only blink back the burning in her eyes and fold her arms over her breast while pressing one hand to her cheek.

Without a word, Sees Far hung the garment back on its hook and stepped away. A muted sob escaped her.

"Mama?" Ginny sat up, rubbing her eyes.

Elinor swooped her up and wept, without shame, into her child's hair.

Georgie could not bring himself to leave the house. Mushaniq also stayed, and Master Cooper and Manteo. Doubtless they all felt uneasy at the strange Secotan warrior upstairs who, with but a look at all of them, had told Elinor to sleep, then stretched out on the floor and promptly himself fell into slumber.

Elinor and Ginny followed suit.

They'd traveled night and day, she'd said, and there seemed to be nothing for it but to leave them to rest.

Mushaniq began the task of sweeping the floor. Georgie helped dust, while Master Cooper and Manteo spoke softly together just outside the door. A little after noon, Timqua and Wesnah came with food, and Margery and Alis to inquire. Elinor made her way sleepily down the stairs, Ginny and the Secotan on her heels. "I thought it was a dream," she said, then stopped, passing a hand across her face. She met their gazes as they all stared at her. "I must be wretched indeed to your eyes."

"No, but a most welcome sight," Margery said, and came forward, weeping, to embrace her again.

She and the man took a little food along with the others, then the women helped her gather things for bathing at the river. The warrior followed, silent, watchful.

Theirs was a story Georgie very much wished to hear more of.

It was evening before they could all gather and sit. Elinor began the tale of the days and nights immediately after their captivity, of Emme being sent away to the Powhatan by Okisco, and the rest of them herded on to the trading town, where they were bought by those who drew copper from the earth.

The men leaned in and asked all sorts of questions about that, but Elinor shuddered and said she knew very little of the mining of it. She had been put to carrying ore and beating out the copper.

She then told how Sees Far had arranged to purchase her from those they had been sold to as captives and led her eventually back here. It was so strange—she said it so matter-of-factly, almost as if she were a sheep or a cow. The Croatoan seemed to be less disturbed by it than the English, who all exchanged glances. "And what of the others?" Roger Bailie asked.

Her shoulder lifted. She was much improved in appearance after washing in the river and combing out her hair and putting on a clean gown, but Georgie could see the weariness—and leanness—carved into her features. "I do not know. I nearly cannot reconcile that God has seen fit to bring me home to you and not them—"

She looked up from the fire and gazed at all of them.

"We are of course so happy you're here," Chris said with much feeling. "But we must needs hear more of the testimony of this one—Sees Far?"

The Secotan spoke, with Manteo translating.

"There is more to say, but at the first, all I could think of was revenge. My father, Granganimeo, had died of the sickness brought by the wutahshuntas. The girl who would have been my wife had also died. This woman—the taking of her was my way to strike at the people who had taken Roanoac from us and who would take more were they allowed.

"But then she and the rest of her people were braver than I expected. Her man thought to rescue her—and I regret the loss of his life, but he also was brave.

"After this—" He slowed, taking more time to think on his words. To Georgie it appeared that he was on edge, as if he expected them to fall upon him at any moment. "Wanchese's hatred of her burned bright. And he could not give proper account of it. It was like"—his gaze skimmed the crowd—"he poured all his anger at your people upon her. But I did not think that was fair." He hesitated. "And she was my captive. Not his."

Georgie gritted his teeth at the man's proud and possessive tone. She had been rightfully Ananias's before he had taken her.

"As time went on, however, I began to ask what gave her courage. I talked to Roger Prat about his god—your God. And Elinor told me much while we were journeying after leaving Ritanoe." He looked around the group again. "I wish to hear more. I wish to know if this is the true God and to learn more of His ways if so."

Silence, then Towaye spoke, and Manteo translated that as well. "We will gladly share what we have learned of Him."

But there was something about the stranger that did not sit well with Georgie.

Coming home was one thing. Returning to any semblance of life as it was before, impossible. They'd received her with overwhelming joy, but in the day-to-day? She felt their looks, heard the whispers.

Worst was trying to recall who was there, who had gone to Beechland. She missed Rose terribly—she and her husband were among those who had made the move deep into the swampy forests of Dasemonguepeuk.

Jane Mannering—now Stafford, since she had married the good captain—was still at Cora Banks and delighted with Elinor's news that she carried another child. Margery was a comfort, and unexpectedly, Alis Chapman as well, both mothers to two each now.

She had also forgotten how much the everyday life of the planters blended with that of the natives. Or was that something that happened over the spring and summer, after she had been taken captive and so many of the men went to search for them, that the women and remaining men leaned more on each other just as a matter of course?

Her return had coincided with the bringing in of the harvest. Over the next few days, Elinor helped and tried to find her place in the rhythm of the townspeople. She carried water, prepared food, and joined the women's morning bath in the river, accompanied by song and prayers. Sees Far saw to his own appearance with his former care, both head and face cleanly groomed, hair carefully knotted and adorned and new feathers behind his ears. The other men, English and Croatoan alike, had wasted no time in sitting him down to examine in more detail his motives in being there.

The women likewise asked so many questions about her journeys. About Ananias's death, her treatment by her captors, about Sees Far himself. She found herself shy and tongue-tied and questioning it all as well. Just what was their future to be? Sees Far seemed to accept the immediate move into her house, and every night he lay down on the floor beside her bed and remained there until morning.

Still her self-appointed protector—or something more?

And what would the leadership say if they knew how familiar their arrangement had been—and still remained?

She could find no words, however, to explain the bond between them—not even in her own musings and much less to any of the townspeople who asked, however kindly their inquiries. From fellow captive Roger Prat's gentle insistence that she go with Sees Far—even after he himself had offered to marry Elinor—to those long days journeying the forested hills. The wonders of trees and waterfalls and far blue vistas. A man who began as an enemy but through his own questions about faith and courage turned into something more—far more. And those days after he revealed his part in the troubles they'd suffered at Roanoac, when all she wanted was to die and join Ananias in heaven, he'd carried her and tended her and exhorted her to live, both for Ginny's sake and that of the child she was yet to bear.

And then he'd brought her home, asking nothing in return for all the temporal wealth he'd expended to buy her out of captivity.

She still marveled that he'd chosen to stay. That, in truth, the townspeople had not themselves fallen upon him in vengeance. But was that not testament to the power of Christ and His Spirit, though they yet failed to walk it in so many ways?

Ananias was gone from her, and she could scarce comprehend that some days. She grieved him still and might always, but Sees Far's presence remained a comfort beyond words, along with his efforts to know and be known by the rest of the town and to fit his life with hers.

Elinor might have returned, but even Mushaniq could see she was the merest shadow of herself. Rounding belly notwithstanding, of course.

And that Sukwoten warrior who was rarely far from her side—none knew what to make of him. They were willing, of course, for Elinor's sake and that of his avowed change of heart, to welcome him among them—or try, at least.

But it was so strange and—difficult. Mushaniq watched him, his attentiveness toward Elinor and now to Ginny, and she felt jealous. Here was this enemy who, true, had returned Elinor to them, but how did that wipe away all he had done before? From taking her to begin with, to however else he had been involved.

She knew there had to have been more.

The men were oddly closemouthed about it—the older women as well. And that alone was strange because her people had always delighted in talking about any little bit of news, of hearing stories and exploits and outright gossip from among their town and the next ones over and the ones beyond that.

So why the sudden silence when it came to Sees Far?

Nohsh had not said a word since his own return about when she and Georgie might be considered able to marry, and neither had anyone else. Everyone's attention was on Elinor and the joy of having her back—and the quandary of what to do with the one who was at once her captor and rescuer.

It made Mushaniq angrier and angrier to even think on it.

Chapter Twenty

There was a place and time for conducting business as the Inqutish, and then there were times when the old way of lingering around a fire with a pipe full of uppowoc was the best.

This, Manteo judged, was the latter.

The Kurawoten weroances—his mother included—and the English Assistants sat gathered, each with their own pipe, puffing and waiting for Manteo to begin. Next to him, the Sukwoten, son of Granganimeo, known as Sees Far.

"We held much regard for your father," Manteo began at last. "It grieved us all to hear of his death."

Towaye translated quietly for those still having trouble with the nuances of their tongue.

Sees Far's brows arched. "Were the Inqutish indeed grieved? It seemed that Rafe Lane used the great sickness to his own advantage."

Manteo drew on his pipe. "Not all were of the same spirit and heart of Rafe Lane." He gestured around the circle. "And these, least of all."

"Is that why you chose to take the Inqutish ways?"

There was both pique and curiosity in the question, Manteo thought. "Even Wanchese agreed, when we were both chosen to cross yapám to their island nation, that these people had great power. He chose to look only at their cunning and the evil in men's hearts, and there was plenty of that. I chose to look at what wisdom they might offer, and those who sought to know us and live with us without guile. There is perhaps less of that, but it has been a worthwhile endeavor."

Sees Far considered the rest of the group. "These have been abandoned here, and yet they do not take the ways of the People."

"They yet expect ships to come with supplies for their way of life. But we are working, helping them adapt where needed."

Pipe stem between his lips, Sees Far grunted. "And what of this about their God?"

"We leave that to each one's choice. True faith should not be forced. I chose—and then felt such joy and peace I could not deny He is real."

Sees Far grimaced. "Ahoné is good. His favor need not be sought. He gives rain and sun on all because of His goodness."

"And this is not untrue. But the way the priests have taught that we must curry the favor of Montóac, the spirits of the land—I have heard the whispers of those spirits. They wish their own way among our people and to blind us to the fact that God did intervene in our history, that He did come down as a man and make the final sacrifice for us."

The Sukwoten's eyes glittered. "I have seen Wanchese driven to rage over a woman merely quoting a prayer from their holy book. And then we passed without discovery, beyond all reason, because of that same woman's prayers, so that I might bring her back to you."

"I am not surprised. Elinor is a woman of great faith. Her father, likewise." Manteo gestured with his pipe. "When he comes, you will wish to speak with him. He is one whose heart is for our peoples to live together in love and brotherhood."

"I look forward to that. When do you expect him?"

"He was expected two summers past. We do not look for him again until next year. They cannot sail during the winter, or the season of storms."

Silence fell. Manteo looked around the gathering. "Have any of you questions?"

They had plenty, he knew, but slowly they came—a cross-examination on Sees Far's part of Elinor's capture, which he took full responsibility for, almost proudly, as was their People's way. Manteo bit back a smile. Would the Inqutish indignation over that be appeased? Or would they choose forgiveness and restraint, as Elinor had begged them to do—indeed, as she had insisted God had led her to extend to Sees Far, for acting in ignorance of His truth and love?

The questions became more searching. How much would the Sukwoten reveal? If he had taken part in the slaying of George Howe—or of those who Greenville had left the year before on Roanoac, before John White and the planters came—would they rise up and demand blood?

Would he blame them if they did?

Sees Far seemed to know the risks and to be calculating honesty. "Our People here on these shores have a long history of making war upon each other, of taking captives and even at times betraying each other. You surely know of the quarrel Pemisapan had with the Pomeiooc while he was yet Wyngyno, how an entire town was invited to a feast and then cruelly fallen upon, with the men slain and the women taken."

A few heads nodded. They did indeed recall that, from the earliest days of the Inqutish landing and exploring here.

Manteo thought back. Six years it was now, at least. Mushaniq had been but a small child.

"You may have heard that Wyngyno thought to ally himself with your people to bring vengeance upon them. This is the way of our people, and none faulted him for it. So it is, when my father died and so many of those I loved, the bitterness that rose up in my own heart would not be denied. Vengeance for their deaths became all my purpose."

He stopped, cradling the pipe in his hand. "I admit, I do not understand this word *forgive*. But Elinor offered it to me even after her husband's death, even after learning of my part in the attack when you first came to Roanoac"—the fear in his eyes was unmistakable now—"and I want to know more of a God who would send you all across the ocean and who would give a woman such courage."

There was a stirring among the Inqutish men. Cooper and Bailie scrubbed hands across their faces, and Sampson's head went down. "How can we tell young Georgie," Cooper said, "that here was a man directly involved in his father's murder?"

"The same way," Bailie said, very quietly, "that young Johnnie knows his father is still in captivity even though Elinor was returned to us." He looked up, tears shining in his eyes. "Do we trust in the grace of our Christ or no?"

Jane straightened from her examination of Elinor's belly and helped her rearrange her clothing. "So—Christmas or before, then?" Elinor asked.

"I would think well before, but these wee babes have a way of coming when they will."

"Too true."

Mushaniq stood in a corner of the room, holding Ginny, who had not wanted to be parted from her mother since Elinor's return—and rightfully so. Auntie Timqua also lingered for her own reasons, mostly having to do with their former friendship, Mushaniq was sure.

"You are, in my opinion, too thin," Jane said as Elinor rose from the bed. "But you seem healthy enough, and the babe is vigorous."

"That he—she—is." Elinor gave a rueful smile.

They all filed downstairs, where apon and yaupon tea waited on the hearth. The women arranged themselves, some in chairs and some on the floor, according to comfort, and after settling Ginny, Mushaniq helped serve. With a hand to her shoulder, Elinor met her gaze and smiled. "Thank you, dear girl. I have missed you."

"We missed you as well," Mushaniq said, and they exchanged a quick embrace.

"So," Jane said, after several sips of the yaupon, "you assure me this child is Ananias's?"

Mushaniq did not miss the sudden stiffness in either Elinor or Timqua. Surely Jane realized the very great insult implied in her words?

Not that the Sukwoten were incapable of such dishonor, but even their enemies understood proper restraint.

"It is," Elinor said firmly. She glanced about at them all. "And before you ask, Sees Far has not touched me in that manner. Nor any of the other native men. Not that I was always used so kindly, but in that wise, never."

"Native men do think much of honor toward women, I will grant them that," Jane said.

"Well they should," Timqua said with pride.

Mushaniq thought of Two Feathers, still sulking that she ignored him and gave attention, however quietly, to Georgie.

"Englishmen are not without their own honor," Jane said. "I'm sure Mushaniq would have something to say about that as well."

All eyes swung to her. If only she could sink into the floor.

"Mushaniq wishes to marry our Georgie," Jane went on.

Elinor's blue eyes lit with surprise—and not a little joy. "Oh? How sweet!"

Timqua coughed. Mushaniq glanced at her, face burning, but her aunt did not look up.

"Well." Jane gave a short laugh. "It is not so easy as that."

She went on to explain to Elinor, while Mushaniq stood, head aching and heart pounding, how Mushaniq wanted to take the name of Georgie's mother, but she would not accept the faith that came with such a name. "And her people will not accept Georgie unless he undergoes that accursed rite they force all their young men through."

"Huskanaw," Timqua said. "And it is not like that."

"Yes, well, they have one for the girls, and Mushaniq and a few others did that this summer, but what they ask the boys to endure is barely short of human sacrifice." Jane stared at Elinor. "You know this?"

"Do I?" Elinor said faintly, while looking between Mushaniq and Timqua. At last her gaze settled upon Mushaniq. "I thought there was something different about you." She beckoned. "Pyas. Sit with me, sweet girl."

Reluctant and wary, she crossed to the older woman, but there was nothing but kindness in Elinor's face. She grasped Mushaniq's hand. "You were not one of those who rushed to be baptized that one night in the sound?"

Mushaniq shook her head a little. Oh, she did not want to stir up an argument with this one, so beloved.

But Elinor smiled. "I was tending Ginny that night, who was sick, and I missed all the excitement." She squeezed Mushaniq's hand. "If I had known, we'd have talked. Did you simply not wish to do as everyone else in the moment?"

Mushaniq granted another nod. "It seemed but madness on the part of my people. Nohsh has explained it to me, but—" She shrugged.

"But you wished to change your name, why?"

Jane started to speak, but Elinor held up her hand to silence her.

"His mother's name was Mary, wasn't it?"

"Kupi. And I wished to—honor Georgie."

Elinor's blue eyes turned shiny, as if with tears. "There is nothing at all wrong with that. Nothing."

Her grip remained firm, and Mushaniq drew strength from it.

Elinor turned to the other women. "Can you not see she cares for him? They should be allowed to marry. They should—" Her voice broke, and she brought her hand up to her face. "Life is far too short."

And then the weeping took her.

Mushaniq knelt beside the chair and put her arms around Elinor. The woman leaned into her, sobbing. Both Auntie and Jane wept as well, looking abashed.

Not too long after, both Jane and Timqua took their leave, but Elinor asked Mushaniq to stay on the pretext of helping with Ginny. "I still tire so easily," she said.

When Ginny curled up for a nap, Elinor sat Mushaniq down and offered her more tea. Dark eyes wary, she perched on the edge of the chair.

Half a year as a captive had much changed her perspective, and certain things seemed not to matter as much anymore—if at all. And one of those things was the avoidance of being direct.

"Does Georgie care for you as well?"

A smile, hesitant at first, then more genuine, stretched Mushaniq's lips, and she nodded.

Elinor's own mouth curved. "I cannot imagine how he would not." She sipped her tea. "What does Timqua say about it all?"

Mushaniq tucked her chin again. "Very little. She has other things to occupy her thoughts. Kokon—who is Bright Star now—she has Dances Wild courting her. Auntie is—concerned."

"I see."

The girl looked up. "I am not trying to be trouble."

"But you do not wish to be pushed, either."

A single nod.

Elinor thought for a time. What could she do in the situation that would be judged helpful and not meddlesome? Mushaniq was not her child, but under the circumstances—if the one who had stood in for her as mother was at best preoccupied by other matters—

"And your father?"

"He admits he would let us just marry, but must respect the ways of both our peoples. And so—we are stuck." Mushaniq spread her hands. "Even if I were baptized, your people will not let Georgie go huskanaw. So he can never be viewed as a grown man among the Kurawoten, not for many years yet."

Elinor would see about that. She leaned forward. "Would he come talk to me, do you think?"

Mushaniq wasted no time in running out to find Georgie and fetch him back. It was not quite what Elinor had in mind, but she would take it.

Life truly was too short. And they were young, but she'd known of couples in England, just as young, committing to each other and managing to make a go of it.

They should have no less of a chance to do so, here in the New World.

Before long, she had the two of them sitting before her. Georgie dressed no better or worse than any other young men of the town, with a shirt and slops displaying both wear and dirt, but being summer, he dispensed with both shoes and doublet. His hair, though pulled back, still curled in wild bits around his face, and the blue eyes watched her, expectant and wary. Strangest, however, was the downy fringe across upper lip and jaw.

His father had been a not-unhandsome man, and though sometimes too quick to judge, he'd a keen mind. Please God that Georgie had enough wit to do well here, despite his father's absence. And he'd enough of his father's looks to cause Elinor's heart to ache even now. "How have you fared, Georgie?" she murmured after a moment.

"Well enough." His voice had taken a decidedly downward pitch over the summer.

"I am in your debt for watching over little Ginny."

He shook his head, exchanged a glance with Mushaniq. "I did so little." He swallowed. "Would that I could have kept you from being taken."

Her eyes burned, but this time she blinked the tears back. "That is not important now. God has seen fit to return me."

Was that a flicker of bitterness in his face?

"Would that He had also brought Ananias back," he said after a moment.

She pulled in a long breath. "Well, I am somewhat at peace about that, though it is a sore enough wound." She hesitated. "We will always miss those taken from us."

His gaze flickered, came to hers again. "Manteo said he acted rashly. I know—I know my da did as well, going crabbing alone, but—" He swiped a hand over his head. "I always wondered what would have happened had I not run off with the other boys that day."

"You would have been slain as well—or taken." Elinor sat back. Shock rippled across his face at that. Good. "Think on that. All our lives might have been different had we landed on Roanoac not at all or passed on to Chesepiok as we'd planned. We might all be slain at this moment. But here we are, still, by God's good pleasure."

She watched the conflict play across his face.

"Do you doubt Him, young Georgie?"

His brows drew firmly together at that. He glanced at Mushaniq, back at his own clenched hands, then up at Elinor again. "What does it matter whether I doubt or not?"

Oh, she must tread with care. "It matters very greatly."

When he did not reply, she let out her breath slowly.

"I asked to speak with you, young Georgie, because I wish you to know that I'll do all I can to aid your cause. If our peoples are to live together in love and brotherhood, as is my father's vision, then unions between us are to be welcomed."

His head lifted, hope dawning in his gaze for the first time. "I thank you, Mistress Dare."

She smiled a little, ruefully. "I'm aware that after so many months a captive, the others may no longer view me as perfectly English. But that truly matters not." She ducked her head. "I will likely—eventually—marry Sees Far. Not yet, of course—it is too soon—" This time she could not quite overcome the tears. "I think," she whispered, "God has a purpose for him none of us will be able to deny."

Chapter Twenty-One

I t was something of a shock to realize that with Elinor returned, he and Mushaniq no longer had a place to slip away to and be alone—with Ginny or otherwise.

The realization came with a wave of guilt, of course. Doubly so because he had not reckoned on her seeing so clearly his own questions about God and the church and their place in the grand scheme of things—but with such kindness and understanding he was quite undone.

"You said she would be for us in this," Mushaniq said softly, as they sat in the dark against the back wall of the smithy. She snuggled against his side. "You were right."

"I was not expecting such fierceness over it. She is much changed."

"As are we all, I think."

"'Tis true. And what is your opinion of Sees Far?"

Mushaniq stiffened against him. "I am glad he brought Elinor back, but I trust him not at all."

"Nor I," Georgie said softly. "We need to watch, and closely."

Ginny slept soundly at Elinor's side, but Elinor could not sleep.

She peeked over the edge of the bed. Sees Far lay perfectly still, his eyes wide open.

"How went the council meeting?"

His chest lifted and fell with a breath. "They have not yet slain me. It was a near thing."

She reached down and let her fingertips rest on his shoulder.

"It may have been better had I not stayed," he said.

She thought of what she had told Georgie that afternoon. "I am glad you did stay."

He huffed. "So you say now." One hand came up to curl around hers. "You are much loved by them. So they are willing to tolerate me at least for now."

She sighed. "And I am grateful for that."

"Who is the youth? The one who came with us to this house on the first day?"

"That youth—" She sat up. Should she—? No, he needed to know. "That youth is the son of the man your band fell upon and slew in the marsh at Roanoac."

His head turned, and he met her gaze in the gloom.

"He is caught in a dilemma there seems to be no answer to. He and Manteo's daughter wish to marry, but for him, the Kurawoten refuse to consider it if he does not accomplish huskanaw. And my people—they see it as a type of human sacrifice not to be even thought of."

He sat up as well. "It is not! There is sacrifice, but huskanaw—it is a symbol."

"Then mayhap you can tell them that."

Sees Far remained silent for a few moments. "What is the objection on the girl's part?"

"She is willful and does not want to accept the faith of our people simply because so many of her family have done so. Not that she should be forced, but it is important to us—it is rather a requirement of our faith that—that we marry only within the faith."

She stammered over the last part because she was all too aware of the implications for the two of them.

"It is not unreasonable," he said at last. "The other men questioned me on this as well. They wished to know what I intended, and I told them I would hunt for you and protect you and your children for as long as you wished it."

Her heart skittered up into her throat. "What did they say?"

"They said it was good enough for now."

'Twas only a matter of time before they pressed the point, however.

"You will not leave the town unless I'm with you," Sees Far warned her. "That includes morning bathing."

"But the other women are there—"

"*You* will not." He bent for emphasis, gazing into Elinor's eyes until she blew out a breath and looked away.

"Very well."

He could see she did not like it but understood his reasoning.

He would not, after everything, lose her to Wanchese or anyone else.

Still, he could not follow her around at all times, and when she was busy with some task, surrounded by the other women, he slipped away to see how the men occupied themselves.

During their first days there, he helped with the harvest. Though not his people or his town, if he expected to dwell there with Elinor, he would share in its resources and would likewise share in its support.

The men tolerated his presence about the town but did not yet trust him. Sees Far did not fault them for it. On this particular day, however, he might have given the appearance of wandering, but he had a very specific purpose in mind.

The blacksmith's fire and tools fascinated him, and the man acknowledged him with a nod, but he did not linger. Near the edge of town, a new house was being built, and in a frame mud was being mixed, smoothed, and cut into what they called *bricks* for the building of that house. The youth of which Elinor had spoken was working there, and as Sees Far approached, the boy looked up and fastened his attention on Sees Far for a long moment.

Sees Far nodded. The youth nodded in response, slowly.

He would return for that one. There was a matter to see to first.

Manteo he found with a group of men cleaning the weapons they called *guns*. He beckoned to Sees Far and showed him the workings, how the pieces came apart and were put back together again. It all stirred memory from when the English first visited years before, when his own father had welcomed them and been shown all the wonders of their curiously made devices.

And now here he was, the stranger, the outsider.

Manteo looked into his face and must have seen something of his thoughts, for he asked, "Do you wish to speak with me?"

"Kupi. I understand I am not trusted yet, but it is a matter between us, so bring who you will, who is trusted."

Manteo spoke to three others, one Kurawoten and two Inqutish, and they set out walking.

"Is it true the Inqutish are refusing huskanaw to their youths?"

Manteo smiled a little, thinly. "It is true."

"Elinor tells me it is because they do not understand the true nature of huskanaw. That they believe it to be a kind of sacrifice."

"It is a kind of sacrifice. But I see the trouble now." Manteo glanced at him. "You have been speaking of Georgie and my daughter?"

"Elinor is greatly distressed that they should not be allowed to marry. Is theirs the first pairing between us and the Inqutish?"

"Mahta. There are two others, but in both cases the men were past the age for huskanaw, and it was not an issue. Georgie and Mushaniq are—young. And I think my mother, being weroansqua, and sisters are more protective of her." The half smile returned. "Not that I blame them. She is very willful."

Sees Far thought of what he'd seen of her so far. Watchful, guarded, certainly protective of Elinor, which he could appreciate. "A weroansqua in the making herself, perhaps?"

Manteo's smile widened. "Perhaps."

"So what of this youth she wishes to marry?"

"He is. . .capable and good. He would make her a good husband, I think."

"Then there should be no obstacle to this. It is not right that his people refuse to allow him huskanaw. Have the Kurawoten youths accomplished theirs?"

"Not yet. We have had too many other things the past few years. But we have been discussing it."

Sees Far brushed a hand over his head. "You should begin preparations."

Manteo watched him for a moment. "It is unwise to do anything before spring."

"Mm, perhaps." Would the boy even trust Sees Far for what he was contemplating?

"Besides, there are other matters. Mushaniq has not yet accepted the faith of the Inqutish. I will not push her, but it is not a small thing in their eyes."

"So Elinor has said."

"Elinor has very great trust in you," Manteo said.

"And I am aware you do not." Sees Far felt the stiffening of his neck and shoulders, the desire to clench his own weapons in his hands. "But to her, I am the one who followed her to Ritanoe, who saved my resources to purchase her redemption from captivity, and who then led her back here."

"None of us are questioning that. We only wish to be sure this is for love of her, not something else."

There was no answer he could give that his pride would allow. Wanchese's rage had wearied him beyond bearing, but in this moment, it was tempting to walk through the opening of the palisade, out into the forest, and not return. But he had already spent too much, risked too much, to throw it aside so quickly.

He pulled in a long breath and forced himself to reply evenly. "Only time will show, then."

Manteo nodded gravely, arms folded, never looking away.

This one—he was not at all what Wanchese had said either.

Sees Far lifted his chin. "Tell me more of this—*baptism*."

Christopher Cooper was Elinor's cousin, the son of her mother's elder brother, and after Papa's departure three years before and failure to return, they were each the nearest family the other had in the New World. And Chris was not about to let Elinor forget that, it seemed.

At every turn, he was there, hovering even when Sees Far watched over her, or mayhap especially then, and sometimes while she was busy preparing food with the other women, when even her Secotan protector occupied himself elsewhere.

After a day or two of it, though, she could bear it no longer, and seizing his sleeve, she dragged him off to a relatively quiet spot. "Out with it, cousin. Why will you not let me out of your sight?"

His brows rose. "You lay blame upon me for this, when you are scarce returned?"

"I can feel that you have something you wish to say."

He huffed and folded his arms. Did he intend the imitation of the native men when they took on the mien of authority? She bit back a smile. He would find no humor in her observation at this moment.

"Where does Sees Far sleep?"

She mimicked his stance. "Anywhere he chooses."

Chris did not move. "And that would be—where, exactly?" When she did not reply, he went on. "I heard the two of you speaking from the upper room of your house last night when I chanced to pass by."

Snooping, was he?

"He has made himself my provider and protector, and I will not gainsay him." She fought to keep her voice level.

"Elinor." He scrubbed a hand across his face. "'Tis not meet for him to sleep in the same house let alone in the same chamber as yourself."

She leaned toward him. "Whether 'tis meet or not, I have slept near his side many a night, and never has he laid a hand upon me in the way you think. His own scruples forbid it."

Chris looked wholly unconvinced.

"The way of the Sukwoten—the Kurawoten as well—is to abstain from intimacy while a woman is with child and then for a time while the child is still suckling. It would be an insult to him—to both of us— to think he would do otherwise." She rocked back on her heels a bit. "Besides. He has agreed to give me due time to mourn Ananias. Their allowance for that I think is much longer than we English even deem fitting. But until this child is born and has grown, he and I have time to sort things out. Until then do not deny him his wish to watch over me. He has seen me used quite ill, and it is not to be wondered at if he seeks to prevent that happening again."

Chris gazed at her with a measure of sorrow in his eyes. "You speak more like them than you did."

She tucked her chin. "When I have lived among them as a slave for half a year, it is also not to be wondered at."

"Do you already consider yourself his, then?"

There was a wistfulness in his tone that brought her head back up. "Chris. Surely you do not—you left a wife behind in London, and children—"

The color came to his face in a rush. He lifted a hand and turned away for a long moment. When he faced her again, his gaze was beseeching. "A wife, aye, that I miss more than I can tell. But how long do we wait for your father the governor to return before we say distance and time have stretched too long, and we move on with our lives?"

His words struck as little else had the past few days. She could not breathe, could not move.

'Twas not such a stretch, the thought of never seeing Papa again. She had already suffered the cruel, sudden loss of Ananias.

"Even you feel it." He stepped closer. "Do not think, Elinor, once Master Johnson and the other elders realize this savage dwells in your very house—"

She drew up to meet him, nearly nose to nose. "He is no savage!" Her entire body trembled, suffused with a heat she could not contain. "They are thinking, feeling souls, every one—shaped by our Creator as deliberately and lovingly as we are convinced each of us, the English, to be. Not savages! We have our own savagery, as you will do well to recall. Or have you forgotten Papa's accounting of the previous expeditions here?"

Silence hung between them, broken only by her ragged breaths in and out.

"Well, then." Chris was suddenly, inexplicably calm. "As I started to say, do not think, once they realize you are dwelling with this man, that they will not insist you marry properly." He straightened. "Whatever the two of you choose to do with that, after, is your business."

"Chris."

Her cousin hesitated and turned back.

"Ginny and I sleep on the bed. He lies on the floor nearby. But if you and the other men are so concerned about what is meet, tell me why Georgie and Mushaniq are denied marriage. Does the town wish to push them to sin—if they have not already done so?"

Chris's face went a little pale.

"What, that had not occurred to anyone?"

Chapter Twenty-Two

Georgie would rather be elbow deep in mud, making bricks or cutting tiles, than have to sit still for Master Johnson with a book before him. In this case, that book was the Holy Scriptures, so he should not feel such pique. But it rose within him, regardless.

The script made his head ache even worse than working sums.

Come to think about it, having to read always put Da into a sour mood, even though he'd a brilliant mind in business and they'd lacked for very little despite the strictures of life in London. A gentleman, he'd been called. Georgie remembered a fine house with servants and a tutor.

Life on board the ship and then on the island had been free beyond imagining.

Did he truly need an education such as Master Johnson envisioned for him here in the New World? Houses and lands and servants in England mattered nothing here.

Here, what mattered were the skills one brought or learned.

Of course, "education" also included fencing lessons for the first time since they'd left England. 'Twas odd to think he was finally tall enough for Da's rapier, and learning to handle it properly was a delight. But this— this seemed sorest torture.

In great irony, the passage Master Johnson had him copying out was the chapter on love. Georgie narrowed his eyes against the swimming script before him and turned the page, then another.

The opening of a previous chapter caught his attention.

As concerning the things whereof ye wrote unto me: it is good for a man, not to touch a woman. . .

His skin washed hot and then cold. He bent closer and kept reading.

Nevertheless, to avoid whoredom, let every man have his wife: and let every woman have her husband. Let the husband give unto the wife due benevolence. Likewise also the wife unto the husband. The wife hath not power of her own body: but the husband. And likewise the husband hath not power of his own body: but the wife.

He sat upright. This was something he'd never recalled being taught in church. The wife belonging to her husband, yes, but according to Scripture, the husband also belonged to the wife?

He skimmed further.

I say unto them that be unmarried and widowed: it is good for them, if they abide even as I do. But and if they cannot abstain, let them marry. For it is better to marry, than to burn.

Was this why he felt so connected to Mushaniq already?

And if this was what the Holy Writ commanded, why would they not allow them to be husband and wife in truth?

Voices at the door of the house heralded the approach of Master Johnson and, in his wake, Manteo and Sees Far. "I will finish my lesson here with young Georgie, which you may observe, and then—" Master Johnson stopped, looking at Georgie. "What is it?"

He rose, one hand splayed across the page. "Why do those who profess to follow God not follow His Word?"

Master Johnson's jaw sagged, while behind him, both Manteo and Sees Far straightened to attention. Then the minister recovered himself. "In what way do you mean?"

"It is here—First Corinthians chapter seven. 'It is better to marry, than to burn.' And a husband and wife owe each other due benevolence not just—not just that the woman is there for the man's use. Why is this not preached? Much less followed?"

The older man's mouth flopped open like a fish again. This time he replied more softly. "It is preached, young Georgie. But folk do not wish to hearken."

He felt himself flushing. "And why are Mushaniq and I not allowed to marry, if this is the case?" His gaze darted to Manteo. Surely his own words would indict him, but he could not keep silent. "It was better, then, when the other boys were running about after the girls with no thought of honor, but she and I—somehow our wish to be together is a thing of shame?"

"N-no," Master Johnson stammered. "It is—it is more complicated with you two—"

Manteo stepped forward, the smile on his face oddly gentle. "It is no shame. And this indeed is why I favor you for her. Because you wish to do what is right."

Georgie's eyes burned. "What difference does it make if the entire town doesn't care? If they do not follow the rule of that which they say is law?"

He turned the page back to the passage he had been tasked with memorizing. " 'Though I speak with the tongues of men and of angels, and have not love, I am even as a sounding brass, or a tinkling cymbal.'"

Manteo and Master Johnson only looked at him mournfully.

The one called Sees Far stood back, arms folded. Was that a gleam of admiration in the Secotan's eyes?

Georgie could bear it no longer. Lessons or no, he was done for the day.

Making for the door, he gathered up his bow and quiver and escaped into the sunlight.

The youth had a fire in him, Sees Far was glad to see.

After Georgie left, the conversation with the town's Inqutish holy man—or so Sees Far gathered he must be—was interesting. He read from the talking pages, the thing they called a *book*, and answered Sees Far's questions as Manteo translated, since Sees Far was still very limited in his understanding of their tongue.

The holy man's full name, Sees Far was told, was *Ni-co-las-jon-son*, or Johnson for short. He confirmed Sees Far's suspicion that *baptism* was, rather like huskanaw, a type of dying to an old life and rising again to a new, and meant *washing*, accomplished by putting oneself beneath water or merely having water that had been blessed poured over one's head. Sees Far could not understand how such a thing would matter—but then, if the Inqutish refused to see how huskanaw mattered to the People here, perhaps it was not to be wondered at.

"Why can your Mushaniq not merely trade baptism for the youth doing huskanaw?" Sees Far asked Manteo.

The Kurawoten weroance laughed. "One would think it that simple."

When the question was aimed at Johnson, his brow furrowed. "There is a certain preparation for baptism that must not be taken lightly."

Manteo translated the words. Sees Far shrugged. "It is the same for huskanaw."

This drew another laugh from Manteo and a shaking of his head, but he gave Johnson the words.

The Inqutish only stared at Sees Far.

"I wish to walk through the preparation for the washing," Sees Far said. He looked at Manteo. "Is there anyone seeing to the youth's preparation for huskanaw?"

Manteo was quiet a moment. "Mahta."

With a nod, Sees Far followed the youth out the door.

"They are not the same thing at all!" Nicholas Johnson exclaimed. "It is heresy to suggest—even to think it!"

Manteo knew this word, *heresy*, from long-ago conversations with Thomas Harriot. "There is much Sees Far does not comprehend yet. But it is worth thinking more upon—that our huskanaw is a rite, a ceremony, necessary to the passage of manhood, just as baptism is a passage to being a Christian, or the marriage rite to being husband and wife."

Johnson chewed his cheek. "I shudder to think what the others will say to that."

"Well, we shall not know unless we say it." Manteo glanced toward the door, where Sees Far had just gone out. "It will take time for preparation, upon any account, so this need not be rushed."

With a sigh, the Inqutish man turned toward the table where rested their holy book. His fingers brushed the open page. "Georgie does not speak entirely amiss. It is not a sin or shame to marry. I struggle with all of this as well."

Manteo stepped closer. He could read most of the script now.

One line caught his eye—

" 'When I was a child,' " he read, " 'I spake as a child, I understood as a child, I imagined as a child. But when I became man, I put away childishness.' " He looked at Johnson. "Even the Scriptures say there is a difference between a child and a man. And huskanaw, as I learned it, provides that time of leaving childishness behind."

"Well. We will present it to the others in that light, then."

Throat still burning, Georgie went out through the palisade opening, nodding at the guards, then setting off downriver. He would not stay to belabor the point with Master Johnson or anyone else. He would go hunt or fish—anything to avoid having to return and trade words with those who thought his view had no merit. If what he could do was all that mattered to them, then he would find something to do.

He'd not gone far before he heard a call behind him. *"Numat! Nuh-maht!"*

Little brother, the word meant. He stopped, tucked himself behind a massive oak, and peered between the branches.

It was the one they called Sees Far. "Numat, I wish to speak with you."

The words were clear enough, although his way of speaking was a little different from the Croatoan. But why had he followed Georgie? Did he intend ill or not?

Sees Far seemed to sense Georgie's hesitation, and he stopped in the center of a small clearing, spreading his hands wide. "I come as a friend. I wish only to speak."

And this was how some of the English had perished previously.

He was no coward, however. Though this one reminded him of Two

Feathers, with all his pride, Elinor had put her trust in him, and that was no small thing.

He stepped into the open, one hand upon his bow and the other on his dagger.

Sees Far nodded and folded his arms across his chest. "You have no reason to trust me. I know this. But I can help you get something you desire to have."

"I am listening."

"I think it a great wrong that they will not allow you to do huskanaw. But I will help you prepare, through autumn and winter, and when the spring is come, you will be ready."

Georgie could feel all the fight going out of him. "Without the approval of the town's elders?"

Sees Far just looked at him for a long moment. "Do you not wish to prove yourself worthy of her?"

"Kupi."

"Then I will teach you what you need."

Heart thudding, Georgie nodded. It was not a complete solution, but it was, mayhap, a beginning.

Or it would be his death.

Either way, he was willing to risk it for Mushaniq.

But what if he betrays us?

It was the question everyone whispered, Kurawoten and Inqutish alike.

His devotion to Elinor was clear enough—or possessiveness, depending upon how one looked at it. Mushaniq could not decide which she thought it was. She wanted to question Elinor about it. The older women certainly had not held back from attempting to satisfy their own curiosity about her experience in captivity, and while Mushaniq had plenty of curiosity to match, she did not want to pester Elinor. Another way she was growing from child into woman, she supposed.

Today, they were out scavenging the last of the foodstuffs from the fields, while the men ranged farther out, both to hunt and to guard. Mushaniq saw Georgie go out with Sees Far and then return carrying a good-sized buck between them. They lowered it to the ground at the edge of the field, and after brief discussion, Georgie began the work of dressing it.

Sees Far rose and ambled toward Mushaniq.

For what purpose would he do so?

"Greetings, *Nuhsimuhs*."

Little sister? Oh, now she was definitely suspicious, especially when he quirked her a half smile as if he thought she should find him handsome. Or perhaps only trying to set her off her guard, which was equally dangerous.

"May I help you gather?"

She made a dismissive gesture. "I suppose."

He lifted a large orange *mahkahq*. "I have wished to speak with you about a matter."

Gathering up an armful of the smaller gourds, she set off toward the town. "Kupi? Speak, then."

"It has to do with your feelings about the God of the wutahshuntas."

That brought her up short. Her stomach sloshed uncomfortably. "They are no longer strangers but family!"

He tipped a hand in an apologetic motion. "*Chumay* can also be strangers."

"Mahta—it is more than that—" She huffed. "But what of it? What are you getting at?"

"I understand that most of the Kurawoten have taken the name of this Christ and accepted baptism. You have not."

"Why does it matter? I have simply not made up my mind about it all yet."

"There is nothing wrong with that. I am simply curious what your questions about it might be. Have these people proved to be like the other Inqutish who were here before?"

Mushaniq set off walking again. "I know nothing of that. These are good people, not without weaknesses but neither are they evil." She shot him a severe look. "It is not because of them that I have not accepted their faith. So do not try to get me to speak ill of them."

That only made him laugh. Was he a lackwit? He did not seem so.

"Do you find humor in that? I assure you, I did not intend it as such."

She marched past the guards at the opening of the palisade, and he kept pace with her. "Perhaps we should wait to speak until we have Elinor and Georgie with us, hmm?"

"I would not object to that."

It was too uncomfortable being the sole focus of his attempts at conversation.

Much later—while the deer roasted, and bits of it had been cut and hung to smoke, the hide stretched to dry and the innards also roasting or buried accordingly—they gathered in Elinor's house.

At the last minute, Manteo and Cooper were also invited. Once they had eaten well, Manteo filled a pipe with uppowoc, and the men passed it about.

"There is a thing I should perhaps have told you all when we first came here," Sees Far began. "Those of you of the People know that huskanaw is a time of purging the body so the heart and spirit can be made more right, and our eyes and ears are more open to Montóac and to learn something of our place in the world." Nods from all around, as they sat or crouched at the hearth, allowed him to know that they understood. "So it was, when I went, I looked to receive something as well." He hesitated. "But what I received was not what I expected. I saw a man and a woman, walking along the seashore, both with hair as bright as the sand itself. They were a long way from me, and however quickly I walked—or ran—I could not catch up. But I could see. And at one point, the woman turned and smiled at me.

"Thus, when I returned from huskanaw, my family and the priests agreed my name should be 'he who sees a long distance.' The priests believed it was a sign I would someday join their ranks, but that is not a thing I ever sought."

The gazes fastened upon him, sharp with interest.

"When your people first came to Roanoac Island, after the father of this one was killed, there was a day when we had come in secret to the island to spy upon you. I hid in the woods, and she"—he nodded toward Elinor—"chanced to be alone for a moment. I stepped out and revealed myself to frighten her."

Georgie sat up straighter. "I recall that day. I was with her—and ran away for a moment to pursue the deer."

Elinor only smiled a little.

"But she was not afraid. And I realized, as she tried to make conversation with me, that she was the woman from the dream I had during huskanaw."

Exclamations and gasps followed all around.

"Much later, when your people moved from Kurawoten to Pumtico, I returned, and over time, as Wanchese sought opportunity for revenge, I determined to take Elinor. But I did not intend for all that was ill to occur after, though I too was bent on vengeance."

He looked at Ginny tucked into the curve of her mother's arms and saw there the reflection of her father's face, the strength and determination.

"It gave me no pleasure to witness the death of her man. To the very end, he looked only to her and how he could shield her from harm." He took a pull of the smoke from the pipe. "I think he was a man I would have much admired."

Elinor's head went down, but not before he saw the sheen of tears in her eyes.

The others looked similarly grieved. He must have been much loved by all of them. How hard it must also be for them to accept his stepping into this man's place at Elinor's side. No wonder they all looked at him with such suspicion.

Elinor lifted her head, wiping her eyes. "He was not a man for niceties, such as some have, but Ananias assured me once that he'd no fear of dying. He knew where he had placed his faith. And yes—he was completely devoted to Ginny and me. To any he had pledged to protect and serve."

"His is a sore loss indeed," Manteo said, and the one they called Cooper—whom Elinor had said was her mother's brother's son—nodded.

"Despite that," Elinor went on, her voice rough with weeping, "I have come to believe that God Himself brought Sees Far to me. For whatever mysterious reasons He may have."

Chapter Twenty-Three

D uring the days that followed, the town settled back into the usual rhythm of life, but all seemed strange to Mushaniq, and a little wrong. Nohsh was solemn and sometimes stern as he saw to the town's affairs and its overall well-being. Sometimes she overheard him arguing with the other men over how best to meet the threat of Wanchese and the Sukwoten and others who were sure to bring war upon them again.

It made her gut twist just to think upon it.

Georgie was suddenly busy and preoccupied, often going out early in the morning with Sees Far to hunt and fish. He remained as sweet and tender and affectionate with her as ever, but there was less opportunity for slipping out to be alone and of course almost never inside the town walls even after dark. She missed him. And she missed Ginny, even though caring for the child was an unlooked-for task and Elinor's return welcome enough.

Auntie Timqua must have taken note of her moping about, because she presented Mushaniq with the suggestion that she offer to stay with Elinor through the birth of the new baby or however long Elinor wished as help and comfort.

For whom specifically, Timqua did not say. But when Mushaniq ran to ask Elinor whether she might welcome such a thing, the Inqutish woman's eyes shone with such obvious joy and relief, it warmed Mushaniq's heart, and she wasted no time moving her things to Elinor's house.

She might have been apprehensive over Sees Far's response. The man acted as if he were already Elinor's husband, though no words had been spoken that Mushaniq knew of or ceremony given by the church. But he merely gave a curt nod and said, "It is good."

Elinor commented on the new doeskin tunic Mushaniq wore most of the time now, especially as the days cooled. Mushaniq explained more about huskanasqua and all the skills she had acquired in the course of preparing so intensively for womanhood.

"I wish I had been here to see it," Elinor said, a little sad. She fingered the upper fringe of the tunic, edged in bits of shell, then the worked copper ornaments at Mushaniq's ears and strands of pearls and copper about her neck. "You were always a beautiful child, but you have grown even more lovely." She met Mushaniq's eyes and smiled. "I do not blame Georgie for being taken with you."

Mushaniq laughed and dipped her head. Would he have been so taken with her had she not pressed the issue? But Elinor did not need to know that.

Though she had witnessed the daily routine of the Inqutish for many moons now, Elinor taught her all that was required of *keeping house*, as they called it. Mushaniq helped care for Ginny and sometimes would arrange Elinor's hair the way the Kurawoten women did, although she did not allow Mushaniq to trim the front and sides the way the women of the People often favored. Sometimes Elinor would let Mushaniq try on her *shift* and *kirtle* and *sleeves*, just so she could feel what it was like to dress as the Inqutish women. But Mushaniq always shed them before anyone else could see her parading about in such borrowed clothing.

Would being Georgie's wife, if his people allowed it, mean she would be expected to dress as the Inqutish? The older men who had married Kurawoten wives did not seem to care, but would he? Even Nohsh still wore the strange garments, though during this past summer he sometimes paired a simple Inqutish shirt with the deerskin kilt and otterskin of the People, one wrapped behind and the other covering the opening in the front.

Of course, such questions meant nothing if they did not eventually approve of their marriage. And that, such as it was, seemed to hinge on her willingness to accept their God and their faith. She would not submit herself to the rite of baptism—the washing—as a pretense, simply to please them, however tempted she was to do so, just for the sake of being Georgie's.

She still most fervently wanted him and no other. Two Feathers had nearly given up asking, although he still sometimes pestered her about it.

He, along with others, was also busy preparing for huskanaw. They would continue all through the winter, and then at the first sign of spring, it would be decided who among the boys would be sent out and when.

Would Georgie be one of those? Her worry over that was enough to nearly drive her to pray to the Inqutish God—a confusion all its own. When had she ceased seeing the prayers and sacrifices to Montóac as the suitable and desired way of seeking divine favor? It was certainly becoming more difficult to do so now that most of the Kurawoten had taken the name of Christ. She almost felt that she needed to go out into the woods, secretly, to accomplish that.

And perhaps she should.

Other worries gnawed away at her heart and mind as well.

In the old days, before the Inqutish, before so many of their people took the name of Christ and it changed how they conducted their lives, it was a common enough thing for the girls and women who did not have husbands to prepare and drink a certain kind of tea to keep their monthly flow regular. The older girls talked about how it was part of the instruction they all received upon their first stay in the women's house—how they might attract the boys' attention, where to find the plants, when best to drink them. Babies were sweet and wonderful, but until they'd husbands to hunt and provide for them, this was the best way.

Had the older women merely forgotten when it came to Mushaniq and the younger girls coming of age, or had they stopped using such things for themselves? She did not know who to ask or how to couch such questions. Grandmother or Timqua—or the other aunts—would certainly want to know why Mushaniq wanted to know, and she was simply not ready to reveal that. Not even with it already presumed by so many that she and Georgie went walking together.

Nor was she willing to give up those sweet, stolen moments with

Georgie. And that was the impossible thing—to think he might stop being affectionate with her according to the customs of the People—

Oh, how desperately she wished she could just become his wife now, and let it be done. For that alone, the subterfuge of being baptized, even though she did not believe in what it represented, might be worthwhile.

The thought of lying, however, curdled in her middle. But so did the thought of drinking a tea simply for the sake of bringing on her regular womanly time.

"We have lived here now for three years," Georgie said, as they paddled the kanoe down the river toward open water, where their weirs stood. "I have learned the names for the different *namehs*—fish. Which ones come at which seasons. Where to hunt for oysters and when." He hesitated. "And when crabbing is the most profitable."

Sees Far nodded. "You have done well, hunting the wutapantam. It is nearing the time of year when the flocks come of the *woanagusso*, the *weewramanqueo*, and all the other waterfowl that come for the winter from the north." He smiled a little. "Now that the weather is cooling, you should dig for oysters and collect the pearls for Mushaniq."

Georgie returned the smile. "I have been."

"Ah! Good."

"I also have deerskins for clothing and hazel rods for making bows and the supports and roof of a house."

"Those are also good." Sees Far paddled with long, sure strokes and pointed where he wished them to go. "Come winter, I will teach you the setting snares for smaller animals—the *waboose*, *arohcun*, and *cuttak*, for their fur." He flashed Georgie a quick smile. "It will please her to have a mantle especially of the waboose, and—perhaps—there will be an infant to swaddle sooner or later."

Something swept through Georgie at the thought. Was that a possibility already, though they managed to slip away together but seldom late? Mushaniq had said nothing of it, and to be truthful, it was not foremost on his mind in the moments when her kiss and touch swept him away.

He thought about how hard it was to not be with her, how he could hardly bear the wait until they were truly married—although he considered her his wife already in his heart. Then he thought of all the men who'd sailed here to the New World and still were without wives, whether they'd left one behind or were yet unmarried. No wonder the Scriptures spoke in such strong terms about men and women needing to be married. He'd never quite understood that before.

It is not good that Adam should be alone. . .

The line from the creation story floated through his head.

And as he had heard it pointed out, it was not as if the masses in England paid any attention to what was good and proper.

Elinor stood at the window, peering at the dark clouds scudding overhead, hands smoothing over the ever-widening roundness of her belly. Thunder rumbled in the distance, then nearer.

On the floor behind her, Mushaniq sat with Ginny, stacking and counting small blocks of wood that Ananias had carved not long after they'd come across the sound to Cora Banks. It made Elinor's heart burn to listen to them, and yet it soothed her as well.

The last couple of months, as summer wore away into full autumn, had been like this, a tangle of conflicting thoughts and feelings. For even as she basked in the delight of having Ginny once again near enough to whisk into her arms anytime she chose, the memories of Ananias assailed her, along with the reminder that never again would he be part of such a scene.

To make matters worse, she fretted about the storm, but she held herself back from voicing it. Sees Far was a man well acquainted with the humors of the weather, as she herself had experienced and not so long ago.

Mushaniq seemed to know her mind, however, even without her saying anything. The girl rose and came to her side. "They will find shelter from the rain if needed," she said softly.

Elinor gave a little laugh. "Was I that obvious?"

Mushaniq smiled, a far more restrained expression than Elinor recalled from her before the events of that spring. "I have my own worries."

She looped an arm around Mushaniq's shoulder and tugged her close, and though Mushaniq was now taller than Elinor by a finger or two, she leaned her head upon Elinor's shoulder. It was sweet how freely affectionate the young Kurawoten woman had been with her since her return.

"Well, speaking of worries, there is a thing I have been meaning to ask. Since you are now of age—and I know your people's way with a woman's time—it has been some weeks, but have you not needed to visit the women's house?"

Mushaniq did not pull away, but Elinor felt the stiffness in her lithe body. A sudden suspicion stole through her.

Stepping back from the window, she drew the girl with her and dropped her voice. "Mushaniq? What is it?"

But this lively creature, never without a laugh or a quick retort, only stood speechless, shaking her head.

Elinor took her shoulders in her hands. "Are you with child?" she breathed.

The girl's eyes went wide for a moment, almost unseeing, then snapped shut, and the tears poured down her cheeks. A thin wail escaped her trembling mouth.

"Oh, sweet one." Elinor gathered her in. "Is it—Georgie?"

Still shaking, Mushaniq nodded.

"Did he—oh, I'll wring his neck for daring to touch you."

"It isn't—like that." Mushaniq drew back, swiping at her cheeks as Elinor stroked her hair. "I asked him. I wanted him to be my first." She flashed a look at Elinor then, so full of defiance that she nearly took a step back. "In the ways of my people—at least, in the old days before your holy book made it all wrong—it was no shame. But"—and she crumpled again—"I did not ask about the tea that brings on a woman's flow—and the older women have neglected to instruct us—and now—" Her hand stole across her middle. "Today, I felt fluttering, as if a *mamankanois* were inside me."

Elinor's throat tightened. She knew—she'd heard talk among the other women, and such things were not unknown in England as well.

It was, after all, why she'd hidden her current pregnancy as long as she could while a captive—for fear they'd force her to drink something to make her miscarry.

"There is much difference of opinion about how these matters should be handled, but our holy book also tells us that children are a blessing—and, I would say, it makes no difference how they have come about." She drew a deep breath. "Have you told Georgie yet?"

Mushaniq shook her head, sorrow overtaking her again.

Oh, these two. . .no wonder they wanted so desperately to be wed.

A sudden fear seized her heart. "You do *want* to keep your babe, do you not?"

Mushaniq's eyes went wide again. "Kupi—yes! Very much. I—I love Georgie and want to make a family with him. But there are yet so many things that must happen." She huffed. "He has yet to make huskanaw. And I—" She shook her head slowly, then with more emphasis. "Nohsh and Nunohum both made it clear that to finish huskanasqua, I must take a new name. And—I want none but Mah-ree." Again that quick, sharp glance. "Just as I want no man but Georgie. But I do not want to be baptized when I am not sure I believe."

Elinor drew her into a tight embrace again. Oh, how she loved this girl for her honesty.

"Also, I am afraid that they may insist I drink the tea. Because until I have a husband to hunt for me—"

Again Mushaniq shook her head against Elinor's shoulder.

"Well, if I know Georgie, he will insist on hunting for you whether they allow him to be called your husband or not."

"It is not just that. *Ai*. . .there is too much. . ."

"Sweet, blessed girl."

Ginny got up from her toys on the floor and ran across to throw herself into their skirts. "Mama!"

Laughing a little, they both lifted her, including her in the embrace as Mushaniq continued to weep.

Mindful of the girl's resistance to their faith, Elinor bit back the urge to pray out loud. *Help us, gracious Father! For all that Thou hast carried me through this past year, I trust that You yet have a purpose in this young woman's life, and this tiny one kindled inside her—and that of Georgie. Help me to speak aright, to lead her to You and not turn her away!*

Please God, indeed, that her words and deeds not be a stumbling block to Mushaniq coming to true faith.

The rain began to fall at last, a mere pattering at first, then a downpour. Mushaniq drew back from Elinor's arms, swiping at her cheeks, and peered out the window. "I do not wish anyone else to know yet."

"Will your family be unhappy?"

The girl shook her head again then said, "They might. Kokon—I mean, Bright Star—and her husband just took up dwelling together, and many said it was too soon after huskanasqua. But some of that was Dances Wild being known for a hasty temper."

"And what happens if he uses her ill?"

Mushaniq sniffed. "Then she casts him out. Puts his belongings outside the house to show he is no longer welcome."

"Things are not always so different in England." Elinor set Ginny down and nudged her back toward the blocks. "But what if before that, Bright Star became with child. Would she be expected to take the herbs to miscarry?"

"No, it would be her choice." Mushaniq frowned. "At least I think it would. Sometimes when the women talk about such things, it is confusing. And I wonder now whether I truly understood all I was hearing before."

Oh, how well Elinor understood that feeling.

"Georgie at least would want to know." She reached out for Mushaniq's hand, and the girl's gaze came back to hers, still mournful. "He deserves to know."

Mushaniq hesitated, then nodded.

At that moment, the door opened, and with a gust of wind and rain, the two stepped through—Sees Far and Georgie. While they set aside bows and other accoutrements, Elinor went to inspect the pair of fish they'd brought—each as long as her arm but already cleaned—and Sees Far playfully shook the raindrops from his wet hair onto her. She squealed in mock protest.

Behind her, Mushaniq crouched next to Ginny again, her back to the others.

Sees Far moved toward the hearth and prepared to broil the fish. Georgie hesitated near the door, looking from Elinor to Mushaniq and back again.

Elinor gave a little sigh. "Mushaniq."

No response, except for the young woman crooning in conversation with Ginny.

She cleared her throat. "Mary."

Mushaniq's head came up, her back and shoulders straightened, then she turned slowly to regard Elinor with wide eyes.

"Mary Mushaniq. I shall call you that henceforth."

She stepped across the room, swooped Ginny into her arms, and tipped her head meaningfully toward Georgie. "I must needs see to something in my chamber," she announced, and exchanging a glance with Sees Far, made her way to the stairs and up.

Chapter Twenty-Four

She could never recall being so afraid of anything in her life. For that matter, she could never recall being truly afraid. Except when it came to the possibility of Nohsh not returning, but then—he had. And not even when the Sukwoten had attacked moons ago, and she and the others had taken refuge in the marsh along the river.

She had managed to survive it all, along with sea storms, but this—this overcame her?

In yet several more moons, she would face giving birth to this baby. Was she not brave enough for that and for whatever might come before?

Was that new life, and her hopes to share a future with Georgie, not worth being brave for?

Across the room, he laid aside his things with deliberate and likely exaggerated slowness, then tugged his wet shirt off over his head and laid it over the back of a chair to dry. Sees Far finished setting the fish to broil over the fire and, without a word, followed Elinor upstairs.

She rose and after a moment padded across the room to Georgie. He turned, looking wary.

A bare arm's length away, she stopped. Her heart pounded so hard inside her chest he must surely hear it.

Dread rimmed his pale gaze now, his mouth pressed flat.

She huffed. She tried to speak, stopped, tried again. "Kuwumádas."

His expression softened. "Kuwumádas."

"I—" She stopped, covered her face with her hands.

She must do this. He deserved honesty.

Lowering her arms, she took another deep breath and met his gaze. "How would you feel if you were to be—a *father*?"

She used the Inqutish word on purpose. His eyes went wide, his nostrils flaring with a deep breath of his own, and his mouth fell open. "You—are—with child?"

She hazarded a nod.

"We're—to have—a babe? Of our own?"

Another nod, and a giggle escaped her. Then he closed the space between them and caught her up in his arms, turning her round and round, his face buried in her shoulder. She clung to him in return, savoring the strength of his embrace, breathing in his distinctive smell of cedar and rain, despite it being mingled at the moment with fish.

At last he let her down, only to swoop in for a kiss.

When at last she could breathe, she pulled back just enough to murmur, "You are glad and not angry?"

"Oh, Mushaniq. I am very glad." And he kissed her again.

"They—the elders—may not wish to let me carry it."

Georgie's eyes went wide. "What do you mean?"

"There are plants that we eat or make into a tea that keep a woman from growing a baby." She cupped his face in her hands, sweeping his cheekbones with her thumbs. "It is the usual way before a girl chooses a husband. But. . .I had forgotten."

"You—no! No, that is not right—"

He caught her into his arms again, so tight she could hardly breathe. But she did not mind.

"I want you. I want any babes we might have. I will not let them do this." He kissed her again. "Please do not do this! Do not let them persuade you."

She held him tightly in return. "I will not."

It was more than she dared believe would happen, and so exactly what she had hoped.

Elinor sat Ginny on the edge of the bed and reached for a comb. The child's hair was not in dire need of it, but it gave Elinor something to busy them both with to give Georgie and Mushaniq a few moments alone.

Sees Far came to her side while she worked Ginny's silky strands. "What is it?" he asked softly.

She smiled a little. "The two of them need a little time to speak."

He gave her a searching look, then padded back to the door and listened. She could not hear the words, but the tone and pitch of the exchanges told her all she needed to know about what was being said. An ache rose in her throat.

Oh, that first time she had shared her expectant state with Ananias! Of course, they were at that point properly wed, so there was no uncertainty, no shame. . .

Things were very different among the native peoples here, she knew well by now, and yet not different at all.

Ginny wiggled away and, before Elinor could stop her, trotted over to the door. She stopped beside Sees Far, looping one arm around his knee.

Elinor's breath stopped altogether. It had been several weeks, and while Ginny seemed to accept the presence of the tall Secotan since the beginning, neither had she been so openly familiar with him either.

Sees Far's hand came to rest upon her head, and for a long moment none of them moved. Then Ginny let go and hovered at the top of the stairs, no doubt spying upon the two below, before running back to Elinor. "Mama! Neek and Georgie kiss!"

She laughed, taking the child's hands and sitting down on the edge of the bed. "Do they, now?"

Ginny nodded, all seriousness, and scrunched her nose. "They kiss all the time."

Sees Far crossed the floor to them again. "What does she say?" he asked in his own tongue.

But the heat rose to her face at the thought of having to explain something so—so simple and yet so momentous, in a certain setting, and she could only chuckle and shake her head.

Ginny climbed up on the bed and bounced about. Sees Far stood so close now his knees nearly touched Elinor's, and with the corner of his mouth quirked, he regarded both her and Ginny in turn before asking the child, "Geenee, what is *kiss*?"

Oh, that was unfair! Ginny perked, instantly understanding, and in all her childlike innocence, ready to enlighten him. "It is this!" She bounded across the bed to Elinor, where she planted a noisy buss on Elinor's cheek. Then she seized Elinor's face with both hands, and turning her head as she leaned nearly into Elinor's lap—she had to catch the child before they both tumbled into the floor—the next one went on Elinor's lips.

Nothing untoward there, of course. It was natural and common even among the Kurawoten for mothers and children to exchange such tokens of affection. But—

His eyes came to Elinor's, intense with growing comprehension. "I did thus the day I brought you here, intending you to return without me."

"Kupi." She could hardly breathe under the weight of his gaze.

"That was. . ." Sees Far hesitated, suddenly appearing as flustered as she had ever seen him. "I was bidding you farewell. Expressing my fondness for you. . .as one would to family. It was all which seemed fitting in the moment." His brows arched. "Among your people, then, it is more? Or—different?"

"More, and different, when two people are—well, when they are interested in each other."

"In love play?"

She choked out a laugh, her face burning. "Kupi."

Ginny continued to flop around the bed, and the babe within kicked and rolled as if in sympathy with the older sister's cavorting. But Sees Far's gaze ensnared her for what felt an inordinately long time before he lifted his hand to touch her face and hair.

Her breath caught again in her throat, nearly a sob. In another time, another place, she might surrender to such a moment—with her insides awash like a sea tempest and not least among it all, the sharp longing to simply be held in a man's arms.

Were that man Ananias, she'd give it never a thought.

But—mayhap it was not unmeet for even Sees Far to serve in the here and now.

Just to be held. Nothing more.

His fingers stirred against her cheek and temple, and shutting her eyes, she leaned into his touch. Turned her head just so and pressed her lips to the edge of his hand when it chanced to brush close. He stilled, then sank to one knee beside the bed and bent his head to hers—yet not in the way she had expected, but his face hovering close beside hers. Inhaling deeply, then a slow exhale as his nose traced the edge of her ear.

"This is the way of my people," he breathed, his cheek against her neck.

She looped her arms around his shoulders, trembling, as his lean form did the same.

It was too soon after Ananias—and she was so heavy with child—and having been a wife, she knew too well how a simple kiss or even this—oh, mayhap especially this—could so quickly lead to more.

And this could not be more—yet.

"Mama! Sees Fa'!" Ginny threw her small, wiggly self over their embrace, arms clinging over both of them.

It was the dash of cold water they both apparently needed. Sees Far's shoulders shook with his chuckle, its rumble mingling with Elinor's own watery giggle.

Supper was a strangely subdued but joyful affair, with Mushaniq scurrying about to help serve, although Elinor tried to do her share, and then Georgie's hand tightly entwined with hers whenever they had opportunity.

After, Sees Far asked many questions about what he had overheard from the top of the stairs. Mushaniq did not care that he'd eavesdropped and would have been rather surprised had he not. To the dilemma of whether or not she should make her pregnancy known, he nodded toward Elinor. "It was for fear of her unborn child's life that she hid her state while we were yet at Ritanoe." He eyed Mushaniq for a moment as if considering his next words. "What is your father's opinion likely to be?"

She lifted one hand. "I do not know."

"Well. Children are a joy and treasure, but they must be fed and cared for." He rubbed his chin. "I have pledged myself to provide and protect Elinor, and so far I have taken more than enough for her needs when hunting and fishing. Today, we caught far more than these two and gave them to the other women before we came here, to feed whoever might need it. It is no burden for me to do the same for you, until such time as you and Georgie may marry."

Georgie straightened, where he sat beside her. "I will provide for her as well, of course, whether or not we have approval to truly marry."

Sees Far bent a smile upon him. "Kupi. I had no thought that you would do otherwise."

Mushaniq squeezed his hand. "Nor did I." She turned to Sees Far. Perhaps she had misjudged him—but then again, accepting his provision did not mean trusting him with all. "I thank you. You have no obligation to see to my care, but it is a generous thing you offer."

Later, when Sees Far had carried a sleepy, sagging Ginny to bed, Elinor in their wake, and both had called *winkan nupes* down the stairs, Mushaniq snuggled closer to Georgie as they sat before the fire. He'd not yet put his shirt back on, and the heat from his bare skin comforted as greatly as did that from the flames.

"He surprises me," she murmured. "Although I still do not know what to think of him."

Georgie remained quiet for a moment. "He seems—true. Despite all I wanted to believe at first. Of course, that has yet to be proven."

Mushaniq sniffed and rolled her head across his shoulder. "I have wanted to hate him but found that I cannot." She peeked up at Georgie. "Do you think he would promise to keep himself only to Elinor?"

"I think he just might," Georgie said slowly.

"I once thought that no one can promise those things however much they wish to. Now I am not so sure."

"Some manage it." His brow lifted. "Are you having second thoughts about—us?"

"Mahta! Not at all. I have only been thinking about it all, how some of my people have kept the same husband or wife for a long time, but no one expects them to keep themselves only to that one. And weroances, they take as many wives as they can afford." She shrugged. "It is just the way it is done. And girls of my people are encouraged—or at least they were, before your people came and brought the teaching of your God—to not limit themselves to one boy. Because after all, how could we know who might suit us? But"—she could not suppress a chuckle at the twitch that went through Georgie as she spoke—"when Two Feathers pestered me to take him, I could not even bear thinking of it. And when I asked you to be my first. . ."

She stopped, took a quick breath, and let it out. Did she dare admit this to him? To bare her heart in such a way?

"After," she murmured, "I could not bear thinking of taking any other. And I still cannot. So—if that is what your holy book means by a love giving itself to one only, it is not so far beyond my understanding."

Arms tight about her, he exhaled with a rush, then inhaled with a sniffle. She peered up at him, and though his eyes were shut, wetness welled from the corners.

He swallowed hard. "How long do we wait to tell—others?"

"Oh, one of the aunties will probably notice before long that I haven't been to the women's house. They are all nosy and meddlesome that way." She gave a humorless laugh.

"Mayhap it would be best to just be out with it, then."

She could find no reply to that but only burrowed deeper into his embrace.

Chapter Twenty-Five

M ushaniq and Georgie sat before him, she composed and lovely, and he grave but resolute. This could not bode well, the two of them asking to speak with him alone.

When, however, had she grown so completely into a woman? So much the image of her mother, although he could see in her face the reflection of his own mother and sisters as well. And in Georgie he could see the shadow of his father, the Inqutish Assistant who had met such a horrible end near as soon as they'd landed on Roanoac.

Not for the first time, it struck him how the two together symbolized much of their peoples' hopes and plans for the future. Would that he could honor their desire to be joined as one much sooner than others deemed it fitting.

He felt a twitch in his hands, a dull craving deep in his chest. Would that they'd uppowoc to share, or even a cup of tea or some other drink. But both of them appeared so determined, so sober.

Manteo waited in silence for one of them to speak.

"We wished to come to you," Mushaniq began, "before anyone else is made aware. Elinor knows—she noticed because I am staying with her, that I have not been to the women's house recently. It has been since the middle of summer, in fact. And if Elinor took note, it will not be long before the aunties also do. But I have determined not to drink the tea to bring on my flow. Georgie and I know we are young. This has not been our people's way. But we very much want this child."

No wonder she seemed more luminous of late.

He swiped a hand across his face, then folded his arms and sat back.

"We were hoping," she went on, "because you are the one who most straddles both worlds—a foot in two kanoes, so to speak—you could tell us how best to go from here. Do we tell the entire town and be done with it? Wait until my belly is so round everyone knows, regardless?" She spread her hands. "Sees Far and Elinor have promised to shelter and care for me until Georgie and I are allowed to marry. But we have determined we do want to marry with no doubts. We want to make a family together."

They exchanged a look, and his heart burned within him. He remembered—oh too well—what that sort of love felt like.

What would have become of him and Mushaniq's mother had she not died?

Gracious and good God, such futile thoughts. But You know all my thoughts. . .

"Georgie is willing to go huskanaw and is preparing for such," he said as gently as he could. "Are you prepared to be baptized and profess faith in Christ? To take the vows of Christian marriage?"

She tucked her head. "I do not wish to lie about where I place my faith," she said at last.

Sourness rose in the back of his throat. "I understand. And I did promise not to force you."

"But I am prepared to promise to be true to Georgie for always," she was quick to add.

He peered at her. "That is not a common thing to our people."

"Nevertheless, we have talked, Georgie and I, and it is what we both want."

It was a beginning, perhaps. Please God it would grow into more.

She tucked her head again. "Are you disappointed in me, Nohsh?"

"Disappointed? Never! Why would you think so?"

Her gaze held his, mournful.

"Never," he said again, and beckoning, drew her to him. "Kuwumádas, Nunutánuhs. Always. No matter what you have done or not done."

She slowly surrendered to his embrace, weeping.

"And I am very, very happy at the thought of being a grandfather."

At that, she hugged him back very tightly.

The entire town was in an uproar.

Though they'd community gatherings aplenty as the weather allowed, with talk and laughter and music around the common fire, they'd never before met together, all the adults in one place, over one common issue. Not since moving to Cora Banks, and at least not while Elinor was present.

They all crammed into the longhouse built as their meeting place, rain drumming on the roof. Lacking room to pace, she stood in the back, swaying and rubbing her belly and hips. The current state of affairs only added to the unrelenting ache.

She had already argued in private on behalf of Georgie and Mary Mushaniq—she could not help but think of the girl by both names already, despite lingering disapproval from the English because it was seen as too papist and by the Kurawoten because, well, it was English and associated with a holy book in which the young woman had yet to confess any belief. All agreed, with varying degrees of reluctance, that she and Georgie had shared somewhat of a particular friendship over the years, and so it was natural, when the girl learned that was the name of his deceased mother, for her to see it as a token of their attachment, at the least.

The Assistants, such as remained, suddenly seemed to recall their duty to the lad—since his father had also stood in that position—and expressed their concern and interest in the matter but in such a way that smacked to Elinor of self-righteousness. Were they still in London, not a one of them would even raise an eyebrow but would chuckle into their cups and congratulate the boy on his exploits.

Suddenly, it became a matter of horror because there was a child and mention of marriage involved. And perhaps because she was Kurawoten and he English.

No less so for the Kurawoten. Elinor had watched with interest as Manteo's mother and sisters bickered with the other women over whose responsibility it had been to instruct Mushaniq on the proper use and timing of their teas and whether it could yet be advisable for her to use it. When it had been pointed out that God as defined by the Christian faith perhaps did not approve of taking measures to end a life even unborn, the entire group fell into a tizzy.

Scripture was not clear on such things, it was true. But deep in Elinor's heart, she felt the wrongness of it.

"Will Mushaniq be cast out if she refuses and wishes to carry and birth this child?" she had finally asked.

All the women stopped, staring. "Of course not!"

"Will the child not be fed and cared for?"

"No, we would feed and care for the child."

"Then what is the difficulty here? Georgie and Mary Mushaniq have expressed their desire to marry, and he is willing to provide even if the community does not give its approval."

That led into a debate over whether Mushaniq could rightfully be called by her new name if the elder women had not yet declared it to be hers.

Elinor was wearied beyond words by it all.

In the present, the Assistants also bickered on. "Perhaps the ones who went to Beechland had it aright, and if we do not well define what we stand upon—the sacraments and the doctrines—then we will soon find ourselves upon sand, washed away by the waves."

"The sacraments and doctrines are clear enough! That is not our trouble here. It is that we wish to administer the letter of the law and not be mindful of the spirit thereof."

"Then how do we do so without appearing to close our eyes to sin?"

"We have already closed our eyes to it," growled one. "Recall the case of William Wythers and the other boys some two years past. The thing is Georgie has now come forward with honorable intentions, and we should gravely consider how to fulfill his request."

"But to let him take part in such a heathen rite—"

Manteo spoke nearly for the first time. "Sees Far has been learning the catechism and creed in preparation for his own baptism, and he and I have been talking of ways to conduct huskanaw so it does not violate

Scripture—or needlessly endanger our youths. We need only to sort out the details—"

"And what of your girl's refusal to accept baptism? Why should we agree to send Georgie on huskanaw while she remains unregenerate in the Spirit?"

"That is a matter for prayer, because I will not force her and it must be the Spirit of God that moves upon her heart. Else it is not a true conversion. You know this."

"But if the will determines, the spirit will follow—"

Elinor pushed herself away from the wall and pitched her voice above the others. "May I speak? As a daughter of our esteemed governor?"

The men stopped, appearing startled that she had dared interrupt. Manteo nodded and beckoned to her.

She made her way to the middle, accepting the steadying hands reaching out to her as she went. The floor was so crowded it was difficult to find wherewithal to place her feet. When she stood at Manteo's side, she paused for a breath, turning slowly to meet the upturned gazes around her.

"We are here because of the vision of my father, John White. It was Sir Walter Ralegh's vision as well, but my father was the one chosen to be governor despite his inadequacy. Who labored to persuade those who would come, who petitioned time and again for supplies and proper support, and even now continues to do the same, if he is at all able. He is, aye, one of few who recognized not only the beauty of this New World but the dignity of her people, and who longed to see us living together in love and brotherhood, to continue the friendship begun so truly, though some tried well to spoil it and nearly succeeded."

Stopping to let Manteo translate, she gathered her thoughts and continued.

"Let us recall that we battle not only natural forces—wave and tempest and drought and suchlike—but also an enemy of our souls who would delight in nothing more than to see us at odds with each other, tearing down with our own hands what we have sought to build. And so I plead with you—let us hold fast to love and to grace. To holiness as well—'without which no one will see the Lord'—but surely our gracious

God would not have commanded that which is exclusive of the other. We can walk in holiness and yet do it in such a way that is loving and gracious! Is not the Lord Himself long-suffering with our own stumbling? This does not mean we wink at sin. But when those who are caught in it are seeking a way to make right what they have done, we do not despise their efforts. We do not make it impossible for them to do what God has told them to do—which in this case, if you know your Scripture, for Georgie and Mary Mushaniq, is indeed to marry."

"And what of you and Sees Far?" John Sampson asked. "'Tis not meet for you to dwell in the same house and not be man and wife."

"We are working on that as well. For us—and for Georgie and Mushaniq—I would beg your patience. For some of this, only time will serve. As he himself is learning catechism and Scripture, Sees Far is preparing Georgie to be considered fully a man by Kurawoten and Sukwoten measure. Master Johnson is likewise equipping him with all that is needful as an Englishman in the New World."

Master Johnson dipped his head in acknowledgment, the lines of his face grave. Elinor knew the difficulty of his position in all this.

"I intend to continue sheltering Mary Mushaniq—and so I have decided to call her, until her new name is fully recognized—for as long as is needful. Sees Far has assured me he will hunt and provide for her just as he does me and my children, and Georgie already assists him in that endeavor.

"I would plead again with you, let us not fail to support one another in heart and spirit. We also have enemies in the flesh who would be too pleased to see us slain or divided. But if we wish to prosper here, let us not be mindful solely of our own interests. All that we do is in care of not our own selves only but that of our young. Let us not forget that they are the ones who will lead our peoples after us.

"And do not disregard me, a mere woman, or my words. As you respect Her Majesty Queen Elizabeth and Manteo's own dear mother, who has led the Kurawoten these past years, so hearken to what meager wisdom I may offer in the tenderness of my age."

With as much of a curtsy as she could manage with her bulk, she again looked about the entire room and then made to return to the wall.

"Here," Roger Bailie said quietly, rising from his chair. "Do sit down among us. It is nothing if not earned. Well-spoken, Mistress Dare."

She settled herself upon the chair, and Master Bailie now faced the gathering. "Elinor has given us a call to be of one heart and mind, to grace and patience. These are words of wisdom, indeed. Would any disagree?"

An uncomfortable quiet settled over the gathering. If she had dissenters, mayhap they were reluctant to speak.

"What of this matter, however," came a voice from the crowd, "of Elinor dwelling with a man not her husband?"

Elinor opened her mouth to reply, but Sees Far stepped from the shadows where he had kept watch and called out, "I am ready to be called her husband if she will accept."

The words were in his own tongue, but so clear, none misunderstood. A rush of murmuring rose in time with Elinor's own blood into her ears, dizzying her.

"You have not yet been baptized," Chris said.

"I am ready to be baptized as well and declare my belief in the one you call Christ," Sees Far answered, unmoved.

His dark eyes caught and held hers across the room.

Another wave of questions. "He is indeed ready," Master Johnson said. "His understanding is perhaps yet unperfect, but which of us comprehends all the mystery of the Gospel when we first come to Christ?"

Murmurs of agreement followed this. Sees Far lifted his hands. "What hinders water being brought and accomplishing this? And what after must be done for Elinor to be declared my wife?"

Beside her, Master Bailie chuckled. "First she must agree."

She could not breathe, could not think. Throat and eyes burned as she gazed across at this man who had laid aside both vengeance and his own community for her sake. Who in their private conversations revealed a depth of passion and understanding in the spiritual that rivaled most churchmen she had known, even to insisting she read to him every night from Papa's own copy of the Scriptures, which she'd taken care to bring with them from Roanoac.

She would always love and miss Ananias. But she could not deny

God's providence in the form of this tall Sukwoten warrior—this son of Granganimeo, one of the first to welcome Englishmen to these shores.

"I do agree," she said.

Georgie popped to his feet from where he and Mushaniq sat near the wall. "Does this mean we also may be married?"

"No," Master Johnson said but not unkindly. "Elinor has spoken on your behalf, and this must be made right first."

The boy's struggle to accept this showed plainly on his face, but he merely nodded and did not reply. Mushaniq, however, also bounded upright, and with a huff even Elinor could hear, she made for the nearest door and stormed out of the meetinghouse. With a dismayed glance at Elinor, Georgie went after her.

"Could that not have been imparted more gently?" Elinor murmured to Master Johnson.

"Perhaps, but their time is soon." He peered askance at her and then Manteo. "But 'twould mean pressing the point with Mushaniq, and is that wise?"

"If she could be brought into the faith for her love for Georgie, however. . ." Elinor let the question hang and hissed softly.

Master Johnson rose from his place and lifted his hands for quiet over the buzzing of the crowd. "I propose we give Sees Far and Elinor a few days to confirm this decision—and it gives us time to prepare more fully."

"I see no reason to delay," Elinor said.

Across the room, Sees Far gave a slow nod and smiled.

"Well," Master Johnson said. "Let us recess for half an hour, while I make preparations."

Chapter Twenty-Six

M ushaniq, wait!"

Gor, she was fleet, even now. She'd gotten just enough of a start on him to stay ahead as they weaved between the houses.

"Mary!"

Even that did not make her pause. As she reached the palisade opening, Georgie caught up with her at last, seizing her arm and hauling her about.

The rain poured down her face as her breast heaved. "It is not fair!" she cried. "We do no wrong in simply wanting to be together!"

Pulling her into his arms, he buried his face against her neck. "No. But they are our elders. Perhaps 'tis best if they go first in this."

She sobbed against him while the rain pattered cold against his hair and shoulders.

"Come," he said and tugged at her hand.

She followed, head bent, as he led her around the perimeter of the town and into the smithy, currently empty but dry and still warm from the fires. Both of them shivering, they sat on the floor next to the forge, where Georgie set his back against the warm stones and gathered Mushaniq into his arms.

"We should run away and just live alone," she murmured after a while.

"It is very tempting."

"Of course they would not agree to us marrying. You cannot yet go on huskanaw."

"Sees Far says I am very close to ready, were the weather to be favorable." He cradled her closer. "Are you—would you—be willing to be baptized and believe in Christ?"

She made a mewling sound. "I am thinking upon it."

He could not help but chuckle a little.

She lifted her head to peer at him in the dusk. "Does it even matter to you? You do not speak much of God and what you think of it all."

He shrugged. It was a topic he would, admittedly, prefer to avoid.

"When were you baptized?"

Another sniff. "As an infant, soon after I was born."

Mushaniq sat up straight. "What? Why?"

Another shrug. "'Tis customary. The parents do this as a sign of their covenant with God and how that extends over their children. Then later, the children confirm their faith."

"Huh. That is strange."

"Both of our peoples have many customs the other finds strange."

"True."

She curled against him again and burrowed her face in his shoulder. "I miss the island."

He snuggled her closer. "So do I."

"Perhaps we should take a kanoe and go back, just you and I."

"That would be wonderful."

She made a sound, whether a snort or a laugh he could not tell. "Another winter, is it, before the ground will grow food again? At least there we would be safe from our enemies."

As many as three years, they had said, was how long it took the soil to recover from being poisoned by saltwater during the sea tempests.

Mushaniq stirred against him, nuzzling his neck. Oh, but she was soft in his arms.

"Careful," he murmured. "Sees Far has also been hounding me about abstaining from sharing affections since you are now with child."

This time she did snort. "What if that is not my wish?"

"He said I must respect your body as it carries and nourishes new life. He was most adamant."

She gave a noisy sigh. "I suppose we should go back and hear the rest of the talk."

Hand in hand, they returned to the meetinghouse, slipping inside and against the wall.

In the center of the gathering, a small table had been set up with a bowl of water, and before it knelt Sees Far, with Master Johnson standing over him, Bible balanced on one arm.

Impulses of passion sometimes drove a man more true than long talk and deliberation. Sees Far had heard this said once, long ago, and while it could not hold so in every case, there were moments when he felt its veracity to his very marrow.

This was one such moment.

All that had led him to this place—how amazing and utterly beyond believing. Yet here he was, on his knees among a sea of Inqutish and Kurawoten, preparing to confess his growing trust in their God and the one called His Son.

He reflected on what some had said about it—the priests and weroances and Wanchese and the others who, like Sees Far, had run with him. That it would be a contradiction, a denial, of their status among the People. He was no longer sure that was the truth.

All he knew in this moment was that this felt right. Just as Elinor had been at the center of his visions, she and the Man he was increasingly convinced must be the Christ Himself, it was in defense of her that he'd been compelled to step forward and speak, to offer to do these things.

If they were to become one people, she and others had said, they must each bend in some things. And realizing he already believed—he'd committed the moment he stepped out of hiding and walked forward to take her hand, there in the field where he'd first snatched her away. This was but the next step.

Johnson spoke the words over him, first in Inqutish and then, haltingly, in the tongue of the People. Sees Far could not help but be impressed that he had gone to such lengths. But perhaps he had practice already, having performed the same rite for some of the Kurawoten.

Either way, it only deepened the meaning for Sees Far. *That Ahoné did send His Son to satisfy the blood debt we owed, clearing the way for us to be sons as well. . .*

It was so simple—too simple, it seemed. And yet Sees Far could no longer ignore it, could not refuse the call resounding through his own heart.

Johnson scooped water and poured it over Sees Far three times. The rivulets washed down his face and neck, across his shoulders—he'd laid aside his mantle for this—both warm and cool. Sees Far closed his eyes.

Wash not just my head but my soul and heart, oh Mighty Creator! Let me be fully Yours. Let me know You as so many others do.

Then Johnson dipped a finger in oil and made the sign of the cross on Sees Far's forehead. "Sees Far, you are sealed by the Holy Spirit in baptism and marked as Christ's own forever. Amen."

A cheer rose from the gathering around him. Johnson lifted a hand and spoke both a prayer and a blessing, inviting the others to welcome him as numat—*brother*—in Christ.

Grinning, Manteo reached out a hand, helped Sees Far to his feet, and embraced him.

"Now," Johnson said, with a smile of his own, "you have declared your intention to make this woman your wife?"

Then Elinor's hand was placed in his by Manteo, and they shifted to face each other. She had braided and coiled her pale hair and covered it with what she called a *coif*, her garments comprised of a thin white *shift* covered with a heavy red *kirtle*. He still itched to see her in doeskin, but on her, it was not unpleasing.

A flush rode her cheeks, the dark center of her eyes wide, and he could feel the tremor in her hand as Johnson began to speak words over them he could not quite catch—and this time, Manteo took over translating them.

And so, you who are greatly loved, we gather to witness the joining of this man and this woman in sacred marriage. . .

That was a combination he had never heard before, the *sacred* and *marriage*. He would have to think more upon it when there was leisure to do so.

There were more words about the purpose of marriage for joy and help and comfort. Johnson turned to Elinor and addressed her. "Elinor, will you have this man to be your husband, to live together in the covenant of marriage? Will you love him, comfort him, honor and keep him, in sickness and in health and, forsaking all others, be faithful to him as long as you both shall live?"

As Manteo translated, she held herself very straight and said, "Kupi. I will."

Next Johnson turned to Sees Far. "And will you, Sees Far, have this woman to be your wife, to live together in the covenant of marriage? Will you love her, comfort her, honor and keep her, in sickness and in health and, forsaking all others, be faithful to her as long as you both shall live?"

He had understood already the duty of man to provide and protect, but to be faithful to her and have none other was something else he had been instructed about, and he was no less prepared to promise that as well. "Kupi."

And then more words, which Johnson said and Elinor repeated and Manteo translated, then Johnson spoke, Manteo translated, and Sees Far had to repeat. Beautiful words, worthy of song, about love and care and abiding by each other through all sorts of circumstances, both good and ill.

He could hardly believe it. This woman, whose strength and courage had won him over, even during the days when all he desired was to see her humbled. . .she would soon be declared his.

She could scarce believe it. This was all happening so quickly—was he truly ready for all he had just vowed? Was she?

Oh, Ananias. . .oh, gracious Lord in heaven! Have mercy on us.

The Assistants and other town leaders perhaps saw it as a solution to one set of troubles, but to a certain extent, it felt like an open door to others.

But I have trusted You thus far, and I cannot shrink back now. If this is what You intended when You first allowed me to be taken. . .

Still, she could not hold back the tears—some for the strong, handsome man she would never more see in this life and some for all Sees Far had left behind to abide here with her.

After all had been declared and spoken, there was a moment of awkward silence, then Master Johnson cleared his throat. "Here I would customarily tell the husband and wife to greet one another with a holy kiss. But there is some disagreement about what is proper under the circumstances. . . ."

Elinor shook her head and gave a broken laugh. "Let us not make more of it than need be." Leaning closer, she put one hand behind Sees Far's neck and, with gentle pressure, drew his forehead down to hers. "I greet you, Sees Far, as my brother in Christ and my husband."

One hand cupping the back of her head, he murmured similar words. Then they straightened and faced the gathering.

Everyone surged forward to offer congratulations—though such were rather subdued from some of the English townspeople—and to greet Sees Far as a new believer in Christ.

Theirs was no typical wedding, but somehow the town managed to make it an evening of celebration even on such short notice. The rain had stopped, a cold, damp fog sifted through the town in its place, but a community fire was lit and food preparations begun. With much fanfare, Timqua ushered Elinor and Sees Far to a mat laid out for them to share and made them sit down together under an awning in sight of the fire. Wesnah brought them cups of sweet spiced drink.

As she sipped, Elinor exchanged a smile with Sees Far over the rim of her cup, then searched the crowd for Georgie and Mushaniq. They were nowhere to be seen. Had they slipped out again, after returning during Sees Far's baptism, or were they only off tending Ginny? She longed for a few minutes alone with them to talk the entire matter over and hear their thoughts.

Sees Far's hand brushed hers, bringing her awareness sharply back to him—and the reason for all the present fuss.

Husband. 'Twas so strange and yet—not.

She slid her fingers across his. Even after more than three years on these shores, she was still uncertain of all the nuances of courtship and love as practiced by his people. They were shy in some ways, shockingly open in others—

His hand turned and clasped hers, rough yet warm and comforting. Startlingly *right.*

She peeked at him and found him watching her—as always. A wry smile twisted her mouth. But there was something about his expression she could not recall seeing before—an awe, a wonder, almost childlike. It reminded her, in fact, of what she'd witnessed in Manteo's countenance immediately following his baptism.

She leaned toward him. "What are you thinking?"

He smiled as well. "That Manteo spoke truly. All is changed now."

" 'If any man be in Christ, he is a new creature.' "

One dark brow arched. "It is so."

Gladness flooded her, even as a tightness rose in her throat. "I feared you would not truly be ready." She swallowed. "But I am happy 'tis done."

A tenderness filled his dark eyes, and he lifted their joined hands. "This as well?"

"Aye," she said, past the tightening of her throat. "But are you sure you do not regret having to take to wife a woman who carries another man's child?"

He leaned his forehead to hers. "What I did this day was of my own will."

Something in the timbre of his voice sent a shiver through her.

The nearby trill of a pipe heralded the beginnings of a hornpipe. "Elinor, come dance!" one of the men called.

Should she? In her rounded state? Grinning, Sees Far tipped his head toward the gathering, hopped to his feet, and helped her up. Dance she did, laughing, sometimes with the English and sometimes with Sees Far and the Kurawoten, the steps of hornpipes and jigs blending with the free dances of this land. They stopped only to eat and drink, and then she was in motion again.

How good it felt to allow the mirth and music to carry her away.

Chapter Twenty-Seven

Not until well after dark did Elinor, wilted at last, beg leave to retire for the night from the celebration in her and Sees Far's honor. Sees Far scooped up Ginny and carried her but also lent an arm for Elinor to lean upon as they made their way back. Just outside the circle of light from the community fire, Mary Mushaniq and Georgie materialized from the shadows and followed them, ghostlike, without a word.

Inside, Mushaniq fetched her rolled-up mat from the corner and spread it by the hearth. Georgie settled himself inside the front door, now closed. Elinor glanced at them both, but neither met her eye. With a little sigh, she hauled her very round and weary self up the stairs, where Sees Far had already taken Ginny.

Elinor saw her daughter settled in her customary place on the bed, then as she removed her coif and took down her hair, she peered uncertainly at Sees Far. He stood, arms folded, watching her nightly preparations with a look she could not interpret. "What are you thinking?" she whispered.

He gave her a small, secret smile. "It is not permitted for me to look at my wife?"

After being carried along with all the events of the day, how was she now to respond? Especially with the way he watched her—it should not unsettle her so, as he'd been in the habit for most of the past year. But this—this was different.

His dark eyes held a gleam, almost a hunger. She slowly set down her brush as he paced across the floor toward her. Her heart pattered—was this fear or something else entirely?

The latter seemed more terrifying.

He stopped less than a pace away and reached to pull a lock of her hair forward. "Is it permitted for me to touch you?"

She swallowed past the thickness of her throat. "Of course. I am your wife now. And you, my husband."

His gaze widened, and his voice took on a strange huskiness. "We cannot yet come together fully."

"That—is entirely up to you. Though it may be your people's custom, it is not ours."

He drew back a little. "No wonder Inqutish men are so brutish about women. They have no proper respect."

She chuckled and shook her head. He had taken her captive and seen her used so ill by Wanchese yet dared make such a statement? "That may be so."

With a deep breath, he took the brush off the table and motioned for her to turn around. With slow and gentle strokes, he worked the tangles from her hair.

"I have longed to do this since the day I first saw you," he whispered. "It truly does shine like sunlight."

She tipped her head and closed her eyes. How incredibly good it felt, despite the lingering ache in her feet and hips. She found herself smoothing her hands over her belly and swaying a little while he continued his ministrations.

"Does the baby pain you?" he asked softly.

"What? No. I am just weary. And he—she—is so big. I feel—so big."

He set the brush aside but continued stroking her hair. "You are—beautiful."

A broken laugh escaped her throat. "I hardly feel so."

"You are."

He bent close—she felt his warmth at her back, heard his inhale against her hair, and could barely resist the urge to sink against him.

They were husband and wife, but how far did that extend? Was it yet too soon after losing Ananias? It was certainly still too soon if he intended to honor his own scruples about her carrying and then nursing this child.

Her eyes burned. 'Twas not the strangest situation she had found herself in this past year. It should not be so difficult, but the differences in their people's ways seemed so beyond odd at times. Ananias had no such qualms when it came to intimacy between them, except for a time after Ginny's birth, but he was gentle with her in all other ways. Although it was not always so for other women with their own men in the day-to-day.

And this one—this wild warrior of the Sukwoten—just his breathing set her aflame.

Was it only her previous acquaintance with the pleasures of marriage that now made her wanton?

Gracious God, how can this be proper and right? Even after vows spoken between us?

"Bright as the sun, you are," he murmured, "enchanting as the moon—or all the stars in the sky."

His hand slid from her shoulder down her arm until his fingers entwined with hers, while the other slipped around her shoulders, his forearm across her upper chest, and from behind, he burrowed his face into the curve of her neck.

Mercy, but it was like that night, barely a week ago, when he'd nearly kissed her. She could not breathe. His very nearness made her dizzy.

"Sees Far—"

He turned her back around and for a moment only gazed into her eyes, his nose almost touching hers. On impulse, she reached up and drew the heron feathers from his hair, set them aside, then untied the knot at his nape. It tumbled halfway down his back, and as he had with hers, she drew it over his shoulder and ran the inky black length of it through her fingers. "Will you not at least sleep beside me on the bed this night?"

Something flared in his gaze. "I am not sure I trust myself to not—touch you." Lashes dipping over his shining eyes, he reached then to cup her belly. The babe rewarded him with a kick. "Oh!" he exclaimed, and she laughed.

With a sigh, he stepped back and swung away, rubbing his hands across his head.

It was far too soon. For both of them. She should braid her hair and climb into bed beside Ginny, already sleeping—

Sees Far loomed close again. "All else between us can wait, but—will you show me—*kiss*? As it is between husband and wife?"

Oh. My. Her insides had gone molten once more in a moment. She smiled up at him. "If I do, I cannot promise I would not want more."

He drew a deep breath and let it out in a rush, his eyes dark pools she could fall into. "I already want much more." Fingertips once more traced the curve of her belly. "Even though I should be repelled by the thought of taking you while you are with child."

Bending, he grazed her ear with his mouth, and every nerve within her sang. His full lips brushed across her cheek, and she turned her head—the most natural thing in the world—and pressed her mouth to his.

He kissed as if born to it. And when he lifted her in his arms and carried her to the bed, she surrendered with all of her heart.

Manteo paced the perimeter of the town, just inside the walls. Oh, how he missed being able to walk the woods and shores of the island. The silence in which to allow himself to hear God's voice, that he might know what actions to take next.

He loved these people, but the constant company wore upon him. Perhaps he could trade a turn with one of the guards at a corner of the palisade—

A voice floated to him out of the darkness, hushed but impassioned. "—and mark my words, if despite all her insistence of the child she carries being of Ananias's get, when she delivers, it bears the stamp of that savage."

Heat flooded Manteo's chest. There was the sound of a blow being struck, and then a second voice hissed, "Have a care how you speak of her! She is my family and a valued member of the community, no matter what her circumstance."

Silence rang louder than anything else could, after.

The dull thump of another blow. "Can you not agree to honor her for

Ananias's sake? At least he did marry her."

He in this case being Sees Far, of course.

Should Manteo reveal his presence and enter the fray or let the conversation play out to its natural end?

"Does marriage mean aught to the savages? I've witnessed them trading partners with the change of seasons."

Manteo started forward, but Chris—it could be no other—answered, "And are the English any better? In truth? Especially in London and at the court."

A wry smile curled his mouth. Good man, despite his faults. Manteo strolled toward them, adopting the most casual mien possible. "I thought we were past all this 'savage' nonsense."

Both Chris and the other man flinched, facing him. It was William Berde, a leader of the guards.

No surprise there, truly.

Before he could speak again, Manteo went on. "I am glad to know the truth of your heart, however. Our peoples still have much work before we are truly one. But unions such as this—Elinor and Sees Far, as well as Mushaniq and Georgie and the ones who married before them—are part of that. Elinor spoke earlier of her father, the governor. Will you not admit her words have merit?"

Berde's countenance fell, and his mouth worked.

"Did you not have confidence in Governor White? Or did you come thinking we would only make war on our enemies and not also try to live in peace?"

He seemed to consider that, but then his gaze flashed, defiant. "I would just have thought with all the Englishmen here needing wives, she'd have considered taking a man of her own kind. 'Twould be more fitting. Not that it isn't sweet and all how this Secotan brought her back."

"And what kind is that?" Chris growled.

"One who is more than barely Christian, at the very least."

Manteo folded his arms. "Are you jealous?"

Berde shifted, and something about Chris's stance drew Manteo's glance as well.

"She is a fine woman," Manteo went on, "and worthy of all admiration. But it is her choice. Do not begrudge her that. She and Sees Far have endured much together, and it is not entirely to be wondered at if she prefers him."

The guard spat. "More like he had already claimed her and 'twas guilt and shame that drove her to it."

These people, they still had much to learn about the ways of the People. But Manteo too must be patient.

"He had indeed claimed her but not in the way you think. Or is it only the coupling of bodies that matters to you?"

Berde did subside a little at that.

"Sees Far has promised to protect and provide for her," Manteo continued, "and had indeed before marriage vows were spoken. That is a noteworthy thing among my people—not common, but promises made are not taken lightly, and if he has spoken it, he will see it done to his last breath."

He knew that much, if nothing else, of a man in whose veins the blood of Granganimeo and Wyngyno/Pemisapan flowed.

Berde tucked his head and said no more. Manteo knew better than to think the matter settled, however.

"Now. It was my thought to go up on the lookout and watch for a while."

"I was just coming back from watch," Berde muttered, and after casting Chris a look, strode away.

Chris gave Manteo a nod and followed the man into the dark.

Suppressing a sigh, he continued to the lookout post and, calling out to announce his presence, climbed the ladder to the platform. After dismissing the guard for at least a short break, he settled in, arms folded, leaning against the posts, gazing out into the night. A light wind smelled of snow, and not a sound but the shush of leaves came to his ears.

He would be lying if he did not admit, at least to himself, how difficult it was to watch that oft-arrogant Sukwoten stake his claim on Elinor. During council, Manteo had not been sure whether allowing Sees Far to follow through on that bold offer was the wisest course of action, but judging by the looks exchanged between him and Elinor over the course of the day and evening, she was not unwilling. Or, she had determined not to betray any lingering reluctance before the assembly.

Manteo let out a long breath. It was no wonder half the men were besotted with her and jealous of Sees Far. He thought back on her quiet, graceful presence at the edges of his early meetings with John White in England. Her marriage to Ananias Dare and ready acceptance of the adventure of sailing over to Ossomocomuck.

And then that moment, when everyone had crowded on deck and to the rails for their first glimpse of what they called the New World, the way her big-with-child self had all but fallen into Manteo's arms.

She was darling and sweet and another man's wife. But he adored her—he and many other men. And at Ananias's untimely death, he'd have snatched up the opportunity to be her husband, but that was never afforded any of them. Instead, the Good God had provided a most unlikely protector in the guise of a former enemy.

Having seen for himself the genuineness of Sees Far's change of heart, Manteo could not find it in him to begrudge the man his joy in settling his claim before both sides of the community. But having to witness that this day and then the secret looks of longing between Georgie and his own daughter when they thought none else could see, he was feeling a good measure of his own longing.

Good and great God, I have not felt the need so much before now—but will You not provide me a wife as well? While Mushaniq is everything delightful in a daughter, I am not yet an old man and would welcome more children. And the delights of a wife too, of course.

Shines Like Sunset had brought with her a joy he expected never to recapture in anyone else. She truly shone so brightly none other could compare. But as Elinor had found it within her to accept another, and so soon after the death of a husband he knew she loved dearly, perhaps there was more joy yet to be found.

Waiting for that joy to come to him, however, was harder than he'd ever believed possible.

Chapter Twenty-Eight

E linor woke in the wee hours. The ache in her lower back and belly had come and gone all night but would no longer be ignored. Untangling herself from Sees Far's arms, chuckling at his grunt of protest, she eased off the bed, stepping over the bundled, sleeping form of Ginny in her trundle at its foot.

She padded to the window and pushed open the shutter just a crack. Outside, a steady snow fell, the wind a soft chush.

Yesterday, rain. Tonight, their first real snowfall.

'Twas so much like another night more than three years before, except the result of that labor lay slumbering across the room, and that night had been so sultry she could hardly bear the touch of her own garments. She chuckled again. No such trouble now.

Sees Far came abruptly awake and, rising, joined her at the window. When his arms came about her from behind, she leaned completely into his embrace.

"Why are you up?" he murmured.

"'Tis nearly time."

He yanked upright. "What?"

She laughed and tried to draw his arms around her again. "Not right away. At least, I do not think so."

But his eyes were wide with alarm. "I should go wake Mushaniq and run for Jane."

"Not yet." She slid her own arms around his middle until at last he relented and held her again. "I wish a few minutes with you first."

He swallowed so noisily she almost giggled. "It is not fitting for me to be present. Are you sure you will not go instead to the women's house?"

"It is fitting for this child to be born here, in the house Ananias built for us. And not unfitting for you to linger a bit with your wife as she prepares to welcome said child."

His arms tightened, fingers weaving through her hair, which he did have a special fascination for in the past days since their wedding.

"Many Inqutish customs I have bent to," he groused, "but this—I am not at all sure about."

She chuckled. "I promise, you shall not have to be here during the worst of it."

He drew back a little, taking her face in his hands. "It is not that. I know well that this is the work of women of which men have no part except—in the begetting."

Holding his gaze, she drew him down to her. How tall he was—but she was learning to delight in that as well. "And the next one I carry shall be yours."

He kissed her long and deeply, with a slow sensuousness that had her melting. Again.

How strange were the Inqutish customs surrounding birth—and, well, everything else. While Elinor seemed perfectly content to linger in his embrace, Sees Far could tell by the catch of her breathing that her labor was becoming more intense—and even if it was permitted for him to remain, he knew nothing of attending a birth.

And so he tore himself away, and after waking Mushaniq and Georgie, he ran to fetch Jane Stafford and the other women who had asked to be told when Elinor's time was come. A good thing too, because by the time Jane, Margery, and Timqua arrived, Elinor had progressed to pacing the floor, stopping now and then to breathe through a particularly difficult pain.

The women gently shooed him out, and he stood for a few moments watching Mushaniq as she tended the fire and set a pot of water to boil over it.

He was not sure he knew how to do any of this. Be a husband. Await his wife to give birth. Be a father to not only one but two little ones.

With a word to Georgie standing over against the wall, his face reflecting Sees Far's tumult of thought, he left the house. Outside, the snow continued to fall, and he simply stood, letting the quiet wrap him about and sink deep inside.

Georgie stepped up beside him. "How can the women bear it?"

Sees Far opened his mouth and pulled in a breath, letting the cold reach all the way into his chest, then held it. "I had never been given cause to think on that before."

Being uncertain of himself, of his path, was not a feeling familiar to him. As long as he could recall, he had enjoyed a certain sense of purpose. He did not like the lack of it now.

Out of the gloom came a man walking, outlined against the snow-fall, who spied them and angled their way. "Sá keyd winkan?" came the inquiry, as the speaker—Manteo—drew close enough to be recognized.

"It is Elinor's time. The other women are here, attending her."

Manteo smiled, including both him and Georgie. "And you are wondering where to go. Well, then. Pyas."

He led them to the smaller of the two houses set aside for the men with no wives, where the sitting area below had a fire burning and food and drink were laid out under cloths for the guards as they would come and go. Furnished with a cup and smoked wutapantam meat, they sat down before the hearth. They'd no uppowoc, but the yaupon was good and strong and the warmth of the flames comforting.

"I have wished since you came for more opportunity to talk with you," Manteo said, sipping. "So this is good."

"And what keeps you awake this night?"

Manteo offered a rueful smile. "The customary burdens of leading a people. Particularly those who are not sure they wish to live peaceably among themselves."

Something about his look and speech gave Sees Far pause. "Does this concern Elinor and me?"

"Some see it as such. But it is much wider, in truth." The Kurawoten shook his head and drank from his cup. "Well were you named, however, to so quickly ask that question."

Sees Far grunted. "It would be slow-witted of me to not ask."

Manteo only chuckled and drained his cup, then went to refill it. When he returned to his seat, Sees Far gave Georgie a sidelong glance before addressing Manteo once more. "We have need at some point to discuss what to do with this one."

"So we do. But perhaps not here."

Sees Far understood that without even asking. The fine points of hus-kanaw were kept strictly secret even among those who had undergone the rite, and not a breath of what was to come was to be spoken to the candidates.

Georgie yawned and stretched. "I could take myself upstairs to sleep, if that would help."

Sees Far regarded him with some amusement. "You are able to sleep? Wait until it is your woman giving birth."

As intended, Georgie grinned at the ribbing, then went up the stairs.

Manteo's expression had gone very grave.

"He will be ready when the time comes," Sees Far said softly.

"I do not doubt that."

"What is it, then?"

Manteo sipped, wagging his head slowly. At last he set the cup aside and, folding his arms, fixed Sees Far with a look. "I have held back from asking you what you know, or guess, at the intentions of Wanchese and others. But I think such a thing is necessary."

"Ah." Sees Far wrapped his hands around his cup and squinted at the fire for a moment. "I wish I could say he will be content to let your people live in peace without making war upon you again sooner or later."

"That is my thought as well."

"Would it be better, then, to go to war at the beginning of spring before the youths are sent on huskanaw or after?"

"It truly is a matter to carefully consider. My heart tells me that the youths need huskanaw beforehand, but it will do us no good if the town is in peril while that is happening."

Manteo nodded. "For huskanaw, what do you feel is needful?" He pitched his voice lower for that question, doubtless mindful of anyone who might be listening.

"What was it for you?" Sees Far asked, also softly.

"On the island? The women carried out their customary mourning while the elder men prepared the bitter teas, which we drank and purged before going over to Wococon for four days and nights of fasting and praying." He shot Sees Far a look. "I have heard talk of the Powhatan making the youth drink to the point of raving insanity, during which time they keep them contained in shelters prepared for that purpose. Then when they begin to recover, they are treated as newborn children, fresh to the community. That any sign of recognition of mothers or other family as they rejoin their people will result in a repeat of the process." He snorted and took up his cup again. "It is no wonder they are considered out of their minds with fierceness."

Sees Far chuckled. "And no wonder they consider the Kurawoten to be so mild and gentle."

Manteo peered at him. "Do you think the harsher path necessary for Georgie?"

"Mahta. But it was something halfway in between for us who lived mostly on the mainland. It likely would be of value to him to undergo something more strenuous than what you were subjected to."

The other man sipped thoughtfully, then nodded. "There is merit in your words."

"Was there any doubt there would be?" Sees Far smirked.

Manteo only laughed.

At last he sobered. "If there is anything to alter, it is our old way of giving honor to the spirits."

Sees Far nodded thoughtfully.

"If we are men remade by the blood and Spirit of Christ, then we should approach huskanaw from that place. It does not make us Inqutish to accept God's Son—but it completes us, Tunapewak, in ways we lacked before.

"And more than this. . .as we fortify ourselves for huskanaw by

219

preparing in the body, we should take great care to prepare in our spirits as well. If the spirits we served before are unhappy about us no longer seeking their favor, then our youths may be vulnerable to them in ways we were not."

Sees Far found he had no reply to that.

Manteo fixed him with a look and another wry smile. "This is a momentous thing, though, whether you realize or not. Just as I was the first of the Kurawoten to believe in Christ, you may be the first of the Sukwoten. Or at least, what I consider true belief. Those fumbling attempts of Rafe Lane and those with him to bring our people to this faith do not count—with the exception of Thomas Harriot, who did have genuine care for our people and wished us to understand more perfectly what it was than even we sought to know."

He could only sit back and marvel at it all.

Just when Sees Far was tempted to roll up in his mantle next to the fire and doze, the outer door opened, and with a little swirl of snow, Mushaniq stepped inside. Both he and Manteo rose to greet her.

Weariness etched her young face, but her eyes were alight. "Elinor has just now given birth to another girl. She wishes for you to come."

All thought of sleep fled. He suddenly felt an unaccountable shyness. "Are you certain?"

"That the baby is a girl or that Elinor is asking for you?" Mushaniq grinned. "Kupi to both." She looked around while giving her father a quick embrace. "Where is Georgie?"

"Upstairs. I can get him for you—"

"Mahta, let him sleep." She laughed softly and beckoned. "You should both come. Elinor would be glad of it."

And so they followed her out into snow that had fallen thick and deep, though dawn was yet a short time away, and back to the house where light still burned both upstairs and down. The celebration could be heard even through the closed shutters above.

Sees Far stepped across the threshold and found himself trembling.

Manteo slanted him a look. "A new creation in Christ, a husband, and a new father in just a few suns. No small accomplishment."

He opened his mouth to reply, but his mouth was too dry for speech.

"Pyas!" Mushaniq scolded from the stairs, and he ran lightly up them.

The room that had been so recently a shadowed haven for him and Elinor alone now blazed with candles, filled with the chatter of women's voices and a heavy scent that could only be afterbirth. And then, to his ears came the most delicate cry. He stood frozen inside the door until Elinor looked up from where she sat propped in the bed and reached out an arm to him. The complete joy in her face stole away his breath.

Ginny came bouncing off the bed and threw herself against his leg as he approached. "Sees Fa', look! We have a baby!"

"So I have heard!" he said to the women's laughter around him.

He thought there was nothing further of his heart that could be stolen, between Elinor and the charm of little Ginny, but when Elinor held up the tiny bundle and he glimpsed the sweet face, he was completely undone. Wide, blinking eyes and rounded cheeks, tiny pink lips, and wisps of hair already the color of sunlight.

"Would you like to hold her?"

Breathless, he tucked the bundle into the crook of his arm. "Welcome, little Sunlight."

Elinor laughed softly, pale eyes shining. "Her name is Johanna Elizabeth. For her father and mine, and her Majesty the Queen. But Sunlight will do as well."

"Another week, and she'd have been born on Christmastide," Jane said. "Although I truly thought she'd come before now."

"They come when they will," Elinor said with another chuckle.

Her voice was rough and raw. Sees Far peered at her more closely. "Are you well?"

As he perched on the edge of the bed, she reached up to caress his cheek. "Yes. It was swift and not easy, but she is here and we are well. And Ginny miraculously slept through it all."

Chapter Twenty-Nine

Perhaps it was that she'd never cared to notice before, but this particular baby's birth seemed the most momentous Mushaniq had ever known. And the joy that bathed them all in the days after—even Sees Far, stern and brooding warrior that he was, laughed so frequently she had to look to make sure it was truly him.

Nohsh remained subdued, although his melancholy ebbed during the moments when he also held little Sunlight—for so they had all taken to calling her after Sees Far had spoken it.

Her official naming day—a *christening*, the Inqutish word—was held half a moon after her birth, with the entire town once again gathered in the meetinghouse. Sees Far stood beside Elinor in the middle, lifting the baby and pronouncing her full Inqutish name—even Mushaniq was impressed at his pronunciation—before adding, "And her milk name shall be Sunlight!"

Did the Inqutish realize the significance of what Sees Far had done? This baby was truly the child of Elinor and Ananias Dare, her first husband, and so it was declared before the gathering, but for Sees Far to present her and speak her name was an honor given only to a father.

Not unfitting, given the circumstances, but so strange. How was it this Sukwoten even yet drew breath among them when none of her people had ever missed an opportunity to take vengeance? Until, of course, the Inqutish had come with their beliefs. Now they seemed all infected by it.

She was still not comfortable with this idea of *forgive*. Some days, she felt she almost understood. Others, it felt too much like simply brushing aside the hurt, that what the person had done was nothing. And Mushaniq could not accept that Ananias's dying was nothing—that Georgie's father's death was nothing. And while she was as happy as anyone else over Elinor being safely home, it still burned that they all carried on as if it were.

And the way Sees Far had taken it upon himself to prepare Georgie for huskanaw—what did he intend, truly? How did they know this was not an elaborate plan to destroy them all from the inside? Even Nohsh trusted in Sees Far now. Ever since that night Sunlight was born and Mushaniq had entered the men's house and found the two of them sitting before the fire together, they had been frequent companions.

It baffled Mushaniq to observe it. Two that she loved most—Nohsh and Elinor—completely under this man's spell. And yet she could not fault the intense passion evident in Sees Far's instruction of Georgie. Nor his generosity toward her, and certainly not his devotion to Elinor and her girls—although for someone who had so lectured Georgie on his obligation to restrain himself in respect for Mushaniq's state, he seemed woefully free with his affections toward Elinor. Too many times she happened to glance aside or walk into a room and catch them kissing—which somehow was even more shocking and scandalous to her now than when she was still a child. Ever since Georgie had introduced her to that initially awkward but sweet intimacy—

Her cheeks warmed, and the babe inside her gave a little flutter.

This little one grew by the week. Mushaniq marveled at the changes in her own body.

What would it be like to hold her own baby? To finally be able to call Georgie her husband? To prove to the entire town—and Nohsh—that she was truly a woman as well and yet had not needed to run after some of the nonsense the other girls had?

Then she thought of all the conditions placed upon them, and her heart fell again.

In so many ways, she was as dependent upon that rogue Sukwoten as Georgie and Elinor. And she liked it not at all.

1591

Spring was nearly upon them. The first green things had emerged, the first flowers appearing.

Sees Far reflected how, a year ago, he had anticipated spring for a much different reason. Now, the woman he had obsessed over was his wife, with two tiny girl-children in his care as well. His heart had never been so full.

And yet as the weather warmed, he felt an increasing urgency to see the final preparations made for huskanaw and to secure Georgie's place in it.

He took Manteo and a handful of the Kurawoten elders, and they walked out from the town to talk about it all. "A conversation such as this one begs a fire and uppowoc, and yet we need secrecy."

They found a place where great, fallen pine trees made a convenient place to sit in a glade open enough to see whether any made their approach. Uppowoc was duly shared—Manteo brought some—and Towaye passed around a gourd of sweetened drink. Perhaps this would not be as difficult as he had expected.

Georgie was awakened before dawn by a hand on his shoulder. He opened his eyes, startling at the sight of a native warrior bending over him, face painted and unrecognizable. His breath and heartbeat seized, and then he remembered this was the morning huskanaw would begin.

It was Sees Far, of course. Without a word, he led Georgie out into the dewy, mist-laced morning, past the meetinghouse and men's houses, and to the blacksmith's shop. A fire burned there, and an array of tools and earthen pots lay upon a low table.

Georgie was made to sit, and Sees Far took up a small pair of shears. He knew not what to expect but held himself very still. With a yank, Sees Far loosened Georgie's hair and began to tug and snip. Out of the corners of his eyes, Georgie saw whole locks of his hair falling to the floor.

"By the time I am finished with you," Sees Far said gruffly, "you will be able to pass as a youth of the People. Except for your hair and eyes." He laughed quietly, hands still working. "Your skin is so pale."

He'd painted his own in irregular patches of black and red.

Georgie felt the tug of a section in the back, across his nape, being smoothed down and left loose. Then Sees Far gave attention to the very top—lift and snip, lift and snip—and more closely to the sides, clipping very close to the scalp. With swift, sure movements, he laid aside the shears and took up what looked like a razor.

"Hold very still," he commanded.

He smoothed something—an ointment?—across the sides of Georgie's head and followed it with smooth strokes of the blade. Was he shaving that portion?

At last he set the blade aside and, taking up an implement Georgie could not see, tilted Georgie's chin upward. "Again, do not move."

Tiny pricks assaulted Georgie's upper lip. He gritted his teeth and sucked in a breath. Sees Far smirked and kept working.

It was then Georgie recalled the practice of Croatoan men to shave the hair on the sides of their head and to pluck the hairs of their sparse beards. Fortunately for Georgie, his had not yet thickened to what he knew it might be once he gained a few years, if the fullness of Da's beard was anything to judge by.

At last Sees Far finished and stood back to study his work, then gave a single nod and gathered a bundle lying off to the side. "Pyas," he said and led Georgie out into the early morning.

The town was already awake, with the large community fire being laid and cooking fires lit here and there. Greeting no one and receiving none in return, though he garnered not a few stares, Georgie followed Sees Far around the perimeter of the palisade, through the opening and past the guards, and into the eerily hushed forest beyond. Not down the usual path but still toward the river.

Georgie reached up to explore what Sees Far had done. As he suspected, the sides of his head were shaved bare, with a short crest extending front to back over the top of his head and a portion hung loose. His cheeks had been plucked bare, skin still stinging from Sees Far's ministrations.

On the riverbank, when Sees Far motioned him into the water, Georgie stripped, leaving his clothing on the bank, and waded in. He grimaced at the mud between his toes and the leeches he knew lurked there, but dipped himself and scrubbed quickly. The cool water was soothing to both his scalp and face. Back on the bank, he picked off the two slimy, clinging creatures that had attached.

Sees Far stood ready with deerskin, which he helped Georgie fasten about his hips with an otterskin behind, covering his buttocks. While Georgie stood trying not to shiver at the morning chill and unaccustomed near-nakedness, Sees Far tied up the back of his hair, then smeared his skin with white paint head to toe.

At last he gathered up Georgie's discarded clothing and the paint pot and again inspected his work. "You will now appear as a Kurawoten among the other youths. Last night Manteo and I informed the Inqutish elders that you would be joining the others in huskanaw. We do not know whether they will try to prevent you. But you may have to choose."

"I am determined to see this through," Georgie said.

Sees Far gave a nod. "Let us return to the town, then, and join the feast."

Mushaniq had been awake since long before dawn, listening to the sounds in the room above as Elinor tended the baby. Sees Far had gone out long ago to prepare but had not yet come to wake Georgie—who still slept on a mat by the hearth while she now used a cot set up in the corner.

Last night Georgie had held her and kissed her. It was the last time they were allowed to embrace, even touch, until huskanaw was complete. Until then, the baby inside would be a reminder, flutters grown to kicking and rolling.

He—or she—was active now, dancing before the day had even begun. She smoothed her hands over her belly, marveling and yet in so much turmoil over whether Georgie would succeed. It was not that she doubted he could do so. But a cold fear gripped her and would not subside.

She curled on her side, back to the wall, watching through her lashes. When the moment came, it was no less terrifying to know the tall, painted warrior who soundlessly opened the door and strode across the floor was Sees Far and not some unknown enemy come to steal Georgie away.

A hand on the shoulder, and Georgie woke with an intake of breath, then rose and followed Sees Far out.

Mushaniq surrendered to the burning of her eyes and the ache of her throat and let herself weep. Later, she would join the other women in public lament of the death of boyhood that must take place for them to become men, but her tears were in this moment for a different cause entirely.

Before long, Elinor came down the stairs, little Sunlight tied across her back and Ginny following behind. "We should go help now with cooking," she said, her voice hushed although they were all awake.

The other women, just beginning their preparations, greeted them with gladness. Mushaniq threw herself into the work and tried not to keep glancing about for a glimpse of Georgie. It was too soon yet.

A hush hung over them all, however. Besides Georgie, Two Feathers and at least three others would be presented as candidates, so nearly all the women here were family or had close ties to at least one of those being sent out. And beyond that, it was a most solemn occasion, necessary to the continuation of their people and ways.

At the great fire, the Kurawoten men began to gather, painted with various designs in both red and white, not the fearsomely solid black and red of Sees Far. Had he borrowed that from the Powhatan or Mangoac? It did not look like what the Kurawoten had always done or even what she had seen of the Sukwoten and others—not that she had seen many, only those who came to visit the islands.

She realized with a start that Nohsh stood among them, dressed only in the deerskin and otterskin of their people, copper and pearls adorning his ears, neck, and wrists, his hair trimmed and crested and pulled back as the other men. Bare-chested but lacking paint, in keeping with the custom of weroances.

He turned and caught her gaze with a smile as she crossed the open space toward him. "Sá keyd winkan, Nunutánuhs?"

"I am well, Nohsh, and you?"

He hugged her, eyes shining, then spread his arms. "Do you approve?"

She laughed even through the heaviness of her heart. "You appear every bit the Kurawoten weroance. Although, what will the Inqutish think?" She tipped her head toward where several of them stood, observing the proceedings with obvious apprehension.

He raised an eyebrow. "The Inqutish have had plenty of days to shine. Today it is the turn of the Kurawoten and of all Tunapewak. Today we show how the old ways may be carried out in obedience to Christ—perhaps in even more fullness than we have known before."

That was an intriguing thought—but she would not admit so to him and only gave him the barest nod.

He stepped closer, his gaze suddenly intent. "I know you still question and struggle. Do not fear. The Good God will lead Georgie through this."

That, she truly had no response to. "I hope so with all my heart," she said at last.

His hand came up to caress her hair and cheek.

"I must return and help with the food," she murmured and darted away.

She needed to save her tears for later.

The first of the food was ready about the same time that five figures—boys in simple kilts and otterskins, their skin and hair painted completely white—were led to the fire and arrayed before it. Mushaniq set aside the platter she carried of roasted meat and stared, heart pounding. Where was Georgie? All these were Kurawoten youth—

Then one moved slightly and turned his head in a familiar way—and Georgie's pale blue eyes met hers. She half covered her face in shock. His sand-gold hair was unrecognizable with the traditional crest, shaving, and binding and drenched in white paint.

Beneath the same white paint, he gave a tiny smile, and she lowered her hands to her breast but could not otherwise move.

Surely he could not fail to gain the approval of her grandmother and aunts, arrayed so. He must gain their approval.

He more than held his own among the other youth both in stature and form. His shoulders were as broad, his limbs as long and well formed, and there was no softness in him at all. A spark sizzled all the way from her toes to her scalp. Had he grown taller and she'd failed to notice these past moons?

Elinor stepped close beside her. "I'd not have recognized him."

"Nor I," Mushaniq murmured.

"He already carries himself as a warrior."

Mushaniq nodded.

Five older men stepped up to face the youths, one of them Sees Far with his bold black and red paint. Nohsh turned to the gathering and waved for silence. "These youths are presented this day for huskanaw, the ritual that will determine their placement in the community as men. We will feast and dance on their behalf before sending them away for their proving—four days in the forest to fast and pray and seek God for their individual paths.

"As each of them has prepared for this in body and mind and will be further prepared, it is very important that they prepare in heart and spirit as well. The Holy Scriptures tell us that *Riapoke* walks about like a roaring lion, seeking whom he might devour. And so each one of these youths must make sure they place themselves under the protection of Christ before they go out."

Mushaniq could see the ripple of comprehension and interest in the Inqutish at those words, the murmuring between them. They had not expected this—and how wise and cunning of Nohsh to perceive this was something they needed to hear if they were to approve of this most secret of ceremonies. It was almost enough to make her believe for herself.

Riapoke—the deity to whom all that was tragic or senseless was attributed. One of many they had been taught they should appease.

But what if it was true that rather than appease him and the other spirits, it was as simple as placing oneself under the authority of the Highest God and the One sent, by the testimony of the Inqutish and their book, as His representative?

She wanted to run away and find a quiet spot to think, but there was no escape from the obligation to stand and witness this to its end. In this, at least, she wished she were still a child.

As Nohsh lifted his arms and in a loud voice began to pray, alternating between the tongues of the People and the Inqutish, the little one inside her kicked, as if reminding her of the reason for her resolve. Kupi, she would stay, and watch, and when the time came, see Georgie off with all the dignity he deserved.

Chapter Thirty

T he day had hardly begun, and Manteo's heart was near to bursting
with pride.

The two of them were unspeakably darling—Georgie, standing among
the Kurawoten youths as if he were truly one of them, and Mushaniq,
watching from a short distance away, deeply affected and yet unmoving.
The two of them had eyes for none but each other, and it was doubtful
either heard much of his admonishment and prayers. But it mattered
little—he would make sure to repeat what was most needful when they
were finally sent off.

The youths remained standing as the feast began, and Manteo
motioned to their attendants to prepare portions for each of them, then
surveyed the gathering. The women tended to their usual work of bringing
out the food, while the younger children scampered about—from what he
could tell, most of the Inqutish women had joined the effort, though the
men stood off to the side, simply watching. And most of them had indeed
showed up to observe.

They still wore expressions of concern, although their initial apprehension appeared to have faded. Please God that they recalled and heeded
his quiet warnings not to be troubled at anything they saw or heard. Manteo would interpret all that he could, but some of this simply could not be
explained. Not yet, anyway.

Chris and Roger Bailie stood nearest, arms folded and their bearded faces grave. As one, they stared at Manteo as if they'd never seen him before—and in truth, he was sure he'd never appeared before them looking so completely as one of his own people. Not since the earliest days of their landing in England, the first time, when he and Wanchese had decked themselves in their full finery for the benefit of Queen Elizabeth and her attendants. He recalled the looks of shock and whispering among the Inqutish then—did they truly see him so differently because he had appareled himself differently?

They would simply have to observe and understand, in this case.

Georgie did not have to force himself to eat. His belly had been growling for hours. He tried not to think about what it would feel like to fast for four whole days. Water would be allowed, of course, they were told—but otherwise?

Prayer and fasting, Manteo had said. To focus on God. That was a worthy enough aim if not entirely comfortable.

What had God to do with Georgie, except to leave him orphaned in this land? At odd moments, it seemed almost a mockery that he had become enthralled with this Kurawoten girl and. . .

And yet, there she had stood and even now flitted in and out of the crowd, so lovely it made his throat ache.

After the food came dancing. It alternated between stomping and chanting, calling down blessings and strength for Georgie and the other boys, to the rhythm of their gourd rattles and clapping, and nearly inarticulate cries and howls. At last the English musicians, not to be outdone, joined in with drum and whistle, providing the wildest sound he had heard yet from those instruments.

The music then alternated between tunes and songs Georgie knew as English and those he'd come to know from the past years of living side by side both here and on the island. It came as a shock to him that he could recognize those as readily now as the ones they'd brought across the ocean.

No less of a shock was it, as the morning wore on, to realize that the

English musicians had joined in—for him. The entire town had turned out by now for him. His eyes burned to think upon it.

Now and again, Mushaniq danced past him, her form still lithe and sinuous despite her rounding middle. Her gaze flashed to his, then away, her expression never changing as she stomped and kicked and swung her arms in time to the fierce beat.

This girl—mahta, young woman—his own *crenepo* as her people said it—displaying her passion and approval for all to see.

About midday, as the sun stood at its highest, Manteo stepped forward and again motioned for quiet. "It is time. The youths will be led out, given their final instructions, and subjected to their last cleansing before facing the death of their childhood."

Though he knew by now this wording was customary and necessary, still it struck a strange dread into Georgie's heart. In the next moment, however, it was followed by a surge of resolve. Perhaps this was what needed to happen. He should die to the past. To England, to the horror of his father's brutal slaying, to all he had known before.

If any man be in Christ, he is a new creature. . .

The scripture came to his mind unbidden.

A sudden outcry startled him into awareness. He had missed Manteo's final pronouncement, and the women had begun their traditional show of mourning.

The rise and fall of their wailing and sobbing scraped across his nerves and lifted every hair upon his body. Nothing in this moment would convince him that their distress was not genuine.

God. . .oh God. . .

He had long ago lost the habit of crying out to the Almighty, let alone formal prayer outside of church gatherings. But he could not deny the present impulse to do so.

The boys beside him were being herded out of the gathering area. Before he could move, Mushaniq was there before him—just out of arm's reach, so he'd not be tempted to touch her—with very real tears pouring down her cheeks and her entire form trembling. "Come back to me," she said at last, very low, but most emphatically.

He was not permitted to reply. A single, hard nod was all he could offer.

"Pyas!" Sees Far growled, and Mushaniq whisked herself out of the way.

Out of the town and roughly up the river they were led. They walked for perhaps a quarter hour, then at a particular creek, they turned sharply inland and followed the smaller stream away from the main river. At last they came upon a camp where two Kurawoten men, painted as the others, waited beside a fire.

The men rose to meet them. "Welcome to your deaths!" called out one, who Georgie thought he recognized as Towaye.

"May you meet it bravely," the other added.

They were made to sit around the fire, facing it but so far away they could barely feel its warmth. Georgie suppressed a shiver. He'd been warned already not to show weakness, but would they give allowance for bodily responses he could not control? He had a feeling he was about to find out.

Behind them, their attendants unpacked the bundles they'd carried. Someone produced cups, filled from a large pot set into the fire, a murky-looking concoction that smelled no more trustworthy than it appeared when Sees Far placed a cup into his hands.

"It is the time now to drink the black drink," intoned the elder of the two Kurawoten who had been waiting at the fire.

Manteo stepped up beside him, his gaze meeting that of each one of them in turn. Georgie shivered again when it speared him and held. "Before you do—before you embark on this journey—you must make sure you have placed all your trust in the Christ, God's Son. Have you done this? Do you believe?"

Georgie jerked a nod. "Kupi. I believe."

Manteo repeated the question with each of the other boys, and all responded similarly.

"It is good," he said. "Drink it all and quickly."

Georgie did, nearly gagging at the first taste, but forced himself to take it in big gulps. Wiping his mouth, he set the cup aside. By the expressions on the other boys' faces, they found it as revolting as he.

His stomach gave a lurch, and the forest around him shifted as well. Across the fire, Two Feathers put a hand over his face with an obvious shudder—or was that only the effect of the drink on his eyes? Because the trees definitely rippled, mimicking the motion of the flames before them.

Two Feathers turned from the fire and crawled away, but he did not get far before his body convulsed and everything he'd drunk—and eaten—came back up. Georgie's own innards heaved in sympathy, but he pushed it down. He would not humble himself in this wise—

A second boy joined Two Feathers in vomiting, then a third. But what was this? Their attendants were, incredibly, offering words of encouragement.

A cramp, then a wave of nausea, shook him. He shoved to his feet and ran away from the fire, away from the others, before his body gave in to the urge that would not be denied. He bent, heaving, dimly registering all the others doing the same behind him, then stumbled a bit farther before repeating the process.

The third time, nothing would come up. The forest danced about him. With a groan, he collapsed on his side in the leaves, then shut his eyes to the growing dark.

He woke—how long later he could not say—to a hand upon his brow and a softly spoken exhortation to drink again. His head pounded with the effort to come upright, but he accepted the liquid from the cup put to his lips until he tasted once again the foul brew of before.

"Mahta. You must drink. Even if only a little."

Oh. . .God. . .they truly are trying to slay me.

Again with the vomiting, this time where he lay because he had no strength to move. How long he moved in and out of darkness, the flames of the fire very far away and the figures of men and trees swaying alike, he could not say. Day passed into night, he was sure. And every time he woke, his tormentor plied him with more of that cursed *black drink*.

This is the way of huskanaw, the voice insisted, hushed. *You do this for*

Mushaniq. For your child. Do not let your courage fail.

Mingled in with it all were prayers, which seemed strangest of all—that someone would pray over him even while they poisoned him—for he was sure now that was what had taken place.

Do you follow the Christ? came the voice again.

But his tongue seemed tied.

Do you believe?

Did he? What did he truly think and feel about all that he had heard in the Church and from Da over the years?

Are you a follower of the Light or the darkness? You will not survive this if you do not determine to follow the Light. The spirits of the land will rend you in pieces.

The whispers made no sense, and yet they lingered in his thoughts, like mist off the river or smoke inside a longhouse.

God. . .are You truly still there? Do You see, do You hear? Am I yet Your child?

The dark of night was a fearsome thing indeed. Curled on her bed, Mushaniq stared into it. After the briefest of slumbers, sleep had fled entirely.

She and Elinor were alone tonight with the girls, and to say she missed the presence of the men—mahta, it was more than that. The house creaked, and the shadows whispered without even Sees Far here.

If she'd thought her fears terrible when Nohsh had gone away, this was so much worse. If Georgie did not return—if Sees Far had taken him away to see him slain—if she and Elinor were left destitute, without care even from the town because Elinor had taken a Sukwoten to husband— Mushaniq had heard the whispers from all sides. She'd had her own suspicions aplenty, but to hear the others say it? It only made her wish to strike someone.

And she—her grandmother and aunties had yet to say much about her coming baby. Nor the Inqutish women, with the exception of Jane Stafford, the *midwife.* Mushaniq fully intended to give birth in the women's house, but there was something oddly comforting about the tall, angular Inqutish woman.

The baby kicked and rolled all night. She hoped that meant all was well.

At last, near dawn, she fell into an uneasy slumber.

Dawn came slowly, thin and pale, full of a fog so thick Georgie was sure it had issued from his very dreams. Shivering, he came to wakefulness and sat up to find Sees Far crouched nearby, relaxed but watchful.

He nodded sharply and rose to his feet. "Pyas."

Georgie followed—or attempted to—but slowly. Every fiber of his being ached. His mouth tasted acrid and yet felt stuffed with cloth. He managed to drag himself to his feet and stumble after Sees Far.

To the creek they went, and here the water burbled over rocks and sand. Sees Far waded in, shedding his garments and gear and tossing them to the streambank. Georgie did the same.

The cold water was bracing and did much to both clear his head and ease the aches. Despite the shock and shivering it sent through him, he found the deepest of the pools and sank into it.

A stream of white flowed away from him as the water washed him clean of the paint. Was that also meant to be symbolic, along with the vile drink they'd consumed last night and the strangeness?

He scrubbed at his scalp and skin, stopped to gulp several handfuls of the clear water, and finally emerged, dripping and out of breath, while Sees Far, washed similarly clean, waited for him on the bank.

As he dressed himself again in the Kurawoten garments provided him, he realized no one else was in sight.

Sees Far's intensity commanded his attention. "The black drink has purged your insides of all that is unclean, and the stream has washed your skin. It is time for you to journey into the forest and seek God."

Chapter Thirty-One

Mushaniq woke far after sunrise, her head still aching but her belly crying for sustenance. Although the house was quiet, a platter of smoked fish and apon lay on the hearth.

Elinor must have left it for her and taken the girls so she could sleep. At least, she hoped it was for her, because she fell upon it and half devoured it nearly without thought.

She slowed, listening to the sounds of the dwelling. Nothing amiss in daylight. Comforting, even.

And where had daybreak found Georgie?

She finished the food, retied her hair, poked about the house for any tasks she should do, and finally with a sigh, forced herself to walk outside.

It was a beautifully perfect spring day, with remnants of mist clinging at the edges of the town and over the forest beyond. The muted buzz of town life seemed a strange contrast to the tumult of yesterday's celebration—but they'd all been weary last night, and she felt she could easily return to her cot and sleep again. That is, if she could sleep and somehow evade the darkness of the night to come.

She found Elinor over by the women's house, gathered with Grandmama and aunties and others. They all looked up as she approached and smiled and greeted her.

Was it possible that Georgie's embarking upon huskanaw had shifted their hearts toward the two of them already?

"We were just talking," Timqua said, "of how you have not long before your little one might be born."

She dipped her head in an uncertain nod and went to sit, a little ungracefully, beside Elinor. Her body ached in unexpected places—likely because she'd joined so energetically in the dancing yesterday.

"Have you given thought to who will attend you?"

"Mahta." It was not completely truthful, of course, but she still stung at their lack of acknowledgment until this point.

She did not miss the exchanged glance between Timqua and Elinor. "She is welcome to give birth in my house," Elinor said.

Timqua answered quickly, "It is the way of our people to give birth in the women's house. But she has need of certain things." She looked at Mushaniq thoughtfully. "Has Georgie brought you gifts yet?"

Elinor was just as quick. "He is preparing to do so but wishes things to happen in proper order." As the other women sniffed, she smiled a little and added, "As much as is possible."

Grandmama gave a little sigh. "Then we will wait to see what he does when he returns from huskanaw." She eyed Mushaniq as well, but there was affection in her gaze. "Hopefully, this little one will wait as well."

The forest was cool while the sun was warm. Georgie went slowly, following the stream, letting himself absorb the sound of birdsong and squirrels chattering, of waterfowl calling from not far away.

He felt light and immaterial, completely poured out, yet strangely at one with the world around him. He walked as if in a dream, bathing in the sunlight slanting down through the trees, forming ribbons in the remnants of mist.

In this moment, the past was far away. Even Mushaniq and the babe she carried seemed part of another life, that belonging to someone else, or only the bits of a dream he'd had long ago.

"Do not venture too far," Sees Far had said. That at least he recalled. *"Find a place to hide, where you have water nearby, where you are safe. You are too pale, too obviously not Tunapewak, and I would have you survive this."*

He would need to find a place soon, and before he encountered any towns that could be hostile.

"The Spanish also still traverse these lands."

Georgie had seen the Spanish—at least he was fairly certain he had, on a long-ago and faraway voyage from England to the West Indies and thus to the New World. He had no desire to see more.

"You are yet young, and if you are discovered, it is likely you would be taken either as a slave or adoption rather than slain. Stay alive, if you can. But if you die, die well, holding firm to your courage."

'Twas not a pleasant thought either, but here—surrounded by deep forest—he could not stretch his mind to comprehend it.

At last he found a likely place, a thicket with several trees growing so closely about he thought it must be a single tree with multiple trunks. Indeed, a closer examination revealed that this was so. In the center of the trunk base was a hollow, just big enough for him to fold himself into. Animal scat, probably arohcun, lay in the bottom, and after he'd cleaned that out as best as he could with a large section of bark, he filled the area with leaves.

Unrolling the bundle Sees Far had handed him just before sending him off, he found a waterskin, mahkusun, a simple knife—one of Georgie's own—and containing all, a deerskin mantle, hair on the inside for warmth. A little distance away from his nest, he filled the skin, slipped the mahkusun on his feet, and with the mantle about his shoulders, made his way back.

Tucked snugly into the cradle of tree trunks, he pulled the mantle over his head, curled up, and fell asleep.

Sleep crept in upon Mushaniq early on the second night and stole her away. But the dark proved even more insidious than before, pressing in upon her dreams.

First it was Grandmama—although this woman was unlike the grandmother she had always known. Yet Mushaniq knew it was her because dreams could be tricky and strange that way. Grandmama sat upon her mat on the raised platform in the longhouse that was her own, shoulders bare and strong, draped with strands of copper and pearls of impossible wealth. "You, oh daughter of my son! What is it you think to accomplish, leaving the ways of your people? Come back!"

"But I have not left the ways, Nunohum! I am faithful. I am still here!"

The woman rose, leaning on a staff that suddenly appeared as a bow, herself as muscled and tall as a warrior—no, taller. "You have clung to the ways of the Inqutish! To that boy who is too weak to survive huskanaw. To his seed which has taken root in you."

Mushaniq trembled. "What must I do?"

"You must take yourself out to the water. To yapám. And there let this seed go."

She began to cry. "But I cannot go to yapám! I am here, land-bound. And—and it is a child, not merely a seed! I do not wish to let it go!"

"Then your weak boy will die. Life is sacrifice. You must give up one thing if you wish to keep another."

In the dream, she fell to the floor of the longhouse, weeping without consolation. Hands gripped her—a pair of other women warriors, dragging her outside...

"Mushaniq! *Mary!* Wake up!"

She opened her eyes to the sound of a thin keening coming from her own throat, which was so tight it felt as though someone had a hand around it. But only Elinor bent over her, concern etched upon her face.

She sat up, gasping for breath.

"What is it, Nuhsimuhs?" Elinor had taken to calling her *little sister* in the same way Sees Far had. "Were you dreaming?"

It all came back to her in a rush, and with it, a wave of weeping such as she had just dreamed. Elinor gathered her in her arms, settling beside her on the cot. "There. All will be well, I promise—"

Mushaniq shook her head, choking on the sobs. "It is not—I dreamed—Nunohum told me—at least I thought it was her—that I am foolish in trying to hold on to both Georgie and this child, and now I must lose one or the other." Her whole body shuddered. "She said—she said I must go to the ocean and—let his seed go—in order to give him strength on huskanaw and bring him back."

The distress tore through her again and came out of her in the form

241

of yet another wail—one she could not hold back.

Elinor embraced her even more tightly. "Oh, my dear one. Do not listen. It was only a dream."

"But—what if it was not?"

She pulled back to look into Mushaniq's face, stroking the tears from her cheeks. "Would your own grandmama say those things to you?"

"M-mahta."

"Then you must consider from whence they come."

Mushaniq could not think, only cry.

"They are not true things, Mary Mushaniq. Only dreams—"

"And dreams sometimes speak true!" She sat up, staring at Elinor. "Or would you despise what Sees Far told you he dreamed about you?"

Elinor's mouth dropped open for a moment, then she slowly closed it. "You are right. But still—I think this is not a dream of truth. That something—or someone—" A flash of comprehension lit Elinor's gaze, then she shook her head—"wishes you to believe it is truth." Her lips compressed with either disapproval or resolve.

"And that would be. . .?"

"The one we call the devil. Manteo named him as—Riapoke?"

The name opened a new horror like a dark hole in her mind that Mushaniq could not escape.

Sacrifice. . .life demands it. . .

The weeping took her again. "She said—she said—I must sacrifice. That it is the only way."

Elinor's arms were about her once more. "Kupi, there is some sacrifice. But our Jesus made all the sacrifice necessary to give us life, and now your sacrifice is to give life to your little one, not take it away. No matter what you are told in a dream."

"But—what if Georgie does not return to me?"

None of her words were having any effect upon the young woman. Elinor rocked her, desperation rising in her own throat.

Oh gracious Father, what shall I do?

The answer resounded through her. *Pray.*

She gulped a breath. *Very well. Our Father which art in heaven—*

But it was not enough. She swallowed. Mushaniq needed more, something—stronger.

The silent prayer could be powerful, but the spoken word even more so, she knew.

With a ragged sigh, she began again. "Our Father which art in heaven, hallowed be Thy name. Let Thy kingdom come. Thy will be fulfilled, as well in earth, as it is in heaven. Give us this day our daily bread. And forgive us our debts, as we forgive our debtors. And lead us not into temptation, but deliver us from evil. For Thine is the kingdom and the power, and the glory for ever. Amen."

Mushaniq had quieted from her wild cries, but sobs still shuddered through her.

"You truly are our Father in heaven," Elinor continued. "A good Father, especially in the absence of those earthly fathers we miss." She too began to cry.

Papa, where are you? Where have you been all this time?

"We beg You now to deliver us from evil. You truly hold everything—power and wisdom and glory and honor. You are the God above all gods, whether in this land or elsewhere. Be the God over our own hearts and even of our dreams. Show us Your truth here."

Mushaniq had quieted. Elinor swallowed again, gaining courage. "Protect this young woman and her child. Protect Georgie. Protect us all, gracious Lord, as we seek to live for You in this land and be a light in the darkness."

With a start—or was that a shiver?—Mushaniq sat up and stared at her, tears still pouring down her cheeks. "How did you know? It was the dark—trying to swallow me."

Elinor wiped her own cheeks. "I did not. But perhaps God led me to pray thus."

Georgie awoke in the dead of night to the rumble of thunder and rain pattering over him. Nothing for it but to curl tighter and hunker down.

At least the rain would hide him. Harder still, perhaps, to conceal himself afterward.

Sleep overtook him again, this time with strange dreams that made no sense. *"Take note of your dreams,"* Sees Far had told him. *"I do not know whether God speaks to the Inqutish in the same way, but it is worth at least thinking upon them."*

Georgie did not know what to expect. Nothing appeared in his slumber, however, that he even could recall, much less remember. When he woke, every bit of his body hurt, and the sky was still grey above the half-emerged leaves.

Mushaniq remembered Sees Far saying that Elinor's prayers had power. She could not say whether that was so, but she could not deny that as Elinor prayed, a calm had washed over her. The terror inside ebbed like storm surge, and for the first time, she could breathe deeply without lapsing back into tears or wailing.

Carrying this babe to birth is your sacrifice, she had said. Mushaniq held those words close to her heart, even as she smoothed her hands over her rounding belly.

Elinor had gone to stoke the fire, then prepared a few apon and knelt to cook them at the hearth. Outside it was still dark, and both Ginny and baby Sunlight yet slept upstairs. It was, for the second night, just the four of them. Neither Nohsh nor Sees Far had returned—but then, they had not truly expected it. It was the way of the older men to stay out as well, to camp and covertly keep watch over the youth.

Mushaniq joined Elinor at the fire. She ate a pair of apon, drank the tea Elinor brewed for her from the mint that had grown outside her door, then crawled back into her bed for whatever portion of the night might be left.

But the tears returned, and sleep did not.

Where was Georgie? Was he well? Had he found a place to shelter, and would he be able to avoid bears and panthers and—

And any people who would be not pleased with his presence in the forest. He could speak well the tongue of Tunapewak by now, but he was so pale, so obviously Inqutish.

Would she ever even know what had happened to him if he never returned?

Chapter Thirty-Two

H is nest was snug enough, but at last he could bear it no longer. Listening first to make sure none were close enough in the forest to mark him slipping from inside the thicket, he edged out, fastened the knife at his waist, drank deeply from the stream and refilled the skin, and looked around more carefully.

If he followed the stream, he could find this place again, but he would also be in danger of encountering towns and other people.

This would be—what? His second full day of fasting? He should devise a way of keeping track. And of making sure he would find his way back. Because—he wanted to go back. There was a girl with a pert grin and teasing eyes and the sweetest of kisses to welcome him—and who soon would be mother of their babe. What a thought, that he would be a father though scarce of age.

A breeze bent the tree boughs above, fluttered the emerging leaves. Birdsong once again filled the forest.

It all whispered to him. *Pyas! Come deeper. Know my secrets!*

He drew in a long breath. Looked at the angle of the sun, the moss on the trees, where he knew the stream behind him lay in relation to the Pumtico River and, generally, the town from there.

Sees Far had, not too many weeks ago, drawn him a rough map of where he and his people had ranged over the years. Had Georgie absorbed it well enough to get himself home if he ranged farther?

And if he did not, would he always wonder what it would look like, what adventures he might have met?

This was his time. Three solid days with nothing to call to him but the wild forest.

And God as well, of course.

Day three since huskanaw had begun. It would be the second day of Georgie's fast.

Mushaniq sat back from the task of molding an earthenware pot and swiped her wrist across her face. She could hardly keep her mind on the task, even when the Inqutish potter promised to show her their methods of fire and glaze, and she truly was curious what might result.

Nearby, Elinor sat stitching while baby Sunlight slept in a basket.

"How slowly can a day pass?" Mushaniq asked, pitching her voice quietly enough to not wake the slumbering child.

Elinor's hands lowered to her lap, and the lines between her brows eased. "Very slowly," she answered softly.

Mushaniq huffed. "It is unfair."

The older woman released a puff of breath to rival Mushaniq's. "Much in life is."

She looked more closely at Elinor. Wisps of golden hair escaped to surround her face, and the lines between her brows had returned.

How easy it was to forget how much Elinor had also endured.

"What was it like," Mushaniq said, "to leave everything you had known and come here?"

There was a tremor in Elinor's hands this time, and she did not look up.

"We thought it a grand adventure," she said at last. "And we were fully persuaded we were doing the work of God. I have had cause enough to question that. But I still believe He brought us here." Her head lifted, her pale eyes bright with tears. "That He brought me here. To you and to the others."

"But—how? How can you believe that, when not all has gone according to what you planned or hoped?"

"He is with us, Mary, even in the hardship. In the sickness and even in the death."

It was so like what Auntie Timqua had said before.

And did Timqua still believe it as well, or had her thoughts changed? "Would He be God if He were not with us always?"

Now that was an angle she had not considered. "I suppose not," she said and returned to her task.

She had begun work on another pot, taking a chunk of clay that the men had dug, rolling it into a long, thick rope, when a commotion arose from near the palisade opening. Though she itched to go look, she stayed at the task. It was critical that she work the entire pot start to finish before the clay dried.

Elinor stayed put as well, but before long, the stir had come to them.

It was Nohsh, apparently freshly in from the forest, accompanied by a warrior of the People, unfamiliar but garbed in a manner similar to Sees Far. Both she and Elinor straightened as they approached.

"You will wish to hear this, Elinor. He brings tidings of what I am certain must be the English. Mayhap even of your father, the governor."

Elinor could not still the trembling in her body.

Mushaniq kept working—she must, because of the wet clay—while Manteo sent for the Assistants. His mother was already informed, the other women busy with preparing yaupon and anything else they had on hand for refreshment. But she could only tuck her sewing into a basket next to the fire, scoop little Sunlight from hers, and clutch the babe against her shoulder in a vain attempt to still the quivering deep within.

Ginny awoke from her nap, and Mushaniq finished about the time the other men were ready, taking a little of their wash water to rinse her hands. They still tried to fetch water only once a day, enough for the entire day's needs, when all went to the stream together for safety. But she looked impatient to hear what the unknown warrior had to say as well.

At the last minute, Mushaniq stayed behind at the house with Ginny. She offered to take Sunlight, but Elinor shook her head absently and simply took along a cloth for bundling the babe to her. She would need to nurse all too soon.

Inside the meetinghouse, she sank into a seat near the back.

After food and drink, uppowoc was passed about and smoked for a bit before the young warrior was expected to even begin speaking. Elinor was glad of her place by the door, with a bit of fresh air. She still could not like the rank, heavy smoke they seemed to favor. At last, however, he began to speak, relating a tale of having roamed about the previous summer and winding up on Roanoac just before the onset of a terrible sea storm. Lightning had struck, starting a fire in the dry grass and wood of the forest. He had gone to investigate but heard voices. Strange voices, he said, speaking words that seemed like those of the Inqutish that had sojourned there under Rafe Lane.

They had seen his footprints on the shore, but because he was alone, he did not venture out to greet them, only watched. They marched up and down, both on the beach and through the forest, making much ado over the markings on a tree overlooking the northern sound. Then they had gone to the place of the old Inqutish town but apparently found nothing of note save several chests that had been buried, then dug up again, and the belongings inside spoiled.

Finally the men, who had been dressed all in wassador like those early Inqutish, got back into their two boats and went away. The tempest had struck shortly thereafter.

"Was there a man with a grey beard?" Chris asked the warrior.

"There were many men with grey beards, but the one who made the most of the markings on the tree and the belongings that had been scattered, he did have a grey beard."

Almost as one, they turned and looked at Elinor.

She could not breathe, could not speak. Somehow, she knew in her heart—she simply *knew*—it had been Papa.

He had returned at last, found the first of their tokens, and then—what? Had the tempest turned them away? Delayed them? Or worse, made wreckage of them?

"We need to go there and carry away what we still can," Master Bailie said.

Manteo appeared to ignore him for the present. "What other news? What of the Sukwoten and Weopomeioc?"

"There is talk of them going to war, but I do not know where or who."

Manteo did not move, but Elinor could read the slight hardening of his features. "We will speak on this later," he said at last.

And with that, he turned the conversation to other things entirely.

Babe in arms, Elinor slipped out and made her way back to the house, wholly unseeing.

Mushaniq was in the middle of cooking a small meal for Ginny when Elinor returned to the house and, without a word, pulled a chair over to the window and sat, staring out at the sky and rocking and patting the baby.

She did not even want to ask.

Before long, however, both Nohsh and Chris Cooper came to visit. Mushaniq let them in, and without a word as well, they went to Elinor and settled on the floor near her.

Chris spoke first. "It might not even have been him—"

Elinor turned on him with a rare passion. "You know as well as I do, it was. It must have been." Her gaze drifted to the window again, and Mushaniq could see the tears welling in her eyes. "None other would have made so much of the token or of—of finding his chests broken into and spoiled." She gave her cheeks an agitated swipe. "All his books—his drawings—I wonder how quickly it was after we left Roanoac that they were dug up and plundered."

It was Nohsh who reached over and placed a hand upon her knee. She clasped it, and a shudder shook her body.

When little Sunlight stirred and squeaked on her shoulder, Mushaniq retrieved the baby to dandle her.

"We all knew 'twas a risk. We knew all the risks. But you cannot blame me for being disappointed and—and a little overcome."

"He may yet come," Nohsh said.

"And he may not." More weeping. "Only God knows."

Nohsh leaned toward her. "And truly God knows. Do we trust Him in all else and not this?"

Elinor's hand tightened on his and her other came up to cover her eyes, but she shook her head.

"I wager your Secotan knows something about when those chests were spoiled," Chris said, a bitter edge to his voice.

The crackle in Elinor's met it for fierceness. "I doubt it not, yet he was guilty of being party to much worse. Do we then rescind forgiveness? Or God's own grace? 'And forgive us our debts, as we forgive our debtors.' Is that to be made of no effect?"

"You can forgive without marrying the enemy," Chris growled.

Elinor sat up straight, glaring at him. "If you cannot leave off, then you may go elsewhere. He is my husband, true, but I chose to forgive him before that was ever a thought in my mind."

Mushaniq kept her back turned, hiding her smile, and kissed the downy head of the sweet baby bobbling a little in her arms.

"My apologies, Elinor. You know my concern is ever and only for you."

There was a rustle behind her, and Nohsh came over to Mushaniq. "Sá keyd winkan?" he murmured, with an arm about her shoulders.

"Missing Georgie," she murmured back.

He hugged her more tightly. "He will do well. Have no fear on that account."

She hesitated in replying.

"What is it?"

"I have nothing but fear."

"Ai, Nunutánuhs." His lips pressed her temple. "You must leave him in the hands of God."

She stiffened in his embrace. "What good will that do, when others have done so but lost anyway?" She tilted her head toward Elinor, making awkward small talk with her cousin. "She and Ananias. Her father's delay in returning."

Nohsh's eyes were grave but understanding. "Are they truly lost if we meet them again after we die?"

When she could draw breath, it hurt all the way into her chest. "Do you truly believe that?"

His gaze was steady. "I do. The Christ defeated death. Nothing else is of sense if that is not so."

Her eyes burned. Why did it always come back to that? And why did her heart always seem to kick against it?

The clouds lay above her, a tangle of grey as far as she could see. Around her feet pulsed the sea, rising, pushing, foaming about her calves. Then receding, tugging at her feet and ankles as she sank a little deeper with each wave.

Come deeper. It is the only way.

Mushaniq caught her breath. She loved yapám, with all its moods. Loved wading out into the waves but feared the open sea with its sharp drop-off not far from shore. But how had she gotten here? Why would she endanger not only herself but the unborn child she carried by flirting with the endless waves?

Her feet took a step as if they had a will of their own.

No! This was not what she wanted!

It is the only way, the voice answered.

It cannot be the only way, she screamed even as her feet took another step. And another.

The waves surged over her knees now. Her toes neared the edge of the great drop-off. And still they wiggled forward. . .

It cannot! I will not do this!

Her body compelled by something beyond her own strength, she was up to her waist now.

The next wave sloshed over her breast.

Mahta! This cannot be!

It is, and will be. Come in, child. Do not fight. Just come. Let the dark water take you.

No! Mahta! Do not do this!

A wave splashed her in the face. She sputtered, gasped.

I do not want this! I do not want to die! I want to live—and for my child to live!

All die, child, sooner or later. It is better to surrender now.

And then the water was over her head, and she could not breathe at all. Her feet lost all sense of the ocean floor, and something had seized her, gripping, yanking her deeper—

Help me! Oh, someone help! Save me—if anyone is there—

Strong hands took hold of her shoulders and tugged her upward.

Save. . .me. . .

The hold on her feet released, and the grip on her shoulders lifted her upward through the water until her head broke the waves and she could drag a breath into her lungs—

"Mary, wake up! Mushaniq! I am here. All is well."

She woke, gasping, to Elinor holding her again and collapsed into the woman's arms.

Chapter Thirty-Three

S unrise of the third day found Georgie high in an oak tree, where he'd initially climbed to avoid a mother bear and her two cubs and then stayed for the simple pleasure of surveying the forest. While there, he discovered a crook in the branches that would afford him a place to tuck in without worry of falling.

He'd put little enough energy toward the seeking God portion of this. As evening fell, however, Mushaniq was strongly in his thoughts, and he spent an uneasy night mulling all the conditions between them that had yet to be fulfilled.

Today and tomorrow, and he could return to her. But if her heart did not soften enough to accept the faith of his people, would it be enough? In truth, he was not sure he himself cared. He could live happily as a Kurawoten, after this.

But the Kurawoten, most of them anyway, now believed in Christ. He knew from conversations he'd had with Mushaniq that even those who did not wish to press her on the matter did truly want her to take this faith as well.

It was curious to him how they'd belief of their own aplenty in God. Several gods, as he understood it, but they suffered no delusions that the spiritual did not exist, or that even in existing it did not touch and affect the natural. And yet, their understanding of such was completely different. Completely wrong.

Manteo had talked of hearing the voices of the spirits of the land. Mocking, menacing. Now that his head was perfectly clear, Georgie thought he could remember an echo of something like that, the long evening and night they'd been made to drink the black drink. Terrifying, it was.

"You must place yourself under the protection of Christ," Manteo said, and Sees Far repeated it the morning after.

What even did that mean?

He knew about praying the Lord's Prayer. There were those who talked of addressing the Almighty as if it were just a matter of everyday conversation. Georgie was not sure about that, but considering some of the psalms he had read, he supposed it could be. Others made it sound as if God would strike a body dead for daring to be too familiar.

Then there were the Tunapewak, as Mushaniq referred to *the People*, who had at least formerly insisted God was so great and high and benevolent He could not be bothered with human prayers to begin with. And yet—the whole of Scripture portrayed a God who revealed Himself to His people, who indeed even became flesh to redeem them.

He had no trouble accepting that. Why then these doubts that God took thought enough to want Georgie's prayers?

Come to think, the ones who warned against overfamiliarity—usually couched in terms such as *proper reverence*—Georgie recalled them as stuffy, robed officials of the church. The same church that winked at or even enabled the misadventures of a king who was not content to have only one wife.

Did any of them have a shred of comprehension of what simple English folk might encounter while trying to build a new life on the other side of the sea? If the merest survival meant the need to throw oneself continually on God's mercies, then surely that same God would not despise the inarticulate prayers flung at Him by His people.

A long-forgotten verse came to mind. *Cry unto me, and I will answer, and shew thee great and high things, which were unknown to thee. . .*

Where was that? How could he be sure it was even Scripture?

And yet. . .

If this is Your Word and not my own imaginings, O Lord, then show me. Show me what I'm meant to learn here. Where You wish me to go and do— even if that is only waiting here until the four days are over.

And oh—above all, Lord, protect Mushaniq and the town!

While tending the apon cooking on a small flat pan in the coals, Elinor considered Mushaniq, huddled on the floor by the window, curled in on herself. She'd prevailed upon the young woman to come lie down upstairs beside Elinor and the girls after awakening her from yet another terrible dream that had Mushaniq crying out in her sleep. Whether she slumbered again the rest of the night was another matter, and this morning she would hardly move or speak.

Georgie was not due back for two more days at the least. If Mushaniq was in such distress now, how would she endure another two nights?

The cakes were done, and Elinor set them onto a platter and moved that to the table. "Pyas, *micis*," she called softly, but Mushaniq did not move.

She blew out a breath. How was it that she herself had endured months of captivity and everything from the abuse heaped upon her by Wanchese and the privations of the journey to the mines and back, but this girl seemed to have no defense against troubled dreams?

Yet, 'twas more than that. It had to be. But she was at the end of herself to be of any use.

...no defense. Her thoughts redoubled on the two words. Was that the trouble? She thought of Manteo's emphatic reminder to each of the boys going on huskanaw to confess their belief in Christ and so put themselves under the authority of the only One who could—and would—defend them from the darkness. From the enemy who, as he had also so rightfully quoted, "walked about, seeking whom he may devour."

Manteo and others had also rightfully insisted Mushaniq not be pushed to make a decision not in line with her heart—that she must choose. But oh, how long would she wait?

She crossed to the young woman and, kneeling beside her, slipped her arms about the bent shoulders. "Tell me again of the dream."

Mushaniq's account, in the shadows of the bedchamber upstairs, had been vague and garbled.

Her head, hair still mussed with the night's struggles, shook a little. "Yapám. Darkness. A voice that told me to come deeper." She shuddered. "It pulled me under and would not let go."

Oh, sweet child. "And what happened? Did you drown?"

Another shake of her head. The ends of her hair tickled Elinor's cheek. "I—cried out. For help. Something took hold of me and pulled me from the water."

Thank You, Father, for that. She stroked Mushaniq's hair. "Who did you call to?"

She sobbed. "I—do not know."

Elinor cradled her a little closer. "Do you not?"

The only response was quiet weeping. Tears were oft better than silence, however.

After a few moments, Mushaniq drew herself up and out of Elinor's embrace. "It could not have been your God. After I have resisted so long, it is only weakness that persuades me to think that a path I should follow."

Elinor held herself steady, watching the younger woman try so desperately to compose herself. "Is it, truly? Could it not be the Spirit of that same God who is drawing your heart, showing you the way to Him?"

Mushaniq shut her eyes, one hand over the side of her face. "Why would He do that?"

She leaned in a little, dropping her voice. "Because you are precious to Him. Just as you are precious to your earthly father and the rest of your family. Just as my own daughters are precious to me. It is why His Son came to the world—to save us. To rescue us from darkness and death. And that carries meaning that is so much more than our lives simply being easier."

Mushaniq was still so long Elinor did not know what else to say. If there was anything else that would be of use. At last the girl dropped her hand and, avoiding Elinor's eyes, shook her head again. She unfolded herself from the floor and, crossing to the table, took apon and began to eat.

It was something. But dear heaven, how long would she remain entrenched in her stubbornness?

She wanted to take Mushaniq by the shoulders and shake her. But she dared not—the girl seemed fragile enough she might shatter completely.

God in heaven, give me wisdom! Give me the right words. And—open her eyes to see You for herself! You are all that saves any of us.

She went to the shelf where lay her father's copy of the Holy Scriptures—the same one she had been reading to Sees Far these past months—and carried it to the table. While Mushaniq continued to eat, Elinor turned the pages until she found Psalm 18.

With a glance at Mushaniq watching without comment, she cleared her throat and read. " 'The sorrows of death encompassed me, and the overflowings of ungodliness made me afraid. The pains of hell came about me, the snares of death overtook me. In my trouble will I call upon the Lord: and complain unto my God. So shall he hear my voice out of his temple, and my complaint shall come before him, it shall enter even into his ears.'"

She straightened, fingertips still on the edge of the page. Mushaniq had gone still, her own hand upraised with a morsel of cake resting there.

The young woman's eyes rounded, her face a little pale—especially for the Kurawoten. "The pains of—hell?"

"*Popogusso*, as you call it. Eternal lostness, away from God."

She lowered the piece of cake and set it back on the plate, shaking her head slowly.

"But see? You called out, and He heard. He does not despise our cries. He is worthy of our trust and our devotion."

Without a word, Mushaniq turned and walked out of the house.

Elinor stifled a moan. Had she done amiss, reading her those few verses?

Sinking into a chair, she covered her face with her hands. *O Lord, show Yourself to her! I cannot.*

The new house was going up well. Though not involved in the actual building of it, Manteo enjoyed watching the progress of first framing, then what the English called *wattle* and *daub*, the brickwork around the fireplace, and the laying of floors.

It made him miss Ananias all the more fiercely, however. And this one would be the home of Jane Pierce—a slightly older woman who had come with the planters and some said had ties to Spain or even Simon Ferdinando, the Portuguese navigator who had caused such trouble on their voyage from England. Jane was to be married soon to Roger Bailie, and all were pleased by the match.

Only one of the women who had come—four years ago now they had sailed from England—was not yet wed. The men muttered between themselves that she was a *shrew* and it would require a man of exceptional patience to be willing to take such a one to wife.

Well, the women were not the only ones difficult to live with at times.

Chris sidled up to him as he observed the brick being laid for the hearth. "I see you have not yet changed back to English apparel since you've returned."

Manteo gave him a cool glance. "It is comfortable and a reminder to me of our youths who need prayers as they finish huskanaw."

Cooper had the good grace to look properly chastened at that. Manteo shifted to face him.

"It seems a good time to ask, however. Is it apparel that makes one English? Or Kurawoten? And does that matter when Scripture tells us there is no difference between peoples under Christ, that we are all one blood and one Spirit?"

Chris dropped his head and appeared to struggle for words. "I am shamed, Manteo, by your grasp of God's grace and how often I must be reminded."

Manteo took hold of Chris's shoulder and shook it. "We are brothers. And I often must be reminded as well."

One of the men laying brick called his name and pointed to the doorway. Mushaniq hovered there, her rounding form outlined against the light. "Nohsh? Are you busy?"

Chris tipped his head toward the door, and Manteo went to her. "I always have time for you, Nunutánuhs."

He followed her outside and to what had become a packed footpath around the inside of the palisade walls, letting her set the pace. She did not speak at first, only folded her arms across her chest, head bent.

"Nohsh," she said abruptly, "why did you take the Christian baptism?"

He frowned. What sort of answer did she seek? "At first, only because it seemed right. But then God Himself surprised me by His presence. By the peace and joy I felt after."

"There does not seem to be much peace and joy lately."

A laugh escaped him. "Oh, it is there, but in a different way. Things change, and we grow—just as what delights your heart now, as a grown woman, are not the things that delighted you as a child." He peered at her. "And there are more troubles as you become older, but you also learn to love more deeply."

She nodded hesitantly. "Does God—as the Inqutish say He is—truly protect us from evil?"

That was a harder question. "He does. And if there is any hard or evil thing allowed to touch us, He promises to work it together with other things in our life for our good." He dipped his head. "That is difficult to understand, to see how it could be, but—He does promise."

Nothing more did she say after that, but thanked him, gave him a quick embrace, and went on her way.

Sunset on the third day. Or was it the fourth? Georgie could no longer say.

He stumbled to a stream and threw himself half into it, drinking deeply, then lay there, letting the icy cold water soak his flesh into numbness.

Once begun, the prayers had become their own litany. *Protect the town. Protect Mushaniq and the babe she carries. . .*

Protect me, and show me Your face.

He yanked upward with a splash and crawled back to higher ground, then tipped his head to the sky.

A surge of frustration brought him to his feet. "Where are You? I have wandered this forest for days, denied myself meat or even sleep—called out to You, and yet You do not answer! Are You even there? Or do the Tunapewak have the way of it, and You simply left us here to do as we will and make the best of it, after You set the world into motion?"

A hush seemed to fall across the forest, as if even the birds stopped to listen.

"If You are God, why do You not reply? I have said with my own mouth that I believe in Your Son. But so did all the English who came here. So did my da, who perished horribly that very first week! Where were You then?"

He collapsed again to his knees, shuddering with dry sobs, then threw back his head.

A scream tore itself from his throat. "Where—were—You?"

A breath, almost a whisper, caressed his skin. *I was, and am, and ever will be—with him, and with you.*

There was nothing—nothing at all—he could do in response to that besides fall flat on his belly on the forest floor. Arms outstretched, face pressed half into the leaves.

His soul, completely undone.

Chapter Thirty-Four

S omewhere in the night, Georgie awoke. He knew what he was supposed to do. Or at least, attempt it.

He rose, turning, listening. There were no sounds but the burbling of
the stream and a distant owl. With a deep breath, he stretched his limbs,
then relaxed.

The thought would not leave him be. It was mad—he'd likely die
trying—but it felt unalterably *right* deep in his heart.

His only hesitation was—Mushaniq. All he needed to fulfill the obligation her family placed on him was to endure this next day—just one
more day—and return to the town. She'd be in his arms by the second
sunset. He need not take this dive off the edge—

Yet if he did not, now that the task had presented itself to him, he
would always wonder *what if.*

Going through huskanaw was supposed to prove him a man, but
what kind of man would he be if he refused something just because it
was difficult?

Above him, beyond the tree leaves now almost fully emerged, glittered the stars. North. He needed to aim straight north. Carry out a bit of
spying, figure out exactly where to go.

Of course, none of that took into account the difficulty of returning
without discovery. He thought back on all Sees Far and Elinor had related
of their journey from *Ree-tah-noh-ay.*

If Sees Far, an experienced warrior born and bred in this land, had difficulty, what hope had Georgie of making the journey there and back, much less to free those who had been taken captive?

He dropped to his knees in the leaves. "If this is of You, Lord, give me some sort of confirmation. 'Tis not wrong of me to ask, is it?"

A hollow ache in his gut reminded him that prayers did not guarantee success, at least not as they measured it. Da had prayed, and look what happened to him.

"Please, gracious Lord," he breathed.

As he knelt there, the conviction that he was meant to try did not ease.

"At the least, protect Mushaniq and the babe. And me, if it pleases You. Lead me and guide me. Because I am all too aware that better men have perished before me."

With a deep breath, he got up, brushed himself off again, and fixing his direction by the north star, he set off.

As the sky lightened with the coming dawn, so did his heart.

Please, Lord, whatever happens. . .protect Mushaniq and our little one.

Of course, it would be surpassing wonderful if he could succeed in this as well.

The sun was well risen when a far-off owl's hoot made him dive into hiding. Among all the other sounds of the forest, this was the least likely to be the call of a real bird. More likely to be human.

Crouching at the base of a huge oak, he waited.

"Hai! Georgie!"

Someone who knew him—this far from the town? He peered out, slowly scanning the forest, and a figure stepped into view a short distance away.

Two Feathers. Of course.

"Today is the last day," the other youth said. "What are you doing out here—and headed north?" He made a scoffing sound. "Are you abandoning Mushaniq?"

Georgie eased out of hiding and made his way closer. "Mahta. I am—on a hunt."

Two Feathers lifted his chin. "A hunt for what? You have nothing with which to take game."

He pulled in a deep breath. "I need none for this one. Only cunning."

Still the other youth waited, so he went on.

"I am going to Ritanoe to bring back the Inqutish captives. If I can."

Two Feathers hissed, but a spark of admiration lit his eyes. "You will die."

"Perhaps. But I have been shown that I must try."

A slow shake of the head met that statement. "So you *are* abandoning Mushaniq." He grunted. "I will be there to comfort her when she is ready."

A burn rose in Georgie's throat. As much as he longed to send back a message to her, he didn't trust Two Feathers not to twist his words. "I would ask you to tell her this was not a task lightly accepted, but I am sure you will only say whatever casts you in the best light."

With that, he checked his direction and set off again.

"Wait. Are you truly doing this alone?"

"Kupi." Georgie stopped for a moment and looked back. "Do you wish to come?"

Not that he wanted to be saddled with his rival in this.

Two Feathers tipped his head. "Then we would both die. Or be taken captive."

"It is a possibility. But I did not think you a coward. Besides," he threw back over his shoulder as he kept going, "you are too noisy, and this requires much stealth."

It would be more difficult for the two of them together to be quiet, wouldn't it?

At the next stream, he stopped to drink and refill his skin. As he crouched to dip his hand so he could keep watch, Two Feathers stepped up to the water, a few paces away, and also bent to drink. Georgie hid a smile.

Gracious Lord, if You are listening—this seems more a jest than a means to answer my prayers. But perhaps You are not as disdainful of such as I have been led to believe.

She had counted the days with care. This was the sixth sunrise. Nearly a week, as the Inqutish reckoned.

Two of the youths returned as soon as the sun was over the horizon, trailing their sponsors. The sound of rejoicing from their families echoed across the town, and food was being prepared for a feast. Another hour, and a third appeared. But still no Georgie. Nor Two Feathers, for that matter.

Everyone ate and danced, and then the sun was standing overhead. Still no sign of either youth or Sees Far. Mushaniq could not breathe, could not think. She could not even go keep watch because they might come at either entrance of the palisade. And the guards would not allow her up into the lookout platforms on the corners, not with her growing bulk.

It was not fair, but they would not be persuaded, and so she stomped away.

Despite hardly being able to stay indoors, she went back to Elinor's house and swept the floors. "They are clean already," Elinor protested, half laughing, but Mushaniq only shook her head and continued, first the upstairs, then down.

After, she gathered her materials for a basket she'd begun for the baby and sat outside to work on it. All the while, worry gnawed at her.

She had never felt so alone in the middle of an entire town. But it seemed everyone avoided her, and she, them. After all, what more was there to say if her talks with Elinor and then Nohsh brought no answers, no comfort? What more could Nunohum and Auntie Timqua add, except to chide her for not acting as quickly as she might have with the herbs?

The thought brought only a jolt of sickness to her stomach and bowed her over her belly.

It made no sense. Their people valued children, bringing them up with love and care. Mushaniq could not recall ever having been misused nor Auntie or Nunohum allowing such behavior to occur—or at least, when they were aware of it. And if they would love this child once it was born and breathed—or was that the difference?

Her head ached to even try to sort it all out.

At least her dreams the last two nights had not been terrifying, although they were still dark and confusing.

They ran together lightly through the forest, across swamps and fording rivers—sometimes swimming—and always northward. At the approach of other people, they hid in the brush to listen.

Near evening, they stopped once again for a short rest. After a drink and refreshing his waterskin, Georgie took his knife, found a likely sapling, and cut it near the base, then began shaping it for a bow. That done, he looked for grapevine and, as Sees Far had taught him, peeled away long sections of fiber and twisted them into a string. Two Feathers watched at first without comment, then set to making his own.

Arrows were a little more troublesome at the moment. They bickered, but quietly, over what to use for shafts and points and fletching. But what good was a bow without good arrows?

"Perhaps we could sneak into a town and steal some."

"I'd rather not steal," Georgie said.

"Heh. You are intent upon stealing back the Inqutish captives."

"That is different."

"Is it? And if this helps you accomplish that task. . . ?" Two Feathers sat back and looked at him. "How is it you think you can do this?"

"I don't know," Georgie answered evenly. "But if God told me to, then He will make a way. Or I will die trying."

Two Feathers sniffed.

"Are you a believer in Christ?"

"Kupi." The Kurawoten boy answered flatly but without hesitation.

"Were you one of those who were baptized that night in the sound?"

Two Feathers narrowed his eyes. "You followed Mushaniq away into the forest that night. I saw you."

Georgie wanted to roll his eyes. Was every move she made marked by the other boys?

Not that he blamed them. . .she was luminous even then.

"Kupi, I went under the water that night with the others."

"And. . .what did you feel after?"

Two Feathers went uncharacteristically thoughtful. "All clean and new inside." He was silent for a moment. "It was not unlike what I feel here and now, after huskanaw."

In the end, they decided to raid for the arrows—and anything else they could find of use.

Before attempting it, however, Georgie found soft, smooth earth and mixed it in his hands with water before smearing it over every bit of his exposed skin—including his hair. Two Feathers helped make sure he was completely covered, then streaked his own limbs and face with the same. Then, fortified with a prayer for God's guidance and protection, they set out.

For three days, Sees Far had remained in the forest, a silent shadow in Georgie's wanderings. During the night before the last day, he had awakened in the dead of night to the youth's impassioned howl, like a wolf crying out to its Creator.

Oh, how well he understood the desperation behind such cries. Had he himself not been in that same place and not so very long ago?

Offering up his own prayer on Georgie's behalf, as he had countless times already, he closed his eyes and let sleep return to him.

The forest was grey and filled with mist when he opened them again. Rising, he washed and made his way downstream toward the place from where Georgie's prayers had lifted to the heavens.

The youth was nowhere in sight. Faint sign led away from the stream, due north. How curious. Sees Far followed until, at the edge of a marsh, all trace of Georgie's passing disappeared altogether.

A straight path would take him across the swamp. Indeed, footprints in the soft ground led as if into the murky water but stopped just before the edge, as if Georgie's track simply ceased to be. Prints of water birds and small animals, however, still marked the mud beyond. Sees Far considered the stretch of water. Too distant for Georgie to have leaped across, and his ending prints were no deeper, as they would have been if he'd used that spot to jump from.

Sees Far spent the rest of the day searching to no avail. At dark he was forced to stop and bed down for the night. Tomorrow at dawn was to have been the end of huskanaw. Had Georgie merely taken to wandering the night before and somehow slipped past him on his way back to the town? Or had something else entirely happened?

Why the footprints that ended at the edge of a swamp?

Great Creator, I do not wish to return without him. You alone know where he has gone. Either guide me to him, or show me what I must do instead.

No answers came to him before he slept, but at dawn, he made another quick search before deciding that going back to the town did indeed seem the best course.

Who knew? Perhaps Georgie would be there before him.

The sun rose to its highest point by the time the walls of the town came into sight, with singing and shouts of joy echoing through the forest. Sees Far ran the last stretch to the palisade opening.

The guards eyed him as he approached. "Has Georgie returned yet?" he called out.

They shook their heads. "You might inquire of the guards on the other side of the town, but we've neither seen nor heard word of him."

He hastened on, greeting those he saw and questioning. Then, as much as he longed to see Elinor first, at a full run he skirted the palisade until he reached the other opening.

Georgie had not entered there either.

He bent, hands to his knees. How would he face Elinor and Manteo? Or Mushaniq?

There was nothing for it, though. He made his way to Elinor's house, heart thudding.

This should have been a joyous occasion. He and Georgie both, freshly washed in the river, entering the town together among the singing and shouting.

Mushaniq sat outside, working on a large basket. Catching sight of him, she stilled, then slowly sat upright, her eyes round and her face going pale. "He is not with you?"

He gave a tiny shake of his head. "I was hoping to find him here already."

She sucked in a long, noisy breath and, pushing aside the basket, rose and stumbled into the house just as Ginny came spilling out and threw herself against his legs. "Sees Fa'!"

He picked up the girl, then went inside to find Mushaniq already in Elinor's arms, wailing and babbling about a dream and sacrifice and her baby—

Elinor pulled her in, fiercely, and met Sees Far's eyes across the room. "Where is he?"

He shook his head, waiting until there was a lull in the girl's weeping. "I do not know."

Manteo appeared in the doorway, his expression severe. "What happened?"

"I followed him and kept watch—just as we planned—but sometime in the night before the last day, he slipped away alone. I tracked him to the edge of a swamp, where his footprints ended with no further trace well short of the water's edge, but there was no sign of where he might have gone after or even of any struggle."

While Manteo thought upon that, it seemed half the town gathered outside.

"Neither Towaye nor Two Feathers have returned either."

The speaker was Swims Deep Water, an older weroance who served as elder beside Manteo's mother, who herself now pushed through the crowd to stare hard at him.

"I have seen neither of them," Sees Far said. He set Ginny on the ground, still holding her hand. "But it is yet early. Georgie had struck out to explore—part of huskanaw is for him to find his way back. He knows how to find the town."

"How do we know there is no connection between him and the other two being missing? How do we know you have not betrayed them and us in this?"

"Why would I return if I were a betrayer?"

One of the Kurawoten warriors raised an arm to gesture at the house behind him. Elinor and Mushaniq had both come to stand in the doorway, embracing each other.

"Perhaps you meant to take them both to wife?"

"I would not!" He breathed in, let it out. "I returned thinking perhaps Georgie had come back on his own. And the fact that he is not—" He surveyed the faces around him. "Is it possible he and Two Feathers came to blows?"

Several broke out talking at once.

"Quiet!" Manteo's bellow shocked them all into silence. "It is only the day after huskanaw ended. We will wait and be patient and give ourselves to prayer in the meantime."

Mushaniq broke into sobbing again, crumpling to her knees on the doorstep. Elinor knelt with her, murmuring, and both Manteo and Sees Far came to their sides.

"Mushaniq, listen," Manteo said, gentle but firm over her weeping. "Did you hear what I said? There is yet time—"

"Mahta! I know he is gone—I feel it in my heart. And—do not call me Mushaniq any longer! Mushaniq is dead. I am *Mah-ree*—bitter, in whole now, as you have said. That is me! Call me Mary, for that is my name."

Manteo and Sees Far exchanged a look. The actual declaration of a new name by any of the People was not to be taken lightly, no matter what the name might be or the circumstances leading to it.

"It will be as you say," Manteo murmured. "Mary. We will call you that."

Chapter Thirty-Five

S imple apon tasted better than he ever thought possible after more
than four days without food. They'd sneaked just a few along with a
handful of arrows—and Georgie wished heartily that he'd some way of
repaying whoever both belonged to. But he could only whisper a prayer of
forgiveness and blessing upon those who had provided, however unwit-
tingly, and move on.

They huddled now in a thicket, far enough from the town that they
could talk very quietly without discovery, and munched their edible bounty.

"Do you even know where Ritanoe is?" Two Feathers asked.

"North," Georgie said. "We can hide and listen and discover more as
we go."

Elinor tucked the coverlet over Mushaniq—no, fully *Mary* now—and
turned back to where Chris, Manteo, and Sees Far all sat or crouched
about the hearth.

The young woman had taken to her bed and, face to the wall, refused
to move or speak, although her weeping could be heard now and again.

Chris's gaze shone with sorrow and not a little frustration. "What,
then, can be done?"

Manteo shook his head. "Nothing. Only wait."

"And pray," Elinor prompted quietly, as she drew near. "That is no small thing."

The men nodded. "It is our strongest weapon, I suspect." Sighing, Chris propped his elbows on his knees and cradled his head in his hands. "It pains me more than I can say to realize we could not better tend the son of George Howe."

"The fault is not in how we tended him," Elinor said. "He was bound to grow into a man sooner or later and launch out into the deep in his own way. It is up to God to lead him and to keep him alive."

None of the men looked happy with that, but they did not argue.

"A matter that we must give thought to now," Manteo said slowly, "is that of defending the town—or taking war to Wanchese. Spring is upon us, and he will not long delay." He looked over at Mary. "Someone should sit with her. I will do so this night."

"I am here and do not mind—"

"You have your little ones to attend. And she is my daughter. I will go speak to Timqua and have her come as well."

"Mushaniq—Mary—has seemed fearful of speaking to her or your mother these last weeks. I wonder if she fears their disapproval."

Manteo appeared to consider that. "I fear more for her well-being, that she might harm herself."

Evening fell, and he had not returned.

He is gone—he is gone, and it is my fault. I should have listened to the dream. I should have—

I should never have chosen him to begin with!

For hours she had been able to do nothing but weep, curled in her bed.

I am Mary. . .bitter. There is nothing but bitterness left of my heart.

She heard others moving about the room, heard their talk over by the hearth. Someone, likely Elinor, covered her with a blanket, and Ginny crawled up and over her legs to snuggle with her for a time before getting restless and leaving. But she herself did not move.

Is there anything left for me except death?

Even Two Feathers had not come back, and she would have expected him to try to persuade her to consider him as a suitor again in Georgie's absence...

It was very strange, both of them going missing at once. And Towaye, well experienced in the ways of the land.

None of them would have simply run away. Which meant they were likely taken or—dead.

A fresh wave of tears overtook her.

Would she ever again see him in this life?

Would she even see him in the life to come?

What if Nohsh and Auntie Timqua—and Elinor, Georgie, and all the other Inqutish—were right, and the way of Christ was truth?

What if... *what if... what if...*?

She had been so stubborn about it all. But was holding on to her stubbornness worth never seeing Georgie again, if not in this world then the next?

For a moment, the nightmare came back to her—the waves, cold and deep, the sensation of being pulled under. She had desperately wanted life for herself and her child. She still wanted life for the child at least. If the gods of the sea and the land were angry with her for not giving it to them, where could she go for refuge?

Or was it a better question to ask *who* could she go to?

Both Elinor and Nohsh said there was only one God strong enough for that. One God, and His Son, and the blood He shed to free them from making sacrifices to other gods. To buy them back from captivity, as Sees Far had ransomed Elinor.

Nohsh had told her these things. But she'd never before considered them all in a row like this. It all seemed different somehow, this way.

She opened her eyes. The room was lit only by a fire on the hearth, and when she looked over, she saw Nohsh sitting by it.

Why was he there? And watching, not sleeping?

Something Auntie Timqua had said came back to her, though she could hardly recall the exact words—*"I do not understand how you can be so tender to your father's love and yet resist that of the Good God."*

There was the love of Nohsh, of Nunohum and the aunties, of Elinor and Ginny. Of Georgie—and oh, how she longed for his arms around her, his voice husky in her ear, his soft but fervent kisses.

She turned back over and squeezed her eyes shut.

The dark pressed in upon her yet again. The baby inside kicked and wriggled as if in protest.

She should be accustomed to this by now, truly. After the onslaught of the first two nights of Georgie's huskanaw—

But this seemed different. Heavier. And she was so weary of it all.

It did not matter what she did now. Georgie was already gone. So why would the shadows not leave her be?

Because she was the one who had gone against tradition. Who had flouted the ways of her people. She deserved to be swallowed up by the darkness—

It is the favor of God we do not deserve. If we did, it would not be grace.

She could not even recall where she had heard that.

Did she dare believe in something that was simply given them? Which she did not have to labor for, did not have to sacrifice her child for? Something for which she only need surrender?

It was too easy. Elinor had said, however, that there was sacrifice but not as she had been told in the dream.

. . .hands, reaching down to pull her from the waves. . .

Was that You, God? Did You truly hear me and answer? If it was, then. . .I am here and listening. Show me. Speak to me. I cannot bear the thought of never seeing Georgie again, so if this is what is required—

I surrender. I am Yours.

Something inside her released. Even as the tears flowed, she fell into a deep, dreamless slumber.

For hours, Manteo sat by the fire, praying continually even as he dozed. Deep into the night, however—he judged it not too long before first light—he felt a lifting of the burden. Wrapped in his mantle, he lay down and slept.

He woke just after dawn to the sound of a baby's cry in the room above, and shortly after, Elinor came down the steps. He sat up to stoke the fire while she brought water to set over it.

"Any change overnight?"

"Mahta. She slept."

Sees Far came in from outside and joined them at the hearth. Casting a glance toward Mary Mushaniq's slumbering form, he shook his head. "He has not yet returned."

They kept their voices quiet so as not to disturb her, but she rose suddenly and wrapped the blanket about her shoulders as she padded across the room. Her hair hung loose and unkempt, and the shadows still lay about her eyes, but there seemed something new in her face.

"Mary! Good morning," Elinor said.

She drew a deep breath, her gaze skimming each of them in turn before lifting to the window. "I am ready. What must I do to be baptized?"

They all exclaimed, and Manteo jumped up to embrace her, then leaned back to peer into her face again. "What made you decide—now?"

Her eyes overflowed, and she reached up to brush the tears away. "I could not bear the thought, if Georgie never comes back to me in this life, of never seeing him again—in the afterlife." A quiet sob shuddered through her. "Days ago, Elinor read to me out of the holy book, 'the pains of hell'—Popogusso—'took hold of me,' and I realized that in my dream this was what was happening to me. The water—the thing under the water pulling me down—it was trying to drag me and the baby to Popogusso." More tears. "I do not want to go there, Nohsh. I want to know I will see Georgie again, if not on this side of death then—after."

As she dissolved into weeping, he gathered her into his embrace. His own eyes burned with tears, Elinor likewise wiped her eyes and cheeks, and even Sees Far did not appear unmoved.

"Let us eat, and then we will go see Master Johnson," Elinor said.

And so it was, the entire town turned out to follow them down to the river—where Mushaniq-now-Mary insisted the baptism be done. Master Johnson waded into the water with her, after having satisfied for himself that she did, indeed, hold to true belief and understanding. He spoke the words over her with all the proper questions, which she had heard often enough before she could have recited them for herself, and then scooped handfuls of water over her head—*one, two, three*—before she lowered herself completely under the water.

It closed over her head, cool, caressing, the muted sounds of splashing beneath the surface a soothing thing and not the terror of her dreams. Then standing, she emerged, drawing in the sweet morning air and pushing back her hair as the town clapped and cheered.

And a wave of something else washed over and through her—a sweet peace and joy, just as Nohsh and others had attested to. She tipped her face to the blue sky, letting tears mingle with the river water on her cheeks.

Why—oh, why—had she resisted so long?

Georgie lost track of how many days it took them, running when they could and sneaking when they must, before they reached the river he and Two Feathers agreed must be where at least the great trading town lay. Here they could more or less blend with the crowd. Georgie goggled at how many different native peoples and towns were represented here. He even glimpsed what surely had to be the Spanish through the gathering. All the more reason to keep his own skin and hair disguised.

They watched and listened and soon gathered the information they sought.

Now they moved under cover of night, though the country grew rougher and the danger of bears or panthers was greater. And then—they were there.

It was no easy task to spy upon the copper mine and the town that lay in the hollow below, where a creek ran burbling over rocks and boulders. The forest was not so dense here as in the lowlands, and it was an effort for both Georgie and Two Feathers to not be distracted by glimpses of far-off bluish hills.

What did come easily was picking out the English captives from among the other people. Roger Prat, John Tydway, and Willie and Tom, he recognized all, partly for the relative paleness of their skin and partly for their bearded faces, though about half of the captives wore deerskins now and not English apparel. He even picked out Libby from among the women—although when she straightened and stood, the rounding of her belly was clearly outlined beneath a deerskin tunic.

Well, Elinor had said that there was talk, before Sees Far had led her away, of Libby being taken by someone in marriage. That would make things more difficult.

He and Two Feathers waited and watched, flattened among the rocks and bushes. Opportunity came unexpectedly in the form of Willie, walking off into the woods to relieve himself. His captors seemed unconcerned and appeared not even to watch. Exchanging a glance and nod with Two Feathers, Georgie grabbed a pebble and threw it.

Finished, Willie stopped, his gaze tracing the stone's faint clattering path across the ground. Georgie threw another. Willie did not move.

"Hey!" Georgie pitched his voice just above a whisper. "William Wythers!"

Willie's eyes went wide, and still he did not move.

Georgie eased slightly from his hiding place. "'Tis I, Georgie."

The other boy's jaw sagged. Or rather—not a boy any longer, but young man as well, with a beard full grown. "What happened to you? You look like—Tunapewak."

He grinned. "I am newly finished with huskanaw and have come to steal you and the others back, if you will come."

'Twas more difficult done than said, of course.

In the end, Libby stayed behind, as Georgie suspected she would. She had indeed been given as a wife to one of the warriors and seemed content to stay, although she expressed regret at not seeing the rest of the English again. But what surprised Georgie was Willie debating whether to remain.

"I could provide a distraction," he said, "and tell them you've gone in the opposite direction."

"That wouldn't work," Georgie said. "They know where we all came from."

"I could say the Powhatan stole you." Willie gave a crooked smile. "They would believe me—the Powhatan keep offering ridiculous amounts of furs and pearls for us, but the weroance here will not let us go for any amount."

Georgie liked it not, but did they have any choice but to trust him if he stayed behind?

They chose the dead of night for escape. Each of the men and boys would slip out to the stream and downriver just a bit.

Clouds obscured the moon, and the wind whipped the trees, driving a few raindrops before it. One by one, the men came, while Georgie did his best not to fret.

Gracious Lord, please aid us, if You will. . . The rain began in earnest, lightly pattering, then turning to a hard, steady downpour. They crowded beneath a spreading oak for Georgie to count. Masters Prat, Sutton, Tydway, and Bright, along with Robbie Ellis and Tom Humfrey. Two Feathers and himself.

"Since we are all here—"

Out of the gloom, Willie appeared. "Is it too late for me to come as well?"

Two Feathers turned upon Georgie, bristling. "Should we let him? After all he has done?"

"We are all guilty," Georgie said. "We all need grace." He fastened Willie with a look. He stood a little taller now than the older boy, he noticed for the first time. "You realize we may all be slain."

"They may kill me regardless if I stay behind," Willie said. He flicked Two Feathers a glance. "He's right. I used you terribly. I would not blame you for leaving me."

"'Tis not your use of me I think of," Georgie said. "But we can speak of that later."

Master Prat offered a quiet, short, but heartfelt prayer, then they set out.

Though their pace was slower than it might have been, they were thankful for the cover of the rainstorm and made good progress. At daylight, with the wind and rain still lashing the forest, they found a place to hide and took turns sleeping.

Despite the foul weather, Georgie was fairly certain someone pursued them. Then at dusk on the second night, as they prepared to move out again, it was Towaye who stepped from the shadows and joined them, silent as the night itself.

Two Feathers was no less astonished than Georgie.

"I have followed you all this way," Towaye said gruffly. "You were my charge before huskanaw, and so I kept watch over you and came after when I saw you were not returning to the town. Sees Far would also have followed, but I think you must have slipped away without his notice." He gave Georgie a brief but genuine grin. "That is not a small feat."

Well. 'Twas nothing if not gratifying. But how angry would Sees Far be when they returned—if they returned?

He would not think of that just yet.

Chapter Thirty-Six

Nearly a moon had passed since Georgie and Two Feathers failed to return from huskanaw. Even Towaye had not come back. Nunohum sent out inquiries—and Mary knew Sees Far and Nohsh still searched on the pretext of hunting—but there was no word. Not a hint. Not even of captives being taken, which usually was a matter of boasting no matter who had carried it out.

Even Nohsh puzzled over the footprints that led to nowhere in the swamp, still visible the next day when he and Sees Far ventured out to where Georgie was last seen. Neither had any explanation for that.

Mary was almost, but not quite, reconciled to certainty that she would give birth and her child would never know his true father. Even so, she regretted nothing.

Nohsh had brought her the bundles of goods Georgie had been saving all through the winter to give her as marriage gifts. She immediately set to sewing the soft waboose pelts into a wrap for the baby and then into a mantle for herself, not only to wear but also to sleep on when the nights turned chilly.

As she worked, the baby wriggled and kicked, and her tears came and went. *Creator—God—I still hardly know how to address You—make me strong to birth this child, and then let him grow strong as well.*

There was no longer the horror of the dark or of Popogusso. A new lightness, even joy, threaded through the sorrow and longing. And in the

280

midst of it all, Timqua and Nunohum were tender with her again, and both assured her they would never have pressed her to drink the tea, not with both Mary and Georgie so delighted with the coming of a baby and so certain they wished to marry. Furthermore, they were talking with the other women and elders how best to address their people's ways in a manner that might be more pleasing to God.

Of course, they were all overjoyed at her coming at last to belief in Christ. Mary could not even be annoyed over that. She still did not understand—she had spoken words, made a decision, went into the water, and let it be poured over her—and now everything was different.

How could that be? Unless Nohsh and the others were right, and this God truly was the Creator, and this Jesus the Christ really was His Son and had come to do all the things the Inqutish holy book said He did.

Unless this God, in all His greatness and strength, did truly love them.

She closed her eyes. *I know now that You are with me. That You even love me and care for the little things. Thank You for showing Yourself to me. I want to see You more and more!*

The only thing that would make life better in this moment would be Georgie returning—and to be back on her beloved island.

Despite the warnings, the women could not always stay inside the walls of the town. There was foraging to be done, water to be fetched, and the customary bathing every morning and sometimes at evening. Elinor found she enjoyed the native standard of cleanliness and craved the daily washing.

They had clothing to wash as well, although Elinor tried daily to take along whatever was needed to their morning bathing. And they did keep watch, with Mary even carrying Georgie's bow and arrows.

It rejoiced Elinor's heart to see strength and joy renewed in the young woman. They all still sorrowed at Georgie's absence, but she could see how the Spirit of God upheld her as she grew in her trust in Him. Just as He had Elinor through all the long year before.

Sees Far and Manteo had gone out with the other men, some to fish and some to range a bit. Two of the three young men who recently completed huskanaw were tasked with guarding the women on their morning trip to the river. The men still expected an attack, but with every day that passed, as the weather warmed more fully and trees leafed out while flowers bloomed, such a thing seemed more and more unlikely.

And yet...each morning the possibility flitted through her thoughts, and each morning Elinor prayed silently for their protection as she carried little Sunlight and whatever washing she had, Ginny clutching at her skirts, to join the other women at the river.

On this particular morning, she offered up the prayers and set out without further thought. Whether from distraction or something else, Mary had gone a little ahead with Ginny, and she lagged behind, Sunlight on her back, when a tall warrior stepped out in front of her, blocking the path.

For the briefest instant—only the briefest, she knew him too well now—she thought it was Sees Far. But the body paint, the cut of the hair, the features and line of his shoulders—all were different.

"So he returned you here after all," the warrior said in a voice that brought a hundred waking nightmares sweeping back. "What magic did you work on him to make him turn betrayer to his people?"

She could not move, could not speak. Ahead, closer to the river, rose a commotion and cry.

Where were Ginny and Mary?

Gracious God, help us!

Mary was not yet to the river when the cries went up from the women and girls already there. Ginny had run ahead a little but came flying back, eyes wide. "Mama!"

Mary caught her, drew her into the bushes beside the path, crouching. "Stay here," she said. "You are waboose—hide like one, kupi?"

Ginny nodded, blue eyes shining with the excitement of the unexpected game.

"Do not move unless your mama or I come for you."

And then she herself was creeping through the forest, bow in hand. This had been so much easier when she was not big with child!

The young men who had been set to watch had their bows up, raining arrows upon the warriors surrounding the women's bathing place. But Elinor—she had left her behind on the path!

Mary hurried back, retracing her steps, weaving through the underbrush. There, just ahead, stood Elinor, facing a warrior as tall as Nohsh and Sees Far—perhaps taller. Elinor backed away, and the warrior swooped in, seizing her by the hair.

Mahta! She would not merely watch as Elinor was taken. She stepped onto the path, drawing an arrow and nocking it to her bow, then put it into the back of the warrior.

He whirled, gaze fastening upon her. It was almost as if she had not just shot him, for he took measure of her and smiled. "You seek to stop me, little mother?"

He was fearsome—and beautiful. A little taller than Nohsh, who easily topped most of the English if not all, and dazzling with his mocking grin and arched brows under the red and black paint. Was this Wanchese? The great warrior who had been chosen, along with Nohsh, to journey across yapám and back and learn the ways of the Inqutish?

Then something inside her hardened. If so, he was the one who led the slaying of Georgie's father. Who had slain Ananias.

She would not allow him to take Elinor.

Another arrow came to her hand. She fit it to the bow and drew back. *Good God, let my aim be true!*

And released.

The arrow took him in the throat, knocking him backward. Elinor had already scurried out of the way, beyond his reach. He clutched at it, as she sent another after, then fell, his eyes wide and disbelieving.

One hand still at his throat, bathed now in red, he flung his other arm out, fingers scrabbling against the ground. Then it went still.

A horrible tightness gripped her middle. Leaning on the bow, she could only bend, half-crouched with hands on knees, and take deep gulps of air.

"Mary!" Elinor, breathless, was at her side.

She was aware that the shouts and cries over by the river had changed. What that meant, however, she did not know—nor could she have moved if another threat presented itself.

Elinor's hands smoothed across her back. "Is the baby coming?"

At last, the tightness began to ease, and she gave a little shake of her head. "I—do not know," she admitted.

When she could draw a deep breath, she straightened, blinking. Some of the other women were coming up the path, and then—Nohsh and Sees Far ran toward them through the forest.

Another wave of tightness gripped her not quite as hard as the first but still taking her breath and ability to move.

"Ai," she gasped. "I left Ginny playing waboose in the bushes!"

"I'll fetch her," Elinor said, and the aunties surrounded Mary in her place.

Manteo and the other men had not gotten far that morning before both he and Sees Far felt a strong urging in their spirits to go back. They ran, arriving just in time to give pursuit to the war party that was already breaking up and taking flight.

And to find that of all things, Wanchese had been felled and slain.

Mary stood in the path, near his body, bent as if in pain. "Nunutánuhs! Are you wounded?" he asked as he neared.

Timqua looked up with a tight smile. "We think the alarm of the attack might have brought on her time." She nodded toward the fallen warrior. "After she took down that one by her own hand." A flash of pride crossed her face. "We knew she was a fine shot with a bow."

Oh—his brave, beautiful little daughter!

And oh, his enemy, once a brother.

Manteo looked upon the bloodied form while Sees Far stooped to examine it, and he could find nothing but relief and sadness in his heart.

Mary straightened with a deep breath and lifted her gaze to his. Tears filled her eyes. "I could not let him take Elinor again and the baby."

Sees Far rose, his own expression fierce. "I thank you, Nuhsimuhs."

"Kupi, we thank you!" Elinor returned, Ginny at her side, and stepped past Mary and into Sees Far's embrace.

Mary stared at the body, looked around at all of them, and with a squeak, bent again with hands on her knees.

Step by agonizing step, the women coaxed, tugged, and bullied her back to the town and to the women's house. It was all a blur to Mary.

She was not afraid of birth—it was a process they were made as women to do, like the wutapantam, or even the *mushaniq* for which she had been called. She had not counted on it being so powerful, so all-consuming, her body taking over as if it knew already what to do, sweeping her along whether she wished it or not.

She paced, swayed, crouched, knelt, all the while encouraged by the other women. Elinor was there, and Auntie Timqua, but the faces of the others were swallowed up in the birthing haze. As from a distance, she heard her own voice crying out—then suddenly the impossible, crushing ache that came and went gave way to an undeniable need to bear down.

On her knees now over a wide, shallow opening lined with soft mosses, she obeyed the impulse of her body until—ai, what a wonder! A tiny person, slippery and wriggling, fell into her waiting hands and that of the women bending around her. With a cry that was half a sob, she gathered the little one up to her breast as the others surrounded her, cooing and squealing, and wrapped her about with a mantle before helping her to sit more comfortably.

The baby gave a soft bleat, and still weeping—she could hardly believe this creature had truly come from her—she shifted the baby and helped it latch on for its first milk.

"Well, what have we?" Nunohum's face appeared among those gathered around to tend her or simply gawk. Her eyes shone with tears. "A boy or a girl?"

Mary peeked—most definitely a boy. "I have a son." Another sob. "Georgie has a son!"

And then all she could do, while her little one suckled, was bend her head and give full vent to her own tears.

Chapter Thirty-Seven

"They will not believe it is truly us," Roger Prat muttered, staring through the trees at the palisade.

The former captives had but trudged their last few miles, refreshed only briefly by a quick bath in the river. Yet now, in sight of Cora Banks, after a moment to take in that they truly had accomplished the journey, they roused enough to break into a shuffling run.

"Ho! The town!" Georgie called out as they came into the open. 'Twouldn't do for them to be shot by overanxious guards who didn't properly recognize them.

At his greeting, two appeared at the opening nearest the river, and another emerged at the nearest lookout platform. There was a whoop and a call, and suddenly half the town boiled out to meet them.

Amid exclamations, embraces, and much thumping of his back and shoulders—and not a few tears—Georgie searched the crowd. No sign of the one he most longed to see. "Where is Mushaniq?" he asked at last, after trying to edge his way inside and utterly failing.

Master Cooper caught him in a tight, double-armed embrace, then pulled back, a huge grin on his bearded face. "Come and see!"

He led off at a run as if Georgie had not just come such a long distance—but he kept up easily, and it soon became apparent they were headed to Elinor's house.

His heart thudded painfully. What was amiss with her that she could not come out with the rest of the crowd?

And where was Sees Far? If either his mentor or the girl he loved more than anything else in the world had come to harm because of him—

But there she stood, just outside the door with Elinor, who held both little Sunlight and another bundle. For a moment his heart dropped to his feet—she wore naught but a skirt and a brace of beaded strands—and her figure was slim again, or nearly so.

What of their babe?

Was it truly her Georgie?

He looked wilder than the day he'd gone out on huskanaw—hair brighter than ever where it had grown out, beard again beginning to sprout, skin darkened with the sun, but still in clothing of the Kurawoten, so that he appeared almost a blend of the People and the Inqutish. He gaped at her as if she were the one who had disappeared for more than a moon.

She trembled so much she could hardly stand. But she could bear it no longer and, with a cry, threw herself toward him.

He caught her and tucked her against him, breaths heaving and muscles quivering. She clung to him in return. "It is you," she murmured. "It is truly you!"

When she gained some semblance of control after the flood of weeping, she reared back, thumped his shoulder with her fist, then took his face between both hands. "Could you not have sent word?"

He laughed through his own tears. "I tried. But Two Feathers insisted on coming as well. And then Towaye followed us."

"And Sees Far came back here, seeking you."

His face reddened as he chuckled, then sobered. His hands came up on either side of her head as well. "I am sorry. I hoped you did not worry—too much."

She pulled him in for a kiss, not caring that they were on display before all, and hardly heard Elinor's chuckle when they finally broke, leaning foreheads together.

"Oh, my sweet Mushaniq," Georgie breathed.

"Mushaniq no longer," she crooned, "but Mary in full. And," she amended, withdrawing just a little so she could look him in the eyes, "I have taken the name of Christ and received baptism."

He squeezed his eyes shut and, with a sob, pulled her into his arms again.

Another soft laugh from Elinor stirred them both. "Do you not wish to meet your son, Georgie?"

His mouth fell open once more as he looked over her shoulder. "Son? I mean—" His gaze snapped back to Mary, then down at her belly. "So you—?"

She took the tiny, squeaking bundle of their baby from Elinor and held him for Georgie to see.

Eyes and mouth rounding, he scooped his arm beneath hers and with infinite care took the baby from her. Tiny lashes fluttered as the baby's eyes closed and opened, then the round little face scrunched in a yawn and the lips worked, a dimple flashing in both cheeks.

"What have you called him?"

She couldn't help a giggle. "Waboose. For now."

He laughed as well and, cuddling the baby closer, kissed the down forehead. "A son," he breathed.

His blue eyes shone with so much love Mary nearly lost herself to weeping again, but Sees Far rounded the corner, Nohsh and Elinor's cousin Chris on his heels—apparently having delivered Georgie to her, he'd gone to fetch the other two. She found herself gathered into an almost too-exuberant embrace between Nohsh and Sees Far, who alternately scolded Georgie and preened that he'd succeeded in getting away without being tracked.

The women insisted on Mary resting for forty days, this being her first baby. During that time, Manteo held councils with all the weroances and the English Assistants, oversaw the receiving of Georgie as a fully grown member of the town—both as Inqutish and Kurawoten—and sent word to the surrounding towns of the death of Wanchese.

The sorrow over that came and went like waves on the shore. From the time they both were chosen to journey with the English, when they were each the only ones able to fully speak their tongue, throughout that entire strange and wondrous year, then the long journey back where they met Spanish and other Native peoples. . .more things than either of them could recall or speak of in a single sitting.

He could also scarce believe it had been Mary-Mushaniq's arm that had ended Wanchese. That girl's passion for life—for those she loved—was boundless.

And then how she had, in the same day, given him a grandson. How sweet it would be to hear the boy call him *Numohshomus*.

Once Mary's days of resting were finished—the English crenepos called it *lying in*—the town had a wedding to celebrate. And high time, it was.

In the meantime, an air of celebration lingered over the return not only of Georgie, Two Feathers, and Towaye but also the captives from Ritanoe.

On the fortieth day after the birth of Mary and Georgie's baby, the women of the town gathered to help Elinor carry everything out of the house, sweep it clean, shake out or wash the bedding, and then carry everything in again.

On the forty-first day, a feast was prepared. Mary wore again the doeskin tunic she had made for her huskanasqua, and a garland of flowers was placed about her head, with her hair loose down her back. Georgie scrubbed and wore a shirt, doublet, and trunkhose saved from his father's belongings.

The neighboring Cwareuuoc came also, bringing all manner of foods and drink, and it was a good thing that the weather allowed for the marriage ceremony to be held outdoors, because the meetinghouse would never have accommodated them all.

Manteo, Timqua, and their mother all stood with Mary, and Georgie stood accompanied by Sees Far, who was dressed to everyone's notice and consternation in a fine shirt and doublet that had been Ananias's—Elinor assured them it was with her most fervent blessing—and both Chris Cooper and Roger Prat. The older man was much greyed by his time as captive, but the joy of the moment shone in his face.

Elinor and the other women gathered nearby, minding the babies. Even the younger children pressed about to watch the spectacle of Georgie and Mary taking each other's hands and speaking their vows, which Manteo translated for the Native speakers.

The music and dancing began shortly after, while baskets and bowls heaped high with foodstuffs were brought out. Georgie and Mary swirled with the others, laughing.

Manteo took a turn dandling little Waboose, as soft and endearing as his namesake, and looked out over the gathering.

Kurawoten, Cwareuuoc, and Inqutish all danced, feasted, and laughed together, from the children to the elders.

He did not know how long the peace would last. With the death of Wanchese, the Sukwoten and Weopomeioc were bound to be angry, especially after what they had done in Pomeiooc and Dasemonguepeuk the summer before. The people of Ritanoe might seek retribution for the theft of their favored pale-skinned captives. Even the Mangoac and the Powhatan could be stirred up. He had already discussed with the weroances and Assistants the possibility of the community either returning to the island or going farther south—or perhaps dividing and doing both. All agreed that keeping such plans in mind could be nothing but sensible, whether or not they were found by ships from England.

They would all savor the joy and contentment of this moment, however, especially those taken captive and recently returned.

Even the last unmarried woman of the Inqutish, usually so sour and difficult of temperament, smiled and laughed as she stood in conversation with Roger Prat—and then Prat took her by the hand and led her into the dancing.

Ahh. . .well, that would be most fitting, were those two to find their own joy together. And what exceedingly good hap, as the Inqutish put it.

Manteo suppressed a sigh at his own longings. This was his daughter and Georgie's day. He would begrudge no one their happiness.

And thank You, most gracious and glorious Creator, for bringing us here!

In the next moment, he chanced to glance across the community fire and caught the gaze of a woman. She was dressed splendidly in a double kilt edged with both shell and wassador and with abundant strands of wassador and pearls adorning her neck, wrists, and ears. Lovely even without that extravagance, she held herself with confidence, meeting his eyes steadily, the corners of her mouth lifting in a hesitant smile.

He smiled back, bouncing the baby and dancing a few steps where he stood at the outskirts of the crowd, then casually made his way through the press and closer to where she stood.

His heart was keeping time with the drums that set pace for the dancers.

She met him halfway, one arm resting in the loops of her necklace, her free hand offering a cup. "Might I offer you refreshment, Manteo of Kurawoten and Roanoac?"

He laughed quietly and accepted the cup. Sweetened, spiced tea slid over a tongue that was suddenly parched. "I thank you. And you are?"

"Light That Dances, of the Cwareuuoc." Her smile went coy, and her lashes dipped as she touched Waboose's cheek. "Your daughter's little one?"

He took another sip. "Kupi."

It was a promising beginning in an evening that already held more joy than he knew how to contain.

Epilogue

Summer 1592

T he sky to the west was a sheet of scarlet and purple, almost too brilliant to look upon, by the time she emerged from the river. Morning
bathing was the ritual of these people, as it had been with the Kurawoten,
but she loved the solitude of an evening dip as well.

Astonishing it was that they gave her such freedom. Perhaps they
thought it worth not having to smell her *Inqutish* stink all night.

Not that they wouldn't find other things to ridicule her about. *Ussac*,
they called her, after the white crane that frequented the waters here—
presumably because it was white and awkward, both traits of which she
still retained even after two years here.

Emme, her name had been. She still whispered it to herself when no
one could hear her, so she would not forget. She must not forget.

Dressed once more in her doeskin tunic—a ragged thing, befitting
her status as slave—and hair braided back, she walked back to the town
and to the lodge reserved for the female slaves and unmarried women.
A bundle lay next to the doorway, and in the dusk, she could just make
out the lean form of a warrior, leaning with deceiving indolence against
a nearby tree.

She should simply walk past. But the spirit that had earned her a
beating all too often rose up, and a sigh escaped her. "She will not accept

your gifts, no matter how often you leave them."

A slight grunt, almost too low to be heard, came from the shadows. "What if I were to tell you it is not by her I mean them to be found?"

Emme had been about to step inside, but his words kept her rooted in place.

"Who is meant to find them, then?"

From the corner of her eye, she could see him draw himself upright. "Ussac. You."

She swung toward him—she couldn't help it. She should go inside, and quickly, ignore both bundle and the tall, handsome warrior who had left it.

It was too far past belief that he'd meant it for her.

"You mock me."

"I do not." His voice was barely above a breath.

"Why would you want the Crane? A slave?"

He took a step closer. Coal-black eyes glimmered in the twilight, his strong features set in proud lines.

He was so tall, so—menacing, she could not suppress a little shiver.

She turned away. The appeal of his gaze was almost too much to resist. "She will be angry if she finds you speaking to me."

"Let her be angry."

Emme huffed. "You are not the one upon whom the beating will fall."

He crossed the space between them in two strides, swooped the bundle from the ground, and taking one of her hands, placed the bundle in it. "Then accept this and be my wife."

She did not move, though she could feel a clinking inside the wrapping of softest rabbit skin. "Wahunsenecawh. Just because your father is the great weroance of all the Powhatan does not mean you can simply have anything you choose. You cannot take a slave to wife."

He smiled, a slow, beautiful thing that made her pulse leap. "Can I not?"

Oh, but this was impossible. And yet. . .to be a wife rather than a slave? Would it not be mad to refuse?

Slowly, she unwrapped the bundle. Two necklaces, one of shell and another of copper.

"I will speak to my father tomorrow about the redemption price for your captivity," Wahunsenecawh said. "Keep those concealed for now, if you wish, but they are indeed yours."

'Twould be foolish to accept. 'Twas foolish to refuse. He was indeed the favored son of the great weroance and would, in all likelihood, be weroance himself someday.

Emme gave another little sigh. Did she truly have any choice in this?

ACKNOWLEDGMENTS

My deepest thanks during the writing of this particular story go to. . .

Steve and Janet Bly: for inspiration, guidance, and amazing stories. . .and a leg up on the publishing industry, a horse I never thought I'd ride again while my children were so young. I am long overdue in acknowledging this debt!

Jen, Lee, and Beth: for prayers, encouragement, and never-failing friendship. I could not do this without y'all!

Cameron and Meeghan: for so much grace and understanding while we're living our best deadline life.

Becky Germany: for inviting me along on yet another adventure! Or should that be for suggesting my latest obsession?

All the staff at Barbour Publishing: for your tireless work in providing quality books to the world.

Ellen: for your enthusiasm and patience for yet another hot mess (this time it really was).

Tamela: for letting me put "represented by" and your name after mine. You are such a blessing!

Troy: for being always steady and faithful while giving me room to be messy and free spirited, even when running off to do research without you.

The rest of my darling family: for making my life so full of joy and excitement.

Most of all, my Creator-God: for the living expression of His love in Jesus the Christ, Yeshua HaMachiach, the One and Only Son. Because of Him, we really can know where we stand.

HISTORICAL NOTE

In the real-life drama of the Lost Colony, historians tend to view the actions of the players through a rather cynical lens, ascribing motives of political or personal gain to their decisions. But was this true in every case?

More specifically, was this true of Manteo in his conversion to Christianity? Was it merely a political move more or less carried out under duress?

Well, what if it started as that, but somewhere along the way, he had a genuine encounter with a real and living God?

Hatteras Island history mentions an old Indian cemetery where the graves were marked with crosses. Such a departure from Native burial custom speaks to me of something more than conversion under duress, especially in a situation where those known as "Christian" were dependent upon the local populace for survival. Real faith lived out with authenticity enough to make unbelievers thirst for the same is rare enough—especially with unbelievers so obviously content with their lives just as they were. I think they'd not have stood for being bullied into conversion—which means at least some of the Lost Colonists did indeed hold such a faith. So just as I decided to portray John White and others as genuine believers in Christ, flawed but sincere, I did the same with Manteo. It's my most fervent prayer that his journey—and that of others—rings authentic to readers of all walks of life.

Native peoples are renowned for their spirituality—for recognizing that God exists, that the spiritual realm is real, and that the seen is affected by the unseen. Often dismissed as superstitious for how it finds expression, such a worldview is, I believe, only a step away from recognition that their Creator is not merely a lofty, distant being but One vitally interested in our day-to-day affairs, who loves us so much He Himself became the sacrifice to satisfy all the wrongs ever done. It only follows, then, that a more supernatural outworking of faith in Christ would be reality for Native believers, especially in a historical setting.

And why, as is voiced and explored by my characters, would there not be spiritual conflict over the People of the First Nations turning to the truth of their Creator and no longer serving their old gods?

We come at last back to the question, what really happened to the Lost Colony?

John White, once merely professional artist and later governor of the fledgling Colony of Virginia, knew by the tokens left that his daughter, granddaughter, and others had removed to Croatoan Island, now known as Hatteras, the location of their most certain allies in the New World. What took place after is anybody's guess.

Everyone has an opinion. Scholars from David Beers Quinn to more recent analyses by Lee Miller and Brandon Fullam offer varying theories. Archaeological efforts reveal the near-certainty that English colonists dwelt alongside and assimilated with the Native peoples, as the early eighteenth-century explorer John Lawson speculated.

Exactly what that looked like, however, we aren't sure.

In *Elinor*, book one of Daughters of the Lost Colony, I explore the first steps of possibility, what led to the move to Croatoan and what might have driven them at least temporarily to the mainland, then the perils sure to follow. So many questions were left unanswered—what became of Cora Banks after Elinor was taken, how did those left behind cope with the loss, and will the townspeople really accept Sees Far when he unexpectedly brings her back? Where the story of *Elinor* held heartbreak with room for hope, *Mary* offers a deep breath of relief, a happy ending despite the unsettled future sure to follow.

There were complications, of course. In the process of researching Native culture, I uncovered customs that honestly should have surfaced in the first story, but as I said at the end of the historical notes there, I knew by the time this story came along, I'd be thumping my head against the wall at things I'd missed. Among other issues, casual intimacy outside of marriage and widespread use of herbal abortifacients were too prevalent in Native life to ignore. Indeed, it provided the perfect ground for conflict between colonists trying to live their faith more perfectly than they had seen others do and the Native peoples they sought to dwell alongside and minister to. (Not to mention individual attitudes toward those of a different skin color and culture.)

Such conflict is not, after all, so foreign to modern life, is it?

Those familiar with the story of the Lost Colony will no doubt recognize nods to different theories and legends. I did lean heavily on several sources while weaving the tale begun in *Elinor* and continued here. Lee Miller provided an intimidating introduction to the entirety of Lost Colony events with a rendering so vivid, it made my early attempts at dramatization seem redundant. She also suggests that John White and the colonists were Separatists and thus considered disposable for such a venture. Brandon Fullam thoroughly explores the timing and effects of hurricanes, which I found very helpful despite disagreeing with his conclusions about the motivations of various historical figures. Scott Dawson brings to bear several generations of local Hatteras Island history as well as personal archaeological research to show that the Lost Colony was never really lost, only abandoned by England. Philip McMullan presents evidence for the community of Beechland, although I took issue with his conclusion that Raleigh secretly maintained contact with the planters. David Beers Quinn's exhaustive work offers an absolute wealth of information I couldn't find elsewhere.

For research on the Algonquian-speaking Native peoples of what is now eastern North Carolina, I first turned to the sketches and watercolors of John White, initially tasked with "painting to life" the sights of the 1585 English expedition to the New World. Thomas Harriot also provided much written detail about the people and land. Both men, despite their use of the term *savage* (a colloquial term of the time), did see the indigenous peoples of America as beautiful, intelligent, and worthy in their own right, not merely as objects of conquest or conversion—or at least, to a lesser degree than others of their time. In *Elinor*, I endeavored to portray both as men of faith—that is, of true faith, not without fault but also not paying mere lip service to Christianity. (Contrasted with, say, the actions of Ralph Lane.)

Other firsthand accounts were helpful—Amadas and Lane, and later Lawson. James Axtell's works, *Bonds of Alliance*, and several titles about Pocahontas and the Powhatan people also proved invaluable, especially in regard to Native coming-of-age, courtship, and marriage customs. (See my bibliography for a complete list.) Some customs are well-documented, such as the use of abortifacient herbs and their concept of open marriage, as well as taboos on intimacy during various seasons of a woman's reproductive life. Other things were harder to pin down, such as specific details on coming-of-age rites, at least as they related to the less warlike tribes. The Powhatan were definitely more heavyweights in that area, much like the Iroquois to the north, but plenty of push-and-pull for dominance or vengeance took place between the smaller tribes. Harriot's work and accounts of the earlier English expeditions discuss this in more detail.

As far as provenance for the Croatoan possibly widening their influence, I would point out that the map drawn by John White shows only the one island with a place name of "Croatoan," while later maps show other locations labeled as such (or the modern spelling "Croatan"). I cannot recall which historian suggested that after the attack on Roanoke, the Croatoan and English might have combined efforts to push back against the Secotan and Weopomeioc, but it presents an intriguing possibility. If the boast of the Powhatan twenty years later of having mostly wiped out the English was rooted in any sort of truth, it might have been sparked by what the Powhatan perceived as a lesser, upstart tribe thinking too highly of themselves and daring to give aid to strangers who almost certainly posed a threat to Native life.

In the middle of all the facts and speculation surrounding the fate of the Lost Colony emerges a particular legend, centering around young George Howe and a daughter of Manteo and later connected with the Lumbee tribe of North Carolina. Rather than try to work with a minimal thirteen-year age difference between Georgie and any child of Manteo born after his 1587 return to Ossomocomuck, I theorize a daughter born from an early marriage. Histories of Pocahontas, after all, state that she was originally married between thirteen and fourteen to the Powhatan warrior Kocoum, so it isn't out of the question for Manteo to have been married as a teen—nor Georgie and Mushaniq themselves.

I also loosely modeled the capture of Elinor and her fellow English after reports given almost twenty years later by the Powhatan to John Smith. I do credit the Native grapevine as being more accurate than to serve up such old news, but historians speculate that at least some of Wahunsenecawh's boasts to Smith were exaggerated if not fabricated outright. So it's very possible that not everything reported as fact was indeed fact, and at the least there is room for dramatic license.

Some will, no doubt, be disappointed that I did not include the Dare Stone—not even the first one—although I can't say the story presented thereon didn't inspire me at least a little. But Outer Banks residents in particular hold such a firmly negative opinion on the veracity of that stone, I couldn't in good conscience treat it as authentic.

Discrepancy enough exists in respected historical records. For instance, two separate dates are given for what year Ananias and Elinor Dare married. Some historians give credence to the earlier date, positing that Elinor must be mother to both John Dare, listed in 1597 as the "natural" son of Ananias (a term referring to illegitimate birth) and to a Thomasyn Dare, presumably left behind in 1587 with relatives. I thought evidence for that scant, however, especially for the existence of Thomasyn Dare. For the purpose of this story, I went with the later date of marriage, with Virginia being their first child and John Dare having been born to Ananias of an earlier relationship. (I couldn't find a graceful way to manage a mention of John in this story, sadly, but he did exist—court proceedings in 1597 awarded him whatever remained of Ananias's estate in England—and hopefully lived a long and productive life.)

For the many nuggets of information about various members of the Lost Colony and earlier expeditions, my thanks to William Powell for his genealogical work, as shared by Roberta Estes. Some men were unmarried; some left wives and children behind. Of the women, we know very little about the unmarried, although shreds of possibilities exist for some. I used local Hatteras Island tradition and stories about the vanished community of Beechland as a guide for which men and families might have moved or stayed.

The fictional town of Cora Banks carries a similar name as Core Point, North Carolina, but is located near the mouth of the Pamlico River, on the southern shore, rather than directly on the Outer Banks.

I owe my initial education in Carolina Algonquian, a language that died out more than two hundred years ago, to the work of the late Blair Rudes and Scott Dawson, later supplemented by John White's drawings and the Strachey/Smith lexicon of the Powhatan language, which is very similar and contemporary to the settlement at Jamestown, Virginia. Thomas Harriot is reported to have compiled a dictionary of Carolina Algonquian, as learned directly from Manteo and Wanchese, but it did not survive. As noted in *Elinor*, I decided it would be easier to render various words phonetically rather than use their spellings strictly. Carolina Algonquian contains one or two strange consonant forms—some Rs are more a flip of the tongue, so they get rendered as a T or a D phonetically, and the language lacks an L entirely (at least in some regions), thus the problem of them saying words like English or Elinor. For "English," I've borrowed the word Dr. Rudes developed for the Powhatan speakers in the film *The New World*. Also, after studying various spellings of names alongside Dr. Rudes's article on pronunciation, I decided to go with John White's own spelling of Wyngyno rather than the otherwise-common Wingina, because I felt it easier to point the reader to what seems a more historically authentic pronunciation of ween-GEEN-ah/oh (hard G like gate), or possibly even wing-ee-nah, than the usual modern win-JEAN-a

Finding names for fictional characters was a major source of stress, especially when writing *Elinor*. I hated using what amounted to cool-sounding groups of syllables with no known meaning, although I did resort to that in a few cases—and one account I ran across states that some Native peoples did actually employ such methods, so we English speakers aren't the only ones who don't always pay attention to meaning when we name our children. Also, for adult names, it seems Algonquian-speaking peoples didn't tend to use words referring to animals or various objects (which would have made choosing fictional names so much easier) but rather personal traits or attributes. We do know that young children were often given a "milk name," which later changed, thus my choice of Mushaniq ("squirrel") for Manteo's fictional daughter, and names like Little Shell and Two Feathers.

Obviously, I've expanded my Algonquian vocabulary and Powhatan by extension, which will come in handy for book 3, but there is always more to learn. For instance, I'm not sure anyone really knows the meaning or origin of the hooded faces carved into the tops of the posts comprising a Native town's dancing circle, but I found an interesting link to similar figures on posts on the far Caribbean island of Dominica.

Understanding the nuances of Native belief about God and the spirit realm has also been a work in progress. Scott Dawson's Algonquian glossary includes the definition of *Montóac* as the Great Spirit or God, but further research suggests this term refers, as my glossary states, to the collective guardian spirits or spiritual force of all living things—of whom *Kewás* may or may not have been one. It's probable that Kewás refers only to the actual idol, not the spirit/s represented thereby. Among the Powhatan (whose language is very similar), the Creator-God was referred to as *Ahoné*, above and separate from all other gods and generally detached from His creation after setting everything in motion. I previously state that the evil god, analogous to Satan, was referred to as *Oki* (oh-KEE), but have since found references to Oki or *Okeus* as a more benevolent God, especially in Powhatan belief, while the devil is referred to as *Riapoke*. The current glossary—and references in this story—reflect that. I would offer my readers the reminder Scott Dawson gave me during an email discussion about the exact meaning of Montóac, that language and concepts were likely more fluid than we know because the Native peoples had no written language. Thus, regardless of how uptight I (or others) might get over wanting things "exactly right," there is a lot of room for doubt as well as artistic license.

BIBLIOGRAPHY

Allen, Paula Gunn. *Pocahontas: Medicine Woman, Spy, Entrepeneur, Diplomat.* Harper Collins, 2004.

Axtell, James, ed. *The Indian Peoples of Eastern America: A Documentary History of the Sexes.* Oxford University Press, 1981.

Axtell, James. *The Invasion Within: The Contest of Cultures in Colonial North America.* Oxford University Press, 1988.

Dawson, Scott. *Croatoan: Birthplace of America.* Infinity Publishing, 2009.

Dawson, Scott. *The Lost Colony and Hatteras Island.* History Press, 2020.

Fullam, Brandon. *The Lost Colony of Roanoke: New Perspectives.* McFarland & Company, Inc. Publishers, 2017.

Fullam, Brandon. *Manteo and the Algonquians of the Roanoke Voyages.* McFarland & Company, Inc. Publishers, 2020.

Hakluyt, Richard. *The Principal Navigations, Voyages, Traffiques, and Discoveries of the English Nation.* Google Books. Abridged edition, *Voyages and Discoveries.* Penguin Books, 1972.

Harriot, Thomas. *A Briefe and True Report of the New Found Land of Virginia: The complete 1590 edition with 28 engravings by Theodor de Bry after the drawings of John White and other illustrations.* Dover Publications, Inc., 1972.

Lawler, Andrew. *The Secret Token.* Anchor Books, 2018.

Lawson, John. *A New Voyage to Carolina.* Google Books, 1709.

McMullan, Philip S., Jr. *Beechland and the Lost Colony.* Pamlico & Albemarle Publishing, 2010 (as a master's thesis), 2014.

Miller, Lee. *Roanoke: Solving the Mystery of the Lost Colony.* Arcade Publishing, 2000, 2012.

Oberg, Michael Leroy. *The Head in Edward Nugent's Hand: Roanoke's Forgotten Indians.* University of Pennsylvania Press, 2008.

Perdue, Theda, and Christopher Arris Oakley. *Native Carolinians: The Indians of North Carolina.* North Carolina Office of Archives and History, 2010, 2014.

Quinn, David Beers, ed. *The Roanoke Voyages 1584-1590, Vols. I and II.* Dover Publications, 1991.

Reader's Digest. *America's Fascinating Indian Heritage.* The Reader's Digest Association, Inc., 1978.

Rountree, Helen C. *The Powhatan Indians of Virginia: Their Traditional Culture.* University of Oklahoma Press, 1988.

Rushforth, Brett. *Bonds of Alliance: Indigenous & Atlantic Slaveries In New France.* University of North Carolina Press, 2012.

Sloan, Kim. *A New World: England's First View of America.* University of North Carolina Press, 2007.

Strachey, William. *A Historie of Travaile into Virginia Britannia.* The Hakluyt Society, 1612, 1849.

Ward, H. Trawick, and R. P. Stephen Davis Jr. *Time Before History: The Archaeology of North Carolina.* University of North Carolina Press, 1999.

A handful of online sites were absolutely crucial to my research as well:

Coastal Carolina Indian Center: CoastalCarolinaIndians.com

Virtual Jamestown: virtualjamestown.org

The Other Jamestown: virtual-jamestown.com

Roberta Estes, scientist and genealogical researcher, particularly this page: https://dna-explained.com/2018/06/28/the-lost-colony-of-roanoke-did-they-survive-national-geographic-archaeology-historical-records-and-dna/

The British Museum online, for their collection of John White's drawings and paintings: https://www.britishmuseum.org/collection/term/BIOG50964

CAST OF CHARACTERS

NATIVE
Historical

1. Granganimeo: Secotan weroance and brother-in-law of Wyngyno; one of those who originally welcomed the English but later died of the mysterious illness caught from them. [grahn-gah-nee-MAY-oh, "he who is serious"]

2. Manteo: Croatoan man who accompanied Amadas and Barlowe back to England in 1584; returned in 1585 with Lane's expedition and stayed to support the English; returned to England in 1586; and part of White's colony in 1587. [probable historical pronunciation mahn-TAY-oh; modern MAN-tee-oh (particularly the town on Roanoke Island); "to snatch"]

3. Menatoan: a Croatoan man, sometimes confused with Menatonon, mentioned in John White's account

4. Menatonon: weroance of Chawanoac; "he who listens well"

5. Okisco: weroance of Weopomeioc, region north of Chowan River [oh-KEE-sko]

6. Piemacum: weroance of Pomeiooc, enemy of Wyngyno [possible pronunciation pee-AY-mah-kum]

7. Towaye: possibly Croatoan; accompanied the 1587 expedition back from England; nothing is known about him besides his name being recorded on the roster alongside Manteo [toh-WAH-yay]

8. Wahunsenecawh: Powhatan warrior, weroance of great influence and renown during the settling of Jamestown, father of Pocahontas [wah-HUN-sen-ah-cah]

9. Wanchese: probably of the Roanoac or Secotan, who accompanied Amadas and Barlowe back to England in 1584; returned in 1585 and disappeared into the wilderness. "To take flight" [modern pronunciation WAHN-cheese; historical probably wahn-CHAY-zay]

10. Wyngyno [spelling from John White]: weroance of Secota, Dasemonguepeuk, and Roanoac; gifted Roanoke Island to the English; changed name to Pemisapan when suspicious of Lane's motives ("he who watches"). Variously spelled Wingina/Wingyno [modern pronunciation win-JEAN-a; historical probably ween-GEEN-oh, with hard G like gate]

Fictional

1. Bright Star: "adult" name of Kokon
2. Dances Wild: young Croatoan man, older brother of Two Feathers
3. Kokon: Timqua's daughter and Mushaniq's cousin [koh-KOHN]
4. Light That Dances: Cwareuuoc woman
5. Little Shell: Croatoan child
6. Mushaniq: Manteo's daughter [MUSH-ah-neek, "squirrel"], about nine to ten years old when colony first arrives at Roanoac
7. Sees Far: Secotan warrior, son of Granganimeo, and former friend to Wanchese
8. Shines Like Sunset: deceased, Manteo's wife, and Mushaniq's mother
9. Swims Deep Water: Croatoan weroance
10. Timqua: Manteo's sister, who helped rear Mushaniq [TEEM-kwah]
11. Two Feathers: Croatoan youth
12. Wesnah (fictional name for real-life wife of Menatoan)

ENGLISH

Assistants for the Cittie of Ralegh (as listed on the ship's roster by John White):

1. Roger Bailie
2. Ananias Dare, husband of Elinor and son-in-law to John White
3. Christopher Cooper, nephew to John White and cousin to Elinor White Dare
4. Thomas Stevens
5. John Sampson, father of John
6. Dyonis Harvie, husband of Margery and father of Henry
7. Roger Prat, father of John
8. George Howe, slain on Roanoac Island, August 1587, father of Georgie

Other men of the colony:

1. Arnold Archard, husband of Joyce and father of Thomas
2. William Berde (guard after attack by Secotan)
3. Henry Berrye
4. Michael Bishop
5. John Bright
6. Anthony Cage, former sheriff of Huntingdon
7. Thomas Coleman
8. William Dutton
9. Thomas Ellis, blacksmith, older brother of Robert
10. John Farre (guard after attack by Secotan)
11. John Gibbs
12. James Hynde
13. Nicholas Johnson, minister for the colony
14. Griffen Jones (wounded by Secotan)

15. Thomas Phevens
16. Henry Payne
17. Edward Powell, husband of Wenefrid
18. Edward Stafford, captain of the pinnace
19. Thomas Stevens
20. Martyn Sutton
21. Richard Taverner
22. John Tydway
23. Ambrose Viccars
24. Thomas Warner
25. Cutbert White
26. John Wright ("more or less in charge of the planting effort" in *Elinor*)

Women:

1. Joyce Archard, wife of Arnold
2. Alis Chapman, wife to John
3. Ann Coleman, wife of Thomas (first name fictional)
4. Elinor Dare, daughter of John White and wife of Ananias
5. Elizabeth ("Libby") Glane
6. Margery Harvie, wife of Dyonis
7. Jane Jones, wife of John or Griffen
8. Margaret Lawrence
9. Jane Mannering, midwife, later (fictional) wife of Captain Stafford
10. Emme Merrimoth
11. Rose Payne, wife of Henry
12. Jane Pierce, later (fictional) wife of Roger Bailie
13. Wenefrid Powell, wife of Edward
14. Audrey Tappen, married to Thomas (Topan?)
15. Elizabeth Viccars, wife of Ambrose
16. Joan Warren, wife of Thomas (Warner?)
17. Agnes Wood [possibly married to John Wood who came in 1584]

Small children and older boys:

1. Thomas Archard, son of Arnold and Joyce, born 1575
2. Johanna Elizabeth Dare, fictional second daughter of Ananias and Elinor, born December 1590; nickname Sunlight
3. Virginia Thomasyn Dare, daughter of Ananias and Elinor, born August 18, 1587
4. Robert Ellis, younger brother of Thomas, born November 1576
5. Henry (fictional name) Harvie, born August 18 or 19, 1587, son of Dyonis and Margery
6. George Howe, son of George Howe the elder, presumed about twelve when the colony sets sail
7. Thomas Humfrey, born October 1573?
8. John Prat, son of Roger?
9. John Sampson, son of John Sampson the Assistant
10. Thomas Smart

11. Ambrose Viccars, son of Ambrose and Elizabeth, born 1583?

12. William Wythers, born March 1574?

Others connected to the colony:

Simon Ferdinando: Simon Fernandez (or Fernandes), navigator of Portuguese birth, originally taken captive as a privateer but pardoned by Queen Elizabeth, presumably for his seafaring knowledge and in exchange for his service. Last name recorded variously as Fernando or Ferdinando but mostly as the latter by John White.

Sir Richard Greenville: English explorer, spelled variously Grenville, Greinvile

Thomas Harriot: English mathematician, astronomer, ethnographer, and translator; accompanied 1585 expedition and learned Carolina Algonquian from Manteo and Wanchese; authored *The Briefe and True Report of the*

New Found Land of Virginia

Rafe Lane: English explorer in charge of the 1585–86 expedition, responsible for the death of Wyngyno, spelled Ralph but historically pronounced Rafe

Sir Walter Ralegh: English explorer, adventurer, and darling of Queen Elizabeth's court; contemporary spelling Raleigh

John White: father of Elinor Dare; professional artist tasked with "painting to life" the sights of the New World on the 1584 and 1585 expeditions (possibly an earlier one as well); later appointed governor of the Colony of Virginia but forced to return to England on behalf of the colony

Moved to Beechland

1. Michael Bishop
2. Thomas and Ann Coleman
3. William Dutton
4. John Gibbs
5. James Hynde
6. Henry and Rose Payne
7. Thomas Phevens
8. Thomas Stevens, Assistant
9. Richard Taverner
10. Ambrose and Elizabeth Viccars
11. Cutbert White

Taken captive by the Secotan

1. John Bright
2. Elinor Dare (later returned by Sees Far)
3. Robert Ellis
4. Elizabeth Glane
5. Thomas Humfrey
6. Emme Merrimoth (sent to Powhatan)
7. Roger Prat
8. Martyn Sutton
9. John Tydway (wife in England)
10. William Wythers

REGIONS AND PEOPLE GROUPS

Aquascogoc (sometimes Aguascogoc) [ah-kwah-skoh-gock]: a mainland region and people adjacent to Dasemonguepeuk

Beechland: fictional English settlement in the region of Dasemonguepeuk

Chacandepeco: "that which is deep and becomes shallow"; inlet at the northeastern end of Croatoan Island (just north of modern-day Buxton)

Chesepiok (or Chesepioc) [chay-say-pee-ock]: Chesapeake, both the people and the region

Cora Banks: fictional town on the Pumtico (Pamlico) River, named after the Corée /Cwareuuoc people

Corée, Cwareuuoc [kwah-ray-yuh-wock]: a people located between the Neuse and Pamlico Rivers; probable derivation of the word "CORA" carved into a tree on Hatteras Island

Croatoan: probably derived from the Algonquian Kurawoten [kuh-ra-WOH-tain]; present-day lower Hatteras Island

Dasemonguepeuk: the mainland peninsula nearest Roanoke Island. Spelled variously Dasemongwepeok, Dasemonquepeu, Dasemunkepeuc, etc. [possible historical pronunciation dass-ay-mong-kway-pay-uhk]

Mangoac: a people of the mainland

Ossomocomuck: Native term generally understood to encompass the present-day Outer Banks and possibly also eastern mainland regions of North Carolina

Paquippe: present-day Lake Mattamuskeet [pah-kwip-pay]

Piaquiac: island immediately north of Croatoan; upper part of present-day Hatteras Island ("people of the shallows")

Pomeiooc (Pomeyooc): mainland region just south of Dasemonguepeuk, north of the Pamlico River

Powhatan: a people group in possession of present-day Virginia

Pumtico/Pomtico/Pumitukew: Pamlico River

Ritanoe: inland Native town where copper was mined [ree-tah-noh-ay]

Roanoac: present-day Roanoke Island

Secota/Secotan: a people group mostly residing upon the mainland but also apparently in possession of Roanoke Island at the time of the first English voyage in 1585; in Algonquian, Sukwoten [suh-KWOH-tain]

Weopomeioc/Weapemeoc: mainland region just north and east of the Chowan River [way-oh-pom-ay-oc or way-ah-pem-ay-oc]

Wococon: island southwest of Croatoan, present-day Okracoke Island

HISTORICAL TERMS

Arquebus: a type of matchlock gun, commonly used in the sixteenth century; also harquebus

Coif: a plain cap that lay across the head, worn by both men and women, snugger than a hood, less ornamented than eighteenth-century women's caps

Doublet: a men's garment for the upper body, a type of fitted vest, worn over a shirt, with or without detachable sleeves

Hose/Trunkhose: a loose-fitting men's garment for the lower body, rather like puffy shorts, tied at the waist and gathered around the thigh, forerunner of breeches

Kirtle: a woman's gown, worn over a shift, having a moderately boned bodice and full skirts, with or without detachable sleeves

Planters: those sent for the establishment of plantations, i.e., the colonists or settlers

Shift: a woman's loose garment of linen, worn as an underdress or nightdress

Slops: a men's garment, like trunkhose but not fitted to the leg, often worn by sailors or laborers

CAROLINA ALGONQUIAN WORDS

Ahoné [ah-HONE-ay]: Creator-God in Powhatan culture, possibly among other coastal Algonquian peoples as well

andacon: evergreen

apohominas [ah-poe-HOE-muh-nahs]: hominy

apon [ah-PONE]: corn bread

arohcun [ah-roh-cuhn]: raccoon

ascopo: sweet bay

chingwusso: channel bass

chumay [chuh-MAY]: friend, said of a stranger or not of one's own tribe [same definition as nitáp]

crenepo [cray-nay-poh]: woman

cuttak [kuh-tahk]: otter

ehqutonahas [eh-kwuh-TONE-ah-hahs]: Stop talking! Hush! or Be quiet!

huskanasqua: coming-of-age rites for girls

huskanaw: coming-of-age rites for boys

Inkurut/Indu(d)und: England

Inqutish [ink-uh-teesh]: English [from Blair Rudes's transliteration of the Powhatan pronunciation

ka ka torwawirocs yowo: How is this called?

kanoe [kah-noe-ay]: canoe, dugout style from trunks of various types of trees, mostly cedar

Kewás [kay-wass]: an idol representing a god of the Algonquian pantheon; Kewasowoc, plural

kupi [kuh-PEA]: yes

Kurawoten [kuh-rah-WOH-tain]: see Croatoan, in place names ("the talking town" or "the council town")

Kuwumádas [kuh-wuh-MAH-das]: I love you [Powhatan kowamánes]

machicomuck: temple

mahkahq [MAH-kahk]: squash

mahkusun [mah-KUH-sun]: shoe (origin of the word *moccasin*)

mahta [MAH-tah]: no

mamankanois [mah-mahng-kah-nwas]: butterfly [Powhatan: Ma-naang-gwas]

manchauemec: croaker (fish)

micis [MEE-cheese]: Eat!

Montóac: gods, spirits, or the collective spiritual force of all living things; attributed by some to be the Creator-God or Great Spirit, but this varies depending on the people

mushaniq [MUSH-ah-neek]: squirrel

nahyápuw [nah-YAH-poh]: bald eagle

namehs [NAH-mace]: fish

nek [neck]: "my mother"

nitáp [nee-TAHP]: friend, said of a stranger or someone not of one's own tribe

nohsh [noesh]: "my father" ([noesh] as in 'doe')

nuhsimuhs [nuh-SEA-muhs]: "my younger sister"

numat [nuh-MAHT]: "my younger brother"

numiditáq / numirihtáq [nuh-mee-DEE-tawk]: "my paternal aunt" (Algonquian differentiated between paternal and maternal aunts and uncles, and male and female cousins.)

numohshomus [nuh-moh-SHOW-muhs]: "my grandfather"

nunohum [nuh-NO-hum]: "my grandmother"

nunutánuhs [nuh-nuh-TAW-nuhs]: "my daughter"

nupes [nuh-PACE]: sleep

nutuduwins [nuh-tuh-duh-wince]: I am called

Okeus, Okee [OH-kee-us]: one of several gods, especially revered among the Powhatan

pegatawah [pek-ah-TAH-wah]: maize, corn

Popogusso: hell, a great pit of endless burning

pyas [pyahs]: Come!

Riapoke [rcc ah-POII-kay]: the devil

Sá keyd winkan: are you well?

Sukwoten [probably suh-KWOE-tain]: see Secotan, in "Regions and People Groups"

Tunapewak [t/dun-ah-PAY-wahk]: the People ("the true, real, or genuine people")

uppowoc: tobacco

ussac: white crane

uunamun: to see (Powhatan)

waboose: bunny, baby rabbit

wassador: precious metals, specifically copper

weewramanqueo: bufflehead duck

weroance/weroansqua: leader or chieftain over a town or towns ("one who is rich")

wingapo: [wing-GAH-poh] How are you? or Hello!

winkan nupes [WINK-on nuh-PACE]: Sleep well!

woanagusso: swan

wutahshuntas [wuh-TAH-shun-tahs]: foreigners, strangers

wutapantam [wuh-tah-PAHN-tam]: deer

yehakan [yay-HAH-kan]: house

yapám [yah-PAUM]: ocean

Transplanted to North Dakota after more than two decades in the Deep South, SHANNON MCNEAR loves losing herself in local history. She's the author of four novellas and five full-length novels, with the honor of her first novella, *Defending Truth* in A Pioneer Christmas Collection, being a 2014 RITA® nominee, and her most recent novella, *The Wise Guy and the Star* from Love's Pure Light, being a 2021 SELAH winner. Yet her greatest joy is in being a military wife, mom of eight, mother-in-law of five, and grammie of six. She's also a contributor to Colonial Quills and a member of ACFW and FHLCW. When not cooking, researching, or leaking story from her fingertips, she enjoys being outdoors, basking in the beauty of the northern prairies.

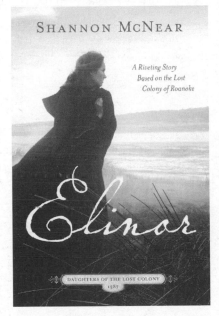